No Christian Grave

Grave

Edmund Power

**SIMON &
SCHUSTER**

TOWNHOUSE

First published in Great Britain and Ireland by
Simon & Schuster/TownHouse, 2002
An imprint of Simon & Schuster UK Ltd and TownHouse and CountryHouse Ltd, Dublin

Simon & Schuster UK is a Viacom Company

1 3 5 7 9 10 8 6 4 2

Simon & Schuster UK Ltd
Africa House
64–78 Kingsway
London WC2B 6AH

Simon & Schuster Australia
Sydney

TownHouse and CountryHouse Ltd
Trinity House, Charleston Road,
Ranelagh, Dublin 6, Ireland

A CIP catalogue record for this book is available
from the British Library

ISBN 1-903650-20-8

This book is a work of fiction. Names, characters, places and incidents are either a product of
the author's imagination or are used ficticiously. Any resemblance to actual people living or
dead, events or locales is entirely coincidental.

Typeset by SX Composing DTP, Rayleigh, Essex
Printed and bound in Great Britain by
Omnia Books Limited, Glasgow

No Christian Grave

CHAPTER ONE

19 August 1982

It was gone beyond the witching hour, the night at its very deadest. High summer, and the air still warm, the land floodlit by a perfect milkbowl moon. Dasher Morrissey and I waited in the shadows by my father's haybarn, about a hundred yards from the dwelling house. We'd been partying and were now hoping to ice the cake. I was just turned seventeen, a novice where drink was concerned, and tonight it showed. But still, I was well up for this. Not so Dasher. Eighteen that very day, celebrating on the double, and worried. As he had been for as long as I'd known him.

'This is a mistake.'

'What is? Nothing's happened yet.'

'Dead right. And I don't reckon anything will.'

'So what are you bellyaching about, then?'

'I dunno. It's just . . . What exactly did she say?'

'Well, as far as I could make out —'

'What? "As far as I could make out"? Jesus! You mean you aren't even sure?'

'The pub was a bit noisy, that's all. And obviously she wasn't going to shout it. But she definitely said she'd sneak out of the house and meet us here later on.'

'Did she sound any way sober?'

'She was stone-cold sober. She hadn't had a drink all night.'

'Right, OK. And does she know where to come to?'

'For fuck's sake, Dasher, she's lived just across the field for the past fifteen years – she ought to have a rough idea. Anyway, it was her choice; she's the one who said here.'

'You're certain she said that, huh? Gimme a smoke, will ya?'

I took two Major from my box, handed him one and lit both. He puffed deeply as he explored some new pitfalls.

'This is a wind-up. She's not going to show. You know her.'

'Her' was Suzy Deane, the only child in the third house of our remote little settlement.

'What d'you mean, "You know her"?'

'I mean you know her. And you know what she's become lately.'

'And what's that?'

'Just about the greatest slapper in the parish, that's all.'

He'd never spoken this way about her before. It must've been the drink. On both our parts, because for an instant I saw red.

'You're the one who's asking for a slap, mate. That's our neighbour you're talking about.'

'Our neighbour? You still fancy her, don't you?'

'No, I bloody don't.'

'Jesus, Billy! I thought you'd got over that long ago?'

'Over what? Stop talking crap, will ya.'

'I mean, watching her going off with every man jack in the village. Old, young, married, single – all the same to our Suzy. And that hasn't put you off at all, no?'

'Oh, shut the fuck up, eh? And be careful where you stub out that cigarette. If you set fire to the haybarn, my old man is likely to suspect that we were up to no good.'

'Yeah, right. Sorry.'

It was the very middle of the hay-saving season. And we were about halfway there – the bales in the barn now rose about twenty feet from the ground, and could only be reached by ladder. Adjoining the barn was the cowbyre, as stonily silent as the rest of the pale surroundings.

'She must've been drunk.'

'She wasn't, I tell you. Chris Scanlon was on tonight and he never serves her.'

'Well, in that case she's having a laugh at us. She has no intention of turning up.'

'Maybe not. But I have a feeling she'll be here. And anyway – isn't it worth hanging around?'

'What – on the off-chance of getting lucky?'

'If you want to put it like that, then, yeah. Speaking of which, I don't know about you, but I've come prepared.' And from my top pocket, carefully as if it was a living creature, I produced a condom. He squinted at it in the half-light.

'What is it?'

'It's a Johnnie.'

'Jesus Christ – show me. Where did you get it?'

'I got it in Dublin.'

To the likes of us, contraceptives were still unavailable in Ireland. But some months earlier I'd been for a weekend to visit my sister, who was studying law in Trinity College. She shared accommodation with three other girls. One day, left alone and having an idle rummage around the flat, I'd come upon a box of Durex. And helped myself to a sample.

'Did you bring one for me?'

'No.'

'Bollox – why not?'

'Because I only have the one.'

'Hmmm . . . maybe it'll do us both.'

3

'Maybe – but I'm getting first go.'

'Well, toss for it, eh?'

'No way – it's mine. You can have it when I'm finished, and be thankful.'

'OK, fair enough . . . ever used one before?'

'No. Never had the chance. You?'

'No, same here.'

When he'd done marvelling at the artefact, I returned it to my top pocket. As I did, something sighed in the distance. Dasher started.

'What? D'you hear that?'

'Yeah. Sounded like a car.'

'Jesus! D'you suppose she's bringing company?'

'She didn't say she was.'

'She didn't say she wasn't either. What if he's with her?'

'He? He who?'

'You know bloody well who. Doran. Ginger fucking Rodger.'

Of a long line of reprobates in Suzy's recent past, Rodger Doran was the latest and by a distance the most undesirable. Now in his twenties, his family had arrived in Lisdrolin some years before from England. The story went that they were the first generation of a traveller family to settle, a story lent credence by their wild, untamed behaviour, their complete disdain for any form of law and order, and their flaming red hair, all of them. This last trait had earned their youngest the nickname 'Ginger' Rodger. Nowadays it was used only rarely, and never, ever to his face.

'You saw her with him in the pub. What if she brings that bastard along for the ride?'

'She won't.'

'She'd better not. If he appears, mate, you're in this on your own.'

4

During what schooldays we'd shared, Ginger Rodger Doran had given Dasher the life of a bad dog. In truth, there were many of us he mistreated, but none with the same relentlessness or cruelty.

'I'm telling you, if that knacker — What was that?'

I heard it too. Footsteps crackling through the loose hay strewn about. We both stomped out the cigarettes and held our breath.

'Billy? Dasher? . . . Lads?'

Dasher looked at me and mouthed, 'It's her.'

'Round here,' I said, loudly as I dared. Presently she sidled round the girder. Her coal-black hair shimmied in the moon, her dark eyes glistened. She wore too much garish make-up, a T-shirt that only just covered what it was bound to, and a leather miniskirt that scarcely covered even that much.

'We thought you weren't coming,' Dasher gushed.

'I said I would, didn't I?'

'It's just that . . . have you come alone?'

'Of course. Who did you think – Rodger? Rodger Doran? Nah – that's over and done with. History.'

'Must be pretty recent history,' I said. 'In the pub you seemed to be getting on fine.'

'That was before. And it isn't what you're thinking – not some tiff that'll be patched up tomorrow. This is it. We're through.'

'I'm glad to hear it,' Dasher said with great sincerity.

'Not as glad as my dad'll be. He was never off my case, telling me to get rid of him. But he's right – it's time I copped myself on, and stopped hanging out with the likes of Doran. I mean, just look at him, for God's sake. Mooching around the parish on his horse and cart, collecting scrap iron. Not exactly the last word in glamour, is it?'

Though he may have been many miles out of earshot, Dasher was still too intimidated to badmouth him. 'Ah, I dunno. It's a job, and he seems to like it.'

'Because it's about all he'll ever be fit to do. Not like some.' She stopped and smiled. 'You've done brilliantly, the pair of you.'

'Not too bad, I suppose,' Dasher mumbled.

'I couldn't really say much earlier with you-know-who around. So sit down and tell me all about it.'

She sat with her back to the rick. Dasher sat beside her. I parked myself opposite them both and began.

'I got called to teacher training today.'

'Wow! Where?'

'St Patrick's in Drumcondra, Dublin.'

'Dublin – God! So when d'you start?'

'Early October. It's a three-year course.'

'So in three years, you'll be up at a blackboard with your stick and your chalk? Y'know, you won't look very much older than some of the kids you'll be teaching.'

It was not bright enough so she could see me blush. And for this I was glad.

'Got a cigarette?' she asked.

I opened my box. There was one. I offered it to her but she refused, telling me to light it up and share it round. I took a few drags and passed it to her. She took a lungful and gave it over to Dasher. After she'd done, she let her hand flop loosely onto his groin area. I imagine Dasher, too, was quite relieved that no one could see what colour he turned.

'And what about you?' she said as she pressed her face close to his. 'What's your story?'

'I . . . am . . . got a place in engineering.'

'Right. And how long'll that take?'

'Four years.'

'Well, at least when you've finished you might look the part. And when are you away?'

'Early October, same as Billy.'

'In Dublin too, yeah?'

'No, Cork.'

'Cork? What d'you want going down there for?'

'I tried for Dublin, but I didn't have enough points. I'm not too worried, though; I'm just glad to have been given a place.'

'So in a couple of weeks' time, you two will be gone in different directions. And I'll be stuck here like always, bored out of my mind. Still, it's great that you both have what you wanted. Strange that you should get the news on the same day.'

'Yeah,' I said. 'And on Dasher's birthday, what's more.'

'Really? How old?'

'Eighteen.'

'Eighteen! Christ, I wish I was eighteen,' she sighed wistfully. 'Old enough to drink, to drive, to vote. Old enough to run away from this goddam place and not have the cops haul you back. You're a man, Dash – imagine! I didn't get you a present, so I'm afraid you'll have to make do with a plain old birthday kiss.'

So she kissed him. And went on kissing him. And then, somehow, she manoeuvred her legs, despite the constriction of that black-leather mini, and straddled him. After an interminable bout of slobbering and sighing, she purred, 'Can we continue this conversation somewhere more private?'

Dasher looked over her shoulder and asked, 'Is it OK to go . . .?' and he pointed up the ladder to the haybench.

'Sure. That's no problem.'

Still in situ she turned her head, smiled and said, 'Thanks, Billy,' then she extended her hand and I helped her to her feet. As I did, her arm went around my waist and she drew me to her.

'Don't go too far,' she whispered. 'I'll be wanting a wee chat with you up there as well.'

Giddy with anticipation, I watched them both disappear up the ladder, then sat myself down on the spot where she'd been sitting. I wished I had a cigarette. In fact, I wished I had two, one for now and one for after. So taken was I with my imminent duck-break that I forgot to expect Dasher back down.

'What?'

'The Johnnie – gimme it.'

'No. It's mine.'

'But you said . . .'

'I said what?'

'You said we both could use it.'

'And what if we can't?'

'Sure we can.'

'We don't know that.'

'Look, gimme the Johnnie, you louser.'

At this, Suzy's head appeared over the top of the bench.

'Problem, guys?'

'No . . . I mean yes. Y'see there's two of us and we've got—'

'I've got,' I corrected.

'Only one Jo — condom.'

'That's not a problem. Those things don't work most of the time. All they do is spoil everyone's fun. Anyway, it's safe tonight.'

8

Dasher stammered, 'How d'you know?'

'You'll just have to take my word for it, OK? That's if you're still interested, of course.'

I elbowed him sharply in the ribs. Still he dithered.

'Tell you what, lads,' she said, and she got to her feet way up on high, 'let's forget all about this.'

Dasher looked at me desperately, then turned and ran, climbing the ladder faster than if he'd been hoovered up it. Suzy lay down again in wait.

I sat there, half trying to listen and half trying not to. With the silence roundabout hanging so heavy, it was hard to blot out the fumbling, the threshing, the occasional whisper, and Suzy's little giggle that chimed every once in a while like a hiccup. There was something vaguely indecent about it all, and I rose to take myself out of earshot until my own turn. But then gradually, there came upon the air another sound, one which could have nothing to do with the high jinks taking place above my head. It was coming from the other side of the barn, a heavy, trundling sort of noise, as if a very large wheelbarrow was being pushed in my general direction. I should've been afraid, but curiosity drew me to the corner and I peeked around. My first impression, I saw, was not far wide of the mark. A car, with lights and engine disengaged, was coming my way, the driver with his shoulder and right arm to the front column as he steered with his left.

When he'd brought the car adjacent to the hay, he went round and opened the boot. Next he reached as high as he could up the rick and began to tug at a bale.

As soon as I saw this, I knew I was going to do something. Drunk or sober, I couldn't not. We weren't wealthy people, my family; my dad did the best he could, but his thirty-five acres were mainly hillside or marsh, so margins were always tight. Only a few years earlier, Dasher's father had thrown in the towel on a similar sized holding and taken a job in a meat factory near town. Making ends meet, then, was an ongoing struggle. I was not about to just stand there and watch someone come in the night to thieve from us what little we had.

My first instinct was to shout the place down, and wake the three houses in the townsland. But I realized that this would leave us with some explaining to do. Instead I took a hayfork I found nearby and hissed, 'You!'

The thief stopped, the bale halfway dislodged from the stack.

'Put it back, and get the fuck out of here!'

Slowly he took his hands away and held them as if it was a gun I had.

'OK, take it easy,' he said. I thought I recognized the voice, but hoped I was mistaken.

'Is that you, Walsh . . . Billy Walsh?' With a laugh, he dropped his arms to his sides. 'Jesus, you had me going for a minute there. Leave down that thing before you take someone's eye out.'

I kept the hayfork at the ready. 'What the hell d'you think you're doing?'

Rodger Doran laughed again. 'Ah now, Billy, you're a smart bloke. Take a wild guess.'

'You're robbing my father's property.'

'Lighten up, pal, eh? It's not that big a deal, is it. And anyway, share and share alike. Come winter, my horse has to eat too.'

'D'you think I give a shit about you or your horse? And if you want him fed, you pay for his fodder like everyone else.'

He studied me for a moment. 'OK. I'll take four. How much do I owe you?'

'They're not mine to sell.'

'So what the fuck are we arguing about? C'mon, Billy boy. Chill out.'

He extended his cigarette box in my direction. It did me little credit that I took one. We smoked a while in silence, then I said, 'This is a bit out of your way, isn't it?'

'Yeah. But I was in the area earlier dropping home the bird, y'know. I couldn't help noticing how close this shed was to the lane. And what a lot of bales you'd already brought in. So I wasn't expecting that you'd miss one or two. Mind you, I wasn't expecting to meet anyone, either. What in God's name are you doing here?'

'Me? . . . Nothing.'

'Nothing? You come out to the haybarn at this hour of the night to do nothing?' He thought it over a while. 'I haven't interrupted anything, have I?'

'No,' I said, suddenly aware that if he were to cotton on there might be absolute hell to pay. 'Look, Rodger, I think the smart thing for you to do is to get in that car and drive away.'

'Yeah, that's a plan. Your . . . ah . . . your father doesn't really have to know about any of this, does he? I mean, there's no poi — D'you hear that?'

'No,' I blurted, a little too hastily.

He raised an open hand and stood stock-still. 'There it is again!' Then he pointed skywards and mouthed the words, 'Someone's up there.'

Before I could contradict, he turned to me with a great broad leer, his face the picture of a penny dropping. 'But you knew that already,' he said, a good deal louder. Still smiling, he stopped again to listen. 'Someone's getting his rocks off! Jesus! Who is it – Dasher? Dasher! Oh, you sly pair of bastards!'

Now more than ever, I wanted to scream. Or run, or do something. The sense of big trouble imminent was overwhelming. It was like I'd just seen an unpinned grenade roll to a halt alongside.

'So c'mon, Walsh – who's he with?'

'I . . . I dunno. Some woman.'

'I should bloody hope so. Where did he nail her?'

'We went to town. To Waterford. It was at a disco there.'

'And Dasher did the business. Or was it yourself?'

'Eh? What d'you mean?'

'I mean have you been up there already, or are you next?'

'I've not been up there, no.'

'Good. Well, in that case, you won't mind if I join the queue.'

'If you do what?'

'C'mon. She's obviously free size – y'know, one fits all.'

More trapped and more terrified than I'd ever been in my life, I could only stand speechless as he blustered on.

'Jesus, what a bit of luck. I struck out myself this night, y'know. My own little mot is normally a flyer but tonight she wouldn't come across, for some reason. Maybe she has the painters in – y'know, the reds must be playing at home.'

I was shitless, almost literally so as the ladder began to creak and Dasher slowly emerged.

'Attaboy, Dash! You're the man. I'd say the oul' cherry is well gone for a hop.'

Dasher heard the voice and froze, rooted to the spot like a deer in the headlights. Desperately, he looked at me for explanation or deliverance. But I could offer neither. Any second now, was all I could think. Any second now.

And sure enough, right on cue a small shower of hayseed gave notice that a head had appeared over the bench.

'Billy, what the — Who's that?'

'Huh? Suzy?'

'Y – yeah. Rodger – is that you?'

'You'd better fucking believe it, sweetheart.'

Slowly, unbearably slowly, he turned his head in Dasher's direction.

'You? . . . And my girlfriend?'

It would've been an idea to try defend himself, but instead Dasher's jaw only dropped further. In a twinkling Doran had swung a right hook, catching him between the ear and the cheekbone and landing him on his back underneath the ladder.

'Get away from him! You leave him alone, Rodger Doran!' Suzy screamed, in a voice so shrill I fancied it could've been heard on mainland Britain. Doran stopped.

'And what's it to you? Since when have you been interested in this piece of shit? C'mon, I'm listening.'

'Well, listen to this, and listen carefully. It's over, Rodger, all over. I'm not going out with you any more, and we shouldn't even see each other from now on.' And then, perfectly casually, she added, 'I've been meaning to tell you for a while.'

'Is that a fact,' he said. 'So, what's the story? You're dumping me for the likes of these two? And what's brought this on?'

'Stuff. Lots of stuff. And before you say it, it's got nothing to do with my father.'

'Oh, I wasn't going to. Cos, like, you're adopted, or had you forgotten. I mean, you dirty little tramp, you don't even know who your father is.'

'Well, at least I know he isn't a tinker like yours.'

Doran didn't reply. Instead he strode with great purpose to

13

the bottom of the ladder and up he went. Suzy, probably recognizing on his face a look she'd seen before, began to whimper.

'Rodger, I'm sorry. Honest, I didn't mean it. I didn't mean any of it. We can still go out together . . . Oh God, I'm sorry.'

'Not nearly as sorry as you're going to be,' he muttered as he advanced on where she lay. I could not see what happened next, but from the dull thud and the winded gasp, I imagine that he kicked her somewhere in the region of the stomach or ribcage. I did see him stoop low and reappear with a clump of that ink-black hair in his left fist. There he held her as he took aim with his right.

'Oh, Rodger, please . . .' she began again, but he cut short her pleading with a clubbing blow that smashed into the side of her face, making a sound like splitting cordwood. Even if she'd been in the whole of her health, she'd not have remained upright. As it was, she was sent hurtling across the shed where she collided heavily with the topmost support and then, dazed – maybe even unconscious – plummeted to the ground, her head splurging against the reinforced concrete base. It had all happened so quickly. Rodger Doran hadn't been trespassing on my father's land for more than five minutes.

I got to her first – hardly surprising, as neither of the others left the starting blocks. I took her head in my hands, looking for a miracle, but got only the flow of blood, warm and sticky through my fingers. On her poll the skin was broken and the skull underneath was in pieces, like a wrapped Easter egg dropped on floor tiles. If there was any sign of life there, I couldn't find it.

Dasher still lay where he'd fallen but had suddenly forgotten his own discomfort.

Doran looked down from above, continuing to talk big but unable to conceal the fear in his voice.

'She'll be OK. There isn't much brain there to damage . . . Well? Tell me, for Christ sake! She's OK, right?'

'No, she's not OK. Her skull is fractured. And she isn't breathing. I think she's dead.'

He hesitated, then came clambering to the ground. 'What are you talking about?' he growled. But when he got close enough to see, all he could manage was a whispered, 'Oh fuck!' Dasher, meanwhile, had risen to his feet and had dared to approach. He lowered his head for a closer look. The blood, the body lifeless and broken, was more than he could take. At once he became hysterical, gibbering loudly and uncontrollably.

'Oh Jesus! Oh my Jesus mercy! She's dead. Poor Suzy is dead.'

'Shut up, Morrissey!' Doran hissed. 'Shut the fuck up, you miserable bastard. D'you want to wake the whole fucking parish?'

'Oh God! Oh God! She's dead. You killed her!'

At this, Doran grabbed him by the throat and rammed him fiercely into the side of the hayrick. The gurgling, choking noises, and Doran's indifference to them, made me believe for a moment that he was about to do for Dasher as well and really make a night of it.

'I'm fed up of you and your fucking snivelling, d'you hear me? *Do you hear me?* Stop that whining, or by Jesus I'll give you something to whine about.'

'Leave it out, Doran!' I snapped. 'Don't you think you've done enough harm for one night?'

He turned his head towards me, held on for another moment and then let go.

Dasher collapsed, a limp sobbing heap on the carpet of loose hay.

'OK, then. So what are we going to do about this?'

'Morrisseys have a phone – we can go ring an ambulance. Although an undertaker is probably what we need.'

'Are you mad? Are you out of your fucking mind? If an ambulance is called, the cops will be right behind. We're not getting the cops involved.'

'What? Rodger, we've got a dead body here. We can't just put it down the back of the sofa. The cops were involved the second you knocked her to the ground.'

'Yeah – and I suppose that's what you'd tell them when they got here. That it was me.'

It *was* you, I almost said but didn't. Better judgement prevailed. I knew that I was dealing with a very volatile character here, an extremely dangerous man. I felt that if I could just keep him at bay, humour him, stop him from digging us any deeper into the hole we were mired in, then we might just have a chance. If we could make it through this night, if that sun would only hurry up and rise, things would be all right. Not *all right* – Suzy was dead, things could never be all right again. But for now, damage limitation was in order. It couldn't be allowed to get any more insane than it already was.

'Look,' I said, 'we can't keep the police out of this, but they don't have to know what really happened. There aren't any witnesses, so if we can get our stories together, everybody walks away from this scot free.'

Warily he looked to me, to Dasher, and to the body. 'Go on. Let's hear it.'

I could tell from the tone of his voice that if it was at all plausible, he'd bite. 'Right, how about this. Dasher, come in here.'

I was kneeling beside the body, Dasher was on the ground where he'd fallen, still weeping. Doran, half mad with impatience, grabbed him by the shoulder and dragged him to our little huddle.

'Here's how it happened. It was a total accident, nobody's fault. We were up in the hay having a bit of a laugh, swapping gossip, smoking a fag or two. She thought she heard someone coming so she went right over to the edge to look. She leaned too far, the outside bales gave way and down she came. We'll climb back up there now, knock down a few, leave them beside the body, and there's the proof. We keep it straight, keep it simple, and stick to that story no matter what.'

He peered at me for an age. Apart from Dasher's sniffling, and the sound of my heartbeats exploding in my eardrums, there was nothing. Then: 'OK. Like you said, straight and simple and we're out of the woods. Morrissey, d'you think you'd have the balls to carry that off?'

Through his tears, Dasher nodded. The poor bastard would've gone along with anything to just get the ordeal ended.

'Let's move it, then,' I whispered. I wanted to hurry things along. I wanted to get the police on the scene and have this lunatic arrested. At that moment we were close, so very close.

'Once more,' Doran insisted. 'Go through the story once more.'

'In the pub, we all arranged to meet here. Dasher and I got here first. Then —'

'Hang on,' Dasher interrupted. 'They'll have to do a post-mortem, won't they?'

'Yeah. And they'll find that she was killed by the fall. They'll have to, because she was.'

17

'But there's, y'know, there's spunk inside her. What if they can tell it's mine?'

'I dunno,' Doran snarled, 'maybe they'll give you a fucking medal. You stuck one on her – so did half the blokes in Lisdrolin.'

'But . . .'

'But what?!'

'It won't take the cops five minutes to find out that she was your bird. And that you and me never ever saw eye to eye. But still, we'll be asking them to believe that I had sex with her, while you just stood there and looked on. Who's going to buy that?'

Doran's shoulders dropped, he put a hand to his foxy mane and scratched.

'He's right, y'know. He's fucking right. That story of ours wouldn't have lasted pissing time. Jesus – now what?'

At that instant, I'd have throttled Dasher myself. Could the bloody idiot not see what I was trying to do? However, I knew I was moving on the right lines. Doran was clutching at anything.

'We can still manage it,' I said eventually. 'All the pieces will fit but, Rodger, you've got to get out of here. We'll give you a push as far as the road, give you five minutes to get away before we raise the alarm. And as far as I'm concerned, you were never here. Dash?'

As before, Dasher nodded.

'C'mon then,' I said and got to my feet. I could see Doran take something from his pocket but I couldn't see what. Then suddenly and without warning, he grabbed Dasher from behind by the hair and the pair inched backwards to the rick. I could make out what it was he'd taken from his pocket: a short-bladed penknife, now held to Dasher's jugular.

18

'Nice try, Walsh. Very nice.'

'What're you doing?' I said incredulously.

'I was never here. So why are my tyre marks all over your lane? You think they couldn't find those? You think I'm stupid?'

'You are fucking stupid! There'll be ambulances, coppers, maybe even reporters crawling all over this place in the next few hours. Your tyre marks? They won't be seen under all the others.'

His suspicions were shaken, but not enough.

'My prints are on the ladder. And God knows where else. There may be blood on the top girder where she hit before she fell.'

'I . . . yeah. I was going to clear all that away when you were gone.'

'You must think I came down in the last shower, Walsh. I know what was going to happen when I was gone. You and your pal were going to scream blue murder. Well, poor old Morrissey here won't be screaming blue murder. Or anything else, for that matter. It's very hard to scream when your throat's cut.'

Dasher whimpered. I had no idea what would happen now, and I could see that Doran wasn't terribly clear about things either.

'Let him go, Rodger. If you hurt Dasher, there really is no way out for you.'

'In that case I'm fucked, which or whether. Cos if I don't kill him, you two will sell me down the river. And, y'see, the way I'm looking at it now, one body, two bodies, even three, it'll be all the same to the judge. I've only got one lifetime to spend in jail.'

'You don't have to go to jail at all. Your name doesn't even have to get mentioned. You just need to trust us.'

'Ah, but there's the problem – I don't.'

Stalemate. And a blade to Dasher's throat. Maybe not an ideal time to call someone's bluff.

'Look, Doran, I've offered to help you cover up your first corpse. I'm damned if I'm going to stand around and watch you make another. Do what you like with him – I'm going to get my father.'

I turned. As I did, Dasher emitted a high-pitched, strangulated whine, and Doran hissed something into his ear.

'Come back, Billy. For God's sake, come back. He's going to kill me. Please.' And the blubbering recommenced. I turned back.

'I've a plan of my own, Walsh. And you're going to help me make it work. Isn't he, Dash?' and he yanked Dasher's head back.

'I'm cut! I feel the blood! Oh Jesus, Billy, do what he says. Do whatever he says, in the honour of God!'

'OK, OK,' I said. 'Take away the knife, and tell me what I'm to do.'

'You see those plastic bags over there?'

Near the gate was a small mound of empty fertilizer sacks, there since the spring.

'Those?'

'Yeah, those. Go get one . . . no, get two.'

'Why?'

'Just fucking get them!' and another savage yank at Dasher's hair.

'Right. What now?'

'Put her into one of them.'

'What?'

'Jesus Christ, are you having trouble hearing me?'

His grip, and his knife, tightened around Dasher's throat.

Half choked and half demented, Dasher could only just manage to sob, 'Do it, Billy. God, do it.'

As I've said previously, I had little or no choice. So I wasn't thinking about what I was doing, why I was doing it or what I might be required to do next as I lifted her ankles together off the ground and pushed them into the mouth of the sack. I then eased it up across her calves, knees and thighs. She was only a wee slip of a thing, so I had no trouble hoisting her by the waistband of her skirt and slipping the plastic over her torso. The bag being quite substantial, the arms and the head folded comfortably inside, so that she was now completely concealed. My chore done, I stood back. By chance, I'd gone out that night clad in a white denim shirt. I now looked like one who'd just come off work in an abattoir.

'Happy?' I said.

'Now go get a shovel.'

'And what – dig her a grave?'

'Just do what you're fucking told.'

Insanity was being piled on insanity – he seemed to want me to bury her. If I was to continue to do his bidding, I'd wind up in almost as much trouble as he was.

'And where am I going to get a shovel at this hour of the night?'

'Think. You too, Morrissey – think,' and judging by the grunt of pain that followed, he was exhorting Dasher to serious contemplation.

'There's one in the cowhouse. I saw it there earlier.'

In the milking parlour adjoining, right enough, there was a shovel. Used only to push the slurry towards the pit outside the lower door, it was big, square and very blunt. As a digging implement, then, it was practically useless. And if this madman had in mind what I thought he did, that v no bad thing. In any case, I fetched it to him as instructed.

He didn't seem the slightest bit deterred.

'Excellent man, Billy. This is what I call being sensible. You comfortable, Dash? No? Ah well, not much longer now. Right, Walsh – you see this?'

With his free hand, he indicated a good-sized area of ground that had been bloodied. 'Gather up all this hay, and shove it into the bag after her.'

That struck me as a rather pointless exercise. In the dark, and in the general chaos, I was likely to miss as much as I collected. Still, with Doran's gaze not leaving me for even an instant, I got to my knees. And it was then I heard it. Not much, but on this night, audible.

'Ssshhh!' I whispered. 'Listen.'

'Listen to what?' Doran asked suspiciously.

'Over there in the next field. Something's in the bushes.'

At the far side of the ditch, on land that belonged to Suzy's family, there was a little rath, a thicket of bramble and thornbush. Ancient mythology had it as the home of the fairy folk, and threatened only misfortune to anyone who dared meddle with it. Untended, then, through the ages, it was clogged and overgrown.

'What? What did you hear?'

'I dunno. But I definitely heard something stir.'

He regarded me with even greater mistrust. 'Don't move,' he told me. Don't fucking move,' and with that, he frog-marched Dasher to the ditch. For a time, they both peered anxiously into the undergrowth. 'There's nothing here, Walsh,' he hissed. 'There's fuck all.'

'I'm telling you.'

'No, I'm telling you. If you try to get smart with me again, your buddy'll be one sorry man. Now get that stuff into the bag and drag it round to the car.'

I took the sack by its mouth and hauled it and its cargo along two sides of the shed. Doran walked alongside, manoeuvring Dasher ahead of him as he went till we arrived at the old Avenger. The boot still yawned open.

'Leave it there, go back and get the shovel. And bring that other plastic bag.'

Dasher let out another whimper by reflex.

'What? D'you reckon the second bag's for you? I can't say I've not been tempted, Morrissey, but you can relax on that score.' When I came back he continued, 'No, Dash, I've got plans for you. Get in.'

'Do what?'

'In. The boot.'

Another wave of near hysterical sobbing broke over Dasher as he climbed inside.

'And shut up, for Christ's sake. Now, we're going to put this bag in there with you. What you've got to do is keep the mouth held high – make sure that nothing drips out. The cops are going to go over this car with a fine-tooth comb when she's reported missing. If they find any blood, any hair – anything – we're rightly in the shit. OK, Walsh, leave that down and grab the other end.'

I rested the shovel against the taillight, Doran laid his knife, still open, on the ground at his feet, and together we hoisted the body in to where Dasher lay.

'Next problem – where can we dump this? C'mon, you're the locals. You must know somewhere.'

I didn't. It had been an exceptional summer, with sunshine and no rain for at least six weeks. The countryside was like granite – I knew of no place nearby where the ground could've been dug without a JCB.

23

'Lads, lads, think. It'll soon be sun-up.'

'I know,' Dasher said. 'The old sandpit. What d'you reckon, Billy – it'd do, wouldn't it?'

Dasher was by now so disorientated and so terrorized that he was actually assisting in this cover-up. But if he'd briefly forgotten what side he was on, there was no faulting his thought process. The old sandpit, which had belonged to his own father till the man quit the land entirely, was pretty well perfect. It had been a quarry in the early days of the century and reputedly excavated at its deepest to about fifteen feet. Over years of disuse, it had filled with putrescent, stagnant water till it came to be a serious health hazard to livestock; some had drowned there, others were poisoned. For this reason, it was railed off with barbed wire as long as anyone could remember, and in time had become partly covered by a robust carpet of reeds, rushes and scrub grasses.

Its location, too, was ideal. Another mile off the beaten track, down a cobblestone lane, and then a distance of four or five fields from the main gate. Being low-lying, the area was almost always marshy underfoot, and scarcely accessible even by tractor. But after the dry spell we'd had, a car could comfortably be driven to within yards of the barbed-wire fencing. Once there, the corpse could be disposed of where no one would ever find it, where no one would think of searching if they searched for ever. And just then, even I wasn't sure whether this was what we wanted.

'Well, Walsh – the sandpit sound OK?'

'Yeah, it'd do.'

'You know where it is?'

'Uh-huh.'

'Good,' and he slammed the boot closed on Dasher and the body. 'Get in, and start navigating. Before you do, put that other bag on the seat under your arse. Like I said, no chances, no traces.'

He started the car like one in a hypnotic trance. All the way down the little boreen he glared straight ahead into the darkness, not looking at me, not talking to me, acknowledging my directions only by following them.

It was a route I'd have found blindfolded. I'd walked that path many a time in bygone days, in other summers. As children Dasher, Suzy and I were to be found there almost daily, wading about in the sludge of the exposed shallows, or daring to trampoline on the mesh of scrub and rush that blanketed the deeper waters. It was on this that I was thinking as the car reached the point where it was necessary to leave the cobbles and make the rest of the journey cross country.

'Here. This is where we turn off.'

'Through the fields?'

'Yeah.'

'Right, get out and open the gate. And walk ahead of me, in case I drive into a boghole. Cos if this car gets stuck, Walsh . . .'

Like the chief mourner in some macabre parody of a funeral, I set off with the Avenger trundling along behind. Though we were now a good way from civilization, he still proceeded without headlights. At last, I led him to a halt beside the spot.

Doran got out and unlocked the boot. There was Dasher, just as petrified, still holding the mouth of the bag aloft. Without a word, I took the other end and lifted. I must've held it too high because as Dasher put his feet on the ground the head flopped out and on to his chest, leaving a circular bloodstain to the right of his breast pocket.

'Leave her on the grass a minute,' Doran said. 'I'll find a stone to keep her weighed down.' He took two and bunged one in either side of the corpse.

'Right, let's get on with it,' he ordered.

We – Dasher and I – slid under the bottom strand of thorny wire, a tighter squeeze than when we'd last tried it, but we managed. We then dragged the sack and shovel along after. I took a step or two away from the bank – the floor sagged a little under my feet, but I knew I'd not sink. When he saw this, Dasher too stepped out.

'About here?' I said to him. He didn't answer.

'Dasher! About here?'

'Huh? Yeah, yeah. Sorry. I can't help thinking . . .'

'I'll do the fucking thinking around here,' Doran snarled from the sideline. 'Now shake a fucking leg – it's almost morning.'

And so I began. Blunt though the shovel was, it was sufficiently sharp to hack a metre-long opening in the surface. Thick, oily sludge bubbled up, covering our feet and ankles. I reached down through the muck, caught one lip of the aperture and lifted it as high as I could. It was enough for Dasher to push in the body of Suzy Deane. Done in mere minutes. Even Doran was impressed..

'Brilliant,' he muttered. 'Just what the doctor ordered. Now one more thing. You'd best get rid of those shirts. Here!' And he threw the other sack, the one I'd been sitting on, over the wire to where we stood. 'Stick them in there, and put the lot into the hole as well.'

It seemed a good idea, better far than having to invent excuses come laundry day.

'That's the way. Now go down to where the water is cleaner and give yourselves a wash – you're both covered in it. Give the oul' shovel a wash as well.'

We knelt beside the pool and began to splash the stale, putrid water over our arms and shoulders. It's not that we were getting very much cleaner, but the blood was washing away.

'Hey, lads, what are we to do about the tyre marks? If they follow the trail to here, they won't be long finding the rest.'

'Don't worry about that,' Dasher told him. 'The Galligans – they own this land now – they're drawing silage from the next field. There'll be tractors and wagons going up and down here all day, almost from first light. They should start arriving any minute now.'

'You sure?'

'Certain. They've been at it the past few days.'

'Well, if you're sure that's the case, Dash, I'll take my leave of you. Don't get up – I can see myself out. I'd offer you a lift but . . . you know how it is. Now it's important that we all stick together on this. I know they'll come knocking on my door. So I'll tell them that Suzy was planning to run away again. That she was just pissed off around here, and she was going to do a flit. Sounds OK? And you two don't have to be involved at all. Boys! Don't ever say I'm not good to you.'

We both nodded. He walked round his car, opened the driver's door, but rather than sit in he put both elbows on the roof and eyed us one last time.

'Oh, but just in case you do decide to become involved – I think you know what I mean – well, there's things you should consider before you try to rat me out. If they do dredge this pit, what'll they find? They'll find your shirts covered in her blood. They'll find Dasher's spunk inside her. And Walsh – I know you. I know you can't wait to get my back turned till you run screaming to the police. But first, think on this. She was my woman, everyone knew that. Why would I want to harm her? I loved her, didn't I. And she loved me. Not you or, Jesus Christ, not you, Morrissey. Hey – y'know what's just struck me? You must've raped her! Yeah, raped her, then killed her to keep her mouth shut. And when I came on the scene, you bribed me to help you get rid of the evidence!' He stopped, his grin widening. 'Have no fear, guys, my story will be at least as good as yours. And another thing – those big prospects I heard you boasting about in the pub earlier. Wouldn't it be a shame if you couldn't take up those fancy university places because you were busy helping the police with their inquiries around this boghole?' He lit a cigarette and inhaled deeply. 'Y'know, before, I didn't know if I could trust you fellahs. Suddenly, I'm a lot more confident. So, all for one and one for all, then. Be seeing you around, brothers!'

He didn't switch on the headlights but by now, he didn't need them. We watched him drive slowly away and disappear into the early morning dusk. Watched our lives, as we'd known them to that point, disappear with him.

We jumped the ditch and set off for home by the short cut across the fields. The air, chill as night became day, tingled where we'd washed and not dried, but our pace was brisk. As it need to be – we could not afford to be sighted half-naked and at large at such an hour. But the path we were taking was remote, so there was little risk for us. I wasn't sure I could say the same for Doran. Then Dasher said it for me.

'Oh Jesus, what if Galligan's silage wagons meet the car in the lane?'

'It's too early for them – the dew's not had a chance to lift.'

'I hope they won't.'

We'd crossed another field before it occurred to me to

wonder why he hoped Doran wouldn't be rumbled. He couldn't possibly be thinking of going through with this, could he? I needed to know.

'Dasher, we can't sit on this till morning. Let's do it right now.'

'Do what?'

'Ring the guards, what else.'

'You're going to ring the guards?'

'You may be sure I am.'

He looked at me despairingly. 'But . . . why d'you want to do that?'

'Why? *Why?* Because there's been a murder committed. Because an innocent girl is dead.'

'No one's ever going to find out – unless you tell them.'

'That isn't the point. Suzy was a friend. She was one of our own. And I'm not having it on my conscience.'

'It's on our conscience now, like it or not. Nothing's ever going to change that. Being in prison certainly isn't going to help.'

'Prison? What the hell are you talking about? We aren't the ones going to prison, I promise you that.'

'But you know how Doran's going to tell it – you heard what he said.'

'Yeah, I heard him. He's talking big, but he's worried, and with bloody good reason, too. Cos when the cops get busy on this, it won't take them long to come to the truth of it.'

'I dunno, though, he does make it all sound very believable. And it'll only be our word against his.'

'Exactly. And there's two of us. When people see that our evidence is the same, we're the ones who'll be believed. Especially if we come clean about it right away.'

'D'you reckon?'

'Of course. Doran said we should all stick to the same simple story. Well, how about you and I go for the simplest one of the lot – the truth. If we tell exactly what happened – everything – I guarantee we'll be OK.'

'And when they ask what we were doing there in the first place?'

'We'll tell them. It's small beer compared to what happened afterwards.'

He breathed deeply, noisily; once, then twice, then: 'What about if they discover that I had sex with her?'

'So they discover that – so what? It's not a crime.'

'Isn't it? Suzy was fifteen.'

'Yeah, but you're only . . .'

'I'm eighteen, as of today. Well, it's yesterday, now. Statutory rape, I think they call it.'

I didn't answer. He turned to face me.

'So, it looks as if I'll be going to jail, one way or another. But hey – you follow your conscience. I'm willing to take what's coming to me. I mean it. Mind you, Doran was pretty much right about one thing; I won't be going to university. Neither will you, for that matter. When it comes out that you were waiting around to take turns on a minor – a child – d'you think they're going to want to train you to teach children?'

Half an hour before, I could not have been more adamant. Now, in this instant, I was certain of nothing. Not another word was spoken till we reached my father's haybarn, the scene of the crime.

'Look, Billy,' Dasher said quietly. 'My mind's made up. I'm going to try to keep this quiet. I can't tell you what to do, but whatever you decide, I'll back you. If you say the truth has to come out, then let it and to hell with the consequences.'

30

And off he went. I returned the old slurry shovel to the dairy where I'd found it and crept indoors. Through the neat little kitchen, then up the narrow stairs and on to the landing – mine was the small room at the far end. On tiptoe past the first door, behind which my sister was sleeping soundlessly. With even greater caution I stole by the next, that of the main bedroom. Inside I could just about hear my father, snoring softly and evenly. I didn't disturb his slumber, not that night.

CHAPTER TWO

With indifference that shocked me, the sun rose as it had always done. I watched it through a crack in the curtains first turn the sky a weak watery red then gradually come into its own. I didn't sleep. I'd not even closed my eyes when I heard my dad come to call me. Then I had to fake it.

He threw open the curtains and shook me by the arm.

'Bill – are you right?'

I turned on to my back, rubbed my eyes and looked at him stupidly.

'I won't even ask what you got up to last night. But throw an oul' shape there, like a good lad. I want to get cracking while the day is fine.'

When he'd gone, I got into my old work clothes and came downstairs. Dad sat on a straight-backed chair by the Rayburn, having a gander over the week's *Kilkenny People*. Mam put a bowl of cornflakes in front of me. With great difficulty, I began to eat.

'There's tea made,' she said, pointing to the hob. 'D'you want toast?'

'No thanks. Tea's fine.'

'Well, did ye have a good night?'

'Not bad.'

'Where did ye go?'

'We went to the pictures in town.'

32

'Any good?'

'Nah. Some war film.'

'Wasn't yesterday Michael's birthday?'

'It was.'

'Eighteen, wasn't he?'

'That's right.'

'He didn't ask to go drinking or anything, I hope.'

'Oh God, no.'

'Good. Time enough ye'll be at that.' Then to my father, 'I think I'll do a bit of washing. They're giving rain for the coming week.'

'Hmmm.'

'I'll see if Mags has anything she wants done.'

She climbed the stairs and left us alone. Dad continued reading, not attempting to involve me in conversation. Which was just as well. One half of my fragile concentration was trained on our front yard, into which I expected to see a squad car come screeching at any moment; the other half was desperately trying to devise some strategy for when the cops did show. Now, in the light of morning, that seemed absolutely inevitable. Maybe because we'd missed something the previous night and had left a trail that led directly to the body. Maybe because Doran had double-crossed us and taken his version of events to the police already. Either way, it appeared only a matter of time. My dad continued to read quietly.

Without warning, my mother dramatically flung open the kitchen door. She strode to the middle of the floor holding aloft my jeans for all present to witness. 'In the name of God, boy, what *were* you doing?'

'I . . . ah . . . came across the field from Morrisseys. I stepped into that drain behind the cowshed.'

33

'I don't know what's going to shift this. The socks are as bad. And I think I may just throw the shoes out.'

'Throw them down in a bucket of water and let them soak,' was my father's tuppence worth. Her lips pursed – she didn't trust herself to respond to that.

'Where's your shirt, by the way?'

'Is it not above in the room?'

'No.'

'I must've chucked it in the laundry basket, then.'

She turned and began to walk away, tut-tutting as she went.

'And what's this in the pocket?' she suddenly stormed, her back still towards me. My nerves, shot as they were, sent me directly to the blindest panic. The condom – she must've found it. A clue, the first link in the bloody chain.

She spun on her heel to face me. Like the nurse drawing the ticket in the Irish Sweepstake, she waved in my face my empty cigarette box. I all but melted off the chair with relief. Then:

'Well – what have you to say for yourself?'

I shrugged.

'And what about you, Murt Walsh. Now d'you see what your big son is spending your money on?'

For a while, my dad and I had had this tacit agreement. I didn't smoke in front of him. And if I didn't mention it or make an issue of it, then neither would he.

'You're a very foolish young lad,' he chided without much conviction.

'"A very foolish young lad?" Is that all you're going to say?'

'You may whistle if it's not,' he said, standing himself to his full height. 'I'll have plenty to say on the matter, don't you worry.' Then to me, 'Get out that door in front of me.'

I did, he followed.

'We'll draw first from the mountain field. I had a look when I was driving out the cows, and the hay is in great shape. Did you put diesel in the tractor last evening?'

'Yeah.'

'Good lad . . . you should give them oul' things up.'

'I know. I'll try.'

'Fair enough. Right, let's go.'

I quickened my step so that I reached the haybarn first. If we had left anything blatant, then I just might be able to dispose of it before he got there. But to my utter amazement, there was nothing. This wasn't a forensic certainty, of course, but at first glance, all appeared to be in order. I paid especial attention to the base of the girder where she'd landed; the better to examine it without arousing suspicion, I pretended to take a lengthy piss there. Last night, this spot would've been running red – today, not as much as a fleck. It hadn't rained in the meantime, this I knew. So, unlikely as it seemed, we must've managed to gather every last thing that was bloodstained. And in the dark at that. It was uncommonly good fortune.

My father cranked up the Massey-Ferguson, I took my seat on the trailer and we set sail for the mountain field. It would've been about half a mile from the house, up a fairly steep and rocky incline. I know it's insane, but once there, I felt safe. The police might call to the house, but they'd come no further. At least, they'd not come this far; up here, I was beyond their reach. However, these periods of immunity were fleeting. As each new load was filled and we made the return journey to the farmyard, I was next door to demented, believing with every visit that the reception committee would be standing in wait. That was one morning that passed very,

very slowly indeed.

At about two we stopped for dinner. I was making sweaty, tortuous progress through mine when my sister arrived in. She'd been walking. Her brown tousled hair, which she sometimes kept tied up, was loose and tumbled to the shoulders of her light cotton dress. There was dust on her sandals, and she carried a small bunch of primroses. When my father had taken his tea to the chair beside the hob, and I was alone at the table, she came and sat by me.

'Mam was saying you went to the pictures last night?' she mumbled.

'That's right, yeah,' I mumbled in reply.

'What did you see?'

'Some war film.'

'Must've been one helluva movie, cos it's left your friend pretty hungover this morning!'

I didn't answer.

'So, where did you really get to?' I checked over both shoulders. But before I could say, she guessed, 'The Heather?'

'Uh-huh. You were talking to Dasher, then?'

'No. I was over at his house right enough. I had a few magazines for his mother, and anyway I wanted to congratulate him on getting called to the Uni. But he wasn't up. And apparently, he has no plans to get up today. So when I heard that, and remembered the state of your clothes, I thought, well – must've been quite a night. Incidentally, what time did you get in?'

'I dunno. Pretty late.'

'About five o'clock?'

'Not at all. It was long before that.'

'You sure? I could've sworn I heard you on the corridor about that time.'

'I might've gone to the jax or something. But I'd been in for hours at that stage.'

'Hmmm. OK, if you say so. By the way, who was it that carried you home?'

'No one carried me. I walked, or didn't you see the state of my shoes.'

'So whose was the car, then?'

'Car?'

'Yeah, there was definitely a car. I heard it in the lane, coming and then going again much, much later. But you saw nothing?'

'No.'

'Curiouser and curiouser. I don't know how you could've missed it. I guess it must've been quite a night.'

The afternoon shift passed no more quickly. Nor was the toil lightened by any great dint of dialogue between us. My father did his best but found his efforts all falling on ears that were deaf and distracted. My mind was in a good many places that Saturday, but up in the mountain field atop a hayload was not one of them.

However, as the shadows lengthened, things began to ease. Again, there wasn't much logic to it, but I truly believed that day one was critical. If the first twenty-four hours passed, chances were that the next twenty-four years might follow suit. But then, as I was putting in place the very last bales on the very last load, I saw him come. From my raised vantage point, I first caught sight of him several fields away, then watched as he came through gates, eased himself over stiles and finally clambered across the ditch

37

till he stood in the field where we worked. Joe Deane, Suzy's father. The hairs on the back of my neck began to bristle.

'God bless the work,' he called as he drew near.

' 'Tis well for some,' my father called back. 'The landed gentry, out running the rule over the estate!'

'Estate, how are ye! I was over in the hill field checking on the barley.'

'And what's it like?'

'Not too bad at all. But by God, it could do with a drop of rain.'

'Who're you telling. Sure the whole country is parched. If it goes on much longer, the spuds won't be as big as ball bearings.'

My father sat himself down on a bale, produced the pipe and was sending great plumes of smoke into the evening air. Joe parked nearby and lit a Woodbine he took from his top pocket. Casually, he shielded his eyes and looked up.

'Well, young man. How are you?'

'Fine,' I said. Then my father, his every word emphasizing that this was no big deal, asked, 'Did you hear the two boys' news?'

'I did not, no.'

'Young Morrissey below is going for engineering. And the lad here is after being called to Drumcondra. Y'know – teacher training.'

'Good God, Murt – you're going to have a schoolmaster in the family!'

'Aye. More in my line to try have a farmer in the family. I dunno what's going to become of this place at all, at all. I'm telling you, Joe, young fellahs today just don't want to get their hands dirty.'

'And small blame to them. Would you rather see them spend their lives foosthering around in all weathers, and in all sorts of muck and gutter like we did? Good luck to you, boy. If you have the brains, good luck to you.'

He was naturally a modest man, my dad, and was uncomfortable with too much praise for him or his.

'Oh, brains indeed! Wait till we see how your lassie gets on – I reckon she'd buy and sell this guy. Her results should be out soon – didn't she do the Inter Cert.?'

'Well, Murt boy, we put her name down for it. And we gave her the exam fee. But after that, I couldn't tell you. She spent most of the time since Easter on the mitch, so I don't know if she bothered her backside even sitting them exams.'

'Would she do something like that?'

'I wouldn't put anything past that young wan. Myself and Rita are at the end of our tether with her – she has our souls blackened. She's gone again, y'know.'

My heart jumped into my windpipe. And there it stayed.

'She's what?' asked my dad.

'Gone. Went in to call her today and the bed hadn't been slept in. Billy, you weren't out last night, were you?'

'I . . . er . . . was, yeah . . . for a while.'

'I don't suppose you happened to see her?'

'Ah . . . I . . . no, I don't remember if I did.'

'Nah, you wouldn't. She was with that pup, Doran.'

'Doran from over Knockowen side?' dad asked. 'The Englishman?'

'The very one. That's the boyfriend.'

'Wouldn't he be a bit old for her?'

'Old? He's nearly the same cut as myself! Oh, I used to put the run on him when I saw him, but I gave that up months

39

ago. For God's sake, what's the point? I can't be watching her twenty-four hours a day.'

'Maybe 'tis over in Knockowen she is with the lad?'

'Well, if she is, he's welcome to her. This is her third time going, and she can stay gone this time. Jesus, Murt, I'm not a young fellah any more – I can't be keeping up with the likes of her. She can run someone else ragged from now on. If they find her, they may put her in a home, or foster her out, I don't care what they do, I'm washing my hands of her. Anyway, she'll be sixteen in a couple of months, so after that she can paddle her own canoe. And no bother to the same cailín.'

'I bet you'll find you're getting all worked up over a thing of nothing. She's only gone as far as Knockowen.'

'She's gone farther than that, I'd say. Her travel bag is missing, along with some of her clothes, all her money, and her passport. She looks like she means business this time.'

'By God, it looks that way, doesn't it. Were you down with the guards?'

'No, I wasn't. The barracks were closed when I was coming from the creamery. I'll drop over to Pat Morrissey's after tea and I'll give them a ring. For two pins, I'd nearly say nothing at all about it, in case they might find her. But I suppose I better, or else the people will start saying 'twas I done away with her.'

At this, they both laughed, but I paid no heed. Because at last, things were beginning to make some smidgen of sense. Small wonder that Suzy had spoken so earnestly about the prospect of running away. Or that she'd stayed sober all the previous evening. And then gone for a midnight hike rather than take to her bed. Obviously, she was just marking time till sun-up, to catch the first of the haulage trucks as they went rumbling through our village on the way to Rosslare ferryport. And from there to Britain and to mainland Europe. She had with her everything she needed; clothes, money, passport, the lot.

Down below, the laughter and the bantering of the two men continued, but their words floated by me like thistledown. If Suzy had packed a bag, then where was it? She'd taken it from the house, according to her father. She lived only a hundred yards or so from the spot where she'd met her death. Yet when she'd reached the haybarn, she didn't have it. So where could she possibly have stashed it on the way? At once, I knew this was about to become absolutely crucial. If we could find it and dispose of it, we'd have ourselves the perfect decoy, the ultimate red herring. Nobody would ever question whether or not she'd legged it. However, if someone else were to find it before us, it would be clear that the girl never left Lisdrolin. In all this, we had one great advantage; we were the only people who knew where to search. Come to that, we were the only people who knew that there was anything to be searched for.

'Suzy Deane! . . . little Suzy Deane! I can't believe that!' Mags kept on over supper.

'Well, there you are now,' my dad said gravely.

'And you say she's done this sort of thing before?'

'Twice! The first time was back there in – when was it, Peg?'

'Early May. The weekend of the Castlegannon show.'

'That's when it was. She thumbed as far as Carlow and got stuck there overnight. The guards found her sleeping rough on a park bench.'

'Wasn't she lucky the police found her. A young girl, all on her own in a park in the middle of the night. She might've run into any sort of lunatic. Or pervert.'

Occasionally, she said things like that for no other reason than to embarrass him. I saw her smile as my dad waited for the air to clear before he would continue.

'Oh sure, 'twas only the mercy of God that she came safe. But d'you think she learned her lesson? Not a bit of it. A fortnight later she made it to Rosslare and managed to get on the ferry. But Henry Culleton, down from Deerpark, drives lorries all over the Continent, and he just happened to see her on the boat. So he rang the station here in Lisdrolin, and when they docked in Fishguard the British police were waiting for her.'

'Little Suzy Deane!' my sister said again, incredulously. 'It's amazing. She used to be the nicest, happiest child.'

'Oh, I don't know. I always thought there was a wilful streak to her.'

'You mean she wanted her own way? C'mon, Dad. What child doesn't from time to time. But this – I wonder what could've sparked it all off?'

'We know well what did that. It was finding out that she was adopted.'

'Finding out? She didn't know already?'

'No.'

'You mean to say that Joe and Rita let her get to fifteen years of age before they told her?'

'They didn't even tell her then. What happened was, her class was going on a school tour to France last Easter. For that she needed a passport, and for that she needed her birth cert. And there it was in black and white; her mother was a northern woman by the name of McDermott, and there was no account of who the father might be.'

42

'And up till then she never suspected? Christ, what a way to learn the truth. You have to feel sorry for her.'

'Joe Deane, Rita Deane, that's who I feel sorry for. I have damn all sympathy for that spoilt little brat. When she found out that these decent people took her in after her own abandoned her, she might at least have shown some gratitude.'

'Doesn't always work like that, Dad. And I don't think it's fair to sit in judgement on her. I mean, how would you have reacted in a similar situation? You don't know, cos you've never been there.'

My mother stepped between the two. 'So, Murt, what's Joe doing?'

'He's going to the guards, but he's not taking her back.'

'No?'

'No. He's after rearing her for fifteen years, and look what thanks is on him. He's going to let someone else take over the job now. And I can't say I blame the man.'

Mags let this one go with him, but then there came to her eye a mischievous glint. 'So, come October, there'll be no young people here in Boher?'

'That's right,' my mother said. 'We won't know the place, we'll have such peace and quiet.'

'Good God,' Mags went on, intrigued. 'Two kids here, one in Morrisseys' and none at all in Deanes'. Round these parts, we really bucked the trend.'

'What trend is that, love?'

'Ah, y'know how it's supposed to be. Good Irish Catholic families, in mortal dread of the church, no contraception, tons of guilt and children by the dozen.' Then with a sly wink in my direction she stood up and excused herself.

43

My mother, looking like one who'd just had a bad fright, came to the table to top up my father's teacup.

'You know something,' she told him grimly, 'she'd say exactly the same if 'twas the priest sitting here.'

Leaving my father to gnaw on his lower lip at the very thought, I too took my leave. I set off at once, my business was too pressing to permit even time for a change of clothes. But barring my way out the back door I found my sister, sitting on the step, head buried in a book. As usual, a mighty bulging tome with the print microscopic.

'Any good?' I asked as I squeezed by her. She lifted it from her knees, turned it over to consider both covers and said, 'Yeah, excellent.'

'Ah. *Covenant*,' I said, reading aloud, edging towards the gate.

'I'll be finished soon – I can let you have it.'

'Thanks all the same, but it's a bit on the thick side for me.'

'Or you for it, maybe.'

'Oh, very funny. Pity your remarks at suppertime weren't as clever.'

'I'm sorry, your honour,' she giggled. 'I wasn't thinking straight. Still amn't actually. I can't get my head around Suzy and her antics.'

I desperately wanted to get away. But for fear she might suspect that I was running from the subject, I stopped.

She went on, 'It's bloody weird.'

'Not really. Not if you'd been here these past few months.'

'So it didn't surprise you, then?'

'No, not much.'

44

'Did you know something like this would happen . . . or *do* you know something about what *has* happened? You stayed very quiet all over supper.'

'And is that supposed to prove something?'

'It just got me thinking. She vanished in the middle of the night. That car I heard must've been involved, somehow.'

'Well, then, how would I know anything about it. I saw no car.'

'Oh yeah,' she smiled. 'I forgot. Pardon me. Anyway, are you going somewhere?'

'Only to Dasher's.'

That smile again.

'Is she coming back, Billy?'

'Suzy?'

'Yeah, Suzy.'

'I wouldn't know.'

'If you were a gambling man, how would you call it?'

'It's not the kind of thing I'd bet on.'

'I suppose you're right. Anyway, will you miss her?'

'Won't we all.'

'Hardly as much as you will – and I would bet on that.'

'Ah piss off, will you.' And now I could reasonably make my exit.

Bridget Morrissey confirmed what I'd already learned from Mags. Dasher was refusing food, refusing to quit the bed, and absolutely refusing to talk about it.

'Ye must've had a bucketful of it last night,' she said, half joking, half accusing.

I didn't comment.

'Oh, don't worry, boy, I'm not going to tell on you, God

45

knows. C'mon, I'll bring you up to this other fellah. Maybe you can coax him back on his feet.'

Morriseys' house was practically identical to ours; Deanes' house completed three of a kind. All had once been servant quarters to a stately home burned to the ground during the Fenian uprising. The lord of the manor fled at once to London, never to return. Subsequently, the estate was divided into small lots and sold off. Which is where our respective ancestors came upon the scene.

I followed Mrs Morrissey up the narrow stairs to the door of her son's room. She knocked.

'Michael, you have a visitor.'

'Wh – what?'

'There's someone to see you.'

'Who?'

She pushed open the door and ushered me inside. In the half-light, curtains still drawn, I could see Dasher had hoisted the eiderdown up to his nose. Peering out above it, his eyes were ablaze, a terror that subsided only very slowly.

'Billy! It's you! Well, the curse of fuck on you. I thought . . .'

'You thought what? Who were you expecting – the pooka?' his mother laughed.

He looked at her, then to me, then back to her as the room fairly cracked with unease. Then: 'Give us a few minutes, will ya? I need to have a quiet word with Billy.'

With a roll of her eyes, she obliged. I allowed her time to descend the stairs, then double-checked outside the door. Satisfied that the coast was clear, I said, 'So – are you getting up?'

'No,' he shivered.

'How long d'you intend carrying on like this?'

'As long as it takes. Until it's safe to go out again.'

'Safe to go out again? What d'you mean by that?'

'You know bloody well. I'm going to lie low till I'm sure no one is looking for me.'

'Really? And just suppose they decide to come arrest you in the meantime – what, you dive under the bedclothes and you're across the state line?'

His hands trembled, his knuckles whitened round the blanket he was clutching.

'Dash, nobody's looking for you, nobody suspects a thing. But if you decide to turn yourself into a recluse on the very day Suzy goes missing, then someone just might start asking questions.'

His eyes twitched as he thought it over. I went on, 'Doran may be a bad bastard, but he's right about this; we're only as strong as our weakest link. All it takes is for one of us to flip and we're all up to our necks in it.'

He opened his mouth to speak, but then hesitated. Mouth still ajar, he squinted into each of the four corners of the room and tried again. But again words failed him. Only after a long anxious stare at the bedroom door did any sound emerge. And even then, not much more than a whisper.

'Did you sleep last night?'

'Eh?'

'Did you . . . sleep?'

'For a short while, maybe.'

'I didn't. I couldn't. I still can't. Every time I try, I keep seeing her face. Not even her face – I mean that thing that looked up at me when the head lolled out of the bag. It looked right up at me – the eyes were wide open. The hair

47

was matted, the mouth was slack and full of blood. And every time I feel myself drifting off, it's there like a fucking jack-in-the-box.'

'That's understandable. But it'll pass.'

'Will it? What makes you so sure?'

'Look, if it's any consolation, I didn't sleep very much better last night. In fact, hardly at all.'

'But it's not just the sleep – being awake is worse. Every car I hear on the main road, every knock at the front door, every time the bloody phone rings. I don't know if it's because of what happened, or because I'm afraid someone will find out what happened. But, Billy, I don't know if I can hold it together much longer.'

'OK,' I said, evenly, firmly. 'Cut out the dramatics and get a grip.' I placed both my hands on his shoulders. 'Listen to me, listen carefully. We've had a bit of luck.'

'Luck? What kind of luck?'

'Joe Deane was over with my oul' fellah today. He's convinced she's done a bunk. And that's what he's telling the guards. Y'see, her kitbag, her clothes, her money and her passport are all missing.'

'Missing – how? Jesus! D'you reckon she was really intending . . . ?'

'That'd be my guess, yeah.'

Now not daring to make any sound whatsoever, he mouthed, 'So where's the bag?'

'I dunno. She must've hidden it somewhere in the field behind our hayshed.'

He sprang from the bed and feverishly began to dress.

'We've got to find that bag. And we've got to find it this evening.' He was tying his second shoe when he stopped. 'Oh shit – a problem. Billy, how are we going to look for it? We

48

can't start searching in broad daylight without someone asking what it is we're searching for. And we'd never be able to find it in the dark.'

'We'd better be able to find it in the dark. It's the only . . . what're you doing?'

He'd fallen onto all fours and disappeared under the bed. He re-emerged, beaming, holding two hurleys and a sliotar. I could not for the life of me tell why.

'Geddit? We go up there now for a few pucks. We "lose" the ball somewhere in the ditch. That way, we can rummage and poke as much as we like, and nobody need be any the wiser. Would it work, d'you reckon?'

'Christ!' I laughed. 'There isn't much wrong with your mental health. It's brilliant – of course it'll work. If it's there, we'll find it.'

'If it's there? Where else could it be?'

'True for you.'

'So what'll we do when we find it?'

'Let's just find it first, OK?'

Straight off, then, to Deane's rath field. And after knocking it for a while from one to the other, I hammered the ball into a clump of bramble that I'd marked with a mental note. Then we both set to work round the margins of the field, prodding, swiping, shaking and flattening till everything that grew thereabouts had been disturbed. We even explored the rath itself, the dense thicket in the field's corner, shaking out every nook and every cranny. But we found nothing; there was nothing there to find. With night falling fast, we scratched our heads and went our separate ways, not knowing what to think. Other than that, even in death, she still had us jumping through hoops.

*

The police did call round next day, but not to take anyone away in irons. Theirs was a purely perfunctory visit, going through the motions and nothing more. Joe Deane advised them that he had nothing further to add to the initial report he'd made. And when he told them how he'd spoken to the neighbours and they'd seen nothing either, this was taken at face value. The cops' response was reassuringly slipshod; working on the premise that she'd left the area and was attempting to skip the country, they were concentrating their search on sea and airports. But given the head start she'd had, they concluded that the odds were against them. If she'd managed to get on the right side of a cross-Channel trucker – a feat she was more than equipped for – she might now be anywhere in Europe. Joe's obvious lack of concern didn't seem to bother them very much. It was common knowledge locally how Suzy had the man's heart scalded.

Some time around midday, Dasher called by. He'd slept. He was back on his food. And having heard how the police were treating the disappearance, he was generally feeling a whole lot better. Now if we could just lay hands on that goddam travelbag, the illusion was complete. He'd been thinking it over, he said, and could only conclude that she'd stowed it in a hedgerow by the road between here and Lisdrolin. To be collected in the early hours as she passed en route to her great escape. I nodded – I could think of no other possibility. In that case, he asked, would I care to come with him for a stroll.

We walked to the village and then back. We travelled the road slowly, checking both sides as we went. And when we'd done, we did it again. Nothing. Which left what? Either it was somewhere else entirely, somewhere we'd not thought to look. Or else some person, or persons, had come upon the bag that night and made away with it. Stolen it, never realizing. If this were the case – well, who knew what would happen. We could only sit back and wait for what twists the plot might take. While in the meantime keeping our eyes wide open. And acting normal.

It was in this spirit of normalcy at all costs that we found ourselves back down the village that evening to meet some of the lads for a drink. Lisdrolin boasted three pubs. The first, heading down the main street (the only street), was Conway's. The owner, Tom, was a middle-aged alcoholic, permanently unkempt and aggrieved: the pub he owned was the most disreputable shithole in the place. And he could not have cared less – he'd serve beer at any time to anybody who could make it through the door under his own steam. So it was here that we'd been chancing the odd bottle of cider ever since our middle teens. But we had to be careful; police raids were frequent. In Conway's pub, you drank at your own risk.

A few doors down on the same side was Ned Law's. This was a very staid establishment, mainly for an older crowd fond of their darts and their twenty-fives. To the likes of us, still some way shy of the legal drinking age, it was strictly out of bounds. We weren't welcome, it wasn't our scene, but more to the point, there was always a strong possibility that you'd bump into your father there.

The third, and best, was the Heather Blazing, at the very far end of town. All cut stone and bog oak, it was pricey, but it had the style and the clientele. It was quite strict on matters like dress, general conduct and of course, age; only recently were we deemed old enough to drink there. But now we were in and making the most of it. It felt like the big time.

Seamus Gunning and Peter 'Leaky' Roche were already there. They'd bagged a table near the fireplace and had reserved some stools. Just as we joined them, Kevin Wrafter arrived in from a match in the hurling field. But as it hadn't involved Lisdrolin, no one was interested in hearing about it. So talk turned at once to Friday night's bender, in which we'd all taken part. Or rather, to the state of the heads next day. Kevin and Seamus, casual agricultural labourers, told how they cried off work in the early afternoon, sick as the pigs they were castrating. Leaky, a plumber, hadn't even stuck it that long; in the midmorning he'd left a burst mains in Buckstown, claiming he needed to fetch a particular washer, and simply failed to return. We laughed, Dasher and I, then kept our own accounts brief and sparing on detail. I said I'd surfaced early, in reasonable condition, and had gone working with my father. Dasher described his day as being quiet and unmemorable. Nothing more.

One of the All-Ireland football semis had been televised that day; it was next up for discussion. In fact, we talked of many things before eventually coming round to Suzy's disappearance. Being her third, it was news no longer. Kevin Wrafter did ask if it was true that she'd taken her passport with her. Seamus pointed out that she'd now been gone for almost forty-eight hours, far, far longer than any of her previous attempts. So maybe she'd managed it third time lucky. Leaky bemoaned the departure of such an absolute cracker, but felt that it was better for the girl herself. Because breaking with Lisdrolin meant breaking with Ginger Rodger Doran. And, he said, no matter where on earth she fetched up, she couldn't do worse than that bastard.

'What bastard would that be, Roche?' came a voice from behind.

All heads turned, like to a brick through a window.

'Rodger! I didn't see you there.'

'I know fucking well you didn't. So go on, Roche. What bastard?'

'Y . . . you wouldn't know him. A bloke I was working for last week. He wouldn't pay me . . . the bastard.'

Doran smiled weakly, then came shambling forward and collapsed onto a vacant stool at our corner table. All around, the conversation died in the throats, as the pints were swigged and then studied with great interest.

'What's the story, lads? You've all gone quiet.'

Unblinking and expressionless, Doran allowed his gaze to drift over the gathering, stopping as it fell on each one in succession. He was well drunk, that was clear. But not so drunk that he couldn't see and enjoy how he'd set the company on edge.

'Walsh,' he said finally. 'Are they putting something in the water supply up your way or what?'

'What . . . what makes you say that?'

'Well, take a look at the head on Morrissey there. Jesus, he's like something that was fished from the sea near Sellafield.' When nobody laughed, he went on, 'Seriously, though, is there some funny business going on up there in Boher?'

'What're you talking about?'

'I take it you heard my bird's legged it again. No note, no forwarding address, into thin bloody air.'

'Yeah,' I said. 'It's odd.'

53

'Oh, you reckon it's just odd, do you? Easy knowing you weren't the one who had the rozzers round feeling his collar at cockcrow this morning. Asking me all sorts of ridiculous fucking questions, turning my fucking house inside out. They even searched my bloody car.'

'And did they find anything?' Dasher blurted.

Doran fixed him with the kind of look I'd seen two nights earlier. 'Yeah. They did. In the boot. They found a car jack and a tyre lever. What the fuck did you expect them to find, you simple cunt?'

When he'd done branding Dasher with his glare, he turned to myself. 'Now where did the coppers get the idea that I'd know anything?'

'Because you were her boyfriend, I expect.'

'Yeah, maybe. You don't supposed someone squealed. Y'know, tipped them off that I might be keeping something dark?'

'I can't think of anyone who'd do a thing like that.'

'Good. Cos if anyone did, it'd be a very, very bad career move. Could seriously damage a person's health.' He smiled at me. He seemed satisfied that our understanding still held good.

'For what it's worth, I'm pretty certain that sad old bastard who says he's her father – but fucking isn't, of course – he put them on to me. Funny that, cos he's been fairly civil to me these past few months. Anyway, enough about that. I've come to ask a favour.'

Nervy glances were exchanged around our table.

'I don't reckon I'll be up in Deane's for a spell – I don't believe I'd be terribly welcome. So if there's any news of Suzy – like if she rings or writes or whatever – I'll have no way of knowing. What I want you two lads to do is, if you should hear anything, keep me posted, OK?'

We nodded.

'Sound, I appreciate it. We'll have a pint on it. Who's behind the bar? . . . Oh fuck, not him.' Chris Scanlon, the senior barman, was very particular about who he served and who he didn't. No one took liberties during his watch.

'Chris,' Doran garbled. 'A couple of drinks when you're ready.'

The barman pokerfaced him a long while. 'I thought I told you never to come back here again while I was around.'

'They're not for me, honest, they're not.'

'Who are they for?'

'For my friends. Him. And him.' Slowly, theatrically, he indicated Dasher and me. 'Him and him, swear to God. Two pints of lager, g'won, good man.'

For a moment, nothing. Then, 'You can pay for them first. And then you can clear off about your business.'

Doran put a hand on the table and began straining to his feet. 'Charming! I must say that is fucking charming. Service with a smile, eh.' When he reached the counter, he emptied some balled-up pound notes and a clatter of change from his pocket. The barman took the money required, then literally showed him the door. In the archway, he stopped and faced round.

'I'll be seeing you, lads. I'll be looking out for you. And you fucking better be looking out for me.'

Following that, Lisdrolin was decidedly off limits. Doran spent his days patrolling the main street in his horse and cart, taking in odds and ends and all manner of garbage. At night, he was liable to show up anywhere. So, save for Sunday mass, we stayed well out of the place. And what little socializing we did we took to Waterford, four miles in the road. It wasn't ideal, but it wasn't to prove too great an inconvenience. Because only a few weeks later we both left home, Dasher for Cork, myself for Dublin's fair city. Almost inevitably, we made our departures on the same day, 5 October. By coincidence, it would've been Suzy's sixteenth birthday.

CHAPTER THREE

St Patrick's Training College, Drumcondra, was a liberal version of boarding school. Room and board were provided within the campus, but the rules were adult; if it was legal under the constitution, it was OK by St Pat's. I checked in there on the blind, not knowing a sinner, then discovered the bloke next door to be in just the same boat. Dwyer his name was from somewhere in Leitrim. He too was a smoker, a sports fan, and one who'd lately begun chancing his arm at various watering holes. Neither of us could boast a steady girlfriend, or even an unsteady one. But with the ladies in St Pat's outnumbering the lads many times over, this was something we both anticipated putting right before too long. From the outset I was among friends, among equals.

As I found my feet in the capital, I occasionally wondered how Dasher might be faring in University College, Cork, some two hundred miles to the south. We'd agreed that, except in case of emergency, we'd not bother maintaining contact. Long-distance phone calls were expensive, while letters were for mammies, daddies and elderly relatives who'd made cash contributions. In any event, midterm was just one month on. We'd pledged that, come what may, we'd make it back to Lisdrolin for the break. And regardless of who might be skulking thereabouts we'd have a pint, compare notes, swap stories and trade any little bit of scandal we were fortunate enough to generate. No, I'd not forgotten him.

And neither had I forgotten *that*. I tried. I roared it away when I felt it close. I crammed my mind, my consciousness, with a million other things. I read, I sang, I whistled, I prayed, I counted bloody sheep. But there was no keeping it at bay. Several times a day, and twice as often by night, I'd be ambushed, visited not by a memory but by flashback. The sound of her pleading as Doran climbed the ladder, the dull thud as she struck the concrete, or washing the blood off our hands in the old sandpit with the deed done. One or many of these would be rampaging inside my head before I'd even had a chance to raise the drawbridge.

In all of this, I wasn't helped by one unfortunate coincidence. Occupying a room on the same floor as myself was a girl named Kay Sharpe who bore the most uncanny resemblance to Suzy. Ms Sharpe was then in her second year, so every morning on my way to the refectory I was presented with a pretty close approximation of how Suzy would've looked had she been allowed to reach nineteen. In height, weight and physique the match was perfect. Practically identical too was the oval face with the snub nose and the impossibly high cheekbones. Every time she walked in the room, she held me transfixed. She was never out of my line of vision, as my eyes followed her like searchlights. All this unbeknownst to myself, of course. I had no idea just how blatant I was being. Not till one day in the common room when she and her friend were playing table tennis. As ever, I was poised nearby, mesmerized by the contest. All of a sudden, I was disturbed by a very rough kick to the underside of the chair where I sat. With a start I turned around, and there was her boyfriend, a great bear of a fellow from third year, and looking particularly bearlike at that moment.

'Hey, asshole!' he said. 'Why don't you take a fucking picture? It'll last longer.'

'Sorry?'

'I've been watching you, pal. Now, consider your card marked. Next time, it'll be a slap in the jaw.' Then, to her, 'C'mon, Kay. I don't like having you around this weirdo.' From that day on, I discontinued my surveillance, and allowed the good Ms Sharpe to go about her business unscrutinized.

Of course, she wasn't the only fish in the sea. And within the first few weeks Dwyer and myself spliced ourselves on to a large clique, country lads all, and we would regularly and in packs set about those other fish. We were, I guess, about as successful as any such disparate group could've expected to be. There were some among us who never made it, some who never missed, and one or two curate's eggs like myself. In that first month, I did just about adequately. Halloween was upon us, and with a little massaging of the truth I could face Lisdrolin, and Dasher, with reasonable confidence.

I reached the village at around six and without bothering to check in with my folks, I made straight for the Heather. He was already there.

'Thumb, did you?' he asked.

'Yeah. You?'

'Course I did. Better things to be doing with my money than handing it to CIÉ. Chris – another pint of your stout.'

He'd changed. There was about him a brashness that was well at odds with the Dasher I'd known.

'So,' he said, 'tell us all about it.'

'No, you first. Where are you staying?'

'A flat in Barrack Street. It's supposed to be for four, but there are eight of us. Which means I have to sleep on cushions in the living room. But it's OK. And the craic is mad.'

'I've got a room in the college itself.'

'A room of your own?'

'Yeah. Everybody does. There are more than a hundred people rooming in our house alone. Girls as well as fellahs.'

'Wow! And these women – what's it like sharing a gaff with them? Y'know, having them around all the time?'

'Ah, you get used to it.'

'You smug bastard. If you knew the lengths we've gone to coax women back to our place in Barrack Street. With very bloody limited success. How about you – how're things in that line?'

'I dunno. So-so, I suppose.'

'You've gotten off the mark, then?'

'Dasher, in St Pat's there are three women to every bloke. You'd need to have leprosy not to hit the target every once in a while.'

'Three to one? Good Christ! I find that very upsetting. D'you mind if we change the subject?'

'Sure . . . let's see. How're you finding the lectures, then?'

'Not too bad. Nothing I can't handle so far. What about you?'

'OK. I'm getting by.'

I ordered another round.

'Quiet here, isn't it,' Dasher remarked. 'I wonder if Leaky and the boys are out.'

'Maybe down the street somewhere. You haven't been in touch with any of them since we left, have you?'

'Nah. I spoke to my mother a couple of times on the phone, but nothing more.'

'And? Anything strange?'

'Like what?'

'Well, did she say anything about . . . y'know, if there were any developments . . . y'know?'

The big city swagger, the mask of the man-about-town, instantly slipped. He looked horrified. 'No. Nothing. And don't mention it to me again. Ever.'

There was an awkward silence, then one or two attempts to restart conversation that floundered badly. So we drank up and left the Heather Blazing to go down the village in search of the others. Sharing only our own company this night would not be much fun.

Conways was practically empty. Tom the landlord was still there and, by the look of things, still his own best customer. We enquired if he'd seen any of our friends that day, but he answered with just a slobber. One of the other patrons, however, suggested that we might try Ned Law's – that they'd been seen there of late. This surprised us; only that summer we'd been run out of there in a very peremptory fashion. And told not to even think about returning for several years.

But that's where we found them. In the darts pub, with Kevin and Seamus involved in a game of 501, Leaky marking the board.

'Hey, look who's home!' Seamus said. 'When did ye get in, lads?'

'An hour ago,' I told him. 'We tried the other two looking for ye.'

'What are ye doing here?' Dasher asked.

'Playing darts, what's it look like,' Kevin said.

'Oh, very funny. I mean, why Ned's?'

'Well, it's an improvement on those other places. One is too uppity, the other's a kip.'

61

'But what brought you here in the first place?'

'There was a darts tournament on one night. We rambled in and asked the bossman for a pint.'

'And he said yes?'

'No problem.'

'The last time we asked, he said something else entirely – remember?'

'Ah, we've done a lot of growing up in the meantime,' Seamus smiled. And then, with a sly wink, 'The tash made all the difference.'

'What tash?'

'Mine,' Leaky beamed. 'What d'ye think?'

He was fair-haired. And the moustache was a wretched effort, barely visible to the naked eye.

'Suits you,' Dasher lied.

'Yeah,' I said. 'And when you hit puberty, it'll be the makings of it.'

'I'll hit you now, you smart fucker. You're not in Dublin a wet day, and already you're starting to act like a jackeen. Which reminds me, I bought an old car since I saw you last. I just want you to know that it won't go over fifty miles an hour.'

'So?'

'So when you're robbing one later on, rob someone else's.'

This got laughs all round. The noise bestirred Ned Law, who emerged from a room somewhere at the back.

'Lads – ye're home! What'll it be?'

Dasher filled his chest and dropped his voice an octave. 'Two stout, please.'

'Jesus, Ned,' Seamus said. 'I'd think twice before I'd serve these guys. I mean, if you turn this place into a students' hangout, you can kiss goodbye to the working man. Am I right, lads?'

'Fucking sure,' Leaky agreed. 'You can hardly expect us to be drinking with wasters like these.'

'They're no worse than some of the wasters here already,' the barman announced. 'Like, Roche, when are you coming back to do those rads for me? And to do them properly this time?'

Leaky blushed puce. 'Monday, Ned. I swear to God. Everything's taken care of.' And, all of a sudden, he became completely engrossed in the darts match in progress.

Our drinks came and were paid for. We rested them on a table near the board.

'So, lads,' Seamus asked, 'how's life treating ye?'

'Fine,' I said.

'I suppose poor little Lisdrolin is a bit of a let-down after Dublin.'

'It's a bit different, that's all.'

'Plenty of beer and craic, I suppose.'

'Yeah, loads.'

'And women?'

'There's a few of them around, right enough.'

'Any sign of Suzy Deane?'

This was so out of left-field, so apropos of nothing, that I thought at first I must've misheard.

'I beg your pardon, Seamus.'

'Simple question – where's Suzy?'

I looked from him to Kevin to Leaky. All three were regarding us with rapt anticipation. I attempted a laugh.

'I don't fucking know.'

'Oh, I think you do. You both do. So what about you, Dash. Will you tell us if he won't?'

Dasher gulped as if he was trying to swallow a grapefruit. 'It's like Billy said – we know nothing about that.'

I felt myself go red, then pale, hot then cold and still they were glaring. Accusing. And prepared to wait. Then Kevin emitted an involuntary snort which instantly triggered a damburst of laughter, loud and rowdy. The three quite literally fell about the place helpless as day-olds, wiping tears from eyes and struggling to catch the breath.

'Jesus, we had ye going there!' Seamus gasped at last. 'You should've seen the look on yer faces!'

And away they went again. Such was my relief – at what, I didn't know – that I joined them in the merriment. But not Dasher.

'What? What's so fucking funny?'

'Ah, it's nothing.'

'It's not nothing. Tell me!'

'Right, here's what happened,' Kevin said. 'Yer man, Ginger Rodger . . .' The mention of that name at once cured me of the infectious laughter. 'He was in Conway's one night lately. Polluted drunk, as usual. But he started rambling on about the young Deane wan, absolute bollox, there wasn't head nor tail to it. But out of the blue he says, "D'you want to know where she's gone? Well, ask her neighbours. Talk to the two college boys. They know a lot more than they're letting on, I promise you that."'

Seamus Gunning drew a long breath, then sighed. 'Dasher, you should have seen yourself! Christ man, you were a picture.'

'That's probably because I didn't see the joke, Seamus. And I still don't. There's things you have a laugh at, and then there's other things. Suzy was a family's only child . . .'

'Yeah, an only child who just packed up one night and fucked off on that same family. *She* didn't give a damn, so why should you?'

64

'And you're sure of this, Seamus, are you? That she's away on some kind of adventure holiday? For all you know, Suzy Deane might be —' and here he stopped himself short.

'She might be what, Dash?'

'She might be in trouble.'

'In trouble, like up the pole? Knowing her, I'd be bloody surprised if she isn't by now. Jesus, Dasher, moving away from home has done nothing for your sense of humour. Leaky,' he called, turning to the dartboard, 'what have I left?'

'One double nine. Kevin has double top.'

So we watched the games. We took our turns at the oche. And we drank a reasonable amount. But somehow the night in Ned's failed to catch fire.

It was an easy decision to take and as we walked to our homes up the Boher road we duly took it. Next morning we both explained to our folks that the rigours of university life demanded that we not stay even one more night away from the slog and the study. And our poor folks, God help them, could not hide their admiration. In fact my dad was just a wee bit concerned, and took me aside to advise against overdoing it.

'Don't kill yourself,' he told me. 'You're only seventeen once. Th'oul books will always be there.'

But turning tail and hotfooting it didn't solve a whole lot. No matter how far or how fast, I could never hope to outrun the demons that I carried with me; those that lay by day just beneath the surface, waiting for night to fall and sleep to come. It was on that very same Saturday I had the dream for the first time.

I was standing outside the front gate of our house, shoulder to shoulder with a long line of complete strangers, though we seemed cordial enough to one another. There was a buzz of anticipation over the whole scene, and presently my paternal grandmother appeared. She'd been dead for a good number of years, but in life I'd been her great favourite. With her she carried a rosette-type thing, possibly a medal with an ornate ribbon attached. And as she walked along the line, surveying, all eyes turned to me; there was no doubt in anyone's mind, least of all my own, who the decoration was earmarked for. But she strode right past me like I wasn't there, and pinned the medal to the chest of somebody or other further along the row. Once more, all eyes turned to me. I tried to make light of my disappointment, to put a brave face on things, but even as I shrugged and jittered I could hear the people whisper that I must've done something wrong. Something terribly wrong. And in the way of these dreams, they moved seamlessly to knowing exactly *what* I'd done wrong. The whispers then became louder and more insistent; he killed her, I could hear. It was him. As yet, no one had dared say anything to my face, so I began to walk away casually, as if nothing were amiss. But it was then that one from the depths of the crowd shouted, 'Why don't you admit it? For the sake of her parents, admit it.' All at once, the whole throng began to take up the chant. I fled through our gates, ducking into a door on my left where I found myself inside the library of St Patrick's College. I started to slalom between the shelves, pursued all the while by my accusers, calling upon me to do the honourable thing and confess. I ran and ran, but the harder I tried the more my feet stuck to the carpet, and the more the crowd was gaining. I continued to struggle on feverishly, but as I looked up I saw I was headed straight for a second mob who were advancing along the aisle from the opposite direction. I now had no avenue of escape, and as this became obvious, everyone stopped and fell silent. Then Fr Hughes, our local parish priest, stepped forward into the clearing. 'Admit it,' he repeated. 'For the sake of her parents, admit it.'

'Admit what?' I asked. 'I don't know what you're talking about. Leave me alone, because I've got work to do.' And saying this, I pointed to the upper shelf, to a big black hardback entitled *Calculus* by Michael Spivak – this was, in reality, one of the main textbooks for the maths degree I was attempting. 'Now if you'll excuse me,' I said, and with a flourish I removed Spivak and began to examine the spine. As I did, the crowd gasped; there, behind the row of books but now perfectly visible, was the severed, bloodied head of Suzy Deane. Her eyes were open and wild, her mouth was contorted into a silent scream, and it was with the baying of an angry mob in my ears that I woke with a scream of my own. When I did come round I was sitting bolt upright, trembling and lathered in sweat that was already turning cold. It had been so vivid, so crystal clear and so real that it took several minutes to fully convince myself that it was not. I switched on the bedside light and mentally noted all the familiar, reassuring features roundabouts; my desk, my radio, my locker, my books were all in the appointed place, with not a severed head nor a lynch mob in sight. Gradually I could feel my heartbeat slow down and some calm flood over me. I checked the clock; it was three fourteen. Reveille was still a long, long ways off. So I quenched the light again and lay back in wait for five more hours' sleep that never did arrive, not that night at any rate.

That was just the start of it. Two nights in three – possibly even more frequently – I'd find myself standing outside our front gate, making polite small-talk with the strangers all about. Knowing full well that I'd shortly be standing in the college library, my guilt being witnessed by the eyes of the living and of the dead. No matter how often the nightmare recurred, it always had an identical ending. There I'd be, staring wildly around my half-lit room with sheets soaked through and my heart pounding like a trip-hammer. And no matter how familiar this routine became, it still took me some time each night to satisfy myself that I had, in fact, been dreaming. There was one other curious aspect to it all. I always awoke at the same time – three fourteen. I couldn't say if this time had any special significance; I'd not been wearing a wristwatch on the night when all these terrors were first set in train. Whatever the case, when I woke to see the clock show three fourteen, I could resign myself to watching another sunrise, minute by long-drawn minute.

Inevitably, sleep so disrupted, so denied, caused my health to suffer. I would arise even more exhausted than when I'd taken to my bed. My waking hours were nothing of the sort; it took me all my time to keep my leaden eyelids apart as I shambled about between the light and the dark. There was a listlessness, a torpor that draped over me like a heavy wet blanket. My appetite went in very short order and I began to lose weight that I could ill-afford to shed. Attending lectures became utterly pointless, as I was forever dozing off and missing the crucial bits. Even when I managed to stay awake, my mind was apt to be miles away, very often in that one place and time I least wanted it. As for general leisure activities, I could no longer be bothered. Eyebrows were raised; I was, after all, a competent athlete and had been selected on the Freshman panels for both hurling and soccer. But now I had neither the energy nor the inclination. Deprived of this exercise, I was no longer able to run off the

ten or so cigarettes I got through each day. I soon had a
raking cough that couldn't be shaken, and an odour of
inertia and stale tobacco that even I began to find objection-
able. Cold sores red and raw took up permanent station
around my mouth, and the acne I'd practically avoided as a
fourteen-year-old made a belated but drastic appearance. I'd
once remarked to Dasher how only leprosy could prevent a
bloke getting lucky in St Pat's. Before long I found myself
regarded by the female element as though I was carrying
something contagious.

For a month or more, I let the situation fester. The day I
decided that enough was enough, Christmas hung heavy in
the air. I well recall jostling through hordes of carol singers as
I made my way down O'Connell Street. From there, it was
the 51 bus to Newland's Cross, and from there a ride hitched
home. The nightmare was killing me, this I knew. I also knew
what had triggered it; that was Doran. Ginger Rodger, drunk
and loud, just about stopping short of telling the world where
the body could be found. Going on to almost say how it was
me who'd helped put it there. But this had been back at
Halloween. How much more might he have disclosed in the
meantime, drip-feeding it to an eager audience whenever the
booze got the better of him? I had to be told directly, from
source.

But he wasn't there. Normally he haunted the main street to
such an extent that local map-makers occasionally pencilled
him into town plans. Now, of all times – mid-afternoon
Saturday – would've been peak trading hours for trade such
as his. Yet today there was neither hair nor hide of himself,
his cart or his flea-eaten horse. A quick head round the door
in each of the pubs yielded nothing either. I wondered if he'd

moved on. Possibly emigrated. Maybe even died. Christmas was coming – it was the time of year to be optimistic.

The Heather Blazing was the last of the bars to be checked. As I came out, no closer to finding my man, a blue Datsun pulled up alongside the kerb. The passenger door was immediately swung open by way of invitation. I couldn't see who the driver was, but accepted regardless. Once sat in I found myself side by side with Pat Morrissey, Dasher's old man.

'I thought it was yourself,' he smiled. 'Are you going home?'

'Ah . . . I . . . yeah, I am. I was just heading there now.'

'I very nearly didn't stop for you. I was driving up from the creamery when I sees this guy staggering out of the boozer in the middle of the day, so I says to myself, "That's surely one of the Walshes of Boher." ' And he chuckled. Same old Pat.

'I didn't recognize the car,' I told him. 'Is it new?'

'New to me.'

'It's smashing. There must be a bloody fortune to be made in that meat factory.'

'Well, if there is, I notice you were in no great hurry to go into it.'

Still smiling, he turned to me full on, his first good look at what he'd received into his vehicle. Immediately the smile wilted and he re-trained his eyes on to the road. Then, 'I'd say somehow that you're home on sick-leave, young fellah. You don't look yourself at all.'

'No,' I said, 'I'm fine, thank God.'

'Well, maybe it's nothing, but . . .' and instead of words, he ran his fingers around the edges of his lips.

'Oh this?' I almost laughed. 'I've a few oul' spots, that's all. Maybe a bit of a rash. I must've kissed the wrong girl.'

'Or too many right ones, maybe. G'won, you rogue!'

'Aye,' I said. 'Anyway, I just came home cos there's not a lot doing around the college this weekend.'

'Winding down a bit, I suppose, coming near the Christmas.'

'Something like that.'

'Are you finding the work any easier?'

I had to think about this, to wonder what he might be driving at.

'The work? . . . It's fine, yeah. Handy enough, mostly.'

'That's good. Cos back at Halloween you were struggling a bit. Sure my lad was the same. D'you remember – the pair of ye went back early to see could ye catch up a bit.'

I laughed a little at how wrong he was. Until Halloween I'd been well in there among the pacesetters. It was only since then that they'd left me for dead, kicking dust in my red-rimmed eyes as they went.

'What're you grinning at?' he asked, catching me cold.

'Am . . . nothing. I was just thinking that this is a strange time of the day to be coming from the creamery.'

'Especially for someone like myself who doesn't own cows any more.'

'That's true! So what's the story?'

'I needed a bearing. Well I didn't need it – JJ Maher needed it for the JCB.' JJ Maher was a local contractor in heavy machinery. 'He's reclaiming a bit of land. Used to be mine once upon a time, but it's Galligan's property now.'

'Really – where, exactly?'

'Bedad, a place you ought to know very well. D'you remember where the old sandpit was?'

An invisible fist hit me behind the eye.

'You know the fields I'm talking about?'

'Yeah. I think so.'

71

'Many's the day you spent down there, paddling your feet in it when you were only a little fellah.'

'That's . . . ah . . . that's right.'

'It was the same in my time. You could nearly swim in it back then. The water wasn't as dirty as it is now.'

'So, like, what's going on down there?'

'Something that badly needs doing, let me tell you. The place is like a swamp this time of year – you couldn't set foot there without going to your balls in it. And sure in summer, when it dries up a bit, that pit is a bloody death-trap. In my father's time we lost count of the animals that went in there and never came out. And 'twas only the mercy of God there wasn't a child in there along with them.'

'But what's Maher doing there?' I snapped.

'He's draining the land. Digging trenches all around the ditches, laying drainage pipes crisscross over the whole area. He's nearly finished, actually. These are the things you miss while you're above in Dublin living the high life and chasing the quare wans.'

'But what about the fucking sandpit?'

'Well, that has to go too. Maher was just about to get started on it when a bearing went on the bucket of the JCB.'

I had to object. However pointlessly, I had to put an oar in. 'And why . . . I mean why the hell are you running errands for JJ Maher? It isn't even your land any more. What were you doing there anyway?'

'Oh God, boy, there's a right crowd around. Including your father. And Joe Deane. He wasn't to be seen all week, but he's there today, let me tell you.'

'Jesus, what is wrong with you people? Where the fuck's the big attraction?'

'Oh sure, the want of something better to be doing,

mainly. But it ought to be fairly interesting. You know the bit
you can see? Well, that's not too bad – it's about four feet
deep, and it won't be much of a problem. But there's a big
part that's covered over with rushes and reeds and the like.
There's no man alive in Boher today who ever saw that clear,
and God alone knows what's down there. But sure we'll all
know in a few hours' time – Maher is digging the whole lot
up.'

I needed air. Without bothering to ask, I began to roll
down the passenger window. As I did, we reached the T-
junction adjacent to our front gate. Straight on was the road
Pat was following, while the right-angled turn would take me
home. He stopped the car.

'D'you want to come down and see the craic?'

'No, I'd prefer to go home.'

'Are you sure? I'll be half an hour, max.'

'Look, I want to get out, OK?' I blurted. Then, catching
hold of myself, 'I mean, thanks all the same, but I'd better go
inside. Thanks again for the lift, Pat.'

'Don't mention it, Billy,' he said, a little taken aback, and
he chugged off down the old cart-track.

The dog barked and barked as I opened the gate, stopping
only when he'd recognized me. Inside, my mother was busy
as always, polishing shoes and making ready the good clothes
for mass that evening.

'Sit in by the fire,' she said, 'you look like death warmed
up.'

'Yeah – I haven't been well.' *So how much time?*

'I'll make tea. Or would you rather wait for soup?'

'Soup . . . that'd be nice.' *The machine would already be
dismantled. To replace the bearing? Ten, maybe fifteen minutes.*

'Are you coming with us to mass this evening?'

'Yeah, I might as well.' *Another five minutes to fill a pipe, smoke a cigarette, get everything restarted.*

'D'you want anything aired or ironed. Or are you going dressed like that?'

'No. I mean, I'm OK as I am.' *Then back to the dig. The area wasn't great, and those JCBs could really shift earth. Half an hour should see the whole place cleared.*

'Don't put your feet up on that chair – those are your father's Sunday trousers.'

Another fifteen minutes as the onlookers examined what the digger had dredged up. And spotted therein two white fertilizer sacks. And deduced from the brand name and design that they'd been put there only very recently.

'Careful now, it's hot. Taste it before you put salt in it. Did you have a dinner?'

'I did . . . not, no.'

'I'll be making supper before we go to mass. Daddy and all the other men are down at Morrissey's sandpit. Or Galligan's, I should say.'

'I know.'

'How d'you know?'

'What?'

'How d'you know? Who told you?'

'Pat Morrissey did. He carried me up from the village.'

Mere moments, then, for those to be pulled from the sludge and opened. For those present to see, to realize, to believe what they'd just found.

'And no sign of Suzy since – imagine!'

Oh, give it an hour or two, woman, I remember thinking. An hour or two, and you'll have every sign of Suzy you could want. Still she went rabbiting on.

'Indeed, boy, you might often be gone the same way as Suzy for all we ever hear from you. Is it asking too much to drop us a line once in a while?'

'Yeah, OK,' I mumbled. 'I . . . sorry, what did you say?'

'I said that myself and your father would appreciate the odd letter home.'

'Fair enough, I'll remember that.'

'Oh you will, I'm sure. You're gone as bad as that sister of yours. We don't know if that young lady is alive or dead half the time.'

And off she went about her business, her thousand tiny cares. Filling this, emptying that, laying out the prayer books, the rosary beads, the jingle of loose change for the church plate. It was like watching the danceband on the *Titanic* rehearse. The greatest hue and cry our little village had ever known was upon us. And she was topping up the sugar bowl.

It was then that we heard the car come up the cobblestones. My mother remarked that the driver must be in an awful hurry. Normally the potholes and the rocks protruding meant that the boreen had to be taken at a snail's pace. But to judge by the juddering and the jangling, there was no thought of caution. Presently it arrived at our front gate where it made a skidded turn, waiting just long enough for a passenger to disembark, and then roared off again. Seconds later a form flashed before the window, then my father came hurtling through the door.

'The keys? What did I do with the keys?'

'What keys?' my mother asked, all afluster.

'The tractor. Where did I leave them?'

She put her hand to the top of the TV and produced the ring. As she did, my dad noticed me.

'Oh, by God – howya?' And before I could answer, 'C'mon till you see something.'

'Ah, it's OK, you go ahead.'

'C'mon, c'mon! Hurry up now, I can't delay,' and before I could decline a second time, he was gone.

'You'd better go,' Mam said. 'He might need help at whatever he's doing.'

I had to follow. I could hear him start the tractor out by the haybarn, and ran to avoid being left behind. I hopped up on the hitch, took hold of either side of the cab and he went charging off with the same dispatch.

'Are you all right there?' he shouted into the wind. 'The ground is a bit bumpy, so you'd best hold on tight.'

'I won't fall,' I told him.

'Good man. I'm glad you're here, cos you might never see the likes of this again.'

'The likes of what?'

'You know the job that's going on down the bog? Pat said he was telling you about it.'

'That's right, he did.'

'They're draining the whole place. And today was the day when Maher was to clear out the sandpit.'

'And?'

'And the JCB is after going down in it.'

'It's what?'

'Gone down in it. Sank. Twenty grand's worth disappearing into the muck.'

'Jesus! And how was he doing? Did he get much of it cleared?'

'He got none at all. It was a simple misjudgement. He just went in too far and the ground gave way.'

By now we'd turned off the lane and were rattling through the hill field, so I could see the pandemonium. The great yellow machine with its huge tracking wheels was about halfway hidden under the surface. A wire rope had been attached, and on terra firma a regular tractor was straining might and main to haul the giant to safety. But it was scarcely holding its own – the wheels just spun on the marshy wetland, while the JCB inched closer to a murky grave. Over his shoulder, my father handed me a length of wire rope.

'Hop off there and run over to the men with that.'

This I did. Frantically it was grabbed from my hold and it too was attached to the sinking machine. My dad reversed his Massey-Ferguson into range and had the other end hooked on to his hitch. Now a second tractor was pulling. The difference was slight but crucial. At once, the slide was stopped. The gradual submerging was checked, and the JCB began to rise ever so slowly. The pair of tractors revved and roared, the wire ropes pinged taut as banjo strings, but the tide had turned. Still, it took time; dim dusk turned to black night before the mighty hulk was back on the bank, half-covered in sludge and looking as shaken as its owner. But like its owner, none the worse for this close call.

The last of the engines was switched off. A harsh winter breeze whistled across the open bog, so one and all took shelter behind the breadth and warmth of my dad's Massey. The excitement past, I got my first proper look at the sandpit. Much of the water had been drained away, so the green reed carpet now sagged like the top of a collapsed soufflé. But, vitally, it was still cloaking everything that lay underneath.

JJ Maher produced the Rothmans and flashed them around. Without thinking, I took one. My father didn't even notice, or if he did, he made no comment upon it.

'Well, men, God bless ye and leave ye the health,' Maher said. 'Only for ye, I was fucked.'

'Don't mention it, boy,' Dad replied. 'We'd do the same for anyone.'

'Sure I know that. And after today, I know the value of good neighbours.'

Joe Deane hadn't been saying much, but it was he who asked, 'So – what're you going to do now?'

They all looked at Matty Galligan, whose land it was and who was financing the operation. But he just looked back at Maher, the driver. The next move would depend entirely on him.

'I wouldn't fancy trying to get to the bottom of that with the digger,' he said. 'Ye all saw what just happened. And there's no telling how deep it is.'

'What you might think about doing, Matty,' Joe Deane now prompted, 'is get a few lorryloads of gravel, tip them in there and fill the whole thing up. Then get a ton or two of topsoil, smooth it over and you have the grandest bit of ground ever.'

Everyone nodded, none more vigorously than I. How convenient if the evidence were buried under several tons of broken stone. And how ironic who that suggestion should've come from. But Galligan was far, far from happy.

'Jesus, I don't know,' he mused. 'Maybe there is something in what the old people say.'

'What's that?'

'Before ever I started this job, my father warned me that there was a draíocht on that bloody waterhole.'

'A what?' I asked.

'A draíocht. It's an old Irish thing. It means a spell. Or a curse on anyone who interferes with the place. It probably sounds right stupid to a young lad like yourself, Billy. But your father will tell you, there are some things better left alone. We're at this job for the past month and we didn't have a single stoppage or delay – not till now.'

''Tis true for you,' Maher said. 'No sooner did I mention than I was ready to get started on the pit than a bearing went in the front bucket. That bearing was new – normally I'd get a year, maybe two, out of it. But this one packs up after a couple of weeks. Bloody strange.'

'Well,' Pat Morrissey butted in with a trademark laugh, 'that bearing was very nearly the least of your worries.'

'I'm driving a digger for the best part of fifteen years, Pat,' Maher went on, 'and that's the first time anything like that ever happened to me. I still don't know how. One minute it was rock steady, the next I was up to my neck in it.'

'You made an escape,' Joe insisted. 'Only for the rest of us were here, you were a dead man. Now, Matty, I told you what I'd do if I were you. It's never worth risking. A few loads of gravel would sort it out rightly.'

'Aye,' Galligan said slowly, more thinking out loud than actually addressing anyone. 'Maybe in time, yeah. But for now, I think I'll just make sure it's fenced off well and leave it at that. It'll be a bit inconvenient for ploughing around, but sure I'll manage somehow.'

This was notice that there was nothing more to be seen here, not today.

'C'mon,' my father said. 'If we don't get going, we'll all miss mass.'

I retook my position standing behind him on the hitch of the tractor. Before he turned the ignition key, he looked round to check I was in place.

'What has you home?' he asked. 'Doctor's orders?'

'No, not at all. I'm fine.'

'Fine? Christ, boy, will you have sense and give up them bloody fags. You're like someone dying of consumption.'

*

Buoyed a little by the let-off, I now set about my main order of business. Doran had to be found. Though he had no religion that I knew of, I scoured the congregation at mass that evening on the off-chance. When I was satisfied he wasn't there, I slipped away discreetly to again check out the pubs. But all I ran into on my travels was an earful of abuse from a drunken, belligerent Tom Conway, who noted that this was my second time in without buying a drink, and if his pub wasn't good enough any more, then I could piss off back to Dublin for myself. He was still ranting when I left his premises for the quiet of the main street, and a chance to consider where I might go from here. Though, in truth, there was nothing to consider. It was tonight or not at all – I'd be leaving on the morrow. So if Doran wouldn't come to me, then I'd just have to go to him. To face him in his own back yard.

His house was about a mile out, on the back road to Mullinavat. I well remember the first day I'd set eyes upon it; I would've been no more than seven or eight, en route to a hurling match in the company of Dasher and Joe Deane, with my dad doing the driving. We'd left the village behind, made the steady climb up Knockowen Hill and there, some way in from the road, was the dwelling. It looked like one decent sneeze would reduce the place to rubble. Only the occasional blob of plaster hung to sorry walls, a good part of the roof was unslated, many windows were broken with only some boarded up, and there was a hole in the bottom portion of the half-door that I could comfortably have squeezed through. Dasher and I looked at one another, both struck by the same bold possibilities.

'Dad,' I said.

'What, boy?'

'Would it be OK if we came over here some day after school?'

'What for?'

'To go exploring.'

'Exploring where?'

'Exploring that old house we just passed.'

'Oh, I don't know if that's a good idea,' Joe cut in, and I can *still* see him wink at my father. 'I heard tell that house is haunted.' Joe winked again. 'You might see a ghost there. You might get a bad fright. You wouldn't be able to sleep at night.' He winked again. 'You might start wetting the bed after it.'

'Ha-ha!' Dasher pointed. 'Wetting the bed!'

'Shut up, you,' I said sulkily. Then, to Joe, 'Anyway, how would we see a ghost? We'd go there during the day.'

'That wouldn't make any difference. The bogeymen who live there don't just come out at night.'

My dad looked across at him quizzically.

'That's where the English people, the Dorans, are living.'

'Are you sure?' my dad asked doubtfully. 'Christ, Joe, who could live in a place like that?'

'I'm telling you now,' Joe maintained. He then turned completely in his seat so he was facing us in the back. 'There's a family living in that old house, lads. The Dorans – they're from England originally. Isn't there one of them in the school with ye?'

'Ginger Rodger!' I mouthed, then turned to where every trace of colour had drained from Dasher's cheeks. Suddenly the thought of exploring Knockowen wasn't quite so appealing.

'A strange breed, I believe,' my dad muttered, not for our ears.

'Filth,' Joe whispered earnestly. 'Take my word for it, them Dorans are nothing but bad news.'

The night was pitch, my eyes were slow to adjust. I was so concerned with finding my way, while watching my step, that I'd reached the rusted gate before getting my real attack of the jitters. But by then I'd come too far to turn back.

The house still had as its main entrance that same half-door, though a large piece of corrugated iron had been riveted to it top to bottom. There was no knocker, no bell – I'm not sure if there was even electricity. Twice I shaped, twice I drew back, then I knocked. This provoked an immediate explosion of barking, followed by a loud and gruff 'Fuck up!' and then the sound of a boot striking something yielding. I braced myself. Rickety and ill-fitting, the door slowly came open, lifted rather than swung. There before me stood a low-sized stocky man, almost bald, unshaven, probably in his mid-sixties. Behind him there shone a weak light which came, judging by the smell, from a paraffin lamp. Though it was early December, there appeared to be no heating of any sort at work inside the house; the man was wearing at least half a dozen layers under the grubby green pullover.

'Well?' he barked.

'Is . . . ah . . . is Rodger at home?'

'I dunno. Go round the back and see.'

'Round the back?' But he was already manhandling the door closed in my face.

Round I went, warily, finding puddle after puddle as I did. But once there I was met by a most improbable sight. There was an old railway carriage, one of the kind that had become obsolete a generation before. The many windows were curtained, all those curtains were drawn, and behind them I could see just the tiniest glow, the merest sign of life. It was all so quaint, so ingenious, so *cool*, that for an instant I forgot to be frightened. I rapped loudly on the carriage door.

'Billy! This is a surprise,' he said, pleasantly enough. 'Won't you come in? I was just having a drink – you're welcome to join me.'

'No, thanks.'

'It's my own make – comes guaranteed.'

'No, thanks.'

'Fair enough, we'll talk here. So, to what do I owe this pleasure?'

'I think you bloody well know.'

He gazed off into the middle distance, stroking his chin, deep in thought. When at last he grew tired of taking the piss he said, 'Sorry. I'm afraid I'm going to have to pass on that one.'

'What have you been saying around the village?'

More furrowed space-gazing, more chin-stroking.

'D'you want to know every word, or was there something specific?'

'You've been mouthing off about Suzy.'

'Oh, I doubt that.'

'Don't lie to me – several people heard.'

'Several – really? I must've been plastered drunk, cos I honestly don't remember. Anyway, what is it I'm supposed to have said?'

'That Dasher and I had something to do with her disappearing.'

'Well, let's face it, you did, didn't you.'

'Now listen to me. I don't know what your game is —'

'Game? Don't talk bollox. This is no game. I got a bit

tanked and maybe said a little more than I should've, that's all.'

I pressed on, determined to be heard out. 'I don't know what your game is, but don't ever forget that it was you – you were the one who killed her.'

'I'll dispute that.'

'Open your mouth down the street again and you'll have to. Cos I'm not prepared to live like this, waiting for you and your loose tongue to drop me in the shit. One more word and I'm going to the cops – we'll settle this for once and for all.'

He smiled broadly. 'How's the teacher training going?'

'None of your business.'

'It'll be none of yours either if you run squealing to the law. And what would a hothouse plant like you do then? You wouldn't be tough enough to hack it on Daddy's farm . . . though I suppose you could always hire someone like JJ Maher to come in and do the donkey work for you. He's been up your way these past few weeks, I'm told.'

I made no comment.

'Matty Galligan's bog, wasn't it?

'How did you know that?'

'It's a small village, Billy boy. Not a lot escapes me. Anyway, I believe he's digging drains all over the place. Did he . . . find anything interesting?'

'Oh God!' I sighed. 'Now I see.'

'You do? What exactly do you see?'

'You were expecting them to find the body. And you were making sure that you got your side of the story out well in advance. You devious bastard.'

'Billy – you're reading too much into this. See it for what it was: a simple case of the drink talking.'

'So how many people did this drink talk to?'

'Just a few. None that you need ever worry about, I assure you.'

'Assure me? So you do know who you told?'

'It's gradually coming back to me, yeah.'

'And you're still saying it wasn't deliberate?'

'Oh, I never said that. I said I didn't remember. But why are we standing here splitting hairs? Why don't you just come right out and tell me the good news.' Another flash of that shit-eating grin. 'They found nothing, did they. And from the way you've been going on, I'm guessing that they aren't going to.'

It was very much to my benefit that he know this. But I just couldn't bring myself to bear glad tidings to such as him. I turned to go.

'Aw c'mon, Billy. I'll find out tomorrow anyway. That's how people are around here – they love to gossip.'

I headed back the way I'd come, picking my steps through the mire underfoot. I'd just about rounded the corner when I felt something press on the side of my neck below the right ear. It was cold metal, circular and hollow. I didn't need to look to know that I was at the point of a gun.

'I said tell me what you know, you miserable little shite, or I'll blow your fucking head off.'

I froze, in no doubt whatsoever that he was capable. 'It's like you said, Rodger. They've found nothing.'

'And?'

'And they aren't going to. The sandpit is just being fenced in like before. It isn't being dug up at all.'

'Why not?'

'It's Matty Galligan – he's afraid to touch it. Y – y'know . . . superstitious.'

'Superstitious!' he roared with a loud guffaw. 'Well, here's

85

to Matty Galligan and his superstitions. Fucking moron, may he never learn.'

He came round to face me. The gun was a newish-looking single-barrel. Both his hands were still in situ, but he'd lowered it to arm's length. He leered at me. 'Well, shame on you! You were going to keep that to yourself.'

'Yeah. Occasionally I find that's a good idea. It's something you might try.'

'On that score, Billy, you need have no concerns. From now on, drunk or sober, I'll be a little more discreet. Incidentally, it wasn't very discreet of you to come barging up here, into a stranger's yard, shouting the odds. If anyone saw you, how were you going to explain this away?'

'Nobody saw me.'

'Doesn't anybody know you're here, then?'

'No – except for your fath – for the bloke in the house.'

'That is my father. A man of few words.'

'I'd noticed.'

'So, how d'you like my new gun?'

'It's nice, I suppose.'

'You suppose? *You suppose?* It's a work of bloody art, is this. Shoots straight as a die, no recoil worth speaking of . . . and the stock. Just look at that workmanship. All perfectly legal, what's more.'

'Yeah?'

'Oh yeah. We've only got half an acre, but I sowed some barley and needed something to keep the crows off.'

'Good for you.'

'It certainly is. One little fault, though. On the more expensive models you can always tell if the gun is loaded. But this one you've got to open if you want to see.'

'Really?'

'Aye. Bit of a nuisance. I mean, take a look at it now, for instance. What d'you reckon?'

'I haven't a clue,' I said with a shake.

He took a step back, raised the gun till the barrel was inches from my face and said, calmly but emphatically, 'Guess.'

The light was poor, but not so poor that I couldn't see the hammer slowly lift. I wasn't sure if he'd do it but, oddly at that moment I didn't care.

'Go on – I insist. Take a guess. Loaded or empty.'

'I dunno.'

The hammer was edging towards the point of return.

'Empty, then.'

He raised the gun a fraction higher, taking even better aim. Then with a jerking motion he squeezed sharply on the trigger. Instinctively, I shut my eyes before there came the most ferocious bang. It was to my great surprise that, an instant later, my head still was where it always had been. I opened one eye a crack, and then the other.

There was Doran, bent double with laughter. Again he raised the gun, roared, 'Bang!' and fell once more into hysterics.

'Oh, Christ, sorry about that! I suppose that's ruined your plans for the night – I'd offer you a clean pair of jocks, only I don't bother much with them myself.'

Before I could reply, the door ground open and his father stuck his head out.

'What's going on out there? Suffering, Jesus, I thought someone was shot!'

'Get back indoors,' Doran hissed. The old man hesitated. 'I said get back indoors or someone will be!'

Mr Doran senior didn't need telling a third time.

'Now, Walsh, all joking aside, you're familiar with the expression "Don't call us, we'll call you"? That's how it's going to work from now on. If I need to speak to you, I'll speak to you. But if you ever walk in here again, making threats and accusations against me on my own turf, I'll see to it that you're in no fit state to walk out. Don't think that I wouldn't. And don't forget that I know a perfect place to hide another stiff. Now get the fuck out of it. And don't show your face round here again.'

That last was surely the most unnecessary piece of advice I'd ever, to that point, been given.

CHAPTER FOUR

Doran's vow of silence wasn't the most cast-iron ever made, but it was good enough for me. Back in Dublin, my life was my own again. My sleeping habits were almost as healthy as ever they'd been, with that dream causing only the most infrequent disruption. Where studies were concerned, I'd soon made up all lost ground, and then some. I reclaimed my place on the college hurling team and made the bench in soccer. I quit smoking – in fact, I quit several times. And I found myself a girlfriend, my first. At my age, I suppose this development wasn't a minute before time. Noleen Gray, her name was. Though tall and blonde, she looked nothing out of the ordinary. But crucially, she looked nothing like Suzy Deane. Nothing at all.

Just over one week to Christmas. The streets of Dublin bulged and bustled, the wrapping paper was six for fifty, and St Pat's was deep into the season of eating, drinking and making merry. It was five o'clock in the common room, lads only, killing time till pub time. My money was next on the pool table and 'Come On, Eileen' was playing on the jukebox when one of the second years stuck his head round the door.

'Walsh! There's a strange bird looking for you at reception.'

Intrigued, I hopped to it, taking the stairs two at a time

then running the length of the empty corridor. It was a severe disappointment to find it was no one more exotic than my sister. But the let-down immediately gave way to some unease. We had, after all, spoken on the phone only a couple of nights before.

'Hiya!' I said far too cheerily. 'What are you doing here?'

'Wow! There's a welcome and a half! Have I wandered into a charm school by mistake?'

'Mags, you know I'm glad to see you, but . . . what's the story?'

'No story. I just happened to be passing.'

'Passing? On your way to where?'

She hesitated. Now I knew this was no chance visit. 'I was . . . I had some business out at the airport.'

'What kind of business?'

'A mind-yer-own kind of business,' she said with a wink. 'And since I had to pass through Drumcondra, I thought we might get a cup of coffee.'

'And that's all that's to it? There's nothing wrong?'

'Wrong? Like what?'

'Like somebody's not died, have they?'

'Died? Jesus, no.'

The denial was too emphatic. I'd not hit the nail on the head, but I'd come pretty close. I wasn't going to like this, I could tell. And I wasn't going to walk all the way to some coffee house to hear it.

'Over here,' I said, and I guided her to the waiting area, and a pair of straight-backed chairs either side of a formica table.

'Right, then. Spit it out . . . C'mon, whatever it is you've come to tell me.'

90

Not so much hesitation now. 'There's been an accident.'

'Who?'

'Dasher.'

'Dasher . . . I see . . . What kind of accident?'

'Well, from what Mammy told me, it sounds like a real freak.'

'Freakishly lucky, freakishly unlucky – what?'

'It was yesterday afternoon, he and a friend had been for a few drinks and were coming home on the bike . . .'

'Both of them?'

'Dasher was on the crossbar. It's not known yet who was at fault, but they were side-swiped by a city bus and shunted into a lamp post. At first it seemed that the only damage done was to the front spokes. The two lads got up, dusted themselves down and walked away.'

'But?'

'But when they got to the street corner, Dasher collapsed. Fortunately, he was right outside a doctor's surgery, so he had expert care from the first. There was an ambulance on the scene within minutes and he was brought to the South Infirmary. They operated on him as soon as they could tell what was wrong.'

'And what was wrong?'

'He'd ruptured a kidney.'

'Fuck – is it as easy as all that to rupture a kidney?'

'Seems to be.'

'And is a ruptured kidney all *that* serious? I mean, we've got two of them, don't we?'

'Most people do. But when they opened Dasher up, they found that his other one was completely withered. It was only the size of a pea, and hadn't functioned from the day he was born.'

'So you're saying he's got . . . ?'

'He's in a coma, on life support. They aren't sure if he's going to make it.'

Each word pounded in my head like a falling piano. I don't know what kind of look came over me, but it had Mags reach across the table and take my hand in hers. At once, I yanked it away.

'Course he's going to make it, for God's sake. All those doctors and nurses, in a big modern hospital, with every kind of machine twinkling and humming – they aren't going to lose a young lad like Dasher.'

She nodded, allowing me on.

'He'll probably be in hospital for the Christmas right enough, but that'll be about the size of it . . . I'll go down and see him, that's what I'll do. I'll go down and see him in the morning.'

'There aren't any visitors allowed.'

'What – none?'

'Only his parents. They were given a police escort to Cork city last night shortly after midnight. Them . . . and the priest.'

'The priest?!' I whispered, barely daring to be heard. She watched, waiting for the full realization to strike home.

'Will you be OK with this?'

'I dunno. I've got to do something. I can't just hang around here waiting for a phone call.'

'Well, there's absolutely nothing you can do in Cork. Why don't you go home?'

'To Lisdrolin?'

'Yeah. That's where all his friends and neighbours will be.'

'Will you come too?'

'I don't think so. We wouldn't be all that close, me and him – I'd only be expected home for a funeral. And I wouldn't want anyone thinking I'd got him dead and buried already.'

'OK, right.'

'So, d'you want to get a few things together, then, and I'll go with you to Busáras. There's a late bus to Waterford every evening – I think it goes at seven. Have you got enough for the fare?'

I emptied my money on to the table, my entire worldly wealth. With just days of term remaining, it was easy enough to carry.

'I think so,' I said. 'It'll hardly be more than a fiver.'

Mags took a couple of pounds from her pocket and threw them on to the pile. 'Take this as well,' she said. 'With the help of God, I won't be needing to find bus fare for any unscheduled trips home.'

Our house was deserted, Deane's too. But there were lights in Morrissey's, which struck me as odd if both Pat and Bridget had taken up station in the South Infirmary, Cork city. So after I'd dropped my bag in our kitchen, it was to Morrissey's I went.

There the rosary was in progress. It was being given out by my mother, answered by Dad, Joe and Rita Deane, Matty Galligan and his wife, Betty Gaule – even Leaky Roche was there. He wasn't awfully certain of the words, but he had the right air most of the time. My entrance caused only the slightest stir, eyes shifting to me and then shifting away again. I knelt by the arm of a wooden chair and praying continued.

Once finished, we stood and stretched our legs. The mood remained sombre, the talk remained low. My mother approached across the room.

'I'm glad you came down. Mags gave you the message, then?'

'Yeah, she called over this afternoon.'

'I was going to ring you, but I thought it'd be better coming from her.'

'That was a good idea.'

'Terrible thing, wasn't it.'

I nodded. 'Pat and Bridget still in Cork?'

'They're due back any time now – that's why we're here. God, I hope the news is good.'

'It will be.'

She said nothing and walked away. As she did, Leaky mooched over.

'Jesus, mate, am I glad to see you. I don't know a sinner here.'

'You're kidding.'

'I know who they all are. I just don't think I've ever spoken to any one of them.'

'Well, it's time to put that to rights.' I said as I saw my father and Joe Deane approach. I did the introductions.

'When did you get word?' my dad asked.

'Just a few hours ago. You?'

'We heard yesterday evening. The hospital rang Pat. I know I said this to you a hundred times, boy, but don't ever leave the house in the morning without saying your prayers. For all you know, you might be standing in front of the Almighty before nightfall.'

We all thought on this for a while, then Leaky said, ''Tis tough. Him being an only child and everything.'

'Aye,' Joe answered furtively. 'That'll be the second only child dead around here in the past few months.'

It was surely paranoia, but I felt as if he'd thrown this out for my benefit, for my reaction.

But my dad got there before me. 'Jesus, Joe, that's an awful thing to be saying.' His tone was that of an older brother, admonishing. 'There's no young person dead around here that I know of.'

'And with the help of God there won't be,' I said, just a little fearful that the words might choke me.

'Aye – God is good,' Leaky chimed in.

With that, the little front yard outside the curtains was lit up by a pair of incoming headlights. Car doors were heard to open, Gardaí were thanked and bidden goodnight, and two sets of footsteps began across the gravel. In the kitchen, a hush of trepidation descended. Hours seemed to elapse between the turning of the latchkey and the Morrissey parents standing before us. He looked exhausted, worryworn and greyer than I'd ever remembered him. And even on her brave face the eyes were puffed and swollen, the nose rubbed red.

'He's still alive, anyway,' Bridget announced. There was relief amongst us, though not a whole lot. 'He hasn't regained consciousness yet. Critical but stable, that's what they're calling it. Fr Hughes anointed him last night.'

She then began to fuss and fooster, asking if we'd all had tea, and without waiting to be told, filled up the big electric kettle for a fresh brew.

Pat said nothing, but came sidling over to where my dad and Joe were standing. As he drew near he gave just the tiniest shake of the head. Among friends, among men, there'd be nothing but the bottom line. And it didn't look good.

'Only a matter of time,' he whispered.

'Ah now, he's still hanging in there, isn't he,' my father

insisted. 'And don't they say that once he's over the first twenty-four hours, he's over the worst of it.'

'He shouldn't have lived even twenty-four hours by rights. They've operated, but his one working kidney is mangled. The other is about as big as a marble, and about as much use to him, what's more. Even the doctors can't explain it – he's got them rightly bamboozled.'

'And who's to say he won't go on bamboozling them,' Dad said.

'Aye,' Leaky agreed. 'God is good.'

Pat Morrissey was looking in an unfocused sort of way at some point on the floor near my left foot. When he emerged from his thoughts he said, 'One kidney. That's all he had. That's all the poor oul' devil ever had. We're watching him here all his life – how did we not spot it?'

'Spot what?'

'That one of his bloody kidneys wasn't working. Jesus Christ, there must've been some signs, some symptoms. If only we could've seen them in time . . .'

'And what was there to see, Pat?' Joe asked, joining the debate. 'In God's name, what should you have been looking out for?'

'That's right,' my dad went on. 'There's none of us ever went to medical school, Pat. We're ordinary people with no education worth speaking of. So long as your young lad had his health and his appetite, you left well enough alone.'

'And that's how we were all reared,' said Joe. 'We knew no other way.'

'Yeah . . . yeah. All the same . . .' But he didn't finish the sentence. He let it hang there, a heavy silence that was ended only when Leaky flashed the Major. Each of us took one.

Then Leaky padded his various pockets in turn before asking, 'Anyone a light, lads? I must've left the matches in the car.'

'This the same car you warned me off robbing because it wouldn't go more than fifty?' I smiled.

'The very one. Have you never seen it?'

'No. In fact, until this very minute, I thought it was just a joke.'

'Well, c'mon, I'll show you now and you can judge for yourself.'

Outside, Leaky rubbed his brow and said, 'Jesus, I'm not sorry to be out of there. It was doing my bloody head in. Like down the street it's bad enough . . .'

'What d'you mean, bad enough?'

'I mean the whole fucking place is in shock. There's talk of nothing else in the pubs or the post office or at the creamery. You go up to the church at any hour and some oul' wan is lighting a penny candle. And the school was closed a half-day today, the children all went to a special mass. Like, I know you see a lot worse every time you open a newspaper, but that's always somewhere else.'

We'd arrived at Leaky's pride and joy. It was dull red, looked a little dated but in reasonable nick for all that.

'Well – what d'you reckon?'

'Looks the business,' I said. I pushed down on the bonnet and kicked a few tyres in a knowing way. 'Very sturdy, isn't she. How much?'

'One hundred and fifty.'

'Christ, that was for nothing. And she's going OK?'

'Like a clock. Sit in, we'll go down the street for a pint.'

Law's, so recently flavour of the month, was in the doghouse. The lads were in serious dispute with the management. One night shortly before, a gathering of huntsmen and women – the local big nobs – had turned up in that pub unexpectedly. Ned, the owner, proceeded to spend the night toadying, tugging forelock, licking arse. And treating Leaky and the lads like they were invisible. So, it was Conway's or the Heather Blazing, then. My call, being the tourist. Conway's, I decided. For old times' sake.

It was dismal as ever. Beside a sickly little fire sat two notorious old rakes, both absolutely hammered, while the one figure on a high stool had collapsed across the bar with the hood of a grimy baseball jacket pulled over his head. Tom, as usual, was perched behind the counter, about midway through his day's consumption and just beginning to have difficulty focusing on the TV. When I called two drinks, he rose grudgingly and went to the taps.

'Any account of your friend?' he asked without looking up.

'No change. He's still not conscious.'

'Must be tough on Pat,' he mused. 'Nice bloke, Pat.'

I wondered as I handed over the cash what dealings he could ever have had with a gentleman like Pat Morrissey. I'd still not worked it out when he returned with the change. It was all in coin, and as he handed it over, his permanent shake caused him to spill a few pence around the counter. The drunk who was sleeping there stirred, then turned his face towards me. It was Doran.

'Walsh!' he slurred. 'How's it going? Howya?' And he extended his hand. To be shaken, I assumed. I extended mine towards it. But before they met, he pointed his index finger at me, made a trigger-pulling motion and went, 'Bang! Bang-bang-bang-bang!' And then he laughed himself breathless.

'Ah, sorry about that. Sorry about that, Billy. Sound man,

Put it there.' This time we did exchange a handshake. 'I shouldn't be messing, really. There's no call for acting the maggot, not after what happened to pour oul' Dasher.'

I made some kind of acknowledgement.

'That's Suzy gone, and now Dasher gone. Just me and you left now, my oul' mucker. And y'know, in a hundred years time we'll be dead too. And it won't matter a God damn who did what down in Galligan's bog, will it?'

I took my leave of him, bolted back my pint and ripped into a bewildered Leaky for bringing me to this dive. From now on, it was the Heather, or Ned's, or nowhere at all. I hoped, I told him, that this much was clear.

So back I went to Dublin next day and waited for the phone call. A call which, happily, never came. Dasher continued to fly in the face of all medical wisdom, stubbornly refusing to die. His time came, and passed, and still he kept on ticking over, till the doctors' curiosity got the better of them and they opened him up for another look. And now the wonder came to light. That withered kidney, the one that had not developed since his birth, had kicked in when the other one gave out. It was so ineffectual, its influence so negligible, that right away the body had lapsed into renal failure. This put him in a deep coma and with a foot in death's door. But over those critical first hours, with the main one disabled, the little kidney did just enough to keep him alive. However, that was only half the miracle in progress. Because following its belated call to service, it was now developing apace and would soon be normal size and fully functional, a perfectly healthy organ. As, indeed, would its partner; the operation was a complete success, the recovery well on track. Surgeons in the South Infirmary were no longer checking their watches, looking at the patient and wondering what the hold-up could be. Instead, they were tentatively predicting a full recovery. Chances were that with both kidneys now in working order, Dasher might even emerge from the whole affair in finer fettle than he'd gone into it.

As it transpired, the timing was perfect. Wednesday, 23 December, the day before Christmas Eve, and the college had just officially closed for the holiday. The few of us that remained were playing penny poker at reception as we waited for taxis to take us to the station. Then the call came.

'Billy?'

'Yeah – Seamus Gunning, is it?'

'That's right. I got your number from your mother. How's things?'

'Fine – where are you ringing from?'

'The coinbox in the Heather. Listen, I haven't very much change so I'll come to the point. You heard about Dasher?'

From the tone of his voice, from the very fact that it was his voice, I knew it could only be good.

'He came out of the coma.'

'Thank God. When?'

'Some time last night.'

'Brilliant. And he's OK, yeah? No lasting damage?'

'Well, I won't know that till I see him. And that's what I'm ringing about. Myself, Kevin and Leaky are going to Cork tomorrow, and we thought you might like to come.'

'How d'you intend to travel?'

'Leaky is taking the car, God between us and all harm. So, what about you?'

'Yes,' I told him. 'I'll be there. Count me in.'

*

Leaky made excellent time that Christmas Eve morning. We arrived in Cork city about midday. After several requests for directions, and much sniggering at the accents that came to our aid, we found the South Infirmary in the early afternoon. And with neither illness nor injury observing Church holidays, we found business as usual.

Dasher was off the critical list, and was now in a public area convalescing. As we entered, he laid down the magazine he'd been reading and bade us welcome. I'm not sure quite how I expected him to look, but it was nothing like this. To begin with, he'd lost weight, a significant amount. His eyes were sunken and black-rimmed, while his cheekbones protruded like those of a man who'd survived Belsen. The white shapeless bag that served as pyjamas hung in places, ballooned in others about his bony, wasted frame.

'Great to see ye, lads. Thanks for coming.'

His appearance had taken the wind from all our sails. We smiled, we shuffled, but nobody actually said anything.

'So howd'ye get here?'

'I drove,' Leaky told him nervously.

'Fair play – that was a bit of a haul. What's his driving like, fellahs?'

'Ah . . . not too bad,' we muttered.

'Well, he got ye here in one piece, didn't he.'

The unease was excruciating. Dasher, desperate to crank things up, went on, 'Jesus, Leaky, this motor must be doing wonders for your love life. Talk about being eligible. You must spend all your time beating the women off.'

Leaky grinned awkwardly; he was still too mesmerized by the talking corpse in the bed to reply. And again the conversation flagged. Then Kevin pushed to the head of the huddle and asked, 'How're you feeling, Dash?'

101

'Fine,' he said. 'Just fine. A bit weak, a bit groggy, but I'm coming around.'

'You must've got an awful fright, did you?'

'When?'

'After the accident. When you felt yourself passing out.'

'I never did feel myself passing out. It all happened much too quickly.'

Now at last we'd have it from the horse's mouth. Our cocked ears urged him to get on with the telling.

'It was like something out of *Benny Hill*. There we were, myself and my buddy, he was pedalling, I was on the crossbar, the few pints were on board, so we may not have been the steadiest going down Barrack Street. Next thing, the bus comes and nudges us into a lamp post. Bent the whole front fork into an s-hook. We thought it was fucking hilarious. The last thing I remember yer man saying was, "OK – so where's the candid camera." Next frame I wake up here with a crowd all around, and more wires stuck in me than a bloody telephone exchange.'

'What was it like?' Seamus asked. 'Y'know, being . . . out like that?'

'I dunno. I slept through practically all of it.'

'Yeah, but . . . did you dream?'

'I suppose I must've.'

'A lot?'

'I don't remember.'

Leaky, who'd been taking everything in but saying little, then asked, 'Was it like being dead?'

'Ah, for fuck's sake,' Kevin groaned, 'now how in the name of God d'you expect him to answer that?'

Dasher slowly ran a hand through his hair, now lank and splintered.

'I guess. It probably is. And y'know, if it is, then dying isn't the worst thing that could happen to a fellah.'

This fairly quietened us and had us examining the flooring once again. Then Kevin, not wishing the ice to reset like before, sad, 'We're bloody glad you didn't die. And we're not the only ones. There were a lot of people down South Kilkenny who were rooting for you.'

'So I believe. My mother said the neighbours were very good about it all. Oh don't worry, we'll not forget anyone who stood by us when things looked dodgy.'

'And you needn't think,' Seamus said, 'that they've forgotten about you just because you're over the worst. You may expect busloads over the coming weeks.'

'Have you had many visitors up till now?' Leaky asked, a little anxious that someone might've beaten us to it.

'No. Well, it's been less than forty-eight hours. My folks were here yesterday, and one or two relatives. But outside my family, you're the first.'

Just then a nurse arrived and, very courteously, asked if we'd mind leaving. Michael, she said, needed his rest and anyway it was time for the patients roundabouts to have their medication, injections, bedbaths or whatever. We said our goodbyes and promised to be back before too long. As we turned to go, Dasher cleared his throat and began with a stammer, nervous and self-conscious.

'Ah, lads . . . Billy – can I have a word . . . in private. Fellahs, I need to talk to Billy for a sec, OK?'

Leaky, Kevin and Seamus looked first from one to the other, then to me. Almost in synch they shrugged, feigning indifference.

Once they'd gone, I sat myself on the edge of the bed and leaned closer.

'I lied,' he said. 'I did have one other visitor who wasn't family.'

'Oh. Who?'

He panned shiftily around the ward. 'There may be a few quid in this for me.'

'Really?'

'Yeah. Y'know – compensation. It seems the bus driver who knocked me down wasn't qualified – he was still taking instruction. Except – being so close to Christmas, I suppose – he didn't have an instructor with him. It puts the bus company completely in the wrong. So they'll probably settle – a court case could ruin them.'

'A bit quick off the blocks with all this, aren't you? I mean, you've only been back amongst us two days.'

'It's my dad. Well, actually it's the shop steward in the factory where he works. Y'know – he's a big union guy and they're very hot on personal injury claims.'

'So how much will you be claiming?'

'Depends. First they'll have to assess any long-term effects.'

'But didn't I hear that, all things considered, you'd come out of this pretty well?'

'That's one opinion. But doctors differ. I'm sure, if it came to it, I could find a dozen who'd disagree. I mean, a ruptured kidney, a spell in a coma, a week on life support; you don't often hear them recommended for a ripe old age. Then, of course, there's my academic career to think of. I won't be out of here for another six to eight weeks. So I'll be writing this year off and starting again from scratch next October. And finally, on a pure cosmetic level' – he lifted up his gown to let me see – 'I've been disfigured for life.' He wasn't exaggerating. A scar ran from the middle of his breastbone to the verge of his navel. It was ugly, wide and stitched with very little finesse in evidence.

'Good fuck!' I blurted. 'What did they open you with – an angle grinder?'

Dasher took this perfectly in his stride. 'Hey – don't knock it. This could be my ticket to the big league. It's a well-known fact that women dig scars.'

'If that's even half true, you're going to be a busy boy when you come out of here. How many stitches?'

'Seventy-two. And you know what I've been told? That when the sums are done, each one of those stitches ought to be worth a grand to me.'

Either I'd misheard, or there was some brain damage to be considered as well. Because seventy-two thousand pounds was a king's ransom. Big farms had been bought for less. British footballers changed clubs for not a lot more. I wasn't even involved in this, and already I felt out of my depth. If, of course, it was accurate.

'C'mon, now,' I teased, 'you're reading a zero at the end that isn't there.'

'No,' he assured me. 'Seventy won't be far wide of the mark.'

'But . . . a grand per stitch – that sounds a little too pat. Who could come up with a formula like that?'

'I thought you'd never ask,' he said ominously.

The sudden edge to his tone made me anxious as I asked, 'Well – who was it?'

'Your friend and mine – Ginger Rodger Doran.'

'What? He's been here?'

'You'd better believe it.'

'Wh – when?'

'Bright and early this morning. It's fucking uncanny, but the bastard can smell money all the way from Cork to Lisdrolin.'

'So what did he want, exactly?'

'Ah, what d'you think he wanted. He gave me his estimate, then just said he'd come to claim his cut.'

'Christ – what'll you do?'

'I dunno. I can't just give him money, Billy. If I start now, where's it ever going to end. On the other hand, there are people I'd be prepared to face down. And Rodger Doran isn't among them.'

Though he was ruling out both, it seemed to me as if he'd be forced into one or the other. So I rephrased the question slightly with, 'Right. So – what d'you reckon you'll do?'

He thought it over, then shook his head heavily. 'No idea. What would you do?'

I had no better idea. And anyway, the nurse was back, this time insisting that I vacate the ward. I apologized and thanked her for her indulgence. I hurriedly scribbled down my Dublin number on the Kleenex box by the bedside and asked that I, too, be kept abreast of all developments.

Outside in the foyer, I told the lads we'd been discussing college business. All to do with the end of year exams, which Dasher would not now be in a position to sit. If they were all sceptical, they were good enough not to let on.

Around Lisdrolin, Christmas that year was holly and ivy, peace on earth and goodwill to all. Dasher was alive, and would soon be well. He was still a long way from a hospital release date, and what a nuisance that must've proved for the staff in general. Because every time we got drunk over the twelve days – which was more often than not – we would pool our small change and place a long-distance call through to the South Infirmary, demanding that our friend be paged, forthwith. And if the night out were to run to extra time – a disco in Waterford say – there might well be several such calls, each more garbled and incoherent than the last. The nurses and receptionists there took it all in good part, but must've been yearning for the end of Dasher's confinement even more than he was.

I saw Doran a couple of times, and he saw me. But in the spirit of the season, perhaps, he didn't attempt to start conversation. All things considered, Christmas '82 is one that I remember for mostly the right reasons. Noleen Gray, my girlfriend of some weeks' standing, even made it down from Cavan to join the festivities as we rang in the new year. Being the quiet sort, without a great deal to say for herself, she got on pretty well with my folks. In fact, my dad was heard to remark that you wouldn't know she was in the house, which I'm sure he meant as a compliment. After the brief stay in Lisdrolin, she and I travelled back to Dublin together and then, just a month or so later and by mutual consent, called it quits.

Late February the news broke. It was my mother, all whispers, high secrecy, and I wasn't to pretend I'd heard this. But in an out-of-court settlement, Dasher's legal team had won him seventy-five thousand pounds in damages. Of this, the solicitors would be taking fifteen thousand for services rendered. Such a cut struck me as downright sinful but then, from the outset, I thought it was all crazy money. And however you looked at it, what remained still left him a very wealthy young man. I knew he'd not be able to contain himself for long. And sure enough, he was on the line within an hour.

'Did you hear the news?'

'No,' I lied.

'It's settled. Give a guess how much.'

'God, I wouldn't have an idea . . . forty?'

'Sixty.'

'Sixty? You're kidding!'

'It was actually seventy-five. But my legal fees were fifteen. Imagine – fifteen grand for a few phone calls and a bit of haggling.'

'Daylight robbery,' I agreed. 'But what can you do, eh?'

'I'll tell you what I can do. I can jack in this engineering and take up law. It's not too late. Not too late for you either, come to that.'

'Nah, I don't think so. I'd rather be a poor teacher than one of those parasites for any money.'

He went quiet. 'Aye. But as bloodsuckers go, they aren't the worst kind.'

'He's not been on your case already!'

'I don't know who or what his sources are, but by Christ they're red-hot.'

'So, what . . . I mean how much is he after?'

'Don't know – we never got round to discussing it.'

'No way! You didn't, did you?'

'What?'

'Tell him to go fuck himself?'

'Oh God no, nothing like that. In fact we had a very civil talk. And we may be close to doing a deal.'

'Eh?'

'OK, here's what he's proposed. I give him a one-off settlement —'

'Yeah, right. Until he's got it all spent, and then he'll be back for another one-off settlement.'

'No. Just hear me out, right. A one-off settlement, that's my end of the bargain —'

'Bargain? So he gets the money – what d'you get?'

'I get rid of Doran. So do you. He's only emigrating to fucking Australia!'

'What?'

'That's what he wants the cash for. He's going to set himself up down under. He's leaving Ireland and he's not coming back.'

'God . . . Australia. A bit drastic, isn't it? Are you quite sure this is on the level?'

'Wh . . . why? D'you reckon it mightn't be?'

'I dunno, Dasher, I'd have my doubts. Very, very grave doubts. Like, for starters, I can't see how he's going to get in there.'

'Why not?'

'Well, it's not like deciding to go to Butlins. The word is that it's impossible to get in unless you've got a trade – even then, it's bloody difficult. And Doran has no skills. None that the Aussies would be interested in, at any rate.'

'No, no, no, that won't be a problem. It's all sorted. Something to do with this Commonwealth deal. He was born in England, so he's entitled to a British passport. And once he has that, they can't really stop him.'

'Right then, OK. So he's allowed in. What's he intend doing when he gets there?'

'He didn't say. And I didn't ask. But I wouldn't have any worries about him on that score. That guy is like a shithouse rat – he'd scratch out a living where another man'd starve. From the little I know about Australia, it sounds as if itself and Doran might just be made for each other.'

'So you'd say he's genuine, then? You believe him?'

'I want to believe him. I know it's not the same, but I want to believe that he'll fuck off to the other side of the globe, make his fortune, and that he'll never set foot in this country again. If only, Billy – wouldn't it be worth money? Wouldn't it be worth anything?'

I couldn't deny that it would.

'I mean, it won't change what's happened, but . . . y'know.'

What we both knew was that with Doran out of the equation, our chances of ever being rumbled were remote.

'You think you'll do it, then?'

'I think so, yeah. Depending, of course, on one or two things. Like, I'll need to hear what kind of sum he has in mind. There's only so much I can give away without my dad or my bank manager becoming curious. And – above everything else – I'll need a guarantee that he will actually go. That he won't just pocket my money, drink it up in my face and be back in six months looking for more.'

'And how d'you propose getting around that?'

'I haven't worked it out yet. But I'll figure something. It's not as if I'm doing a whole pile at the moment, and won't have time to think about it.'

'When are you getting out of that place, by the way?'

'It's just a matter of days now. Then it's back to Lisdrolin for the fresh air and the home cooking.'

'To Lisdrolin? Are you sure that's a good idea?'

'Oh, it's OK. Because Doran won't be there. Next weekend he's away to England to sort out his passport and visa. And after that, he says he'll need about a month to settle some unfinished business with a brother of his who lives in Cricklewood. Now for Doran, that could mean anything. But for me, it means I can go down the street and begin enjoying this dosh without having to spend every other minute watching my back.'

'And dead right too. If he's off the scene, you want to make the most of it while it lasts.'

'Don't say "while it lasts". Pretty soon we'll be rid of that vermin for good and all.'

CHAPTER FIVE

Not long after, Dasher was released with a clean bill of health. Immediately, he was on the phone, urging me to come home a weekend, telling how Lisdrolin had returned to its former idyll, all sweetness and light once again. But I declined. I can't quite remember why; it's possible that I'd work to do, or there may even have been a new woman in the frame. For whatever reason, I said no.

But when next he rang, he was not to be so easily dismissed. The word had come; Doran was back in Dublin. But it was only a brief stopover, so brief that he was demanding a rendezvous there for the very next morning. He'd got his passport, he'd got his visa, now he wanted his airfare and some start-up capital. Once he'd his hands on that lot he'd be on the first flight to Australia, that same afternoon if at all possible. Hearing the agitation, the high anxiety in his voice, Dasher was of the definite opinion that he was on the run and fleeing these shores as a matter of priority. Whatever the case, they'd arranged to meet the following day at noon in O'Neill's pub, Suffolk Street. Did I know it? And, as he was still some way off full strength, would I show up to lend moral support? Yes, I said, I knew the place intimately. And of course I'd be there, I'd not have him face this alone. One other thing – his bus got in at eleven thirty. Could I meet him at the station? That'd allow us half an hour to ourselves, as there were certain matters he needed to get straight with me beforehand. I told him I thought this an excellent idea. There was some hard bargaining to be done; we had best prepare a united front.

But we never got the chance. When I arrived at Busáras next morning, Doran was there before me. He'd grown an uneven foxy beard, just visible behind the upturned collars of a dirty fleece-lined bomber jacket. At once he came towards me, briskly, furtively.

'Small world,' he growled. 'Any harm asking what the fuck you're doing here?'

'I might ask you the same question. This isn't O'Neill's of Suffolk Street.'

'Just a precaution – I've decided on somewhere closer.'

At that moment, the Waterford bus swung into the forecourt.

'So get your boyfriend and follow me,' and raising his collar higher still, he went to the main door. Inside the bus, Dasher had witnessed everything and wore the look of a man trapped in a burning high-rise.

'He was waiting when I got here,' I mumbled as I helped him gingerly down the steps. Doran took one glance around, seeing if we were ready to take up his trail. Then off he set. He didn't go far – midway along Eden Quay, he turned into the Horse and Tram. When we got there behind him, he'd just secured the attention of a barman.

'A Harp for myself,' Doran called, 'and . . . ?'

'Two Guinness,' I told him.

He then took a step away from the counter. 'Look alive, for fuck's sake, Morrissey. I wouldn't dream of insulting a man of your means by paying for them.'

Presently, we took our seats at a table in the most remote

113

corner. I noticed how his hand shook a little as he dragged on his cigarette.

'So,' I said, offering some smalltalk, 'you're off to Australia?'

'That's the general idea, yeah.'

'Nice.'

'And expensive. If it wasn't, I wouldn't need this loan.'

'What? This is a loan?'

'Naturally it's a fucking loan. Do I look like someone who'd accept charity?'

'I never suggested that.'

'I should fucking hope not. All I'm after is a few quid to get my ticket and to tide me over till I've found my feet. Does that sound unreasonable?'

'Not at all,' I said, and I let that be my last word on it.

For a time, no one spoke. Doran twitched, scratched his left ear with his right hand, took a swig and lit another cigarette. Then, 'Dasher, I want ten grand.'

Dasher stared at him, open-mouthed. 'You're shitting me now, right?'

'I'm deadly serious. I've worked things out, and it's the very least I'll need.'

'Ten grand? That's a bloody year's wages. How long d'you intend taking to find your feet?'

'I have to allow for a slow start.'

'No way, Rodger. Not a hope. If that kind of money vanishes from my account, it will be missed. And I won't be able to explain it away. I'm sorry, but if that really is the amount you need, then you've got the wrong bloke. I'm wasting your time.'

Doran took several deep breaths through his nose. No more than I, he could scarcely believe the composure of the man across the table. The pressure was on him now; from how many sides was anyone's guess.

'OK then. How much d'you think you can spare?'

Dasher twice cleared his throat. 'A grand.'

'Get the fuck out of here! That'll hardly buy the ticket.'

'A grand and I'll buy the ticket.'

'Five grand and you buy the ticket.'

'That's not possible. There's only so much money I can put down to miscellaneous. A grand plus the ticket is the very best I can do.'

Breathing short and shallow, Doran got to his feet. 'In that case, you are wasting my fucking time here.' He yanked his old jacket from the stool where he'd draped it. 'Keep me a seat on the bus, Dasher my old mate. I've got things to do now, but I'll be home to Lisdrolin with you this evening. Won't that be fun.'

He began to pull the zipper, then to do the fasteners. I watched for any sign that Dasher's bold front was slipping. Both wanted the same thing, the same end result. It was just a question of who wanted it worse.

'You'll regret this, Morrissey,' Doran snarled, clipping shut the last fastener. 'You'll regret you were ever fucking born,' and after he'd kicked a low stool from out of his path, stormed for the door. Then suddenly he stopped, turned again and came raging back.

'Two grand, the ticket, and may you die without the fucking priest!'

Dasher regarded him calmly. An eternity went by.

'Well, you miserable bastard?'

Another eternity, this a longer one. At last there came the merest nod as he whispered, 'OK, deal.'

Together we left, with Doran again leading the charge.

Quayside Tours, close to O'Connell Bridge, was the nearest travel agent. The man with the money went alone to do the business, leaving us to stand by Ellis Quay, not exchanging as much as a syllable as we watched the Liffey go by. In less than half an hour, the transaction was completed. Dasher rejoined us by the bridge and handed Doran a medium-sized white envelope.

'You're flying out of London tomorrow at ten.'

'Which airport?'

'Heathrow. So you've got to catch the half eight flight from Dublin this evening. There's a stopover in Singapore. And your eventual destination is Sydney. I hope that's all right.'

'Yeah, yeah, smashing,' Doran said absent-mindedly as he opened the envelope and began to examine the contents. A cursory glance, then a double-take, and then, 'Hey, what's the fucking story? These are all one way!'

'I know. Is that a problem?'

'It's just . . . no, I suppose it's OK. Anyway, how are we going to organize this other money?'

Dasher, still bossing matters, now looked to me.

'The Central Bank is just across the river,' I told him.

'Fine,' he said. 'Now, Rodger, I'm giving it to you in travellers' cheques. You'll need to come with me, because they've got to be signed in the presence of a cashier.'

Doran eyed him, almost respectfully. 'I've underestimated you, Dasher. You've got everything worked out.'

'You've not quite heard everything yet.'

'No?'

'No. About our settlement; you're not getting it all right away. Half now, and when you reach Australia I'll send you the rest.'

'Like fuck you will. I want my money up front and in full – that was our agreement.'

'We made no agreement about this. And I just want to be sure.'

'Sure of what?'

'Sure that you go, like you said you would.'

'Oh, you don't trust me! So why the fuck should I trust you to send me that money when I'm ten thousand miles away and well out of your face?'

'Because I know the kind of trouble you could make for me if I don't.'

'Morrissey, if I don't get that dosh . . .' Here he temporarily ran out of words and began to jab the finger. 'If I don't get that dosh, and soon, well . . . you just remember that no matter how far down on my luck I am in Aussieland, I can always manage a reverse call to the Lisdrolin copshop. They'll be happy to accept the charges, when they hear what I've got to tell them.'

On that note, we walked towards Dame Street and the Central Bank. There was some argument over whether the two thousand pounds negotiated was sterling or Irish punts, but the differential was small at the time so Dasher relented. I waited on my own outside, where a street artist was reproducing *The Birth of Venus* in chalk on the pavement. I couldn't say how long I stood there, but after a time Dasher returned. Alone. Doran had taken the money and slipped away in the crowd. As to where he might surface next, we could but wait and see.

For all our misgivings, he did get on that plane. We soon had a postcard from an address at a boarding house in Kogarah, a suburb of Sydney. The accompanying note told nothing of what he was doing or who he was doing it with. It simply read:

This used to be a penal colony at one time. So I could probably have got out here for nothing. Then again, couldn't we all?

It was a clear reminder that, though he was far from home, he still had a card or two to play if the need arose. But that was never going to be necessary. By return of post, his second instalment was duly forwarded. This was to be the last shilling ever he extorted from the estate of Michael 'Dasher' Morrissey.

Now it was official, now the coast at last was clear. Little Lisdrolin, so long a forbidden zone, was back on the map with a broad smile on its face. Taking up Dasher's invitation with a will, I made that trip home. And many another besides, so many that to find me in Dublin of a Saturday night soon became something of a rarity. Easter arrived, and the college closed for ten days; I brazenly awarded myself three full weeks. My folks were worried witless, constantly reminding me that the exams were no length away, warning me that complacency had been the undoing of better men than me. In truth, I didn't feel complacent, I just didn't feel like leaving this life of ease for a return to the grind. Furthermore, there was Dasher's money to be considered. An amount so vast was clearly too much for one man to hope to get through in a single lifetime. He needed help from somewhere. And what are friends for.

After Easter, those exams were not long in coming – certainly not after the Easter I'd enjoyed. But I knuckled down, doggedly clawed back the lost time, got very lucky with one or two question papers and somehow scraped through. Now the summer lolled before me, hazy, lazy and long.

And so the party began in earnest. Days by the sea, by the

coves and sands of the Atlantic coast, nights wherever the fancy took us. Our time all our own, money no object, and all with the name Rodger Doran fading fast from the memory. He was gone, departed from our world. Since he'd had his final payment, there'd been no contact of any description. It was out of sight, out of mind; by that summer's end, we'd pretty much forgotten all about him. We were young then.

Only very grudgingly did I return to college when lectures resumed that October. The two years that followed, which took me to – and through – my finals, were a breeze, the calmest of plain sailing. I developed an uncanny knack of doing just the bare minimum required and not an iota more, clearing the bar by a whisker at every call. But it was enough to get me by and get me into a job, a position earmarked for none but myself from the day I first signed up to teach. Old Master Keating, Tom by name, had been educating the youngsters of Lisdrolin for the previous half-century. He was gone several years beyond retirement age, but hung in there till one of his own protégés could take on the baton. Now that handover could be made. On 1 September 1985 I began life as second assistant in the local three-teacher Boys' National School.

I'd not severed all links with Dublin; early in the next month, I was back there twice. First there was my own graduation ceremony – mortarboard, cape, parchment, the works, with the whole family in attendance. The following week the entire clan was again present to attend Mags' conferring in Trinity College. A far grander do, this, than my poor passing out, and my folks were never entirely at ease among what my dad called 'all this quality.' They were itching to get away, and had the perfect excuse when my mother began to complain of feeling unwell. It was no

119

pretence; our journey home was repeatedly halted as Mam needed to get air or to get sick, or both. But in between her bouts of nausea, she was positively delighted with herself.

'Isn't it grand,' she'd repeatedly ask my father. 'Isn't it powerful to live to see the pair of them set up.'

I thought this a little odd, nothing more; but I really should've had it figured. She'd been suffering – suffering dreadfully – from ovarian cancer, diagnosed shortly before I began my finals and too far advanced to be operable. My father had been sworn to absolute secrecy; she was afraid that if word got out she might be prevented from witnessing these great, great days, from watching her children become qualified professionals, set fair for a better life than she'd ever known. Now that she'd seen this, she'd seen enough. Within the year, she was gone. Old schoolmaster Keating wasn't the only one who'd been holding on.

Dasher never did go back to finish that degree. He just got too lazy about it all, too set in the ways of the idle rich. And for a time, he really did play the overprivileged waster with a relish. He would sleep till midday and beyond, then pass the afternoon . . . actually, I'm not rightly sure how he passed his afternoons. But when evening came, he was anybody's, and no invitation to a few pints or a night on the tiles was ever refused. Or was ever even required. His weight ballooned, his dodgy kidneys were hardly the better for it, and his parents were beside themselves with concern. But he was stone deaf to them. With resources like his, he needed to take neither lectures nor shit from anyone.

Where his parents failed, however, fate scored a direct hit. It was following another three-day razzle in and around Waterford city. He woke one afternoon, as was his custom, to

120

find in his pocket a phone number he couldn't account for. It turned out to be that of a woman named Mary Hayes. Dasher didn't know the name; it later transpired that when he'd chatted her up, he hardly knew his own. It must've been some kind of modern-day miracle, but he somehow managed to strike lucky. Extraordinarily so; Mary Hayes was lovely. A nurse in Waterford Infirmary, she was a single mother to two small children and a couple of years older than her bloated suitor. But she had looks, personality and far, far too much going her way to give the likes of Dasher Morrissey a second glance.

But when you're talking miracles, these things do happen. In no time, Dasher was a man transformed. It began in small ways; a little walking, a not-too-drastic diet, an occasional night's abstinence from the pub, and a gradual return to normal waking hours. He bought a car – his first – and even condescended to get off his backside once in a while and do a bit of light work. He bored easily, though, and didn't stick at any one thing for very long. Then again, he didn't need to.

It scarcely even broke his stride when Mary discovered that she was carrying his child. Where I come from, that limits a man's options; they were married that summer. The do itself was a lavish affair that must've cost plenty and put a severe dent in Dasher's stash. Then when they bought a new bungalow just outside the village off the Boher Road, the job was complete, the coffers finally emptied. Sixty grand gone west. Financially speaking, Dasher was back to square one. And beyond.

Now reality bit hard. His wife couldn't afford to stop working, while he couldn't afford to stay idle. But he'd dropped out of college without any qualifications, and he was unfit to hew wood or draw water. Along with general living expenses, there was also the cost of day-care for two young children to be considered. With, of course, a third on the way to exacerbate matters further.

But again at this point, things fell nicely into his lap. Tom Bookle, owner of the village petrol pumps, needed an attendant. And if Dasher had hand-tailored the post, he'd not have made it to better suit. There was nothing much involved, as the operation had recently gone self-service. And his kiosk was quite spacious, affording him room to read, to watch TV, and to fence in those of his babies he'd been left holding. One stone, two birds down, everything sorted at a stroke. It may not have been life in the fast lane, but all things considered, it could've been a lot worse.

Later that year, our new policeman arrived. The old one, Sergeant Laherty, had grown very old indeed, and by the end of his tour of duty had become good for nothing much. So the fresh blood was welcome. He was Conor Furlong, and word quickly had it that he was a native of Boolavogue, Wexford, not long out of training and still a bit raw. After a brief posting on the meaner streets of West Dublin he was said to be delighted to find himself in South Kilkenny, hurling heartland, because hurling was his game.

Indeed it was at a match that first we met one frosty morning in November. The final of some trivial local tournament was down for decision, with Carrigshock providing our opposition. The game itself was a complete irrelevance, a glorified friendly, though there wasn't very much bonhomie in evidence; with the freezing fog that hadn't yet lifted, and the inevitable hangovers that were being nursed on both sides, tempers were short. Furlong and I were among the subs, though for differing reasons. He'd only just arrived in town and nobody had yet seen him play.

Whereas they'd seen me several times, which is why I found myself held in reserve, for emergency use only.

'Not really hurling weather, is it,' he remarked as we watched the combatants trying to exhume the ball from the sodden pitch.

'No,' I agreed. 'You need the hard ground.'

'I imagine our lads are better than this in the summer,' he said, 'cos to be honest with you, they don't look up to much today.'

A crushing understatement this. Without seeming to be even trying, Carrigshock were beating us for fun.

'We're a little better, but not a whole lot,' I told him as another opposing forward sauntered through our back division and planted the ball in the net for the umpteenth time.

'How come you aren't playing?' he asked.

'I wasn't picked.'

'You don't sound too put out by that.'

'No. I didn't really expect to get a game.'

'Good Christ, are you mad in the head, then? I mean, what's got you togged out and sitting here on a morning like this?'

'I dunno – honour of the parish pump, maybe. But hey, what about you? It isn't even your parish pump. So what're you doing here?'

'Well, first and foremost, I enjoy it. I'm fuck-all good, but I enjoy the rough and tumble. And then there's the social side. When you're new in a place and you don't know very many people, it's your gateway to the community. And to the better side of the community at that. There's usually a decent, respectable crowd involved in the GAA.'

We became so engrossed that we neglected to follow the

game. And failed to spot that our centre half back was being helped from the field of play with blood trickling from his eyebrow. We hadn't even noticed that a sub had long been summoned, not till the referee ran towards us, whistling furiously as he came.

'Hurry up, whoever's going on,' he shouted. 'We haven't all day.'

Conor turned to me. 'What about you, oul' stock?'

'No,' I insisted. 'You go ahead.'

With gusto, he whipped off his tracksuit and sprinted on to the pitch, charging headlong into the thick of the fray. He'd been absolutely spot on; he did appear to revel in the hustle and bustle. And he was fuck-all good. Still, he did his best in the face of a rout, a comprehensive humiliation. And the indignity didn't even end with the blow of full time, for as we queued to receive our consolation prizes we were told that the box was a trophy short; one of our substitutes would have to go empty handed. Furlong, as last man in, was the obvious choice but it seemed to me a shame to have all that enthusiasm go unrewarded. So I protested that he be given one; that he be given mine. He argued, of course, and did all he could to decline, but I stood adamant. Eventually, after much toing and froing, he relented, packed the little figurine in his kitbag, and asked if he might take our discussion to the nearest pub and continue it there.

Back in the Heather Blazing, players from both teams were randomly grouped in small knots around the bar. Furlong and I took our drinks to an unoccupied table near the fireplace.

'You're a native of here, then?' he asked.

'That's right. Born and bred in the place.'

'Must make things a bit difficult for you, being local. I

know I could never go back to Boolavogue and be a cop there.'

'Well, they do say that, don't they. That a guard or a banker can never work at home.'

'Between ourselves, I don't know how a teacher can work anywhere at all in this day and age. I wouldn't do your job for diamonds.'

'What's the problem – d'you not like kids?'

'Oh no – I think they're great. But in small, small doses. Hey – would it be OK if I called round to the school to have a word with them one day this week?'

'About what?'

'This and that. Road safety, maybe, bike maintenance – anything at all, just to let them see my face and know that I'm about.'

'Sure. You're welcome to drop by any time you feel like it. You do know where we are, yeah?'

He smiled. The boys' school and the police station were side by side, separated only by a block wall.

'I'll find you. Probably on Wednesday.'

Leaky Roche appeared at the table. He alone of the three original musketeers was still on the scene. Seamus Gunning had completely vanished from the public eye since getting married to a girl from Glenmore. Kevin Wrafter, meanwhile, had gone to London, and several different accounts of his marital status were doing the rounds. Leaky remained, much as he'd always been.

'Well,' he asked me, 'did ye win?'

'We came second.'

'Christ, some things never change. You should be bloody well ashamed of yourselves.'

'Easy for you to talk – the hurler in the ditch.'

'At least I had the decency to take to the ditch as soon as I realized I was no good. Pity you wouldn't do the same, Walsh.' He took a sip from his pint. 'How are you, Guard?'

'The name's Conor – I'm off duty.'

'Oh, I beg your pardon,' I said. 'Conor Furlong, this is Peter Roche. Leaky to his fans.'

'Leaky?'

'He's a plumber,' I explained.

'And a good one, so don't go listening to this fucker. By the way, I'm in the phone book if you ever need any jobs done in that station house.'

'I don't, thankfully,' the policeman told him. 'For such an old building, it's in remarkable order. Like everything else since I've been here – I couldn't ask for better.'

'You're enjoying it, then?'

'Bloody right I am. And if you'd just come from the part of Dublin I did – or Knackeragua, as it's more commonly known – you'd enjoy it here, too.'

'Yeah, I can imagine that it must be easy enough to keep an eye on things in Lisdrolin.'

'Other than sticking my head into the odd pub after closing time, there's nothing much. I even read back through the station records the other day, hoping for some excitement, but there's bugger all there either. No murder, no armed robbery, not even a decent rape – nothing. Apart, of course, from the Suzy Deane case.'

I didn't know if my sharp intake of breath had gone unnoticed. In case it hadn't, I smiled a puzzled wee smile and asked, 'Suzy? What about her?'

'Well, I was kinda hoping one of you might be able to tell me,' he said breezily.

'Jesus, you certainly chanced on the right fellah,' Leaky told him.

'Who?'

'Billy there was her next-door neighbour. And a big admirer in his time.'

'Really?'

I tried to sound enthusiastic, anxious to help, and said, 'She used to live just across the field from home.'

'So what was she like?'

'To look at?'

'That too, yeah.'

'Let me see. She was small, dark —'

'She was a fucking beaut, God bless her,' Leaky interjected. 'I promise you, Conor boy, you wouldn't kick her out of bed for farting.'

'And a bit of a wild one too, I believe.'

'*Wild?*' Leaky whooped. 'The girl was as cracked as a frog's arse.'

Furlong mustn't have heard the expression before, because he spluttered a laugh that made some beer go with his breath. When he'd coughed it up he continued, 'And one night, she just vanished into thin air.'

'No,' I told him. 'Three nights she vanished into thin air. Twice she reappeared and was brought back home.'

He nodded intently, as if this was news to him. I guessed that it wasn't.

'Hmmm. And I understand that, for her age, she was quite . . . promiscuous.'

'I dunno about that,' Leaky said gravely. Then, out of the corner of his mouth, 'But between ourselves, the same girl used to bang like a barn door in a gale.'

It was curious how Furlong was largely ignoring this. He

127

seemed interested only in what I had to say. 'Is that right, Billy? Was she?'

'I may be wrong, Conor,' I put it to him, 'but I reckon you know a lot more about this than you're letting on.'

'I wouldn't say a lot. But the first night I arrived, Sergeant Laherty – or rather ex-Sergeant Laherty – came over to welcome me to the place and we opened a bottle of whisky. And we talked. And we emptied the bottle and kept on talking.'

'All about Suzy?'

'Mostly, yeah. It's a strange one. On the surface, it's your classic teenage runaway. Young girl with big notions and itchy feet takes the high road. Money, clothes and passport go with her.'

'And what's so strange, then?' I asked.

'The case should've been closed right away. But Laherty wouldn't close it. And all because one other name kept cropping up too often. A Rodger Doran.'

Leaky sucked hard through his teeth.

'Woah! Now there was one bad bastard. A real can of piss. And I don't know how, but I'm sure he had something to do with it all.'

'Well, that's the point. So was Laherty. Still is.'

I frowned and said, 'Really? What exactly did he think Doran might have done?'

'He didn't know that. It was just an instinct with him – y'know, a gut feeling. He was a man who didn't believe in coincidence. Now, this young, vulnerable girl gets involved with a man who's known to be violent and dangerous; the next thing you know, she's disappeared off the radar. *That* is a coincidence.'

'And what, if anything, did Sergeant Laherty do about it?'

'He went through the Doran house with his fingertips. Found nothing. Not that that proved a great deal. Because of Suzy's record, the missing person's report wasn't taken seriously for a few days. So Doran would've had plenty of time to cover his tracks.'

'And after Laherty had drawn a blank on the house search?'

'He set up discreet surveillance – had the guy watched for a couple of weeks. The hope was that if he'd stowed her somewhere, he might try to make contact. Or if he'd killed her, he'd visit the body where it was buried. It happens sometimes.'

'Well?'

'Nothing there either. Oh, they observed him going out by night to steal hay from around the village. Or to siphon off diesel from farmers' bulk tanks. He even drove up Tory Hill and stole a sheep one night. Broke its neck there and then, and chucked it into the boot of his car. By all accounts, he was some piece of work. Hardly a murderer, though. Or if he was, he must've been the shrewdest, most nerveless killer ever. He didn't know he was being watched – he couldn't have known. But as far as Suzy's disappearance was concerned, he came up clean as a whistle. Never put a foot wrong.'

'And Laherty still wasn't convinced?'

'And I'm still not convinced either,' Leaky said. 'It wouldn't surprise me if, somehow, he'd managed to smuggle her out to Australia.' Then, to the Garda, 'You know he cleared off shortly after she did?'

'I heard.'

'Well,' Leaky said by way of summing up, 'that's what I think anyway. The pair of them are living together down under.'

'It'd be nice if you were right,' Conor said. 'It'd mean I could draw a line under the whole affair. Cos I'm another man who likes things neat, tidy and squared away. But I don't suppose there's any hope we could find out from Doran himself. I mean, he hasn't been in contact with anyone around here, has he?'

I laughed a little and said, 'I certainly haven't heard from him.'

Smiling mischievously, Leaky studied me for a long while. 'Oh-yes-you-have!'

The blood in my eardrums began to throb.

'Huh? No, I haven't.'

'Dasher has. And I know you two tell each other everything.'

'Dasher? No way!'

'Dasher got a postcard from him shortly after he moved out there.'

'How did you know?' I blurted, and immediately realized how bad, how guilty it sounded.

'It was a postcard, for fuck's sake. Anyone that wanted to could read it. Like for instance, the postman. He's the one who told me.'

Furlong was watching me, not accusingly but not uninterested. I can only imagine what shade of red I turned as I stammered, 'That's right, now that you mention it. Dasher did have a card from him. Didn't say very much – only that he was living near Sydney, if I remember correctly. Maybe Leaky can check that out with the postman the next time the pair of them are snooping through other people's mail.'

They both chortled, though I'd not intended it to be funny. Then Furlong asked, 'So this Dasher bloke – is he a big mate of Rodger Doran's?'

'Are you joking!' Leaky laughed. 'None of us liked him, but poor oul' Dasher was absolutely shit-scared. He would've crawled into a mousehole from that cunt!'

The policeman slowly shook his head. 'So . . . why? Why did he write to this Dasher, of all people. Why him, and no one else?' And again, the eyes bore down on me.

'Well – y'know, of course, that he visited Dasher in hospital after the accident.'

'Did he?' Leaky asked, astonished. Only then did I recall that this, too, was highly classified.

'He did . . . well, so did dozens of others go down to Cork to see him after the crash.'

'I know,' Leaky said. 'But I didn't think Doran was one of them . . . are you sure about this?'

'Yeah!' I snapped, wishing to Christ that we could change the subject.

'There!' Furlong smiled and said, 'That probably explains it.'

But his tone said different. And his expression concurred that there was a rat at large here, stinking to high Heaven.

CHAPTER SIX

But whatever his suspicions, Furlong kept them to himself, and following that conversation we didn't discuss the matter again. We didn't sit on Lisdrolin's bench for very much longer either, both deciding that there were limits to the humiliation we were prepared to endure. Supporting from the sideline was very nearly as degrading, but we continued to follow them the length and breadth of the county. Not so much for any on-field entertainment, but for the few pints and the bit of craic that always ensued. And scarcely a Saturday night went by when we didn't meet up for more of the same somewhere around the village. Then there were his visits to the school, which became a weekly observance and very eagerly anticipated by one and all. Despite what he'd said, he had an excellent way with youngsters. They listened when he spoke, as he usually managed to root his little talks in their own interests and experiences.

But however friendly we became, there was one area on which we could never be reconciled. In hurling, Kilkenny and Wexford enjoyed a rivalry as old and as colourful as the game itself. Furlong was a staunch Wexford man, based now in Kilkenny, surrounded on all sides by the enemy. So as the championship clash approached each year, he'd be getting it from every quarter, and giving it back just as hot and as heavy. Then, come match-day morning as the chartered minibus rolled into Main Street, he'd be there festooned in purple and gold, sticking out like a sore thumb in the sea of black and amber. 1988 would've been his first excursion to Croke Park among the Lisdrolin horde, and it was a case of beginner's luck; our lot went into the game as strong favourites, but came home a well-beaten side. Next year, however, it was business as usual, normal service resumed. Wexford were outclassed for most of the game, didn't begin to play until they had a man sent off, then came storming back and would've won but for a desperate goal-line clearance deep in injury time. Sweet revenge, then, huge relief, because to the very last puck the tension was great. For some, too great; one hundred miles to the south, and just minutes after the radio broadcast had ended, my father died.

For several hours I was incommunicado as our bus hardly missed a tavern on the route, pub-crawling from Dublin all the way home. It was almost one when the coach touched down at base. I bade the others farewell and went reeling up the Boher Road, dog-tired and drunk as a lord.

The fact that almost every room in the house was lit up set the first alarm bells ringing. I smartened my step through the darkness and all but went headlong into a car parked flush in our front gate. After a step back and a quick once-over, I saw that it was Mags' BMW, left where it was because our yard was already full. She'd been last to arrive – barring myself, of course. Clearly, something was not quite as it should be. She must've heard me attempt to get my key into the hole, because the door opened from the inside and she stood in my way.

'Hiya,' she said.

I shook my head, spread my arms and slurred, 'Grand. What's . . . ?'

She beckoned me outside, away from the door and the big front window. 'Billy, he's gone.'

'Dad?' Another head-shake. 'Gone where?'

'Gone to God. He passed away a few hours ago.'

I suddenly became very disorientated. Nothing at all to do with the drink, I just couldn't remember for a second which direction was up.

'Oh,' I said vaguely. 'Passed away . . . right. How did it happen?'

'He was in Joe Deane's house at the time, sat in an armchair by the fire. Without any warning, it seems he just drifted away. It was very sudden, but very peaceful. He didn't suffer at all.'

'That's something, anyway. I'm pleased for the poor oul' devil. Where is he now?'

'Tebbits, the funeral directors, are looking after everything. There wasn't much point in bringing him back here to this house.'

'No, none at all . . . none at all.'

'You'll miss him.'

This was certainly true. Since my mother's death, there had been just the two of us. We were never especially close, nor given to great displays of affection. But I knew my father to have been a decent, gentle man, who wanted nothing from life other than to do right by his family and by his faith. A man like that would be missed at any time.

'You OK?' Mags asked when I wasn't answering.

'Me? Oh, yeah. I'm fine. It's like I said, I'm pleased for him. Y'know, wouldn't it be great if everyone could go like this. Live a good long life and when your time comes, slip away quietly one Sunday afternoon in your oldest friend's armchair.'

Pleased for him I may have been, but there was nothing I could do about the hot tear I now felt trickle down my cheek.

'C'mon,' she said then. 'Come in and say hello to your neighbours.'

'You go ahead,' I told her. 'I'll be after you in a while.'

'In a while? Billy, it's almost two in the morning. They're only waiting to sympathize with you so they can go to their homes.'

'Gimme a few minutes to sober up.'

'You're not drunk.'

I wasn't drunk, not any more.

'Hey,' she said, 'I know you probably want to look the hard man in front of everybody. But your father's just died. So it's allowed.' And she passed me her handkerchief.

Inside, the small crowd came to its feet when I entered. Everyone present was well known to me, all good and trusted friends of the family. One by one they sidled forward to offer muffled condolences. Then, mostly, they left – the hour was late, and next day was a working day. However, before they did they assured us that they'd see us at the removal next evening and at the funeral mass on the morning after. And if there was anything we needed in the meantime, we only had to ask.

Though from what I could gather, everything had been pretty well taken care of. Mags had called the death notice in to the newspapers. She'd also seen to the catering, organizing refreshments in the Heather for anyone travelling a distance to the ceremonies. Neither Dasher nor Leaky had been to the big match; both had come round and volunteered to dig the grave. The undertakers would look after the rest.

When the main commotion had died down, only Dasher and Joe Deane remained. I was glad that somebody stayed – with both parents now gone, the house would be empty soon enough.

'So how did it happen, Joe?' I asked.

'Well, boy, I don't know. All I do know is that your father died contented.'

'I can well imagine.'

'You were at the match, and I'm sure 'twas hard enough to watch. But Jesus, listening on the wireless is fifty times worse. And that escape Kilkenny made in the last minute – 'twasn't good for anybody's heart.'

'So you reckon it was a heart attack?'

'Sure I don't know, I told you. 'Twas in all the hullabaloo after the game ended. One minute he was full of his fun, the next . . .'

'Just like that?'

'Just like that. This day will come for us all, boy. You should pray to God that when it comes for you, it comes as easy as it did for your dad.'

'Don't worry,' I said, 'I already did.'

Dasher smiled weakly and said, 'Well, whatever, he's at peace now.'

'He is,' Joe agreed. 'And he's due a little peace and ease, because he had a hard life. People nowadays have no idea what it was like growing up during the war, with the rationing and the terrible shortages and all. Or in the years before, when the British wouldn't buy our cattle, and every second young fellah was leaving the land and catching the Rosslare ferry. The lads like your father who stayed behind saw some hardship, let me tell you. Trying to scratch out a living from a few miserable acres on the side of a hill, and provide for a family at the same time. But by God, he never left ye short of anything. The man did ye proud.'

We nodded and agreed that, yes, we owed him much. Mags then left the discussion and arrived back with a large bottle of scotch. I declined – I'd had enough all day. But the others were in no way inhibited. Before too long, old Joe was a wee bit tipsy. And in very, very forthright mood.

'So, boy,' he said sternly to me, 'after the trouble your father went to, keeping this farm in your family, you'd better not let his name die out.'

'I have no intention of it,' I told him.

'Well, for the love of Christ, then, when are we going to see a few of his grandchildren running around that yard, eh?'

'All in its own good time, Joe.'

'I'd say it's bloody high time. How old are you now?'

'Twenty-four.'

'Well, you'd want to be getting on with that business. You're not a chap any more – you're the man of the house now.'

'That remains to be seen – I don't know what's to become of this house.'

'I do, faith. I'm an executor of the will, and 'tis often Murt and I spoke of it. I suppose I shouldn't really be telling you yet. But sure where's the harm in it.'

With a low grunt, Dasher stood up. 'Listen, I should be going. This is none of my business.'

'Ah sit down out of that,' Mags told him. 'For God's sake, you're nearly family.'

I said, 'Yeah. You never know, there might be something in it for you.'

'And even if there's not,' she went on, 'it isn't as if you're going to hear anything that might topple the government. So go ahead, Joe. What's the suss?'

'Well now, girleen, there was never anything crooked about your father, and his last will is as straightforward as you could ever want it to be. He left a few quid to the church in the village. After that, he only had the two of ye. So for you, me boy, there's this house, this farm and everything he owned. Except for his savings – he had an account with the ACC. And Mags, that's for you.'

'No, no, no.' she said hurriedly. 'This isn't right. I never lifted a finger around this place. Any money that may be in my dad's account is there because of him,' and she pointed to me. 'He's been working on this farm from the time he could walk, and for the past eighteen months or so he's been running the place single-handedly.'

This was far from being the case. All I ever did was the donkey work, providing the muscle as my father's waned. But he was always the one giving out the instructions, pulling the strings. Left alone, I'd not know where to start.

'Joe,' I said. 'What am I to do with the farm of land?'

'Now, if the man himself was here, he'd say, "Do what you like with it. It's yours now." But we both know it'd break his heart if it was let pass to some stranger.'

'I'm not accepting this,' Mags harped back. 'If there was one thing Dad always drilled into us, it was that you should get nothing for nothing. That money is there to be earned and to be respected.'

'And a man's last wish – isn't that something to be respected? Mags, if your father didn't want you to have that money, he wouldn't have left it to you.'

'I know that, but . . .'

The bequest embarrassed her. She didn't want it, and she sure as hell didn't need it, not the way she was coining at the time. My dad's poor nest egg would scarcely have covered a decent morning's work for that lady, ever since she'd put a foot under the top table of Ireland's barristers. Following a first-class honours degree and outstanding potential displayed while serving her apprenticeship – devilling – she was rapidly making a name for herself defending upmarket lowlife. Drug dealers, stick-up merchants, career criminals of every stripe, but only the biggest wheels, as only they could afford her. Expensive she may have been, but she was good. There was more than one of the nation's thugs who owed his liberty to her and to her alone.

'I can't take this money,' she repeated when the other two had left. 'It's just . . . ah . . . what was the expression daddy had?'

'Fat meat to the fat pig's arse?'

'That's the one,' she laughed. 'Mind you, I've been called worse since I've started defending the gangsters.'

The burial passed off quietly. A great crowd attended. Included in the congregation was a carload of old college mates I'd not spoken to in a few years, but who'd seen the notice in the paper. Similarly, there were several from the legal world present, some of whom I partly recognized from TV appearances and newspaper coverage.

I took a week off work, as was my entitlement. Mags too hung around till the following Sunday. In due course the will was read, the details being identical to those Joe had leaked to us. By then we'd both come to accept that if this was how the old man wanted it, then this was how it would be. It didn't stop Mags carping about her cut (almost three and a half thousand). And it certainly didn't alter the fact that when it came to farm management, I was next door to clueless.

In those early months, I did my best. It was summer, there was hay to be saved and cows to be milked twice daily. At first, things didn't go badly, but soon my lack of know-how told. I brought one lot of bales into the shed too early, before the hay had a chance to bleach or dry properly. The result was that it went rotten, and the rot quickly spread to what good stuff I'd already taken in. Before long it began to give off a dangerous gas and to overheat, which in turn carried the risk of fire. So I didn't just lose my entire hay crop, I had to pay a professional to come and dispose of it for me. Then one of my cows came down with mastitis, a contagious disease of the udder, but I failed to notice till most of the herd was similarly infected. The cost of the veterinary treatment was absolutely staggering, and as the produce was now contaminated by antibiotics, no creamery would touch it. I could only watch as the peak-season milk yield ran in torrents down my drain.

This farm was proving to be just the poisoned chalice I'd feared, and the harder I tried the more out of pocket I seemed to find myself. It was difficult not to be demoralized and I was sorely tempted to wash my hands of it in those dark, frustrating early days. But, honour-bound, I soldiered on.

Naturally, I kept these troubles to myself. Where I grew up, a problem shared was not a problem halved, it was a problem multiplied many times over; a setback only because a calamity within the neighbours got wind of it. Still, I had to unburden myself to someone, and over a few pints with

Furlong one night in that late autumn, I let it all come tumbling out.

'And you're dead set against selling, yeah?' he asked when I'd done.

'I could, I suppose. But . . . y'know.'

'What about setting the land, then?'

'How d'you mean?'

'Set it. Rent it out. If you can't hack it, give someone else a go.'

'Hmmm . . . yeah, it's an idea. I could do that, couldn't I. But . . .'

'But what?'

'Well, I was maybe the worst farmer there's ever been, I'm not sure I'd fare much better as a landlord. Demanding money from people wouldn't really be my long suit.'

'It's not like you were letting out a flat, for God's sake. Land leases usually last a year, maybe more. So you'd only have to collect rent every twelve months or so. Christ, Walsh, even you'd manage that.'

'R – right . . . and how much d'you think I should charge?'

'I don't know, but it wouldn't be impossible to find that out. There's plenty of leasing going on already around the parish.'

'The only thing is, the land's not great; some of it is bog, more of it is mountain, and even the good bits aren't all that hectic. As well, it's a bit out of the way. Not really convenient to anywhere, and trying to move heavy machinery in and out of those little fields can be a right pain in the arse. To be honest, I can't imagine who'd want to pay good money for such hassle.'

'If you can't find any takers, come back to me. I might just know a man.'

Much as I'd expected, I couldn't. So back I came. The man turned out to be a friend and neighbour of his named Houlihan. Mr Houlihan was a sheep farmer who'd fallen on hard times and had defaulted on a loan. His creditor was a national bank who'd promptly foreclosed on the little he owned and, for good measure, had him listed in *Stubbs' Gazette*, with the result that, having gone under on this first venture, he couldn't now raise the capital to start a second. So the proposal was as follows: if I would allow Mr Houlihan – Martin – the use of my land with immediate effect, he'd see me right for the rent when he could. Furlong was prepared to vouch for this man personally, even offering to go guarantor should he ever leave me with monies owed. I told him I needed no such safety net; his endorsement was good enough for me. We had a deal.

My end of the deal could hardly have been sweeter. Martin Houlihan was a dream tenant, quiet, hard-working and unassuming. And honest with it – any time I saw a livestock lorry arrive to take animals to market, I knew for sure that another instalment of my rent would not be far behind. He was about twice my age – late forties, I'd have said, and married with four children. He wasn't much of a talker and though I met him daily, it would be a while before we spoke in any meaningful way. But when we did, he explained how things had been running pretty smoothly in Boolavogue until a truly wretched run of luck. There was an outbreak of a disease I'd not heard of, followed by some trade dispute involving live exports that caused the price of lamb on the hoof to plummet. Given time, he felt he would've turned things round. But the bank was calling all the shots and it didn't share his optimism. Typically, it cut its losses.

142

Furlong called to the house fairly regularly at the start, usually on some flimsy pretext, but all three of us knew that the object was to keep tabs on his man. We didn't resent these random inspections, however, because invariably we'd all end up in Ned Law's, drinking pints and watching the sun go down behind Tory Hill. Life was good then. And financially, my tide was on the rise. Around the farm I'd abandoned all lost causes and stopped throwing good money after bad. My teacher's salary was quite substantial and guaranteed each week. Added to what I received from Martin and coupled with my complete lack of dependants or responsibilities, it gave me a disposable income the equal of any twenty-four-year-old in South Kilkenny. Then one Friday in spring there came the auction of my late father's fixtures and fittings. Some of his old tractors, ploughs and the like were in danger of gathering rust, they were no good to a shepherd like Martin and they certainly were no good to me. The proceeds didn't send me laughing all the way to the bank, but they did pay for a brand new Ford Sierra Laser, my very first car and not at all bad for starters.

Suddenly, and without doing a great deal, I'd become a very eligible bachelor. And back then I was not slow to take full advantage of this status. Oh, around our village some tongues did wag. And I let them. If these gossips had nothing better to do with their lives than be scandalized by mine, then they were more to be pitied than feared.

And so my middle twenties jollied along just nicely. This, I thought, was living, all right; this was as good as it got. And then, out of the blue, it got better. One evening Dasher and I were sitting on the paddock gate while Jamie – his wife's eldest – was down below us playing among the lambs. We were talking about this, that, and nothing at all when the squad car came trundling along the lane. In the distance I could see Furlong behind the wheel, alone and out of uniform. Coming for yet another progress update on my tenant, I assumed. In which case, he'd be out of luck.

He drew alongside and wound the window down.

'You missed him,' I called. 'He left about an hour ago.'

'It was yourself I wanted to talk to.'

Dasher jumped to his feet. 'It's time we were leaving anyway,' he said excusing himself. 'I'll go and round up this young fellah of mine.'

'No, Dash,' said the policeman. 'The two of you together would be even better. Hang on till I turn the car and I'll join you.' And off he went to swing it.

'Now what the fuck d'you suppose he wants?' Dasher hissed through unmoving lips.

'Relax,' I told him, 'if he'd come to arrest us, he'd not have come alone. We're big blokes.'

'With big fucking mouths, some of us!'

His tone caught me on the back foot a little. 'D'you mean me? You got a problem, Dash?'

'We're within spitting distance of where it all happened, with a copper on the plot, and you have to start cracking wise about the pair of us being arrested!'

'Oh, lighten up, why don't you.'

'And shut up, why don't *you!*'

'No, you shut the fuck up. Your stupid paranoia would make anyone suspicious.'

The squad car came juddering back towards us, so it had to be smiles all round.

'By God, it's go-go-go around here, what?' Furlong

remarked. 'A right hive of activity.'

Dasher laughed forcedly and said, 'Yeah . . . What d'you want, exactly?'

'Well, I can see that you're busy men. But d'ye think ye could spare me a minute? Hop in here.'

I sat in the front, Dasher the back.

'I have a bit of a problem, and maybe you guys can help me. It's about Suzy Deane.'

My stomach turned a somersault, as it always did at the mention of that name. I then looked over my shoulder, expecting that Dasher had turned to plasma and was puddling the back seat. But no, he was sitting quite erect, if a little pale.

'Willie O'Connor was in to me in the barracks earlier today. Himself and the bird are just back from a fortnight in Greece.'

'So?'

'He says that on the day he arrived there two weeks ago, he ran into a crowd of backpackers who were just leaving the place. They were doing the Inter-rail deal, roughing it all over Europe. And there in the middle of them was the bould Suzy.'

Dasher's eyes all but came out on stilts. 'That's imposs —' he began.

'Brilliant!' I exclaimed, cutting across him. 'It's marvellous news. Isn't it marvellous news, Dash.'

'Marvellous, bloody marvellous!' Dasher gushed, over-doing it entirely. Furlong frowned, watching for a while in the rear-view mirror. He looked away, then found him again and said ominously, 'Well, Dash?'

Dasher reddened, swallowed, shifted and squirmed before finally stammering, 'Well . . . what?'

'Well, aren't you going to ask me how she is? What she looks like? If she's married? Where she lives?'

Again, I cut in.

'I assumed that after driving all the way up here, you were going to volunteer that much. But go on, then – how is she?'

'I'm very sorry,' he smiled. 'I'm afraid I don't know. O'Connor didn't actually get to speak to her.'

'Ah why not, for God's sake,' Dasher demanded, continuing to lay it on far too thick.

'He only saw her for a couple of seconds, just as herself and a gang of mates were boarding a train heading north. There wasn't much time for any great conversation – he just called to her out of the crowd, she acknowledged him and waved back. It's not what you'd call conclusive. And it has been more than ten years. But O'Connor seems like a pretty reliable bloke. And he swears it was her.'

'The main thing is that she's alive and well,' was Dasher's summation. 'And thank God for that.'

I thought a note of caution would've rung more true, so I said, 'I dunno. I think I'd need other evidence.'

'Well, apparently it did look like her,' Furlong said. 'And by Christ, it sounds like her.'

'How?'

'Everyone that knew her tells me she was as mad as a snake. And you'd want to be off your rocker to do that Inter-rail thing. Holiday my arse, it's nothing but punishment. Pure lunacy, and absolutely made for a screwball like Suzy Deane, wouldn't you say?'

'So are you taking it as a confirmed sighting?' I asked.

'I can't really, can I? But I can ease off a bit with my enquiries.'

'Enquiries? You've been making enquiries?'

'Naturally. Suzy is the biggest mystery ever to hit this parish. In fact, as far as I can gather, she's the only one. Of course I'm going to be asking questions.'

'Yeah, but . . . what questions? And who have you been asking?'

'Oh, nobody from Lisdrolin, I can assure you. That line was well and truly exhausted when she vanished all those years ago.'

'So what *have* you been doing, then?'

'This and that. Whenever I hear of a body being unearthed in Ireland or Britain – or anywhere in Europe, come to that – I try to follow it up. And if it's female, in her teens, I send on a photograph and some hair samples on the off-chance of a match.'

'Where did you get those from?' Dasher asked.

'They were on file when I got here. The hair came from a brush she left behind when she took off.'

'And is it possible to establish a match just from that? I mean, even if you did hit the jackpot, you'd still be talking about a ten-year-old corpse.'

'No bother – they could make an identification almost beyond doubt. You wouldn't believe the advances recently in forensic science. They've discovered a chemical that's present in everything about a person; in hair, skin tissue, saliva, blood, bone, the works. DNA, they call it – I've no idea what it stands for. But not only have they isolated this, they've found that no two people have the same DNA configuration. Imagine – unique as a fingerprint. It's not in widespread use yet, but take it from me, it's the future.'

'And so far, obviously, they've come across no corpse that matches Suzy's . . .'

'DNA? – No. And please God they never will. I'm an

optimistic sort, me – I guess if you follow Wexford hurlers, you have to be. But I do believe that she's out there somewhere. Alive and kicking. And probably just biding her time before a dramatic reappearance.'

'And is there any way of following up a hunch like that?'

'It's difficult – hit and miss at best. Whenever I'm doing business with another copshop, I just enquire if there's any quare wan, mid-twenties, who's settled on that patch in the last couple of years, and whose past doesn't entirely check out. Y'know, who maybe can't produce a birth cert. or a schooling record – you get the picture.'

I did. It was impressive. And a little disconcerting. 'By Jesus, Furlong, a bit of a dark horse, aren't you. I wouldn't have had you down for being so thorough.'

He smiled distractedly, as if weighing something up. Then, 'Call that thorough? You haven't heard the half of it. You know nothing about the other hours, hundreds of them, that I've spent traipsing the boreens and cattle-tracks of this parish, looking in hedgerows, under bushes, behind ditches – searching all the time for something I hope I'll never find.'

Dasher gulped audibly. 'What's that?'

'The travel bag. The goddam travel bag – the peg the whole case hangs on. Y'see, apart from some hearsay, it's the only thing we've got to suggest that she actually ran away from home.'

'Yeah, but a pretty significant thing, I'd have said. I mean, I'm no expert, but – she's running away, so she packs a bag and takes it with her. Where's the snag?'

'If she did, why hasn't her passport been used these past ten years?'

'Hasn't it?'

'No. Not as far as we can tell.'

'OK, I'm still winging it here,' I continued. 'She's got clear, she wants to start again, new life, new identity, so she gets herself a new passport. It's been known to happen.'

'Of course it has. And long odds on, that's exactly what did happen. But just say that bag were to turn up. Just say it was here in Lisdrolin all the time. It'd mean she must be here somewhere too.'

I nodded, feigning intrigue. 'It'd mean . . . that she's probably dead?' I suggested.

'Correct. Very dead. And buried not too far away, I'd guess. Worst of all, the likelihood would be that the killer was local – or locals. Probably people I know. Maybe even friends of mine.'

'That would be awkward,' I brazened.

'So you can understand why I didn't particularly want to find anything. Although I had to search, didn't I?'

I could sense that in the back seat the pot was on the point of boiling over.

'But you're not searching any more? I mean, O'Connor swears that she's alive, right . . . *right?*'

'Yeah, that's right,' Furlong said without turning round.

'So what's your fucking problem, then? You said you came here cos you had a problem – what the fuck d'you want?'

The policeman recoiled dramatically. 'Mother of God, Dasher, you might as well kill me as frighten the life out of me! What's gotten into you – was it something I said?'

Dasher blushed puce, then spluttered pathetically as he tried to make light of it. 'Ah, y'know, I was just wondering if . . . if I could help you at all.'

'That's very civil of you,' Furlong laughed. 'Actually, I was hoping ye might be able to advise me, seeing as how ye know them a lot better than I do. Should I tell Joe and Rita what O'Connor says he saw?'

'Oh, I dunno,' I said. 'You don't want to get their hopes up until you've got something definite.'

'I thought about that,' he replied. 'it's just that they've been in limbo for so long, without so much as a glimmer. Wouldn't you agree that they're entitled to know about anything we've got – anything at all?'

Dasher, sounding unusually sure of himself, then said, 'Tell them. It's important that you do.'

'Really. Why's that?'

'Cos my own missus has been up in that house quite a bit recently. Poor oul' Rita is in a bad way. To tell the truth, she was never the same after . . . y'know. But this past while, she's been going downhill rapidly, and she doesn't seem to have any great will to battle on. News like this might be the tonic she needs. Even if it should come to nothing.'

Furlong looked at me accusingly. 'You never told me she was unwell.'

I said, 'I didn't know.'

'Of course you didn't. You're too busy chasing skirt around the south of Ireland to bother about your poor neighbours.'

'Seriously, Dash,' I said, 'why am I only hearing this now?'

'Y'know how old people are. They'd die before they'd let on that anything was wrong. Rita won't go to hospital, she won't see a doctor. She allows my Mary to take a look at her, but even then it's under protest.'

'So how bad is she?'

'She caught TB as a youngster, and had one of her lungs removed. Then last winter she went down with pneumonia. It's April now and she still hasn't managed to shake it off. The fact that she's well into her seventies isn't helping matters.'

Furlong was quite a while thinking it over. 'You're right,' he said then. 'If I wait for something more definite, chances are she won't be alive to hear. I'll do it this minute.'

'D'you want us to go down with you?' I offered.

'No, I can manage. Anyway, I don't want them to know that I'd been discussing it with anyone; fair is fair, if there's a development, they ought to be the ones to hear about it first.'

At this, Dasher and I disembarked. Before pulling away, Furlong rolled down the window and called, 'Dasher, if you want a lift home, I can call back here for you after I've my business done.'

'No, thanks all the same. The walk will do me good.'

When he'd gone, Dasher whispered, 'Well – what d'you make of all that?'

'I dunno,' I said. 'A stroke of luck, I suppose.'

'Bloody right it is, if it stops that fucker snooping around, poking his nose into things. Imagine – he's been at it all the time and he never let on. Sneaky bastard.'

'He was only doing his job.'

'Doing it a bit too well for my liking. Billy, I know he's a big buddy of yours, but the guy gives me the shits.'

The look on his face – so stressed, so worried about so little – caused me to splutter with laughter.

'Oh, yeah, it's a scream, this. A real fucking hoot.'

When at last I caught my breath, I said, 'Dasher, if you can't find a smile on a day like today – well, you have my sympathy. Don't you realize? We're in the clear. It's all over.'

'You reckon?'

'Bar the shouting. The cops don't want this to drag on any longer than it has to. So you'll see, after this news, a line will be discreetly drawn under the whole affair. Trust me, Dash. We've heard the last of it.'

'Yeah, right. And I suppose you've forgotten about . . .' and he pointed emphatically downwards.

'Yes, I have, if you must know. And I'd advise you to do the same. He's on the other side of the world, and nobody's heard from him since 83. There's every possibility that he's dead too.'

'You think he might be?' Dasher asked, brightening.

'Chances are. Or maybe he's copped himself on, and gone all respectable. He won't be the first cut-throat to turn over a new leaf in Australia.'

He looked at me warily. Then: 'I dunno, I don't think I'll be opening the champagne . . .'

'Jesus Christ!' I snapped. 'You're the same as long as I know you – always the prophet of doom. Well, to hell with you – I'm happy this evening. Joe and Rita aren't the only ones in limbo all this time; we've been there every bit as long. But at last, the ball's hopped our way. And I'm going down the village right now to drink a few pints on the strength of it. Are you on?'

He checked his watch and puffed his cheeks. I stood, poised, daring him to object that it wasn't yet seven o'clock and far too early to go on the razzle. But after a moment's consideration, he squared his shoulders and said, 'Now you're talking! I'll just return this young lad of mine to the bosom of his family, and . . . this won't make Furlong a bit suspicious, will it, if he sees . . .'

I glared at him.

'Yeah, fuck him!' Dasher crowed in answer to himself. 'Fuck him, he can't touch us now. Like you said, we're in the clear.'

I haven't the vaguest idea how or when I got to bed that night – all I can say for sure is that I woke up in my own house some time around eleven next morning.

There was no school, at least not as far as I was concerned. My mouth and throat were dry as the Kalahari so I made my way very gingerly to the bathroom, and there came upon Dasher. He was sprawled across the carpet, his trousers round his ankles and an unflushed toilet behind him; obviously, he'd slipped from his perch some time during the night and had found himself more comfortable lying than sitting. I let him snooze on, drank all the water I could hold, and returned to my bed.

I've since heard of a footballer who, having turned in a man-of-the-match performance in an FA cup victory, drank nonstop for sixteen hours after the game. What odd feelings of both nausea and euphoria must've greeted that young man when eventually he regained consciousness. I fancy I know – I shared those feelings on that happy, hungover April morning.

I swore off the drink indefinitely, but was back in action less than two weeks later upon hearing the news that Rita Deane was dead. She'd thrown in the towel quietly on Thursday evening as Joe kept vigil by her side. The priest had been, earlier in the day, to administer the last rites; not the only time he'd brought that sacrament to the same woman. But it was somehow fitting that she should leave this life as she'd spent the greater part of it, with her husband and with him alone.

Of the outside world, I was first to know. I'd had the phone installed, something the Deanes never got round to. So it was to me Joe turned in the immediate aftermath to make arrangements. Tending to his wife in her final illness, he'd been almost as housebound as she, so I'd not seen him in a while. And I'd never had the chance to discuss with him the bombshell that Garda Furlong had so recently dropped at his door. But now was neither the time nor the place. I merely took from him a list of those people to be notified and got busy.

When Mags showed up, she had with her the latest suitor, one Dermot McGee. I'd not heard her mention the name before, and now that I met him I could understand why. He was ten, maybe fifteen years older than my sister and looked every day of it. In appearance, he wasn't anything to write home about, being a bit on the short side, slightly overweight and greying. By trade he was a gardener, though he confessed to having lost interest there some time before. Which was a polite way of saying that he was on the doss and living off my sister. All of this I could take, but not the man himself. For though he was pleasant enough, there was about him a blandness, a general mediocrity that made time in his company very tough going indeed. Still, for Mags' sake, I did try my best to be civil, confident that I was unlikely to ever see much more of him. That he'd not be staying the course.

Sunday morning was bright and fresh for the burial. We'd finished our decade of the rosary, the coffin had been lowered, and the slatted artificial grass drawn over the hole.

'That pal of yours should stick to pumping gas,' a voice whispered from behind, 'and leave the medical side of things to the professionals.' It was Furlong.

'What are you on about?' I asked.

'Dasher's advice: "Tell them. Rita badly needs a lift, and this might just do the trick?" By Jesus, it did a trick all right.'

'Ah well,' I said breezily. 'You can't win 'em all.'

'Indeed. Doctors differ and patients die. Are you coming for a pint?'

No reply necessary, we both began down the steep chapel road towards the village.

'You did give them that news, then?'

'Oh, yeah.'

'And how did they take it?'

'Well, it's the oddest thing. Joe was all excited. Wanted to find out where, when, how – y'know, really prepared to believe. But Rita, God be good to her, wasn't buying it for a minute. She was sat there, huddled up in an armchair by the fire, shaking her head. Saying, "You can fool yourself, but you can't fool me." Kept repeating this, over and over.'

'Who was she talking to – you or Joe?'

'I'm not sure. She wasn't looking at either of us.'

'I see. So, did you get it wrong? About deciding to tell her, I mean.'

'I wouldn't think the news killed her, but it didn't do much towards curing her either.'

We stepped into single file to allow the first cars leaving the church to go by. Then Furlong said, 'I'm absolutely convinced that O'Connor is mistaken.'

'You what?'

'It wasn't Suzy Deane he saw. It couldn't have been.'

'Why not?'

'Suzy Deane is dead.'

'H – how can you be so sure?'

'Because the old woman was. She wasn't guessing, she wasn't supposing – she knew.'

'But whatever it was she knew, Joe was completely in the dark about?'

'That's how it looked, yeah.'
'Conor, d'you really think that's possible?'
'No.'
'So . . . what're you saying, then?'
'Joe knows as well.'

CHAPTER SEVEN

When Kathleen Madden, our vice-principal, retired that summer, I was promoted to second in command. Deputy head of a three-teacher school didn't make a gentleman of me, but what with my other little irons in the fire, I was very, very comfortable. My tenant, too, continued to thrive. The wheel had come full circle, there was money in sheep again, and Martin Houlihan was lifted on the rising tide. So healthy were his finances that he'd just had his eldest daughter enrol in UCD on a four-year science-degree course, confident that he could meet any expense involved. It was prosperity beyond anything he could've envisaged a decade earlier.

Mags too was dogged by a prosperity that no amount of wilfulness or bad judgement could shake off. She went on stepping out with Dermot for a number of years, after which the pair did the unthinkable and got married. She then set her new husband up in business, buying him a garden centre in Clondalkin, a suburb six miles from Dublin. There, new houses were shooting up like acne – a garden centre was a no-lose bet, a nailed-on certainty by anybody's reckoning. But that would've been to reckon without Dermot, who had the kind of business drive that made some of his plants look dynamic. The place lost money from day one. Still, it kept the man happy, and that was all Mags worried about. All she needed to worry about, either; now an established senior counsel, she no longer accepted a brief for anything less than the proverbial king's ransom.

Even Dasher, by now a father for the second time, was making hay. What had started out as a few hours a week pumping petrol and making smalltalk had, with time, grown into something more substantial. Tom Bookle, the garage owner, was a disaster around paperwork and accounts. He was by inclination a mechanic; not overly skilled but very game, a relentless tinkerer and meddler. If the car wasn't running at peak, he'd want to dismantle it to repair the fault; if it was, he'd want to dismantle it to discover why. Under the bonnet of some rustbucket, swearing like a trooper and covered from top to toe in grime – that was Tom in his element. Balancing books just didn't interest him. To begin with, Dasher would total up the day's takings, nothing more. But then gradually, and on his own initiative, he began to review the slate, that custom of giving goods on credit. This involved the chasing down of bad debts and bad debtors, deciding which accounts should be maintained and which written off. Before long, he'd also taken sole charge of the ordering and pricing policy, and it was with him that suppliers and reps would deal directly. Unleaded petrol, LPG and a powerhose next found their way on to the forecourt, and his office-cum-crèche became a small outlet for motor accessories, in due course stocking soft drink, confectionery and daily papers. Business was booming like never before, and Tom Bookle didn't even have to get his hands clean.

But Joe Deane was faring badly. Like most, I expected him to die, broken-hearted and before very long. But no: he lingered and he weakened and he withered, but he lived. Already somewhat reclusive before the death of his wife, he hardly set foot across the threshold thereafter. Nor was he at all happy to admit any feet from the other side. The parish priest called monthly to administer communion; he was entertained only on sufferance. The same was true of the district nurse. Old friends and neighbours would visit, but met with no better reception. It was as if he'd said all he had to say, done all he had to do, and was now sitting around waiting for his number to come up. Waiting, irked by the unseemly delay.

Despite little cooperation and even less gratitude, I did my best for him. For years it was I who collected his pension and took him groceries on my daily run from school. I'd cast a discreet eye over the place, and occasionally read him a match report from the *Kilkenny People*; his eyesight had failed to a point where even the banner headlines were a strain. But whether seeing to the upkeep of the house, or apprising him of what the papers had to say, I was never permitted to stay for long. My being there made him uneasy, and he made no attempt to disguise this.

It was a sunny Sunday afternoon and the River Suir was reeking at low tide. I'd just come from a housecall on Joe, it had been typically difficult and thankless, and I needed a good drink. But first I needed to get money, and the nearest ATM was here by the Waterford quayside. I'd replaced the cash card in its wallet, thumbed through the sheaf of fresh banknotes and turned to go when, behind me, I heard a call. A beggarman, I guessed – the area round and about the Banklink was infested with them. So I quickened my step away, to indicate that I'd prefer not to make a donation. Behind me, there came another holler, but I proceeded without a backward glance. Whoever it was would eventually get the message.

I never heard him close on me, why I don't know. But as I rounded the corner into Barronstrand Street and was trying to locate where I'd parked, a heavy hand fell suddenly on my shoulder.

'Jesus Christ, where's the fire? Slow down, will ya.'

He struggled for breath; I struggled to produce a single coherent thought as every wire crossed and crackled, every fuse blew on impact.

'Don't say you don't know me!'

Oh, I knew him. A little paler and more gaunt that I recalled, the odd fleck of grey in the still unruly carrot-top, but it was him. Words inched forward, cowering like nervous conscripts.

'Y – yeah. I mean, of course I do. How are you, Rodger?'

'I'm fine thanks. You don't look at all pleased to see me.'

'It's not that. It's . . . I just didn't expect . . . I thought you were in Australia.'

'I was. And now I'm home.'

'For a holiday?' I implored.

'I wish. But no, it's for good. All down to the wife, I'm afraid.'

'The wife? So . . . *you're . . . married?*'

'By God, Walsh, nothing gets by you, does it! Yeah, I'm married. To a nice Waterford girl, what's more. Gas, isn't it – you travel halfway round the world, and wind up getting hitched to a neighbour's child.'

'Gas,' I said weakly. 'And you're definitely home to stay?'

'I am, God dammit, I am. Against my will and better judgement; Australia has been very good to me.'

'Really? How so?'

160

'Well, I took up scaffolding down there – even had my own little company. Doing all right, I was. Doing all-bloody-right.'

'But?'

'But you know how it goes – the missus decided she wasn't happy.'

'Got homesick, did she?'

'Not so much. It was more to do with the kid being born. She wanted to bring him up in Ireland.'

'The kid? There's, like . . . a child?'

'And what's so unbelievable about that?' he cackled. 'Don't I look capable?'

'No, no, it's . . .'

'A bit of an eye-opener? You never had me down as pipe and slippers material, now did you?'

I squirmed and blurted something or other.

'I can't say I blame you. I did some foolish things in my time . . .' he paused, 'things I regret. But what's done is done; best to put it behind you and try to start over. Anyway, when you've a family of your own, you realize that the future is all that matters. Not that you'd know anything about that.'

'Eh?'

'You aren't married, mate. You couldn't be. Not with all that hair you've got left. And hardly a grey rib to be seen. Nor a wrinkle or a worryline, come to that, you jammy fucker! Go on – tell me I'm wrong.'

'Well, you're right about the not being married bit.'

'Course I bloody am. So what have you been up to, then? You were doing teacher training, right?'

'I finished the training, got myself qualified, and that's what I've been up to ever since.'

'Never! You? A farmer's only son? Heir to all that

property? I thought you'd get bored with the study, and come home to live off the estate.'

'No,' I said, 'not for me.'

'So your dad still looks after that end of things?'

'My dad died a good few years ago.'

'Oh God, I'm sorry to hear that. He was a good bloke, your father.'

He'd never actually known my father, but the sentiment was nice. I thought I'd better reciprocate.

'How's your own father keeping?'

'Not good. He lives here these days – y'know, in Waterford. He got a council house in Ballybeg, and it doesn't suit him at all. Too much noise, too much smog, and not nearly enough room to stretch his legs. He's been poorly this last while.'

'That's a shame.'

'Yeah . . . he's an old man now, so there isn't a lot anyone can do. But go on, you – you qualified as a teacher and then what? Where are you working?'

'Back home. In Lisdrolin.'

'Not our old concentration camp!'

'The very place.'

'Good Jesus – it's happened! The lunatics really have taken over the asylum. Fuck's sake! Mind you, it always was run by headcases, if you ask me. I can tell you, I got some pretty bad hidings in that school.'

'You handed out a few as well, if you don't mind me saying.'

'I had to, didn't I? It's bad enough being a messer – that just gets the teacher on your case, and I could've coped with that. But being an *English* messer meant that the whole bloody world wanted to come take a swing. I didn't enjoy Lisdrolin BNS.'

This was absolute bullshit. He was despised, not because he was a messer, not because he was English-born, but because he was a ruthless and sadistic bullyboy. Indeed, for an instant it was hard to reconcile that young cur with the affable, mannered man who was smiling at me so disarmingly.

'Still, I'm sure it's a much more enlightened place now that you're in charge.'

'I'm not in charge – I'm vice-principal.'

'Vice-principal? That's no mean achievement. And you still find time to do a little farming on the side?'

'No, not any more. I've got the land leased.'

'Oh, you crafty bugger! You mean you've got another man making money for you. Christ, Walsh, you must be rotten with it.'

'Not in your league, I'm sure,' I said (as I did, he rolled his eyes and shook his head ruefully), 'but I can't complain.'

'I'll bet. There's no money like money for old rope. Anyway, who else did I mean to ask you about. Wrafter?'

'Kevin?'

'Yeah, him.'

'He went to London. We lost touch.'

'And there was one of the Gunnings – Seamus, was it?'

'Seamus, that's right. I don't see very much of him either, not since he got married.'

'Married, is he? And what about your mate . . . that plumber?'

'Leaky Roche? Oh, still very much a single bloke.'

'Now why doesn't that surprise me. Not the sharpest tool in the box, if I remember.'

'Not the worst either, though.'

'You know him better than I do, I guess. Now, there was

one more . . . Oh, Jesus . . .' He scrunched his eyes, pointing and clicking his fingers at the same time. 'Ah, yer man . . . y'know, Rockefeller.'

'Who?'

'What the hell d'you call him. Dodger? . . . Dasher! Mr Moolah. Is he the richest man in the Republic of Ireland, or did he go away and buy a little republic of his own?'

'God, if you only knew how that's changed! Poor oul' Dash hardly has two red pennies to rub together.'

'Really? And what became of all the dosh – drugs?'

'Drugs? Christ, no! He's married with four kids. It's an expensive business, I hear.'

'Expensive, but not *that* expensive. Not for an engineer – isn't that what he did?'

'It's what he started – he never finished the course. But, y'know, he gets by. His wife is a nurse, and he works at Tom Bookle's pumps.'

'Bit of a comedown, eh?' He checked his watch and said, 'Billy, I'd love to stay, but I can't. I must collect the woman and the little fellah. She brought him to mass in the Dominican. I reckon she's daft, filling the poor child's head with all that bollox.'

I nodded. I myself was a pretty devout atheist by then too.

'Listen, Bill, I'm gone. I'll drop out to Lisdrolin some night when I get properly settled. We'll have a pint, and talk about old times.'

With that, he crossed the road, nipping between cars stopped at red. I stood a while outside the shoeshop window and watched him go. Somehow, I'd always known that this day would come. Oh, I'd spent many years deluding myself to the contrary, and when Dasher's mind needed easing, I'd talked a great game. But I'd never doubted that, sooner or later, he'd turn up again. Now he was back. And he was plausible. And he said he'd changed. And he'd made no direct mention of . . . of that other thing. All in all, first impressions had been positive. But where Ginger Rodger Doran was concerned, I had far more to go on than first impressions.

All the way home, I agonized over whether or not I should tell Dasher. As it happened, I'd arranged to see him for a drink in the Heather later that night. He deserved to be told, certainly. But then again, did he deserve to be worried when, in all likelihood, there was nothing to worry about? And what of Conor? As a policeman, he'd be more than interested to hear what I knew. And I expected that he'd ramble into the pub at some point of the night as well. Maybe, if the moment was right, I might casually mention my encounter to the pair of them: maybe, just whisper it to Dasher on the quiet. Saying nothing to anybody was by far the most appealing option, but somehow it didn't seem the thing to do.

When I entered the bar-room that evening, I found Dasher alone at the counter but in a state of high excitement. He'd spent the afternoon, on behalf of his boss, in negotiations to buy the field behind the garage. To develop there a full-scale forecourt supermarket. To 'blow every other shop in the street out of the water'. He was still so charged with adrenaline that I could hardly squeeze a word in edgeways. And just as he'd done outlining his next step towards eventual world domination, in walked Conor and Leaky. They were accompanied by three local youths, all five of them wound up for an assault on a certain night-spot in New Ross. They asked if I'd care to come aboard: when I declined, they

165

seemed to take against the whole idea and joined us instead for a few quiet pints. Once or twice, at lulls in the conversation, the opportunity did arise for me to go public. But every time, I balked. Somehow I could find neither the words nor the courage, not in this company, not on this night. Still, tomorrow was another day. It'd be easier once I'd had the chance to sleep on it.

But sleep that night would only haul me back over old familiar ground. Not since my dim and distant college days had it surfaced, and I was entitled to think that I'd dreamt it for the last time. But tonight I was there again, outside the front gate, among a good-humoured gathering of neighbours and friends. Then, as my late grandmother appeared flourishing the medal of honour, all eyes turned to me, all eager to share my moment of glory. But when Granny passed me by to make the award to another, the talk behind hands began. I must've done something – something pretty serious, the whisperers speculated. The whisperers concluded. The whisperers *knew*. I tried to make light of it all, tried to play the good loser, tried to steal away unnoticed. But noticed I was, then noted, then pursued with a quickening step. I ran through the yard gate, ducked left and into the library of my old alma mater. Up one aisle I darted, down another with the breath of the mob on my neck. My final bid for escape took me between tall shelves where I found some men in wait. I attempted to double back, but that route too was cut off. As the crowd closed from either side, the parish priest stepped forward and challenged me to do the decent thing; to confess to my involvement, and to tell what I knew. But I still had one last stand in me, one final front. I could tell them nothing because I knew nothing, I protested. I had no involvement in this or anything else. I'd only come in here to borrow this maths book: *Calculus* by Michael Spivak. With that, I reached up and removed the weighty tome from its shelf. And there, through the gap left behind, could be seen the severed head of Suzy Deane. Blooded, decaying and putrid, what remained of her face still contorted in terror.

As before, it was at that point that I awoke, with the clock on the bedside locker showing three fourteen. All about me the room was strange, unrecognizable from the library I'd surely been in just seconds earlier. The lights now were extinguished, the books and bookshelves vanished, and my accusers too were fled from sight. Though they'd probably not gone far – from beneath the covers, I began searching every half-lit nook and cranny for an ambush in wait.

Only gradually did reality dawn. And when it did, my mind was made up. If learning of Doran's return could spook me to this extent, then I dared not imagine what it would do to a fretful neurotic like Dasher Morrissey. In time, he might well be forced to confront his bogeyman; I'd let him cross that bridge when he came to it, and not a moment sooner. As for Garda Furlong, it was his business to be aware of what miscreants were on and about his turf. It was his business to keep tabs on them, on their movements and associations. But what I knew about Doran's whereabouts was my business entirely. And if I wasn't telling Dasher, then sure as Christ I wasn't telling him.

It was a ridiculously poor decision, one I'd soon be made to regret. As I recall, Martin Houlihan and I had just spent an evening dosing lambs. The job done, we leant upon the paddock gate and lit a couple of cigarettes, though the light

167

was fading and the night chill almost down. We were discussing the very high cost of free education; I'd known it all along, he'd only discovered it since his daughter had begun her science degree. Already he was fearful – with three other children to provide for, supporting the one in University would be touch and go.

Out on the main road we heard a car gear down, then take the left-hand turn and come chuntering up the lane. The headlights were blazing so we couldn't tell it was the squad car till it pulled alongside. Conor Furlong got out, dressed in full regalia.

'Ah take a break, lads,' he smirked. 'I know that hard work never killed anyone, but – hey!'

'Have you just come to pester us, or was there something you wanted?' I asked.

'A cigarette could be nice, if you're offering.'

I handed him one and lit it from mine.

'So, what's new, lads?'

'Devil a thing,' Martin told him.

'How's the scholar doing in Dublin, all right?'

'We're just talking about it. She's getting on pretty well, but by Jesus it doesn't come cheap.'

'You're feeling the pinch now, Houlihan. Wait till your next lad decides he'd like to go to college too.'

'My next lad takes after his father, thank God. He's as thick as a ditch.'

'In that case, let him join the cops,' I suggested. 'He'd be a natural.'

'Now you're talking,' Houlihan agreed. 'Cos them fellahs earn a bloody fortune, and all they do is sit around scratching themselves all day.'

'D'you hear this pair of wasters,' Furlong said, highly

indignant. 'Chatting like oul' wans, smoking fags and counting bloody sheep. Here's me, in the dark of the night, with the winter nearly on top of us – and still on duty.'

'You're on duty?' we both replied.

'Sort of. I came up to look in on Joe Deane.'

'Right. And how is he?'

'Hard to say – he wouldn't let me in. It's not awfully important, all I wanted was a quick word. Cos I doubt if he's aware that your old friend is back in town.'

I knew beyond a doubt which old friend he spoke of, but I had to sing dumb; as I'd never mentioned anything, I couldn't now admit to knowing anything.

'Which old friend would that be?'

'Rodger Doran.'

'Doran? No way!'

'True as God. You hadn't heard?'

'No.'

'That's weird.'

'What is?'

'He told me he'd met you.'

'Huh?'

'I ran into Doran the other day – he said he'd been talking to you. That he'd met you one evening when you both happened to be taking money from the ATM on the quay.' He paused, took a long draw on his cigarette and waited. It was my move.

Before I could, Martin cackled, 'I think this Doran character is playing you for a bit of a mug, Conor boy!'

'Maybe. Odd thing is, though, he seemed to know a lot about what's been happening around Lisdrolin. An awful lot. So he's definitely been talking to someone.' Another draw on the smoke, this time with a sidelong glance in my direction.

169

'Are you quite sure you didn't meet him, Billy. Like, I can't imagine it's the kind of thing you'd forget.'

It was checkmate. I could not go on lying. But I couldn't just cave in and tell all. However, either was preferable to standing here, open-mouthed and foolish, looking as guilty as sin.

'I . . . em . . . I did meet him actually, now that you mention it. It was on the quay, yeah, one Sunday evening. We talked for a short while . . .' and then, from God knows where, 'but I didn't know he'd moved back to Lisdrolin.'

'He hasn't.'

'Didn't you just say that my old friend was back in town?'

'I meant Waterford town.'

'I'm sorry. I assumed you were talking about Lisdrolin.'

'Waterford.'

'That's no secret. He's been back in Waterford for a while now.'

'You never said.'

'It slipped my mind, I guess. Anyway, why should you care? It's not like he's on your patch or anything.'

There. I'd squirmed off the hook. Not with any great honour, but I'd weaselled clear. Furlong knew it, and was beyond anger. For a time he just glared; when at last he spoke, each word came only after an effort.

'Did you tell Dasher?'

'I can't remember. Actually, I can't remember if it was he that told me. A good many people have been . . .'

Furlong flung down his glowing stub and stomped it venomously into the gravel, then stormed to his car and roared away. I watched the red taillights disappear, cursing my earlier lack of judgement. Cursing my downright stupidity. He'd always harboured a flicker of suspicion; I'd only succeeded in dousing that with petrol. It might now be difficult to contain the fire.

Dasher badly needed to be put in the picture; I intended telling him whenever next I might catch him on his own. As it transpired, I was spared the trouble – he learned it straight from the horse's mouth.

I'd just come in from work, made the tea and opened the newspaper when the phone rang.

'I need you to come down right away,' he gasped.

'Sure, yeah. You in Tom's garage?'

'In the garage, that's right.'

'And . . . what's the matter?'

'Something's come up, OK? I've got a small problem here, I can't really discuss it over the phone . . . can you hurry on?'

'I'm on my way,' I told him, wondering what earthly use I might be in the event of a problem at a filling station.

'Just one other thing,' he said, his normal breathing still not returned. 'Can you bring some money?'

'Course I can. How much?'

'Every penny you can lay hands on. Please.'

'What?'

'Jesus, Billy, don't start, there isn't time. Will you help me or not?'

'Yeah, yeah, it's just . . .'

'Well, fucking do it then . . . sorry, but it really is an emergency.'

'Fine. I'll see you in five minutes.'

I hung up an began to rifle through pockets, drawers and cubby-holes. In all, I could muster less than fifty pounds. That was never going to avert very much of a calamity, so I took my chequebook with me. Even though I'd got the impression that it'd be strictly cash only.

The garage was deserted. All of the pumps were padlocked, all of the other facilities closed down or stowed away. The door to the little accessories shop, where Dasher held court, was bolted, the venetian blinds slanted to deny even visual access. Further down the street, the lights were on; I saw a woman walk out of the grocery store and across the road to the post office. There it was business as usual, here it was the *Marie Celeste*. I was puzzled – intrigued, even, but nothing more. And I was on the point of returning to my home when from behind the closed door, I heard the cry of a child. Gently, I tapped. Not till I whispered, 'Dasher, it's me,' was the door opened. He looked left and right, the length of the village, before admitting me and relocking the door at my back.

Inside it was almost pitch dark, but I could make out the shape of his little son Niall, strapped into his buggy and sobbing gently in the corner.

'So what's going on?'

Dasher took two, maybe three deep breaths, but the tremble all about him would not be stilled.

'He was here. Right here in this office. Up came the white Astra . . .'

'The what?'

'The white Astra – it's a fucking car. Driven by some bastard friend of his. Came in, roughed me up, threatened the little fellah, and cleaned out the till. Tom Bookle is going to be back any minute, how . . . Jesus, how am I going to explain this, huh? *Huh?*'

And now all the Morrisseys there present were sobbing.

'Easy,' I said. 'take it easy. Start again, slowly.'

'He must've been watching the place, waiting for Tom to leave. As soon as he did, the car pulled up outside. He came in. Told me he needed money . . .'

'Doran, I presume?'

'Of course, Doran. Who else d'you . . . You knew he was back, didn't you? You fucking knew!'

'I heard a rumour.'

'How long? How long have you known?'

'Dunno. A couple of weeks, maybe.'

'A couple of *weeks?* Christ Almighty, it never occurred to you that I might want to be told?'

'Now calm down,' I said. 'Blaming me for this won't do you much good.'

Again he inhaled deeply, still feverish. 'OK. You're right. How did you come to find out?'

'I . . . kinda . . . met him in town one day.'

'You actually spoke to him?'

'He . . . he seemed to have changed. He was collecting his wife and child . . .'

'You spoke to him. Did you tell him where I worked?'

'All I said was that you never went back to the Univ —'

'Oh, Jesus, I knew it. I knew someone must've tipped him off. He didn't even slow down coming along the street – he screeched in here directly, robbed the place, in and out in a minute. How could you be so fucking stupid!'

Little Niall began to wail. Dasher knelt before him, briskly rocking the buggy, hushing and cooing as he did so.

'How much money did he steal?'

'I don't know. The only way to find out is to total up, but I can't do that till we close.'

'Roughly how much?'

'Like I said, I don't know. How much did you come up with?'

'Forty-five, maybe fifty quid.'

'Ah Je-sus!' he cried. 'Fifty scuttering quid? I'd taken that much by ten o'clock this morning.' He slumped into the swivel chair by the register and began to laugh, a deranged, lunatic falsetto.

'This is it, isn't it? For years and years it's been hanging over us, and all we've been doing is buying time, staving off the evil day. Well, Buddy, Happy Evil Day! Let's welcome all our chickens home to roost!'

Suddenly, he was deadly, desperately serious again.

'Think, Billy, for fuck's sake. Think. You're better than I am in situations like these.' Not that that was any great boast.

'OK,' I said. 'Here's what we do. Total up now.'

'I can't, now until . . .'

'Will you just do it!'

'But what's Tom —'

'Tell him you pressed the button by mistake, tell him the baby pressed the goddam thing. It won't bother him – he's not going to be out of pocket.'

'He's not?'

'Just find out how much money should be in the till, will ya?'

He hit a particular key. There followed much clicking, whirring and grinding as a one-foot length of white ribbon emerged.

'Three-eighty-three. And thirteen pence,' Dasher announced. 'Now how d'you propose replacing that with your fifty?'

'Shut up a second,' I said as I did some quick calculations. I then took my money from my pocket and counted

174

forty-three pounds and thirteen pence into the till. Next I produced my chequebook and wrote one, made out to cash, for three hundred and forty pounds.

'Here's the story. The tinkers called to my house. I bought some furniture off them. They insisted they be paid in readies. So I came to you. And . . . I dunno . . . as you were giving me the money, you pressed the "TOTAL" button by mistake.'

'Hey – yeah! Or I could say I wanted to be sure I had enough in the till to cover your cheque, so I totalled up deliberately . . . Yeah . . . D'you think he'd believe that?'

'Why wouldn't he? Though mind you he is bound to suspect something if he comes back and you've got the whole place locked up.'

'Oh fuck!' he said as he grabbed his big ring of keys and ran into the forecourt. 'Give me a hand, will ya.'

It took only a matter of minutes. In fact, Dasher was contented that he'd not had a single customer call while he'd been indisposed, and so stood every chance of the entire incident going undetected. I wasn't hanging about either; there'd be no danger of our stories conflicting if Dasher was the only one telling. As I turned my ignition key, he leaned in the driver's window.

'Thanks, Bill,' he said, still a little breathless. 'You really pulled that out of the fire. I'm very grateful.'

'Don't be too grateful – you do realize what all this means?'

'What's that?'

'It means you can't work here any more.'

'But . . . we've just fixed everything good as new.'

'Dasher, today he took you for four hundred quid without even breaking sweat. D'you think he won't be back for more? If you stay at this, you may as well start paying Tom's takings directly into Doran's bank account. It'll save you the hassle and him the journey.'

He shook his head, a little dazed.

'This . . . this is my job. It's what I do. I can't just pack it in. I can't afford to.'

'Well, maybe you know some way around all this. Offhand, I don't.'

I drove away, leaving him with plenty to ponder.

Very next weekend, Mary Morrissey was at my door. She looked ashen and drawn, but determined. I showed her in, sat her down and offered her tea. But she would not be distracted.

'What's going on, Billy?' she asked, her first words to me.

'With what?'

'With my husband. Is he in some kind of trouble?'

'Trouble? What gives you that idea?'

She studied me intently for even the merest glimmer of foreknowing.

'You hadn't heard that he's given up working for Tom?'

'He has? Why?'

'Just quit, no reason. Well, none that he told me. I thought you might . . .'

I shook my head and said, 'It's only a guess, but maybe he wants something more. You know he's an intelligent bloke, and that is a bit of a dead end.'

'Not the way he did it. He was running the show, and he loved it. Now, overnight, he's no longer interested.'

'Could be a career crisis – it does happen, you know. Out of nowhere, he suddenly decides he's in the wrong job. And acts on impulse.'

'What?' she shrieked. 'Dasher Morrissey, decisive? *Impulsive?*

Jesus Christ, the same man needs advice about which leg to put in his trousers first!'

That summed him up so aptly, I thought about laughing. Then I saw the tear fall from the corner of her eye.

'I'm scared, Billy. I didn't think we had any secrets. But now . . . there's something there. Something he won't trust even his own wife with.'

I didn't like to lie so barefacedly, but I said, 'Mary, it's probably nothing. Some silly little figarie he's taken. It'll blow over in a week, you'll see.'

'Fine, but what is it? And what's sparked it off? When he mentioned it last night, I really did fear the worst. God forgive me, but I thought – I was certain – that he'd done something terrible. Something criminal, even.'

'Like what?' I flustered.

'Like that he'd tried it on . . . y'know, interfered in some way with Claire Bookle. She may be only fourteen, but she's very, very well developed. And she bloody knows it.'

'Not a chance,' I smiled. I sighed. 'I mean, I doubt it very much. Dasher mess with the boss's daughter? That wouldn't be his style.'

'Yeah. Then I wondered if maybe Tom had done something to our little lad, Niall. But Heaven knows, that wouldn't be Tom's style.'

'You do suspect, though, that the problem lies between Dasher and Tom,' I suggested, gently trying to lead her astray.

'Not now. Tom, the decent poor oul' devil, arrived at our house yesterday with a bottle of brandy under his arm. The pair of them sat in the living room all evening, drinking themselves stupid, watching the racing, laughing and joking – and at the end of it all, Dasher still wouldn't change his mind.'

177

Again she studied me, waiting for my attempt to explain this away. When all she got was my best baffled look, she asked, 'Has he said anything to you about emigrating?'

'Emigrating?'

'Obviously he hasn't, then. But that seems to be part of his plan. He wants to leave Ireland.'

'And go where?'

'Anywhere. It doesn't matter, as far as I can tell – all he cares about is getting out of this country.'

'Good Lord. And when he gets there, what does he intend to go working at? I mean, he isn't exactly weighed down with qualifications.'

'Get this, Billy. Just get this. He says he'll look for work running a filling station – something he enjoys doing, something he's got a flair for. Which is all well and good, except he's just walked out on that very same job here in Lisdrolin. Now, you've been his friend a long time; don't you try tell me that I've no reason to worry for him.'

Mary sat a while, lost in her thoughts, not far from the end of her tether. I went to the kitchen to make that pot of tea. As I waited for the kettle to boil, I called, 'So, are you considering emigrating, then?'

'Like hell I am!' she shouted back. 'He expects me to sell the house, uproot the family and move to another country – without even telling me why? When he comes up with an explanation for all this – and a bloody good one at that – then we may talk about it.'

Twelve to twelve thirty was religion time for fifth and sixth classes, the confirmation candidates. On this particular afternoon, the subject was fortitude, the exemplar Fr Raymond Kolbe. He was the Auschwitz priest who'd given his life in place of a married prisoner randomly chosen for execution. The topic was engaging, the teacher and pupils for once rowing in the same direction. Which could only mean that major disruption was imminent. Sure enough, halfway through, the knock came.

Petie Keeffe, one of the slow learners, was my meeter and greeter. I allowed him to answer the door as it was about the only thing he ever could answer. No sooner had he heard the footfall in the corridor that he was up and to his post.

'A man to see you, sir.'

'Who is it?' I mouthed.

'I don't know,' he replied aloud.

Hardly a local then. I quietly cursed him, whoever he was, bade my children read ahead and out I went.

'Sorry to disturb you,' he smiled. 'I'm sure you want to get right back to your teaching, preaching and working miracles.'

I didn't answer. I should've been shocked or intimidated; that surely was the purpose of the tactic. Instead, all I felt was anger, sharply rising.

'I didn't think that even you would show your face around here again.'

'Why not?'

I bit my lip, mindful that twenty-five pairs of ears were well within range. Then, 'Dasher told me everything.'

'Dasher is the reason I came back. I've just been up at Tom's garage, but he isn't there.'

'Of course he's not there. He quit.'

'What – for good?'

'Yeah, for good. He didn't fancy waiting around for you and your pal to come and stick the place up again.'

Doran took a step back, the picture of injured innocence. 'Is that what he told you?'

'Don't insult my intelligence, Rodger. I know what happened.'

'No, you don't. Cos it was nothing like that.'

'Oh, really? So what was it like, tell me?'

He took a moment to compose himself, then, 'It was my dad. He died the night before.' Here he paused, waiting – I think – for condolences. After several seconds of complete silence, 'I haven't been able to find work since I've come home, the social welfare didn't come through yet . . . the cost of the funeral ate up what little savings we had left. I didn't want to have to go cap in hand to anyone but – c'mon mate, you know what it's like to lose a father. I'd been up all night on the bottle, I knew there'd be people back at the flat after the church – and I couldn't even afford a few cans or a drop of whisky for them. To tell the truth, I didn't have the price of a plate of bloody sandwiches. OK, maybe I shouldn't have gone to Dasher. But I was desperate. And I had nowhere else to turn.'

'And is that supposed to excuse everything? You robbed the day's takings – and you knew damn well that Dasher would have to replace that money somehow. Not only that, but you threatened to harm a small child just to get your way.'

'I what? That is an absolute fucking lie!'

Inside the room, where the noise level had been swelling steadily, a deathly silence now descended. I reached behind and pulled the door shut.

'Now you listen to me,' he went on, thankfully in a lower register. 'And you listen good, because I will not have my name blackened like that. I knocked, I walked into that office and asked for a loan of a hundred quid. A hundred lousy quid. But before I could explain why I needed it, he went hysterical. Picked up the baby and cowered in the corner, screaming at me to take what I wanted. "Take it all," he kept saying. "Take it all, but don't hurt the little boy." I'm there, trying to convince him that I have no intention of hurting anyone. But it's no good – he won't listen, he just keeps on hollering, "Take it all, take it all." By now, I'm starting to panic, cos somebody is bound to hear this commotion and maybe that somebody gives the copshop a bell. With the reputation I once had around here, you tell me – how's it going to look?'

I let him continue.

'I took what was in the till like he told me to. I didn't realize how much was there, not until I got back to town. As God is my judge, that's the story. And that's why I'm here in Lisdrolin today; to see Dasher, and put everything to rights with him.'

It did sound reasonable. And if he had come to make amends, I could at least show a little civility.

'Fair enough, then,' I said. 'Leave the money here with me. I'll see it gets back to where it should.'

Doran shot me one quick sidelong glance, then averted his gaze to his feet as he shifted them uneasily.

'You've come here to pay that money back, right?'

'Not exactly.'

'Well, what exactly?'

'I came to make arrangements with him about returning the money. And . . . one other thing.'

He reached into an inside pocket. From there he drew out a smallish slip of paper folded in quarters, said, 'I was hoping he might . . .' and with that, he handed the slip on to me. I opened it, as I assumed I was meant to. The letterhead was that of a doctor's practice in Grattan Square, Waterford. Underneath there was a collection of shapes, signs and squiggles that could've been anything.

'A prescription?'

'It's Jordan, my little lad. He's got eczema. This stuff is a lotion, a kind of rub. It only gives relief for a short while, but it's better than nothing. Without it, he can't even get to sleep. He really, really needs to have it and a month's supply costs less than a tenner, but . . .'

And now, without having noticed the hook go in, I was being reeled ashore. I felt foolish, ashamed at how easily he'd gotten past my guard.

'I'm expecting my dole, and the medical card, to come through tomorrow. But I couldn't wait another twenty-four hours. Have you any idea what it's like to live with a child who cries all the time? I wouldn't ask, Billy, but I'm absolutely potless. I don't even have bus fare. I had to hitch all the way out here, and I'll have to do the same on the way back. Be a pal, and don't make it a wasted journey.'

Inside the classroom door, the children – unsupervised now for a full fifteen minutes – were near running riot. I could argue the toss no longer, I had to get rid of Doran and get back to work. The cost of doing so would be ten pounds.

'Christ, man, you're a lifesaver,' he said as he stuffed the note into his jacket pocket. 'By the way, I've got the promise of a job in Clashmore, starting next Monday. If that materializes, I'll be in the pink. And when I am, I promise you'll have this back.'

'It's OK,' I told him, 'that's a gift. And a speedy recovery to your son. But Rodger, let's get one thing straight. Never, ever call to this school again. You do, and I won't see you, because it's in my contract that I must not leave those children unattended. If anything were to happen to one of them while I'm out here, the insurance won't cover the damages. I'm the one who'll end up in the dock.'

'When you've managed to avoid that up till now, I reckon your luck might hold,' he said with a grin that still, all these years later, raises hairs on my neck.

'But you see what I'm saying – I just can't do this,' I gulped.

'Of course, of course – point taken,' said the new, reformed Rodger, reasserting himself. 'Well, I'd better head. Bye now, Billy, and thanks again. I do appreciate this.'

And off he went. As he did, the main school door was pushed open and in walked a uniformed Conor Furlong. The two passed in the corridor with a curt 'Mr Doran' and 'Guard, how are you?' Furlong waited till the door had been well closed from the outside before he spoke.

'What brings him here?'

'Nothing much, really. Old times.'

'Why was he thanking you?'

Good Christ, I thought, how *did* he hear that.

'He, erm, I ga — He's looking for work, and I promised I'd keep my eyes open for him. Anyway, what brings *you* here?'

'I got a wee bit worried when I saw Gixer Weldon lurking around the school.'

'Who?'

'Gixer Weldon. You must've heard of the Weldons – the criminal family from Ballybeg. Not the kind you want to get mixed up with – although it was inevitable that Doran would seek them out. He seems to be retaining Gixer as some kind of chauffeur.'

'Chauffeur? You mean he's driving Doran about?'

'Yes. It's what chauffeurs do, generally speaking.'

183

'R – right. What kind was the car?'

'An Astra. A white one. Why?'

'Ah . . . nothing. No why. Listen – as you're here, why don't you come in and say hello. You've not been round in a while.'

'No thanks – not today.' And he turned on his heel. Obviously, he wasn't yet ready to put our recent spot of turbulence to one side.

CHAPTER EIGHT

Doran was back, then, in every sense. Back among us, back to his erstwhile ways, and back to me with his hand out. Or he soon would be; of that I was certain. He'd touched me once, and where in all of Ireland would he find a softer touch, a more immobile sitting duck. Not only did he hold the upper hand, I'd even been so helpful as to suggest where he might engage me to his greatest advantage. Anywhere else I could stand tall, shout back, give as good as I was getting. But not in the corridor by my classroom door. Not with nearly one hundred children at ringside. Not with Garda Furlong on the other side of the wall, twitching like a bloodhound at the whiff of anything shady.

Work became damn near unendurable. I was never the most enthusiastic of teachers, but this was beyond all. The thought of school each morning would fill me with terror, with a dread that sometimes made me physically ill. Once in class, things were no better. Every noise in the hallway, every knock on the door, every person who passed by the frosted-glass windows set my heart turning cartwheels, convinced as I was that he'd returned. I waited. Time passed, grinding slowly by, and still I waited. Hoping, praying even, that I'd seen the last of him. Knowing I had not.

Late that November, Joe Deane suffered a stroke. Naturally enough, it was I who found him as I dropped by with his provisions one evening. At the time, he would open the door just wide enough to take his parcel through, then shut it again in my face, often without as much as bidding me the time of day. When, on this afternoon, there was no response at all, I knew I'd better investigate. There I saw him, lying face down on the quarry tiles at the bottom of his staircase. All doors were locked and, to gain access, I had to break the kitchen window. Once inside, and once I'd established that he wasn't past all helping, I covered him with some blankets I found, then hurried home to alert an ambulance.

As they go, it was a mild enough stroke, resulting in very slight restriction of movement down his left-hand side. More damaging was the fall – he happened to be climbing the stairs when it took hold, and on the granite-hard surface broke his arm, his collarbone and his hip. There was some concussion, but within hours of being admitted to Ardkeen Hospital he was conscious and fairly coherent.

When she heard, Mags asked if I thought she should come south and pay a visit. I told her that I thought not, as Joe wasn't very keen on visitors, even while in the whole of his health. So instead she had me pass on her best wishes. She then demanded to know why I still had not made the trip to the capital to see her new house. She'd lately paid an obscene amount for a property in Clontarf, a very swish bayside address and home to many of Ireland's more beautiful people who, like herself, earned money wildly in excess of their actual worth. Almost all of my thirty-odd years had been spent among the good folk in Lisdrolin, so I was quite taken with the idea of finding Bono at the next urinal down the local, or sticking my head over Van Morrison's wall to borrow a cup of sugar. But I knew that, in all likelihood, I'd end up saddled with her husband Dermot, still a grey boring man who hadn't become a whit more interesting with the onset of his middle age. So I thanked her for her offer and swore that I'd take her up on it when I could. But I warned that this might not be for some time. For some considerable time.

Meanwhile, around the village, the word spread about old Joe, and the way he was receiving his hospital visitors. Some he'd refused entirely to entertain, others he'd admitted only long enough to tell them they weren't welcome. It was, of course, exactly how he'd been behaving ever since the death of his wife, so to some of us it came as no surprise. But to most people it was real news. The young folk thought it was hilarious. The older ones saw it as a sure sign that he was raving for death.

Though I knew I could expect no better reception, I thought I should at least try to see him. I was his nearest neighbour. And having tended to him all this time, I knew his likes and dislikes, what he could eat and what he couldn't stomach. Anyway, after so many years spent in his service, I was pretty much immune to his boorishness. And I'd managed to persuade Dasher to come with me, for solidarity.

When we arrived on the ward, the nurse asked if we wouldn't mind waiting, as Joe already had a caller. So we sat on some steps nearby, saying very little. Neither of us liked hospitals especially, Dasher with good reason. On the wall opposite, a big yellowing clock ticked round: five minutes passed, then ten, and still we sat and waited. It was encouraging, in a way, that Joe was agreeable to tolerate anybody at such length. But both of us just wanted to get this whole business over and done with.

Coming to the quarter hour, a set of footsteps – leather

soles on the polished wood floor – came clip-clopping to the door. Though we couldn't see whose they were, or whose bed they'd left, we got to our feet in expectation. And it did indeed signal that our turn had come; the man departing was none other than Conor Furlong.

'Well,' I said, a little surprised. 'You were with Joe, I take it.'

'That's right.' He was guarded, defensive. This had been no mercy call.

'Very good of you,' I went on. 'I mean, the man's not even a friend of yours.'

'I do what I can.'

'Shame you didn't tell us you were coming – we could've travelled together.'

'Yeah.' He half-smiled. 'Maybe next time.'

'So how is he?'

'All right. He'll live.'

'That's not what you expected, though, is it? Otherwise, you wouldn't be here. You came for your deathbed confession. Well? Did he break down and tell all?'

The half-smile became a little more sheepish, a lot more pained.

'It must be obvious, even to you, that he's got nothing to tell. So why don't you leave him alone, for fuck's sake.'

'Mr Deane will see you now,' the nurse's voice called from the ward door.

Furlong straightened his cap and said, 'Be seeing you, lads.' Then he disappeared down the stairs we'd been sat on.

Throughout the exchange, Dasher had been looking from one of us to the other like a kitten watching ping-pong.

'Now what the hell was that all about?' he demanded through his teeth.

'Tell you later.'

'No, now.'

'He's got it into his head, somehow, that Joe Deane knows where Suzy is.'

To mention that name without any forewarning was like hitting Dasher with a wrecker's ball from behind. 'Jesus!' he gasped. 'And . . . y'know . . . does he?'

'What?'

'Does Joe know?'

'I think it's unlikely now, mate – don't you.'

'Yeah, yeah . . . I don't mind telling you, though, that fucking cop gives me the willies.'

Joe was propped up in bed, packed in pillows all round. He shifted his eyes and clocked us both, though I couldn't say what registered on his face, it being partially paralysed and badly discoloured. His broken collarbone was being treated by a large sling and plaster, while the damaged hip was under the blankets. As we drew near, the eyes again stared hard forward. Tentatively we seated ourselves, I on a chair, Dasher on the next bed.

'How are you, Joe?' I asked firmly. Though his mouth didn't open fully, there was no mistaking his words.

'What're ye doing here?'

'We've come to see you.'

'And have ye seen enough yet?' Then, with a slight nod of the head to indicate the bag I was holding. 'Bring that stuff off with you when you're going.'

'It's only a couple of things I know you're fond of,' I said, and I began to place them one by one on the bedside locker. The Fig Rolls and the Golden Syrup he spread on them. The fresh orange juice, and the Andrews' Liver Salts he stirred in. The Bovril that he ate raw by the spoonful.

189

'I said I didn't fucking want them. Now get them away from me!'

And one by one, I began to put them back.

'Was it you that found me?'

'It was,' I told him.

'You were lucky he did,' Dasher added, his first contribution.

'Oh Jesus I was,' he growled sarcastically. 'You need only look at me to see that. I can't walk, I can't stand, I can't feed myself. I can't even make a bloody shit on my own any more. Sure, 'tis blessed I am.'

The atmosphere was poison as he stopped to take breath. Then, with a tortuous groan, he turned himself to face me.

'Why couldn't I be dead before you poked your nose in, eh? Why?'

'I'm sorry, Joe. Maybe it just wasn't your time to go.'

'He's right . . . It's all the will of God,' said Dasher. Immediately, the old man creaked round a little further to light fiercely upon him.

'Oh, you're an authority! And you're telling me there's a God in it?'

Dasher sidled a little further back on the bed and stuttered, 'Well . . . yeah.'

'What has you so sure?'

'I dunno. It's just . . . I suppose there must be somebody up there to watch over us.'

'To watch over us? And he sees everything, does he? No matter what you do, or where you do it, the man above always has you sussed?'

It began like a cough, like a loud emission from the lungs, maybe his last ever. But it became a laugh, long, low and hearty.

'Morrissey,' he wheezed, 'for all our sakes, you'd better fucking hope not.'

He then turned away, sank back into the pillows supporting and slowly, pointedly, closed his eyes. Not sleeping, but not saying another word. We may have said goodbye, we may not, but quickly and quietly we left that ward, never to return.

We were back in the car before Dasher whispered, 'He's gone cracked, hasn't he?'

'What?'

'Joe. He's lost it. He's fucking loony. Obvious, isn't it?'

'Yeah, he's not well.'

By my side, I felt him shift uneasily, then he blurted, 'But what d'you think he meant when he said . . .'

'Nothing! He's old, and his mind is going. That's all there is to it.'

He drew a faltering breath, nodding anxiously as he did.

'It's that goddam cop. I bet he's talking out of turn, filling that poor man's head with all sorts of shit, trying to . . .'

'Shut up, will you, for fuck's sake,' I snapped. 'Joe Deane is gone a touch senile. You were right first time.'

And I pulled away, not at all sure if that second guess wasn't nearer the mark.

Sooner than anyone could've expected, Joe was cleared to leave Ardkeen Hospital. He was still a long way from full fitness, but the prognosis was good. In time he'd walk again, and recover almost totally the use of his left side. But it was in the short term that the problem lay. His eyesight was continuing to fail, and he was still wheelchair-bound. He'd need regular sessions of physiotherapy, but, more crucially, he needed twenty-four-hour care and attention. A full-time nurse was far, far beyond his means. And while his brother's adult children – those based in London – seemed perfectly amenable to someday inherit the farm, not one of them could be persuaded to uproot, move to Ireland and look after the old man. A most unwise decision, one that Joe quickly caused them to regret. With no forewarning, delay or fuss, he sold the place, lock, stock and barrel. In his haste, he let it go cheaply; thirty-five thousand pounds for that lot was chicken-feed. A retired accountant from Dublin it was who nailed the bargain. He and his wife took up residence there in the late spring. Joe, meanwhile, checked himself into a private nursing home in nearby Thomastown. His haul from the sale of the property, topped up by his weekly state pension, would cover things; there'd be just enough in the kitty to see him out with a modicum of luxury. And anyone depending on him for a legacy could whistle for it.

The waiting was the worst part. But, small mercies, Doran didn't keep me on tenterhooks for long. And, predictably, he chose that venue where he would always be playing with the slope. Upon seeing him, I came storming from my classroom, my intention being to hoosh him before me the length of the corridor and out of the building. Warning as we went that the cop had seen everything. And was very likely on his way over. That we could meet later, but it'd have to be in another place.

However, my ploy was scuppered from the off. Doran was drunk. Very drunk. Some minutes short of midday it may have been, but already he was reeling like a top and smelling like a small brewery.

'Hiya!' he garbled, then staggered forward, colliding against my chest.

I pushed him from me and growled, 'I thought I told you not to come here!'

'Yeah, I know.' His hand went to his jacket pocket. 'Sorry, boss, I've only the one fag left.'

'Well put it away. This is a no-smok —'

But already he was in the act of lighting up.

'I don't have time for this, Doran. I've got a class to teach,' and I took a step away.

'I know, I know. Yeah. Sorry. Only . . . hang on, will ya? This is a bit of an emergency. The baby – the cough is after coming back.'

'What?'

'Th' oul' cough. It's going round again. D'you remember, you gave me a few quid to buy some cough bottle a couple of weeks back. Only it's all gone, and he needs more.'

'Last time it was a skin complaint.'

'Was it? Jesus! Are you sure? Well, whatever – who's counting, buddy. A child's health – who's counting.' And he went shambling backwards till he met the wall. The devil came to my shoulder, whispering that I'd never again have a better chance to punch his lights out. I took a very deep breath.

'How did you get here?'

'I thumbed.'

'Same as last time?'

'That's right. I haven't even the price —'

'Oh, bollox! I know all about you and that Gixer Weldon.'

He smiled foolishly. 'Sound man, Gixer. A decent skin.'

'Is he out there now?'

'Aye. He gave me a lift. The kid isn't well, y'see. I need a score.'

'A score?'

'A score, yeah. Twenty quid.'

'I know what a score is. And I know there won't be much

193

of it left for the kid by the time yourself and Gixer have your skinful drank.'

He tried to straighten himself in indignation, but keeled to his left and had to grab the windowsill for support.

'Where's the jakes, eh?'

'Why don't you go back to where you've been all morning and piss there.'

'Ah, fuck it, then, here'll do.'

And with that, making no attempt to find cover, he undid his zipper and let fly. The urine arched almost to the opposite wall, then began to fall randomly and erratically as he jigged this way and that to maintain his balance. By the time he'd finished and zipped himself up again, a steaming, frothy rivulet was running between the floortiles.

There are some things that defy reaction. I stood like one made of marble.

'Ah, what of it! Better out than a man's eye? Hah!'

'Get away from this school!' I trembled. 'I want you out that door this instant.'

'But . . . what about my dosh? I need a score.'

'I haven't got it. I don't bring money to school. That's why I told you there was no point in calling here.'

He looked at me groggily. 'Just get the fucking money, OK?'

'I don't have any.'

'Listen, you miserable cunt – I don't want to cause a scene, but if I have to, I will.'

'Cause what you like. I can't give you something I haven't got.'

Down the corridor, a door opened and the middle infants began to file out, lunchpails under arms. The little leader marched at the head of his line, proud and ramrod straight.

But he hesitated as he reached the sizeable wet area barring his way.

'Hang on there, young fellah,' Doran mumbled. 'Careful where you step. There was an oul' dog here a while ago. And he couldn't hold it.'

All the infants who heard laughed at the thought of a dog choosing to relieve himself outside a teacher's door. Joining the merriment, Doran lowered himself to a squat.

'You're a great chap. What's your name?'

'Jason.'

'Jason, by Jaysus!' And the toddlers laughed some more. 'Jason what?'

'Jason Hickey.'

'Jason Hickey. Tell me, would you be a brother of little Tommy Hickey?'

'Who?'

Doran got to his feet and, attempting a kind of step in time to the rhythm, began:

' "Little Tommy Hickey had a ten-foot mickey,
He showed it to the girl next door.
She thought it was a snake and she hit it with a rake,
And now it's only five foot four." '

Among his audience, there were hysterics. Not so much the bad language, but bad language within my hearing. I wasn't fazed. I'd let him clown all he wanted, wait till he tired of it and then show him the door.

'So you see, Jason. Never show your girlfriend your you-know-what. Tell me, have you a girlfriend?'

'No!' said the boy emphatically.

'Good man. Neither have I. But Mr Walsh here has. Well, he used to have. D'you want to know where she is?'

All the little children were now looking at me, all nodding

their heads, some stifling giggles behind open hands. Doran got back down to his hunkers and stage-whispered, 'She's in a bag.'

And again the corridor rang with laughter. One of the kids, catching the mood, piped up, 'D'you mean like a lucky bag?'

'Well, sonny, 'twasn't very lucky for the girl. Not lucky at all. But no, it's a plastic bag. A big old fertilizer bag. And d'you know where the bag is? Go up the Boher Road about a mile or two . . .'

I grabbed him by the lapel, lifting him to his feet and hauled him out of the children's earshot. From my pocket I took a disorganized clump of banknotes and small change. Mercifully, there were a couple of tenners among the chaff.

'That's strange. A minute ago you said —'

'Take the money and fuck off. And you listen to me, Doran. This is the last time.'

'Oh now, Billy old pal, I think I'll be the judge of that.'

'If I see you near this school again, I'm sending for the police, and you can tell them whatever you like. Then I'll have my say, and we'll see what happens.'

He smiled, smug and contemptuous. He knew what I knew; if it all became public, we were both in the mire. For me, that would be a disastrous fall from grace, whereas he was pretty well there already.

'Doran, you just see if I'm joking,' I blustered.

His smile broadened and he winked at me. 'Billy, even you don't believe that.'

So saying, he turned to go. Seeing him on his way, the children did as they'd been programmed to do whenever an adult was in the act of leaving their company. In unison, they chorused, *Slán leat a dhuine uasal*. Doran spun round, open-mouthed.

'A dhuine uasal? That's the nicest thing anyone's ever said to me! Well, you're toppers, all of you. And I might call back to see you again very, very, very soon. Would you like that?'

'Yes,' came back the unanimous response.

'Well, I will, then. And that's a promise.'

It'd be nice to report that Doran kept to the habits of a lifetime and reneged on his word, but this was a promise he doggedly observed. Once a week, almost always on Wednesday; Thursday was dole day in Waterford city, and he must've had trouble making ends meet. Sometimes he'd brandish a prescription, a note from the district nurse or a half-baked excuse. Other times he'd simply tell me how much he wanted, and leave the rest to my imagination. For a long while in the beginning, he was content with twenty pounds. Then one week I found he'd awarded himself an increase of a fiver. I didn't object; well, not nearly as much as I should've. Because when he saw how easy that was, he upped it again. So in no time at all, I was forking out thirty pounds every Wednesday. It was cheap enough, considering the alternative. But it was not a situation I could tolerate indefinitely. And it was not going to escape Conor Furlong's attention for very long either.

Still the visits continued. That is, until the Wednesday they didn't. All day I stood by, three o'clock arrived but no Doran. Grateful for the respite, I was locking up when I caught sight of Furlong waiting for me by my car. The exchange would be brief and mannered. We'd given up conversing any other way.

'No sign of that friend of yours.'

'No.'

'Strange. It is Wednesday.'

197

'So it is.'

'Maybe he's found that job he had you looking out for.'

'Maybe.'

'Actually, he hasn't. For your information, he's up in court.'

'That right? What for?'

'Shoplifting. He's been doing quite a bit of it recently –
and been caught more than once.'

'Why was he not prosecuted before, then?'

'The store owners were always slow to press charges.
Especially when they heard he was one of the Weldon's
mob.'

'What was different this time?'

'He tried it on with Dunnes Stores. Swiped some silk shirts.
And then assaulted a security guard, for good measure. But
Dunnes don't scare easily. And Doran got himself eighteen
months.'

'Eighteen months?' I whooped, then remembered I must
try to sound indifferent. Must try to keep from bursting into
song. 'Really – eighteen months, by God. In that case, I don't
think I'll be seeing him for several Wednesdays to come.'

'I'm afraid you can think again.'

'Wh – what d'you mean?'

'In view of his guilty plea, and his previously good conduct
– bit of a laugh, that – the sentence was suspended.'

'Suspended? So he . . . ?'

'Was fined a hundred pounds and put back on the street.'

It hit like a kick in the stomach, exactly as Furlong
intended it to. Now, it was even more important to keep the
poker face. To not let him see my heart in my boots. The
smile was so forced, so hard to hold, it caused my eyes to
burn.

'No doubt about it,' I grimaced, 'the guy's got nine lives.'

'Well, he used up a few today. He knows now he's a marked man in these parts. He knows that nobody is going to think twice about taking him to court. And he knows that if he as much as farts, he's got eighteen months coming to him.'

Then a very appealing possibility suddenly struck me. 'With all this hassle in store, I can't see him sticking around. I reckon he'll just pack up again and emigrate.'

'Yeah, but to where? With a criminal record now, he can't go to Australia, or to America. And from what I hear, he trod on some pretty big toes last time he was in England. No, I reckon we're lumbered with him. Now, with the drugs . . .'

'Eh?'

'The drugs. He's a heroin user. You didn't know that either? For people who meet up so regularly, you two don't talk a whole lot, do you? Yeah, he's got a habit. And that habit's still got to be fed somehow. All along, he's financed it with his petty crime, but . . . it'll be interesting to see how he goes about it from now on.'

He stood a while, stiff and stony-faced, just watching me. 'I will find out what's going on here, y'know.'

'Let me save you the bother. There is nothing.'

'Well, that's what I intend to find out. In the meantime, don't do anything stupid.'

He reached out and grabbed my driver's door just as I pulled it shut. 'And if you already have, remember that throwing money at it won't make it go away.'

I really should've prepared for what happened next. Or at least seen it coming. It was the Monday after, not later than nine thirty; the class had not properly woken to its week's work, any more, indeed, than I had. All at once, the door was thrown open with such force that it crashed off the wall

199

adjoining and almost reclosed itself. It was pushed wide again, this time not so fiercely. And there he stoood.

'Money!' he growled, and he held on to the jamb for support. The children in my care that year tended to be a skittish lot, but this provoked not as much as a titter. And small wonder – Doran really was a frightening apparition. His eyes were red-rimmed and bloodshot, he had a growth of stubble which suggested that he'd not shaved since his day in court, and his hair stood in tufts like he'd slept in a wind-tunnel. His cheeks were a dangerously high, ruddy colour and, all in all, he didn't look far away from dying. Or killing, if it came to that. At first the kids were mesmerized, then, slowly, some began to look in my direction. Not one of them could've been unaware by now that something very peculiar was at play.

I strode across the room and shut the door behind us both. When I got up close and saw in his face how crazed he looked, how wired, I knew I must tread softly.

'Are you OK, Rodger?' I asked.

'A lot you fucking care.'

'You don't look at all well.'

'I didn't come out here for a fucking medical, you cunt!'

Obviously, I could say nothing that wouldn't antagonize him. So I said nothing and for a few uneasy seconds, neither did he. Then, 'Just give me the money so I can get the fuck out of here.'

'Fine,' I said, still on eggshells. 'How much d'you need?'

'You know how much I need. You read the fucking papers, don't you?'

If he was referring to the hundred pounds he'd been fined, he'd be well out of luck.

'I'm, erm, I'm not sure . . .'

'Oh, aren't you now. Well let me make it simple then. *You*

– give *me* – one hundred pounds, and be fucking quick about it. Clear enough for you?'

'Rodger, I'm afraid . . .'

'Aw my Jesus!' he drawled, wearily. 'Not this fucking rigmarole again.'

'Sorry, but I just don't carry that kind of money around with me.'

He shaped to speak, as his entire face became contorted in anger. I swallowed a lump and said, 'I'm serious.'

He drew a quivering breath. 'You're serious? And you think I'm not? You think I've come all this way to be pissed about!'

'Rodger, we can work this out. If you come back tomorrow, I promise I'll have the money for you.'

'Good Christ!' he shouted, which must comfortably have carried through to every classroom in the school. 'Tomorrow is no good. I've got to pay by noon today, or they're coming to get me.'

I thought this unlikely. But given the state he was in, I wasn't going to argue.

'So, do you see, you dumb fuck! I've only got a couple of hours to come up with the cash, or else I'm going to jail. And let me tell you, Walsh, if I go down, I'm not going alone. Now d'you understand? D'you see it's important that I get that money?'

'I do, yeah. But you won't get it here. Because I'm telling you again – I don't have it.'

'But you can fucking get it.'

'How, for God's sake?'

'There are two other teachers here. Ask them.'

'No,' I said flatly. 'I'm not getting any of my colleagues involved with you or your blackmail.'

I think it must've been the word blackmail that tripped the switch. With both hands he grabbed me by the throat and ran me backwards into the school wall. The jolt – along with the surprise – completely winded me, while the stippled surface opened a small cut on the back of my head.

'Do you think you've a fucking choice?' he ranted. 'D'you think you get to say who's involved in this and who isn't? Huh?'

I'd still not caught my breath sufficiently to answer. Or to stop him as he took one hand off my windpipe and began to pad my trouser pockets.

'You've got money, you lying piece of shit. Take it out. Take it all out and show me!'

I did, and held it on my open palm for him to inspect. I could've told him it would include no paper money, just a fistful of silver and copper, amounting to not very much. He examined it, growled something through clenched teeth, then swatted the whole lot from my hand, sending coins skittering all over the corridor.

'Bastard!' he snarled. 'Fucking bastard! Where's the rest of it?'

'I told you, that's it.'

'Say that once more and I'll fucking burst you!'

And he now ran his free hand into the various pockets of my jacket. He came upon some permission slips, one or two sticks of chalk and a playing card sized laminated calendar, each of which he discarded with growing desperation. Then from inside he produced a small plastic wallet.

'What's this?' he demanded. 'Well? What is it?'

Then little by little he assumed the look of a prospector who'd just seen a glint in his grading pan. Slowly, he let me go and took a step away.

'Problem solved,' he purred. 'I can sort everything out with this.'

And gently, lovingly, he drew from the wallet a credit card. I didn't know it was in that jacket: to this day, I don't know what it was doing there. It had only arrived days earlier, and I'd not had a single chance to use it.

'That's no good to you,' I said. 'Honest – you can't get any money with it.'

'Oh, don't be too sure about that,' he grinned.

'But . . .'

'No buts, Bill. Everything'll be just fine, don't you worry. I'll get this back to you when I've done with it. Until then, you don't report it lost, you don't report it stolen. If this little card gets cancelled, mate, I will fucking ruin you. But you're an intelligent man, right? So you won't let it come to that.'

Prior to this, I thought I was in trouble. *Now* I was in trouble.

CHAPTER NINE

After that, things happened pretty quickly. Some weeks later, my first ever Visa bill did not make comforting reading. Doran had been good to himself, and the total came to about half the sum I'd actually earned over the same period. He'd also been crafty, not using the card in Waterford where he was known. Instead, he'd been to New Ross, Kilkenny and to Carrick-on-Suir, all good-sized provincial towns, all well within striking distance. He'd favoured the electrical stores, the perfume counters and the high-class jewellers, buying merchandise that was easy to transport, easy to flog, and very expensive. It was all there in black and white on the itemized statement. There too was the warning that if I hadn't paid in full within twenty-eight days, I'd find myself subject to interest charges I wouldn't have believed legal. But that was never a worry – I squared this one away comfortably enough. My deposit account was in a fairly healthy state, and that very week Martin Houlihan came forward with a couple of months' back-rent, a tidy little sum. But the next bill did take a bite. Predictably, Doran pushed his luck a little bit further this time. All in all, he'd very nearly run through the equivalent of my aggregate income. Worse still, I saw from his shopping list that, along with the usual, he'd invested in a mountain bike and sit-on mower. This could only mean that he'd begun buying to order.

Three months on, and I was contacting my bank to arrange a meeting. This was tactical; I was merely beating them to the punch, as before very much longer, they'd have been the ones demanding an audience. I was broke. I was beyond broke. They'd given me one month to clear a debt of more than two and a half grand. I did not have an earthly hope of coming even close.

These were uncharted waters. In the charmed life I'd led to this point, I'd always managed to stay out of the red. Though not born to wealth or privilege, I'd owned a house, owned some land and traded up to half a dozen new cars, all without ever owing anyone a shilling. Debt to me was a bit like Aids. The thought of it scared me plenty, but I just couldn't imagine that I'd ever have to confront the real thing. Suddenly, this was as real as it got.

And so I was called to present myself and to plead my case. This too was virgin territory, and mightily embarrassing with it. However, I knew the bank had just as much cause for concern as I had. Till then, I'd been a valued customer – a model customer, I dare say. Now I was on the other side of the ledger. A debtor. One who, if current trends were to continue, would soon be a big, bad, possibly defaulting debtor. Small wonder, then, that a meeting was convened with some haste.

The official I would deal with was a young man named Greene. I fed him this line I'd cobbled about being in the middle of a small personal crisis, one I wasn't prepared to discuss but one that was strictly, strictly temporary. He barely batted an eyelid before granting me an overdraft of three thousand pounds. And thus he thought to bring our dealings to an end.

However, I'd found him so accommodating, so personable and so understanding – especially when I'd explained practically nothing – that I sensed an opportunity. So I instantly invented a younger brother, wild and wilful, who was at the root of all my current difficulties. We'd fallen out, he'd left home and gone to ground, but he'd taken my credit card with him and wasn't sparing the horses. I didn't want him arrested, or in any trouble come to that. Nor did I want to do anything so calculating, so heavy-handed as to cancel the card, that would cause a rift between us that might never be bridged. Was there some way I could call a halt to this, and have it look like an accident, a genuine mistake or oversight?

The gentlest way, he told me, was to simply neglect to pay the minimum, the ten per cent of the total that had to be met by a date specified. This would provoke one or two reminders which, if ignored, would lead to the card first being suspended, and then being decommissioned altogether.

It seemed so easy, so blindingly obvious, that I pressed him for the catch. He conceded that there might well be a threat of legal action against myself. However, between the card being taken out of service and any court appearance, there'd be ample time to settle the bill to everybody's satisfaction. I thanked him and walked from the building a far happier man than when I'd entered. This had to at least be worth a try.

Upon my return home, I took the offending bill from the mantelpiece and consigned it to the flames beneath. A second letter duly followed, warning of the consequences if I didn't at least pay the minimum. It too came to a fiery end. As indeed would every scrap of correspondence until I was satisfied that the company's patience with me was exhausted, that all former arrangements were void.

It'd take some time for Doran to realize he'd been double-crossed, and when he did it would not be pretty. Fretting about that day, of course, wasn't going to make it any prettier.

But it was near impossible to shut it from the mind, or even force it to the back. However, I did try. I began to socialize more frequently, to drink more heavily. I threw myself with gusto into the stewardship of the school's two hurling teams. For the first time in a long time, I asked a woman out; a rather unremarkable teacher from Ross that I'd met on an in-service course. And I can't recall being particularly offended when she turned me down. I even began contemplating a change of car, and took to browsing in the city's showrooms. That may have smacked of unhatched chickens being counted, but where was the harm in looking.

The reminders from Visa continued to arrive till finally they wrote to say that they had now placed the matter in the hands of their solicitors. And that my credit card was no longer valid in any way, shape or form. So far so good, I thought. Now for the hard part. Now for the sparks to fly.

When the doorbell rang on that unseasonably warm evening, I braced myself. I didn't know if I'd find him drunk, sober or stoned; and I didn't care. I was ready, ready as I'd ever be.

But when I opened up, it was Garda Furlong who stood silhouetted in the blood-orange sunset. I was so thrown, I almost invited him in for tea, just like old times. But I checked myself and settled for a very formal, 'Yes?'

'Hello,' he replied. 'I just happened to be passing . . .'

'On foot?' I could see no squad car anywhere around.

'That's right. It's so nice, I thought I'd stretch the legs. I took a walk over to Dasher's on the way here, but he wasn't in.'

'So what can I do for you?'

He looked to the ground for a while. Then, 'I got an anonymous phone call last night.'

'That so?'

'Whoever it was claims to have information about Suzy Deane.'

'Yeah?' I said keenly.

'He says that Suzy never got out of here that night. That she was raped, murdered, and buried somewhere in the parish.'

'Good God! And . . . how does your caller know all this? And why has he taken fifteen years to come forward?'

'The way he tells it, he was there. Saw the lot, but had nothing to do with it. The reason he was afraid to come forward was because he played a minor part in disposing of the body. He says.'

'And did he say where?'

'No. He wants a deal – immunity from prosecution in return for his story . . . Any idea who he might be?'

I gave it a moment or two. 'No. Not a clue.'

'There was more. I told him a deal might be possible. He said, "I'm going to need that in writing. Cos you won't want to keep your end of it when you hear the names I give up. One is a very good friend of yours."'

'Isn't that interesting,' I said, matter-of-factly.

'I've got a feeling he may be a little out of date with that last assumption.' And having said that, he looked back to the ground, where he began manoeuvring a pebble to and fro with the toe of his brogue. Then he lifted his head and glared. 'Is it you?'

'No.'

'No?'

'No,' I repeated and stood squarely, daring him to take another shot. He retreated a little, biting his lower lip, considering his next move.

'I notice Rodger Doran hasn't been near that school for a

while now.'

'That's hardly a crime, is it?'

'No. Not at all. Well, I'll be on my way. I must take another ramble over to Dasher's. Maybe he'll be there this time.'

'It's not him either. He was with me the night Suzy left town. So don't waste your energy.'

'Thanks for your concern,' he said, ice in his smile.

I watched him out the gate and as far as the bend of the lane. Then I sprinted for the phone. Mary, Dasher's wife, it was who answered. I told her I needed to speak to the man of the house, and quickly. When she heard the urgency in my voice, she didn't ask why.

'Dasher?' I blurted. 'Now don't talk for a minute. Just listen and listen good.'

'What the −?'

'Look, shut up, OK. I haven't got much time.'

'S − sorry. Go on.'

'Furlong was here. Doran's been on to him − anonymously, of course. Dropping hints, stirring shit, feeding him scraps, but at the end of the day nothing significant. And that's why I'm calling; to let you know that Furlong has nothing. He's guessing, he's stabbing away in the dark, but he knows fuck all. Nothing that's going to hurt us, at any rate.'

'Fine. So why are you telling me all this?'

'Cos right now, he's on his way down to you . . .'

'Oh my Jesus mercy!'

'Dasher! Three little words: I don't know. Give him those, give him no more and there won't be a problem. That's what I did, I just denied everything point −'

I stopped mid-sentence, because I thought I heard something at my back. Instinctively, I pressed the phone to my chest and spun round. Furlong.

'Sorry,' he said quietly. 'The door was open. I gave a little knock, but . . .' And as his words tailed away, there followed an interlude during which we both seemed to lose all brain function, and gaped at each other like a pair of tailor's dummies.

'Sorry,' he said again, quieter this time.

'What d'you want?' I trembled.

'I was going to ask if you wouldn't mind ringing Dasher's house, to find out if he'd be there on my way back down. Obviously he is.'

'Yeah. He's . . . em . . . he's there.'

Minutes elapsed, to that I would swear. Then, with no change of expression, Furlong whispered, 'Right so,' turned smartly and was gone.

I waited a decent length of time before collapsing on to the ornate phone-seat, the receiver still pressed tightly to my chest. Slowly, I began to take stock, to survey the wreckage of that last quarter-hour. Only after a while did I realize that I still had Dasher on the other end.

'Hello? Hello? Hello? Billy, what's going on? Where are you?' His voice quivered with a growing desperation. And he hadn't yet heard the worst.

'All right, Dash, I'm back. Sorry about that.'

'Sorry about what?' he demanded. 'What the hell's happening at your end?'

'I . . . think I may have harm done.'

'Harm? What d'you mean, harm?'

'Furlong overheard some of our conversation just now?'

It took a couple of seconds as the spark ran noiselessly along the fuse before reaching the barrel of gunpowder.

'What!? How . . . ?'

'I thought he'd gone. But he . . . he hadn't.'

210

'Oh, for fuck's sake! You fucking moron! How much did he hear?'

'I can't say – I don't know how long he'd been listening.'

'Did he cop that it was me you were talking to?'

'Yeah, he —' here I was interrupted by a loud whimper down the line — 'at least I think he did. But – hey – I rang you for a chat; no law against that.'

This argument did nothing to ease the wheezing, the hyperventilating on the other end. Between gasps he spluttered, 'Did he hear you mention Doran's name?'

'No,' I lied. 'No way.'

'How can you be so sure?'

'I just am. Trust me.'

'Trust you? After the way you've landed me . . . ?'

'I fucking said trust me, didn't I? Furlong knows nothing. He'll be with you shortly, so don't let him rattle you. Stand up to him.'

'That's easy for you to say, you've got your grilling over with. But, Billy, you know I'm not very . . . Oh, Jesus Christ, I hear footsteps.'

'Dasher, that can't be him. It's not been five minu —' But my parting cry was cut short by a thunderclap in my ear as the other receiver was slammed back into its cradle.

I too replaced my end and remained seated. There wasn't a murmur now, not a breath. I shut my eyes tightly, all the better to gather what I could of my thoughts. So, how much had he heard? He certainly knew who I was speaking to. I could remember calling Dasher by name when his wife picked up the phone. If Furlong had been listening from that point onwards, then he'd heard the lot, every last word. But he couldn't have been there from the very beginning – it wasn't humanly possible. More likely, then, that he'd come in somewhere around the middle. If so, what had he happened upon? Well, there was me, calling for a complete denial of everything. And me again, asserting that he didn't have enough information to hurt us. No matter how I looked at it, he'd caught this much at the very least. Yes, sir, I certainly had harm done.

I'd still not budged when, beside me, the phone rang. I caught it on the first chime. The voice was not unfamiliar.

'Very quick on the draw there, Bill. Feeling a bit jumpy, maybe? I'm not surprised, after the day you've had.'

'What d'you know about my day?'

'Call it an educated guess if you like. But I'd say you had a very . . . interesting encounter with your local sheriff. He did drop in on you, yeah?'

'He kinda had to, you bastard, after everything you told him.'

'Everything? Billy, Billy, Billy – I told him nothing. Well, not nothing, exactly. But just enough . . . for a first instalment.'

'This is about the credit card, right?'

'Yes. The credit card. Trouble is, all its credit seems to be exhausted. Very, very inconvenient. There was a chemist's shop in Kilkenny where one young employee even spoke about cutting it, if you don't mind.'

'And . . . what happened?'

'I told her I'd cut her fucking throat if she even attempted to. After that, she was most obliging. Handed it back to me without a quibble. I still can't use it, though. That's the problem.'

'And it's going to remain a problem. Because Rodger, you've fucked up. Royally.'

This rocked him on his heels. Even after some moments'

consideration, he could do no better than, 'You're going to pay that bill.'

'No. Not this time.'

'You're going to pay it. And you're going to pay it quickly. Or else.'

I laughed. 'Or else what? You've had it mate; you've played your ace. What more can you do?'

'I can make another call to that copper friend of yours.'

'It doesn't matter a damn whether you do or not. You've given him the lead he needed – he'll get to the bottom of this now, with or without you. And if you think different, you don't know much about Conor Furlong.'

'I know more about him than you do.'

'Yeah? Like what?'

'Like, he's been promoted, Billy. Leaving Lisdrolin in the next week or so. He's going to be a sergeant. Stationed right here in Waterford city.'

'Where did you hear that?'

'Let's just say that one of my associates is very close to a source inside the Ballybricken station. It's perfectly true, I assure you.'

'Does Furlong himself know?'

'Naturally. He's known for months. Why d'you think he's so anxious to wrap things up? Christ, it must be doing his head in, he's that close to cracking it.'

'Especially when you've nearly done it for him.'

'Nearly, but not quite. He'll never do it now, not in the time he's got left there. Unless, of course, he gets another tip-off. One with more detail in it: names, times, places . . . but personally, I can't see that happening. Cos, I'm confident, Billy my old pal, that you'll do the right thing. You've got till noon on Tuesday.'

I didn't answer. He'd claimed the last laugh.

'Now that's what I like to hear!'

'This once,' I said bitterly. 'But it can't go on.'

'And why not?'

'Cos you're spending money faster than I can fucking earn it!'

'Bollox! Don't come the poor mouth with me. I know all about your other interests, remember?'

'Other interests? The land, is it? The rent I collect from those few acres? Get real, mate! That brings in less than two grand a year. It'd hardly keep you in clean needles.'

He went to speak, but my mention of that figure seemed to throw him. It was a while before he said, 'Less than two grand? That's genuine?'

'Yeah.'

'Not a lot, is it.'

'I'm glad you agree.'

'What's the point in keeping it, then? It makes no business sense and from what I hear, farming isn't the great love of your life. Sell it!'

On the handset, my knuckles whitened. 'Don't you dare tell me what to do with my property.'

'Oh, just a suggestion,' he softly replied. 'I don't care what you do, so long as that card goes back into credit and stays there. Cos if it doesn't, Bill, it won't be your thirty acres that'll be bothering you. It'll be a space about ten feet by eight. Remember – noon on Tuesday.'

I smartly drew my horns in and said, 'You're talking a lot of money here. There's a mountain of interest on that bill by now.'

'So? That's hardly my fault.'

'It's just that I'll need time to get it together.'

'How much time?'

'Give me two weeks.'

'But by then Furlong will be gone to pastures new. And his replacement won't be a big buddy of yours, will he? Now grassing you up to a complete stranger – where's the fun in that. Noon on Tuesday, Billy.'

It would be morning before Dasher rang the school to recount how he'd fared the previous night. Hearing Furlong at the door, he'd lost his nerve and pushed his wife out front to cover for him, to say how he'd been unexpectedly called away again. I told him I thought this a very foolish move, and that he should visit the station with all haste, before the station came back to visit him. He dithered and he grumbled, so I passed on to him Doran's gossip; that Garda Furlong would shortly be moving to bigger and better things. Down the phoneline, I could smell the relief. No need to go near the barracks at all in that case, he concluded. Only a matter of staying out of Furlong's way for the time being. Once he'd taken up his new posting, the cop would be far too busy to be bothered chasing shadows around his old stomping ground. I repeated that I thought this strategy ridiculous, but already he was adamant. If Furlong wanted to interview him, then so be it. But Furlong would have to find him first.

In Waterford that afternoon I made the necessary transfer of cash. The original principal, plus the interest that had now been accrued, left me overdrawn beyond even the prearranged limit. But at least the credit card would be validated again.

My next port of call was to Hanley and Keogh, estate agents. I explained that there was some land I was keen to offload, and wished to engage them to handle the sale. Two fields, each roughly one acre in size. Ideal for housing sites, both being situated by the road. And since the road in question was a quiet secondary, planning permission would surely be a formality. Mr Keogh, with whom I dealt, was quite enthusiastic and advised me to obtain that planning permission without delay. Once obtained, the sites would, he predicted, sell themselves. And he'd have someone out within days to make a valuation. So I began the surrender of the smallholding where generations of my people had eked out a livelihood; something that famine, uprising, civil war and years of British misrule had all failed to bring about.

Authorizing the sale was one thing. Explaining to Martin Houlihan that he'd be losing part of his leasehold – and why – would be quite another. I grasped the nettle one afternoon in the paddock behind the house. He was immersing some lambs in a very rudimentary dip that he'd fashioned from an old watertank. Even as I approached, I'd not quite decided on the finer details. And finding him chirpy and cheerful as always wasn't going to make that task any easier.

'Good God!' he shouted as I drew near. 'Don't tell me you're finished up already.'

'I am.'

He checked his watch. 'A quarter past three? How many kids d'you teach?'

'About thirty.'

'Well, let me tell you, if the thirty of them were standing on you till now, it's still money for jam.'

'Martin,' I said, trying to discourage all smalltalk and pleasantries. He didn't seem to hear.

'Y'know something? If I was back again, 'tis I'd learn my lessons and do my homework. Cos this is only . . .'

'Martin, there's something I need to tell you. I'm selling

the land opposite Gaule's lane – y'know, the two fields by the road there. Selling them for sites.'

He released the animal he'd been manhandling, raised a quizzical eyebrow and scratched the stubble under his lower lip. He then lifted his flat cap and scratched under that.

'And what would you want to do a thing like that for?'

'Cos I need the money.'

'You're codding me, right? *You?* Need the money?'

'I can't say too much about it just yet, Martin. It's early days, and I'd appreciate it if anything I tell you now should go no further. But we – that's myself and few friends – have our eye on a small hotel in Galway city. Things are really booming over in the west at the present time, and we think it's an excellent investment opportunity.'

'Well, good for you!' he said earnestly. 'That's the way to do it. Diversify. Put as many fingers as you can in the pie. That way, if one gets burned, you'll still make out all right. A good many years ago, I staked everything on one big gamble and went for broke. That's exactly how I ended up – broke.'

'So long as you understand.'

'Understand? Good God, boy, if only I had a few quid myself, I'd wade right in there along with you.'

'Yeah, I did think it was too good to pass up. Anyway, about your own situation here – obviously I'll be reducing your rent.'

'Oh, there's no need for that.'

'Of course there is. You'll be getting less land, so it stands to reason you'll be paying less money.'

'Listen, young fellah, when I started leasing this place from you nearly ten years ago, the rent was buttons. And since then, you've not put it up even once.'

'Because I never had reason to.'

217

'Fair enough – but can you think of anything else that costs the same now as it did in '89? I was lucky to get this land first day, but I was even luckier to get it from the most easygoing landlord in the country. And, Billy, I mightn't always show it, but I am grateful.'

'Ah, will you stop it outa that!' I said, hoping to Heaven that he would.

'I'm serious – let's call it inflation, what? I'm more than happy to go on paying you the same as always – it's still a good deal for me.'

'Martin, I insist. I won't see you out of pocket over this. So when you've finished here, come into the house – we'll work something out.'

And I left, feeling small as ever I'd felt; shamed by this decent man, his good humour and good grace, and his misplaced good wishes. Making matters worse was the suspicion that, before too much longer, we'd be having this conversation again. Or at least something very, very similar.

Unless in the meantime my prayers were answered. Questionable prayers they were, for one brought up a Catholic. For one whose religion forbade wishing ill on another. But I did whole novenas, pleading for poison in Doran's heroin. Or a contaminated needle. Or that he'd be knifed by one of his many, many admirers. I'd have settled for a simple traffic accident; even natural causes would've been more than acceptable. But I wanted that man dead, God knows. God knew – I'd told him often enough.

The silver lining to the episode was flimsy, but at least I now had a pretext in order. So when Leaky, drunk as the entire House of Lords, accosted me in the Heather one night shortly after, I was prepared. I drew him to one side and explained, sotto voce, that all the money I could lay hands on was being poured into this brave new venture. He was mightily flattered to have been taken into such a confidence. I emphasized that it *was* a confidence, and asked that he tell nobody. In hindsight, I should've asked him to tell everybody. That way, fewer people would've found out.

But with respect, Martin Houlihan and Leaky Roche were pushovers. My sister would provide the acid test.

'Those sites for sale that were on the Indo last Friday,' she asked. 'Do they belong to anyone we know?'

'Might do,' I said. 'Why – are you interested in one?'

'Billy, what the hell is going on?'

'I have to get my hands on a few grand in a hurry. A hotel's just come up for sale at the right price in Galway city.'

'No! Which one?'

'It's . . . ah . . . Well, it's closed at the moment for renovations.'

'Yeah, but what's it called?'

'The . . . amm . . . Corrib Arms Hotel.'

'Sounds impressive. Whereabouts in the city is it?'

'I couldn't tell you – I don't know Galway at all. But I imagine it can't be far from the Corrib. Y'know, the river.'

'Yeah, I suppose that'd stand to reason. Now, I take it this isn't a solo venture – that you've got partners.'

'That's right. You wouldn't have met any of them, I don't think. They're just a few guys I was in college with.'

'I didn't know you kept in contact with any of the old St Pat's mob?'

'You didn't? God, I can't think why I wouldn't have told *you*.'

'OK, wiseguy, I'm curious, that's all. I'm a little bit sad too

– I mean, it's none of my business, but did you really have to sell? If you needed a loan, why not go to the bank?'

'Mags, it's like I said, the hotel has to be gutted and refurbished. It could be eighteen months, maybe even two years before we see a single penny back on our investment. That's a long time to be paying bank interest rates.'

'You're right, I suppose. It's easy for someone like me to be sentimental about these things.'

'Exactly. Especially when you're living in Dublin, one hundred miles away.'

'Which, I ought to point out, Billy, is less than two hours' drive. It is not the dark side of the moon.'

'I know, I know, I know. I haven't been up to see the new house yet.'

'Obviously you're a man of many parts these days, but you'll come sometime soon?'

'Yeah – I promise. Although I imagine you're very busy at the moment,' I said, delighted with myself at finding this side-track. It so happened that a former client of hers had recently been making the headlines, all of the wrong kind. I'd not had a chance to study events in any great detail, I just assumed she'd be on the case. But I could almost see her frown as she said, 'Busy? No more than usual. Why?'

'Isn't yer man, Cappocci, in some bother?'

'Oh, now there's the understatement of this calendar year so far.'

'And are you not defending him?'

'No.'

'I thought his lot always retained you?'

'Up till now, yeah. But they don't own me. This isn't *The Godfather*, and I'm no Mob attorney.'

'But . . . what's different about this time?'

220

'You've heard it said, "The Lord helps those who help themselves"? Well, I try to work on the same principle, where I can. You're familiar with the story?'

'No, not really.'

'But you know of the Cappoccis? They're crime bosses from the Northside – have been for three generations now. The secret of their success is that they employ an army of hitmen, enforcers and general-purpose thugs to do their dirty work. Which, along with a little luck and the odd backhander here and there, is how they themselves have managed to more or less stay out of jail for those three generations. So what does Benny – the eldest boy, the son and heir to the dynasty – decide to do? He gets involved in a small turf war with Wayne O'Toole . . .'

'Is that Stitchie?'

'Yes. Stitchie O'Toole. A nobody. Not even a speck on the radar. But Benny reckons this is one that must be sorted in person. So he shoots him dead on Berkley Road in broad daylight. D'you know Berkley Road?'

'No.'

'It runs right in front of the Mater Hospital. So there were about five hundred windows facing. With heads in most of them. And a small crowd congregated on the steps. All bearing witness to this goddam idiot in full cry. And making no attempt to disguise either himself or his actions.'

'But why did he not get one of his heavies . . .'

'To show he's a man to be reckoned with. To make a point. Well, he's got plenty of time to consider what a point he made. He was in custody within the hour. He'll be there for the next fifteen years.'

'So you're definitely turning it down?'

'Jesus, Billy, how could I defend that? How could anybody?'

'Not even for the money? Cos I understand these guys pay well.'

'Nowadays, I get paid well, regardless. And that's because I've maintained a good batting average. So wherever possible, I steer clear of lost causes like this one.'

'How do the Cappoccis feel about you deserting them in their hour of need?'

'Oh, they aren't happy. There's been representation, some phone calls, a certain amount of pressure. In fact, I know it's October, but I've been considering taking a short holiday. In a nice little hotel, maybe, somewhere that shower won't be able to contact me . . . hey – now that you're in trade . . . ?'

'If you're prepared to wait a year or two, I guarantee you the very finest suite in the Corrib Bridge . . .'

'Arms.'

'What?'

'Arms. Earlier you called it the Corrib Arms.'

'N – no, I didn't.'

'I'm afraid you did, y'know.'

'It's Bridge. The Corrib Bridge Hotel.'

'If you say so, sunshine. If you say so.'

Leaky's dissemination of the story was impressive; in no time at all, he'd spread the word far and wide. I wasn't surprised – I'd heard enough tittle-tattle from him over the years to know his form, to know that this scoop he'd stumbled upon would eat him from the inside out if he didn't pass it on to everyone he met. In the pub, on the street, at the hurling match or wherever, I found myself being congratulated on my foray into the property market. Or simply being asked how 'th'other thing was going', often by people I hardly knew. But what was satisfying from my point of view was that the story seemed to be meeting with no doubt or scepticism. Even Dasher swallowed it whole. And if it got by Dasher, who was uniquely positioned to entertain at least some misgivings, then I felt it stood a good chance of throwing everyone off the scent.

Cautious to the point of neurosis, he'd allowed more than a week to pass before he dared make contact with me again. And even that was a chance encounter on the Boher Road one evening as the leaves were swirling. I was stretching my legs during a particularly poor hour across all the TV channels, he was pushing his youngest son up the hill in a buggy.

We both repaired to the low block wall that bordered the bungalow across the road. There I produced the cigarettes while he kept a hand on the pushchair, rocking gently and occasionally.

'I heard your news.'

'From Leaky?'

'No. The missus heard it at work. Some patient in the hospital told her.'

'Fuck's sake, what did the guy do? Take out an ad in the *Munster Express*?'

'Why – were you trying to keep it a secret?'

'If I was, d'you think I'd have told him?'

'I suppose not.'

'I was trying to contain it. But if it's out, it's out.'

'Well, here's to your first million, eh? I wish you the very best of luck. Better luck than we're having with Sergeant

Shithead below. D'you realise he hasn't budged yet?'

'Who?'

'That asshole down in the copshop. He's meant to be gone by now but no, not a bit of it. What's keeping him here still, eh? It can't be the great affection he's held in.'

'Last time we spoke, I advised you to go straight down to the barracks. I don't suppose you went?'

'I most certainly did not.'

'And did he ever call back to you?'

'Yeah, he was round again next evening. I just did the same as before – pretended I wasn't there.'

'And what did he say?'

'He said to the wife that he'd like a word with me, and would I drop in to see him if I got the chance. But he can go fuck himself if he thinks I'm going anywhere near . . . What? Why are you looking at me like that?'

'He asked you to come see him – and you ignored him?'

'Well . . . yeah. He didn't say I had to. And he's not been back since.'

'Of course he fucking hasn't! Cos you've told him everything he needs to know.'

'What? Unlike you, mate, I've told him nothing.'

'Jesus Christ, Dasher, don't you see? Now he'll know that you must be avoiding him for a good reason. That you – that we – must have something to hide. That he's on to us – he'll know for a sworn fact that he's on to us!'

'But . . . we do have something to hide. He is on to us. And it's fucking well he knows it already.'

'Suspects, Dasher. It's like I keep telling you, he knows nothing. And he won't know, unless we're stupid enough to confirm those suspicions for him.' I stopped, trying to think of what might be done. Of anything, it didn't matter how drastic. 'Dash – let's go down there now.'

'Wh – what? Surely you can't be serious.'

'Why not? You've been invited, and I'd like to say goodbye, and to wish him well with his promotion.'

Dasher looked like a man being lowered into a snakepit. 'Billy, this is a risk not worth taking. In just a few days, he'll be transferred away.'

'Only as far as Waterford. Four miles in the road. Not much of an obstacle for a bloke as persistent as him. But if we march down there, like everything is normal and we've nothing to be scared of – well, he might just start to doubt himself. To wonder if he's on the right track, and if he really did hear what he thought he heard. Dasher – that's how I want him leaving Lisdrolin. And not going away absolutely convinced that he'd got his men. C'mon, we can brass this out one last time.'

No condemned man on his way to the gallows ever whimpered or whined like Dasher did on that walk down the hill. But one way and another, our party of three made it to the station house intact.

I was about to knock when I saw the door was slightly ajar. At a beck from Dasher, I came to the corner of the building and there saw Furlong's old Mazda, its boot raised and one or two brown cardboard boxes sitting inside. We'd clearly timed it to a nicety. The black patent-leather shoe came snaking round the door, the left leg then manoeuvred it open. Upon seeing us arrayed directly outside, he all but dropped the box he was struggling with.

'Going somewhere?' I asked.

He stopped in his tracks and, a little warily, said, 'That's right. I've been transferred to Waterford city.'

'We had heard a rumour to that effect.'

'I'm sorry – I didn't get a chance to call round and tell you in person.'

'You should get yourself a phone,' I smiled. 'I reckon they'll soon be all the rage.'

But his mood never lightened.

'Have you come here for something specific?'

'We've come to say goodbye,' I replied, determinedly cordial.

'Oh. Goodbye, then,' and he lowered the box he was holding to the ground between his feet, then extended his hand. 'And thanks. Thanks for being there for me these past few years.' We shook, not at all warmly. He then took a pace or two in Dasher's direction.

'Bye, Dash.'

Dasher took his hand and, speaking for the first time, said, 'Just glad we were of help.'

Furlong immediately let go. '"Help"? I did not say "help".'

His face was set, cold and steely, and bristled like his words. No more masks, no more pretences, no more strained civility: these were true colours. We were enemies now, and enemies we would remain. We who'd seen other days. We who were once friends. The thought caused something inside me to stir, to flare, to not just stand silent and permit such a last farewell. Desperately, I began looking around and about for anything – anything at all – with which I might ignite some little dialogue. And there, among his personal belongings on the ground, I reckoned I spied it; a hand-sized figurine, a hurler with his caman, who stood proudly on a plinth of white marble. Furlong had won this on the very day when first we met. Strangers till then, we'd found ourselves side by side on the subs bench for the final of some tuppence ha'penny local tournament. So far down the list were we that when the trophy-box was discovered to be one short, it fell between us as to who should go without. More from disinterest than good grace, I'd not contested matters, insisting instead that the prize go to the newcomer. Through all the years intervening, and all the murky water under the bridge, he'd kept it still.

'Mullinavat Fete Tournament, 1988,' I indicated.

'That's right. Should've been yours, if I remember correctly.' He stooped and removed it from among his other effects. 'Here – have it.'

'Not at all. You keep it.'

'I don't want it. My hurling career isn't something I enjoy being reminded of.'

'Well, hang on to it as a memento of your time here in Lisdrolin.'

'No, thanks. This isn't a part of my life I'll enjoy being reminded of either. Failure is never easy to swallow.'

I knew better than to have him elaborate but Dasher, as usual, could really pick his moments.

'Ach, I dunno – I reckon you left your mark around here.'

'But by Jesus, nothing like the mark you two have left. So take home that trophy, Billy. Or you have it, Dasher, if he won't. Stick it up on your mantelpiece for all the neighbours to see. Then they'll know you're men of achievement, men who've *done something.* Cos you've been hiding your light under a bushel for too long.'

He picked up his packing case and proceeded to the car, where he laid it with the rest of the luggage. And there he stood, facing into the boot, not looking, not examining, but plainly waiting for us to go. I was left with the small statuette; it felt like blood on my hands, like I was holding the thirty pieces of silver.

'I told you, didn't I?' Dasher hissed as we made our way out through the front gate. 'I told you it was a bad idea coming here!'

I didn't answer. But to show that I now conceded the point, I carried the trophy with me as far as the Mill Weir and, as we crossed over, I let it drop into the fast-flowing stream beneath.

CHAPTER TEN

Furlong went to Waterford. I went into very deep denial, and no amount of evidence staring me in the face properly convinced me that the worst would come to the worst. I could see a large 'For Sale' sign adorning the gatepost at the fields by Gaule's lane. I could see the cars pull up in their twos – those of the viewer and the estate agent travelling in convoy. I could see the drivers pace the borders, inspect the quality of the soil, and take in the magnificent view of Tory Hill to the south. I just refused to believe it would actually amount to anything. Fate, or destiny, or my overworked guardian angel would intervene. And the property would not fall into the hands of another. Something would turn up.

Not surprisingly, nothing did. It was the last Friday in October, the beginning of the Halloween half-term, and the prospect had me in reasonably good humour. Then, not long before school ended, a phone call came through from an exultant Mr Keogh. The land was sold – they'd had an offer which was almost two thousand pounds in excess of their most optimistic projection. If I could make contact with my solicitor as soon as possible – that very afternoon, preferably – then the remaining i's could be dotted, t's crossed and the entire deal sewn up in jigtime.

I returned to the classroom more than a little rattled, my mind no longer on the job. Luckily, I was doing nothing too

229

strenuous; all afternoon, the kids had been contentedly making masks for the weekend's high jinks. And I'd been contentedly letting them, intervening only when the voices or the scissors were raised. Now all of a sudden, my concentration was blown, the leash was slackened. Inevitably, the noise level upped by several notches and the general conduct became more boisterous. Not that I gave a toss – I sat back and simply watched it deteriorate. Then, not long before the final bell two youngsters approached me, each laughing up his sleeve, each volunteering the other to pass on the joke. I snapped from my torpor and growled, 'Well?'

'You tell him.'

'No, it was you who saw it.'

I gave them a look they'd come to know as signalling that I was not in the mood. 'You saw what?'

'Ah, sir, there's writing on the toilet wall.'

'Is it fresh?' I asked.

'It's . . . em . . . I dunno. I didn't see it till now.'

Which meant that it was probably there for some time. And that they could've brought it to my notice far earlier. But it wouldn't have been nearly so much fun as waiting for a moment like this, when the class was already close to chaos.

'Fine,' I said evenly. 'So what's written there?'

'I wouldn't like to say, sir. It's a bit vulgar.'

Well, there's a real turn-up for the books, I thought, as I rose from my seat and went to inspect the damage. Having ensured that the lavatory was unoccupied, I sidled in. The floor was swimming, the whole place smelt deplorable, but there was nothing new in that. What was new, however, was the crude scribbling on the wall just below the cistern. There, in garish red marker, someone had daubed 'Willy Woofter Walsh.' Willy Woofter, I understood, was playground slang for a homosexual. Walsh, no doubt, was my good self. So it appeared some young commentator was outing me.

At my back there was another muffled explosion of laughter, and in the doorway stood my two informants. Andrew Neary stepped forward and, obliging to a fault, pointed to the writing and said, 'That's it there, sir.' I was sorely, sorely tempted to knock some smiles to the other sides of mouths, but as I didn't want to cap the day entirely by losing my job as well, I merely shooed the pair ahead of me back to the classroom. There I was confronted by an epidemic of slack bladders, with every man jack suddenly desperate to use the toilet. It wasn't ethical, I know, but I'd had enough for one day. So I packed them all up and sent them home several minutes early. Once they'd gone, I broke out the Brillo and set about the offending graffiti. Scrubbing my name off a shithouse wall wasn't how I would've chosen to begin my mid-term break. But it was no worse than what was to come next; that visit to my solicitor in Waterford city.

The Prentices, with offices near the clock tower, had been acting on my family's behalf for a good many years. Liam, the current incumbent, had all the documentation at the ready. He was full of congratulations; twelve grand, he said, was a wonderful price, and the agents had done well by me. With regard to that money, I should have the cheque in the next couple of weeks. I'm sure he puzzled why none of this could wipe from my face the disgust that, on this day, I could not manage to conceal.

When I emerged from the office, I needed a drink. In fact, I needed several. Nothing would do me but to commandeer a high stool for the evening and get horribly, mind-numbingly drunk. But nowhere near Lisdrolin; I didn't want my neighbours wondering why I was breaking the habits of a lifetime by getting tanked in the midafternoon. So I settled on Monaghan's by the quay of Waterford. It was a dockers' hangout, and not famously overfussy where its clientele was concerned. There I'd be served so long as I had money and could remain at or about vertical. My car was parked at the back of the cathedral; I just hoped that when the time came, I'd have retained enough wit to leave it where it was and get a taxi home.

The drink dulled the pain and eased the guilt. It also helped with the self-justification, something I'd been struggling with while sober. It was my land, I was soon telling myself, to do with as I pleased. What my forebears didn't know wouldn't trouble them. And anyway . . . it wasn't just about me saving my own hide. In all of this, I'd not once forgotten Dasher and his predicament. He was weak, he was vulnerable, and having a wife and family, he stood to lose a lot more than I ever did. But he was my friend, my oldest friend, and I was not about to see him thrown to the wolves. What would I do, then, but protect him with all means at my disposal? The more I thought about it, and the more I drank, the more I came to realize what misery I'd succeeded in averting. And what credit my sacrifice really did me.

That land was mine to sell. There was nothing dishonourable in its sale. Now it was sold, end of argument. Recrimination was pointless. Better to think about something else altogether. Like the writing in the wall of the boys' jakes. Willy Woofter Walsh. Willy Woofter Walsh, eh? Hard to believe that I'd earlier let it upset me. Because the last thing it was, was upsetting. Funny, yes. Downright hilarious, in fact, to think that a generation was emerging who reckoned that I – *I* was some kind of arse bandit. Granted, I didn't have a wife or a current girlfriend. It wasn't something that bothered me, and these days I rarely went out of my way in search of either. But for the record, I'd been with a woman as recently as . . . God, now that I thought about it, it was quite a long time. Almost twelve months – I was certain it was Christmas, because Dasher's youngest had just been born and . . . And that meant it hadn't even been last Christmas, but the one before! December '95? Coming up for two years?! Not possible! I mean, where had those years gone? And how could middle age have edged so close unnoticed? Like never before, the scales fell away and I could see. This was how it happened; how eligible bachelors became confirmed bachelors, how bright young things grew into sad old men, how time caught up with the likes of me. The writing, quite literally, was on the wall.

It was nearing closing time and I was buckled. I drained the last pint pot and determinedly brought it to rest on the counter. The drunk's defiance – I'd show 'em! Those yahoos around Lisdrolin could think what they liked, I had more going my way than most of them could aspire to in ten lifetimes. And if I didn't have a bird, it wasn't because I couldn't, it was because I couldn't be arsed. And right now I'd prove that. I'd show 'em.

A staff member asked if I was OK as I slipped off the stool and began tottering around the bar, seeking out a suitable target. But there wasn't a woman to be seen. Plenty of rough, but all of it male. Which was just as well, because if Peig Sayers had been in Monaghan's pub that night she'd have been in the running for an indecent proposal. But I was going to proposition someone before the night was out, on that I was set. So I took my leave and went about retracing a path I'd not trodden in an age. The Bridge Hotel at the other end of the quay, was my stomping ground of yore. I'd heard that, in the years intervening, it had become home to a much younger crew but – hey, I was young. I'd show 'em.

However, I'd badly underestimated just how juvenile that crew might be. No sooner had I come shambling near the mile-long door queue when a voice called out, 'All right, sir!' in greeting. There then came a second 'All right, sir?', this one an enquiry after the state of my health. I mumbled something that even I didn't catch and walked on by with just a sidelong glance. And with the certain knowledge that I was being regarded like some curious, pathetic museum piece.

Which marked me down as a natural candidate for Leeza's. Leeza's was the last resort. Dirty, squalid and dangerous, mainly for those willing to sell and those willing to pay. Occasionally money changed hands, but often it took no more than a bottle of the awful wine punters were compelled to buy in lieu of an admission fee. Hardened pros and sluttish amateurs, all preying on the big-earning foreign sailors who came in randy as jackrabbits and just as indiscriminate. No local man with a glimmer of common sense or self-respect would ever dream of setting foot in the place. But on this night, I'd run out of both.

I'd only taken my first sip when a short-skirted bottle-blonde came to join me. Or it's possible that I came to join her, I can't be certain. In any case, I gladly livened her glass, then went on refilling as fast as she could empty it. I can't say what we talked about or if we talked at all. But I do recall noting how garish the trowelled-on make-up looked, even in the near-dark. However, I allowed that, by this time, I was no matinee idol myself. So when, some indeterminate amount of time later, she invited me to accompany her home I did.

I'm assuming that we took a taxi, proceeded directly to the

bedroom and did the deed. All I know is that I woke next morning shortly after seven feeling hungover, a bit tender in parts and mortally ashamed of myself. The cold light of morning is rarely a woman's best friend: now that head on the pillow beside me looked positively fearsome. With no sound and only the most gradual movement, I slipped out of bed and dressed. The bedroom door was slightly ajar and I glided through without disturbing anyone. The situation, I felt, was well on the way to being retrieved, with no real harm done and no strings attached that might trip me up.

But as I tiptoed through the living room, just yards from safety, I was halted in my tracks. There, atop the TV, was your average, innocent family snap. My paramour from the previous night, but younger and more comely. Holding in her arms a toddler, about a year old, I guessed. And standing beside the pair was the husband, from whom the child had clearly inherited his head of flaming red hair. But it was here that the composition became noteworthy; the adult male was none other than Rodger Doran.

Now I was sure we'd gotten straight down to business the previous night – if we'd dallied in the living room long enough for me to see this, then I'd have dallied in that flat for not a second longer. Even now I should've run and kept running; after all, I knew what happened the last time someone laid hands on one of Doran's women. But instead I stood rooted, and there I remained till I heard footsteps on the bedroom floor. At once I realized that my clean getaway was foiled.

'What's wrong – couldn't sleep?' she asked as she came out, tying up her dressing gown.

'Yeah,' I said. 'Something like that.'

'When I saw the bed empty, I thought you'd done a runner.'

Without looking around, I gave a tiny scoff at the very

notion. Then as her wits came about her she twigged.

'Listen,' she said softly, 'if you'd asked last night, I'd have told you. Only it's something from my distant past. And I don't much like to talk about it.'

'It isn't that. It's just . . . I know him.'

'You do? How?'

'We . . . we were in school together. Primary school.'

'In Lisdrolin?'

'That's right.'

'Knew him well, did you?' I didn't care at all for her tone.

'No, not really,' I said. 'We were never friends.'

'We were, once. We were even married.'

'In Australia?'

'Yeah, in Australia . . . How'd you know that? Have you been talking to him lately?'

'Not lately. But I did bump into him in town one day.'

She eyed me suspiciously, as if Doran and I might somehow, someway, be in cahoots.

'Honest, there's nothing more to it than that. Anyway . . . how's the little fellah?'

Immediately the woman (I still didn't know her name) seemed to wilt, her gaze lost in the middle distance, her expression glazed and gone-away.

'I . . . I heard he wasn't very well,' I stammered. 'I hope he's better.'

It began with a quiver on the cheek, spreading to the shoulders, and then she was stricken by the most frightful, hysterical wailing. Huge tears ran, and she appeared to lack the strength to even raise a hand to wipe them. Awkwardly, I guided her towards the sofa. There she keeled over, her face buried in one of the scatter cushions, as the wailing went on. I stepped away and said, 'Maybe I should leave.'

Without lifting her head, she turned her face to me and sobbed 'Please, don't. Stay a while. Just hold me – please.'

It wasn't the most enticing offer I'd ever had, but I sat myself next to her and helped her upright. She snuggled under my left arm, her face now almost disfigured with grief.

'Jordan's dead,' she faltered.

'I'm so sorry,' I said. 'When . . .?'

'Oh, nearly eight years ago.'

'Eight years?!' I almost shouted. Are you su— I mean, where did this happen?'

'Back in Sydney. And the reason it still hurts so much is because it wasn't just Jordan who died. It was me, and it was him – it was us. It killed us stone dead . . . but you don't want to know about any of this.'

'Please – I very much do.'

She cleared her throat, sniffed loudly and ran the sleeve of her dressing gown roughly down her face.

'It all started so well. My brother was already out there, and after I finished my Leaving Cert. he paid for me to come visit. I didn't intend staying, but one evening at a football game I met Rodger. Imagine – a Kilkenny man and a Waterford woman meeting up at a Gaelic football match.'

'A bit unexpected, that.'

'Unexpected, yeah. At the time, I was convinced it was fate, nothing less. He wasn't that good-looking, he was a bit older than I was, my brother didn't approve – my brother, as a matter of fact, knew him already and seriously disliked him. But I dunno, I thought he was kinda . . . dangerous.'

'I can well believe that.'

'Dangerous, yeah. He had, y'know, attitude. He didn't give a fuck about anybody. And he always seemed to have money.'

'I have no trouble believing that, either.'

'But what impressed me most about him was his ambition. He already had a good number on the buildings, but that wasn't enough. When I met him, he was going to the local Tech by night, doing a course in scaffolding. Specialist work, that's where the big bucks were.'

As she spoke, I recalled hearing this very story from Doran himself on the quay that evening, our first encounter following his return.

'For a while, there was no stopping us. He qualified, set himself up, and couldn't keep the jobs done he was so in demand. Before long, he had his own company with two full-time employees. And,' she smiled, remembering, 'three or four others who'd go along if things were busy and they were sober. Me? I wrote home and told my folks in Waterford that I wasn't coming back.'

'They were upset?'

'Not really. They knew that Kevin – my brother – had done well for himself down under, and anyway there wasn't much for me in Ireland.'

'But you'd only just done the Leaving.'

'And my mother had only just got the results. They were pretty dire. I was next door to unemployable.'

'And did you get work out there?'

'Picking lettuce at first. I was only seventeen. I couldn't have cared less, but Rodger persuaded me to look for something better. In the end he was able to pull a few strings and get me started as a childminder. By then, we were going out together pretty steady.'

'What did your brother make of this?'

'It's hard to argue with success. Everyone could see that Rodger was raking it in, and once I'd got the diploma and started my own pre-school playgroup, I wasn't doing badly either. So Kevin didn't object. He never really warmed to the guy, but he knew that if he opened his mouth, he'd lose us both.'

'You went ahead and got married?'

'That's what we did. My mum and dad came out for it. Nobody from his side made the trip – his mother died when he was little, and he said his father was too unwell to travel. Although looking back, I'm not sure if he ever even invited him – and I'm not sure I blame him. I met his dad years later, and I wouldn't have wanted him there either. But then —' She stopped abruptly. 'Sorry. I shouldn't have said that. It's wrong to speak ill of the dead.'

'His father *is* dead then?'

'He died last year. They were never close, but for Rodger it was the last straw. Last time he ever walked out the door of this flat, what's more. I've barely seen him since.'

'I'm sorry,' I said.

'I'm not. There was nothing between us by then. Like I told you, it died when my baby did.'

'Look, I'm sure you'd rather not . . .'

'It was Christmas Day, '89. Jordan's first Christmas. There was just the three of us – my brother came up with some excuse for not having us over, and some other obvious lie for not eating at our place. God, if only there'd been more people around, everything would've been different.' Here she faltered a little at the thought of what might have been. And what might have been avoided. 'We'd had a bit of a heatwave that December. It wasn't comfortable for anyone, but it was murder for the little guy, with his fair complexion. So Santa brought him a paddling pool. A little inflatable thing. And so *shallow*. Honest, you could've walked through it in your streetshoes and not got your socks wet. So while I saw to the dinner, Rodger brought Jordan out the back garden and began to set it up. But typical Rodger – even on this one day, it was business before family, money before everything. He was waiting for a phone call. He'd put a price on some bloody job or other, and he couldn't wait to hear if he'd got the contract. Sure enough, just as he was filling the thing, a call came through. So he turned off the water and came inside.'

With a long quaking breath, she forced the tears away a distance.

'The news was good. He got the work. If he hadn't, he mightn't have come to the kitchen to tell me all about it. And I mightn't have opened a bottle of wine to celebrate. And he'd never have left . . . Anyway, when he did eventually go back out, Jordan was dead. Drowned in less than six inches of water. It seems he toppled in face first, banged his forehead and was knocked unconscious. When he was laid out in his coffin, they dressed him in white silk, with a wee garland of flowers around his head so the bruise wouldn't show. It was . . . nice.'

I hated that baby's father as much as it was possible for me to hate, but I could never wish this on anyone. My heart went out to her, to him, to all of them.

'You think things can't get worse,' she went on. 'You think you're in hell. Later, you realize you'd only arrived at the gates, and that your troubles were just beginning. After the funeral, Rodger couldn't sleep. He'd come home from the boozer well oiled, knock back half a bottle of vodka and still he'd spend the night tossing and turning. So he tried out some pills that a friend of his recommended. And when he found he liked these, he tried out some more. From there, it was just a few easy steps to heroin addiction. From heroin addiction, it was no distance at all to losing the business, the

240

home, every scrap of self-respect . . . to eventually finding ourselves destitute and on the wrong side of the world. Then Rodger began getting involved in all sorts, and the police were taking note. In the end, we had to get out of Australia.'

'Well, you yourself could've stayed.'

'That's true. And I did think long and hard about it – y'know, have done with Doran, cut my losses and start over.'

'Why didn't you?'

'Now, this may shock you after last night, but I'm a good Catholic girl, brought up to believe that marriage is for life. I wanted to give ours another shot. You have to hope, don't you? I imagined that when we got back home, back among our own people, things would fall into place. Y'see, I was under the impression that there were no drugs in Ireland. Maybe just a little in Dublin, but we wouldn't be going anywhere near Dublin. We'd be settling in Waterford, and I thought Waterford was clean.'

'Good Jesus, were you in for a shock!'

'Once we arrived back, it didn't take me long to find out different. And it didn't take Rodger long to find the Wild Boar pub up there beside the Applemarket. And become its most dedicated regular.'

'The Wild Boar? I've never heard of it.'

'You're obviously not a user, then. Because if you were, you'd bloody well know the Wild Boar. People say that the beertaps there are only for show. I'm not sure if he pays rent in the place, but that's where he lives these days.' And she laughed a wistful little laugh as she contemplated the ruins of the life she'd just walked me through.

'Thanks for being a shoulder to cry on . . . I'm terribly sorry, I don't remember your name.'

'Billy,' I told her. 'And don't feel bad about it – I don't remember yours either.'

'I'm Angela,' she said. And, bizarre as it was, given that we'd just spent the night together, we now exchanged a handshake.

'How did I get into the story anyway? Oh yeah, you asked me about Jordan. What exactly did Doran tell you about him?'

'He called out to me once or twice, said that he wasn't well, and that he needed money for his medicine.'

'He what?' she gasped.

'He told me he had a prescription that he couldn't afford . . .'

I didn't need to finish – she'd heard me first time. For a while she said nothing, lost in her thoughts. And then, sounding dazed, 'I was married to the guy. I knew from day one that I wasn't getting an altar boy. But I really did believe there were some things that not even he would stoop to. Now you come and tell me . . . *this*? He's been using our dead baby to cadge money?' A tremble came to her voice as her breath quickened. 'He's been using our little angel's name to feed his filthy habit? Jesus Christ, I'm not having hair nor hide of that bastard in my home.'

And with a kind of strangled howl, she leapt from the couch, lurched to the TV and swept the framed photograph into the wall adjacent. It proved sturdier than it looked, because while the glass shattered the border remained in one piece. Undeterred, she retrieved it from the floor where it lay and brought it slamming down on the top of a large hi-fi speaker. This time she succeeded in dislodging one side of the rectangular frame, but in doing so gave her hand a nasty scratch on a glass sliver that had come loose. Small droplets of blood began forming, but she'd done herself no serious injury. Not yet.

'Leave it, Angela,' I said evenly. 'Take it easy a minute. Remember your child is in there too.'

'Yeah,' she replied feverishly. 'Yeah, you're right.' So with great care, she slid the photograph from under the broken glass and fingers trembling, she tore the image of her former husband from the right-hand third of the picture. When she'd done, she took what remained, kissed it, said, 'Sorry, sweetheart. Sorry. I'll get you fixed up again later,' and left it back on the TV again.

I said, 'I really have to go now.'

'OK. And thanks again.'

'Don't mention it. If I've helped you at all, then I'm glad you did.'

'Billy . . . I'm not very good at this, but . . . you seem like a decent bloke, and Christ knows I'm due a decent bloke. If I gave you my phone number d'you think you might ring me sometime?'

'Sure,' I lied. 'I'd like that.'

There was a biro at her side on the table. She picked up from the floor that portion of the photograph she'd just discarded and began to write on the reverse. 'This way, you won't forget whose number it is, will you?'

I agreed that it ought to prove a most effective reminder. And with great ostentation, I took out my wallet and placed the number inside, while making a mental note to get rid of it at my earliest convenience. No more than her, I didn't want hair nor hide of Rodger Doran about me.

'I'll be in touch,' I lied some more, and I made my way out of the building.

*

The drive home was not pleasant. My head pounded, my stomach churned, and my gorge rose with every turn of the wheel. I'd just come through the front door, sick, sore and sorry, when the phone rang. It was Mags.

'Billy – how's things?'

'Fine. And you?'

'All right. I've been better,' she said, listless and deflated. She'd been opposed to the sale of the land, I remembered. And I only just remembered that, the previous day, the sale had gone through.

'It was a good price, though,' I ventured in my defence.

'What was?'

'The twelve grand.' Blank, impenetrable silence.

'Y'know – that's what I got for the two small fields.'

'Oh they've been sold, then?'

'They have – isn't that why you called?' More silence, broken only by a sniffle and then a sob. 'Mags, is something wrong?'

'Yeah,' she choked. 'Plenty . . . everything.'

'D'you want to talk about it?'

'Not over the phone.'

'Well, take a spin down then, why don't you hop in the car and . . .'

'I'd love to. But I've been drinking.'

'What? Already?' It had only gone eleven.

'Will you call up here to Clontarf? You promised me you would, remember?'

I was in no mood for going anywhere other than directly to my bed. But I had made such a promise.

'It's just a two-hour journey. And it'd mean so much.'

In her life, she'd never asked much of me, so I could hardly let her down this once. Maybe a bracing two-hour drive would be just what the doctor ordered. And it certainly couldn't hurt to take a short break away from Lisdrolin, and those 'For Sale' signs at the roadside that still taunted me every time I passed by. So, with all the enthusiasm I could call up, I said, 'I'd love to. See you some time in the afternoon.'

'D'you know where the house is?' she asked, brightening.

'I don't.'

'When you get to the waterfront, there's a public phone. Give me a ring and I'll come meet you.'

On the waterfront by Dublin bay, Mags thanked me again for making the journey as she bade me follow her to her home. A left turn at the next lights and a small maze of sidestreets later, we were both parked on the cobbled forecourt.

The house was – and is – a semi-detached Georgian mansion. Two huge reception rooms, one her study, dominated the ground level. A great cavernous kitchen with a smaller – but by no means small – TV room off it comprised the basement, while the six bedrooms were variously located on the first and second floors. At the rear, once part of a half-acre garden, was a full-sized, fully equipped gymnasium, put in place by the previous occupant but in total disuse under the current ownership. Dotted around the house there were at least three, possibly as many as five bathrooms, one of them bigger than the entire quarters I'd occupied during my time in St Pat's College.

Once she'd given me a very perfunctory tour of the premises, we both descended again to the basement. After I'd forcefully declined the offer of a drink, she ushered me through the kitchen to the TV room adjoining. There I came upon Dermot, draped over a sofa like one of the Salvador Dali's clocks. He looked as if he must either be dead or asleep with his eyes open as he gaped at the set where some Formula One was showing. I'd approached to within touching distance before he acknowledged me with a start.

'Jesus Christ – where did you come from?'

'Just a social call.'

'Good, good,' he said. Then, in a whisper, 'Can't say much for your timing though, Bill. Herself is like an antichrist. I have the feeling that there's something . . . oh, hello love.'

'Did Ewan McNulty ring?' she asked, frost in her tone.

'He did, aye. He left something on your voicemail.'

She strode towards the far end of the room to access her message. Nothing earthshaking, it merely confirmed a meeting in the Law Library for early the following Monday. But as it played, Dermot was glancing nervously over each shoulder in turn, as if he expected to have a hatchet buried in the back of his skull at any moment.

Her message received, Mags sat herself down at the upright piano and, looking strangely intense and pre-occupied, began to tap repeatedly on the same white key somewhere around the middle C. Dermot looked edgy, his head still unmoved but his eyes now finding every corner of the room. Then, all of a sudden, his face broke into a smile as nervous as it was oafish.

'Did I hear someone mention that there was a drink on offer?'

Mags allowed her finger to come to rest on the note she'd been striking and said, 'D'you want a drink?'

More foolish grinning and, 'Begod, I wouldn't say no.'

'Go down to the pub then and get yourself one.' It took him some seconds to catch her drift. 'Go on!' she told him sourly.

'But —'

When he saw in her eye a look that would've blistered paint, he cut short his objection.

'OK, fair enough. Billy, d'you want to come or . . .'

The invitation went unfinished. He took his cigarettes from the table and made a well-advised exit. I heard the outside door shut and then watched as he shuffled up the steps and across the cobblestones.

'D'you mind if I switch this rubbish off?' she asked, pointing the remote at the TV and the motor racing.

'No. Be my guest.'

'How anyone with even half a brain functioning could sit through . . .'

'Dermot seems to enjoy it.'

'I rest my case.' That last she slurred slightly. There were drinks on her breath when we'd met earlier at the bayside.

'You have been drinking, haven't you?'

'Drinking: good man! I'd almost forgotten. What'll it be? I've got Guinness, Smithwicks . . .?'

My innards still felt delicate. Something short and stiff was called for. 'A brandy would be nice.'

'Ooooh! Brandy! Is that the tipple of choice for the young hotelier these days?'

I eyed her blankly. It took several, disastrous seconds for the light to come on. When it did, I smiled sheepishly and hoped I'd not done any irreparable damage. Her expression gave nothing away as she went a trifle unsteadily towards the kitchen. She returned with a litre bottle of brandy, a bucket of ice and a pair of tumblers, all clinking and rattling on an ornate silver tray. She then proceeded to pour two enormous measures. At the second attempt, after she'd slightly misjudged her distances first time of asking, we clinked glasses.

With a single swig, she half emptied the glass before the bubbles had even settled. Drawing in a long, cool breath, she blinked twice to clear her welling eyes and said '*Sláinte!*'

'*Sláinte,*' I said back, and watched as she took another mighty swallow. 'Mags, weren't you taking a bit of a chance earlier, driving when you'd drink on board?'

'I was, wasn't I. A big chance, at that. Cos at the present time, if a guard were to even catch me without a light on my bike, I'd spend Christmas in jail. I've not told anyone yet, but I think I'll be taking that case after all.'

'Cappocci?'

'Yes, sir – public enemy number one.'

'And what's brought about this change of heart?'

'Well, the family have never let up. I've represented them a few times in the past, and things have always gone my way. So now I'm the only one they'll hear of; they won't even consider a different SC. I know it's ridiculous at my age, but I suppose I'm a little flattered.'

'And why not? It's always nice to be appreciated.'

'Indeed,' she said ironically. 'Let's celebrate.' With what was only a third draught, she drained the tumbler and gasped, 'Ready for more?'

'No, not yet.'

She took her glass, now refilled, and slumped back in the deep leather armchair. 'That's not the only reason, though. I've heard whispers around the Law Library, saying I'm nothing but a sunny-day player, that I only take the cases when the money is huge, the dice is loaded and I'm guaranteed to come out looking good.'

'But that's not true.'

'I know it's not. But if I turn this one down, it'd always be said.'

She sat, not speaking, not looking left or right, her breath hard and heavy, interrupted only by frequent sips from the glass.

'So that's what was on your mind?' I asked. 'That's why you asked me here?'

'Partly. That and one or two other things recently have caused me to step back and take stock. Call it a crisis of conscience, if you like.'

'I'm . . . not with you, I'm afraid.'

'Why should I defend Cappocci? Why should anybody? The dogs in the city pound know he's guilty. People deserve to be protected from him and his sort. Why should I be trying to put him back on the streets?'

'But that's not going to happen, is it? Didn't you say he's not got a chance?'

'Neither did the druggie who killed the German tourist in the Phoenix Park a few years back . . . but walked free because there weren't enough bodies in his identity parade. Nor the thugs – the so-called queerbashers – who kicked the young lad to death in Fairview, and wound up with suspended sentences and a victory parade through town the night after. Billy, in this game, the technicalities and the loopholes are far more important than innocence or guilt. And there are judgements handed down all the time that have very, very little to do with justice.'

'So you're saying he might get away with it?'

'I'm saying it's not beyond the bounds of possibility. If he's in the right hands.'

And again she was reaching for the bottle. More to distract her than anything else, I said, 'I wouldn't take it to heart, if I were you. Cos it's like you said – only a game. And if Cappocci does get the verdict, big deal. From what I can gather, he's done this city a favour. I mean, there won't be very many tears shed for his victim.'

'Which victim?'

'The O'Toole guy. Why – has there been more than one?'

'There's been at least a dozen. Oh, not all seen off personally. And not all lowlife like Stitchie O'Toole. Benny Cappocci's put several good people in Glasnevin cemetery during the course of his glorious career. And he's finally been caught red-handed, but what of it? He must get the best legal counsel that money can buy. Because this great justice system of ours has to work for everybody – not just those poor bastards who want nothing more than an honest living and a decent world to rear kids in. Cheers!'

She raised a glass to me before smartly downing the contents. This brought on a bout of hoarse, chesty coughing but didn't stop her going again for more brandy.

'Mags,' I said, 'I think you ought to give that a rest.'

'Ah, why?' she groaned. 'What's the point? Who cares, for Christ sake?' Then, when she'd done pouring, 'What's there to care about?'

'What's there to care about? Jesus, girl, take a look at the car you drive. Take a look at the address on your mailbox. Take a look at this house, why don't you. Go on – just look around!'

Without looking anywhere, she said, 'It's rotten. Every brick, from the ground up. Paid for by criminals and their dirty money. I'm just a better class of prostitute, Billy. A slut in a wig and a gown. If you've got the readies, I'll turn the trick.'

'This is drink talking. Anything you've got you've got because you're bloody good. You didn't make the rules, you just play to them better than anyone else. And that's nothing

250

to be ashamed of. I know, I've always been proud of you.'

This seemed to take her by surprise, to embarrass her just a little. She looked at me a long while, then let her gaze fall to the floor.

'I suppose I had to be good for something,' she garbled. 'Cos I was fucking crap at everything else.'

'Like what?'

'Well, fellahs, for example. I was a bit of a disaster around them.'

'I remember you having boyfriends.'

'Pray God you don't remember what they were like. The nice guys ignored me, the other guys used me, mostly. It's not an area where I've improved greatly over the years. As I'm sure you'd agree.'

'Ah come on – Dermot's OK.'

'Please! I know what you think of him, so don't patronize me.'

She then shaped as if, I thought, to take me into some very personal confidence. But at the brink she drew back and flopped into the chair once more. Then, after a moment's thought, she brought her glass down hard on the table and said angrily, 'How come your life runs so bloody easy? And it's always been the same – clean, straight and uncomplicated.'

'What're you talking about?'

'Look at the job you do, f'rinstance. It's honest, it's worthwhile, it's never cost you your integrity and it never will.'

'It's never afforded me a lifestyle like this. And it never will.'

'But does that bother you? I mean, is money so big a consideration?'

'Depends. If you've got vast amounts of it then no, it's not important. But if you're not getting enough, you can think of nothing else. It's like sex.'

'He's having an affair, y'know.'

'What?'

'An affair. He's having an affair. Or at least he's trying.'

She did seem to be talking about her husband, but the very idea was outlandish.

'Dermot?' I asked, incredulously.

'One and the same.'

'Who . . .?' . . . in her right mind would have him, I began to say, but checked myself.

'Who with? She completed. 'Someone young, I'd guess. The day before yesterday, I found condoms in his jacket.'

'You did?'

'Uh-huh. He didn't even have the wit to keep them hidden from me.'

Though I was still struggling to take very much of this in, it at least explained her need of a kindred spirit, a shoulder to cry on.

'So . . . Jesus . . . what're you going to do?'

'I dunno. Sometimes I want to just throw him out and have done with it. Other times I want to cut his balls off while he's sleeping – which, by the way, leaves me with no shortage of opportunity. Occasionally, I find the whole thing absolutely hilarious, and God knows I do appreciate a good laugh these days. But mostly, it's not him or what he's done that I question – it's me. What kind of person am I, who can't even keep a bloke as ordinary as Dermot McGee. Billy, it's like I told you earlier; everything that could be wrong is wrong.'

Mercifully, the doorbell rang.

'Ah! He's back. This time, he's only overlooked his latchkey.'

'He didn't stay gone for long,' I remarked.

'He's run out of money.'

'How d'you know?'

'Cos I didn't give him any.'

There came a second chime, and as my sister was making no move, I rose and went. Outside, where I expected to find Dermot looking suitably sheepish, I found nothing of the sort. There stood an elderly man, early seventies, most likely. His thick grey hair was slicked back with a little too much Brylcreem, his face and shoulders were square. He wore a black silk neckscarf and a heavy sheepskin coat, while his discreet aftershave mingled agreeably with the aroma of cigar smoke.

'I've come to see Ms Walsh. Margaret Walsh, the Senior Counsel.' The accent was old Dublin.

'Yeah, sure,' I said. 'Come on in.'

I ushered him through. It was only as I showed him to the TV room it occurred to me that I ought to have least enquired his business. But it was too late to ask now – he already had his hand on the doorknob.

'Through here?'

'That's right,' I said, and as if it would make all sorts of amends I shouted, 'Someone to see you, Mags.'

With difficulty, she got to her feet, turned towards the open door and then froze.

'Ms Walsh – sorry to show up announced like this. I won't sit down, I don't intend taking much of your time.'

She'd still not stirred. She'd hardly dared blink.

'I'm afraid, Ms Walsh, that I'm still waiting on your decision.'

'Yes, I . . . em . . . I know.'

He didn't ask why, but even I could tell that an

explanation – a *good* explanation – was expected.

'I was occupied with matters of a personal nature. You've, ah, met my brother Billy?'

He shook my hand. 'Pleased to meet you, Billy. Benito Cappocci . . . senior,' he smiled grandly. And now I well understood my sister's unease.

'Billy's been here this past while, so between one thing and another I've not had the chance . . .' She didn't finish, fearing this excuse was far more likely to insult than to appease.

'I've never hidden my admiration for you, Ms Walsh, or my gratitude for all you've done for my family in the past. Which is why I'm so disappointed that you've not felt able to give me an early answer. Early, and of course, favourable.' Then from an inside pocket he produced a black silken casket, not much bigger than a ring box.

'This is a small token of . . .'

'No. I appreciate the thought, Mr Cappocci, but I can't.'

'Ms Walsh, I'm afraid I have to insist,' and he began to approach her.

'Mr Cappocci!' she snapped, at last finding her voice and her fire. 'I've told you, no. Now please put it away.'

'But it's only . . .'

'I don't care what it is, I don't want anything from – That is, I've already been paid in full for any work I've ever done you. Accepting gifts wouldn't be ethical.'

He paused a moment, opened the little black casket and examined the contents. He looked hurt, though not surprised.

'Not ethical,' he repeated softly before snapping shut the lid. 'Ms Walsh, my son, y'know, he's not a bad lad. He's inclined to be hot-headed, and he's made mistakes – but which of us hasn't, eh? When this is over, and with your help he's still got his liberty, we're sending him out of the country, possibly for good, certainly for the best. To leave this land and his past far behind him and begin again, fresh and clean. Don't you think he's entitled to a second chance?'

Mags nodded, but in acknowledgement, not agreement. I wondered who'd be next to speak, knowing only that it wouldn't be me. Cappocci, meanwhile, was rummaging again in an inside pocket. At last he located what looked like a small beige business card.

'I'll stay no longer. Thank you for seeing me like this. I'll leave you my number and look forward to your call. If there's anything – anything at all – I can do to help make your mind up, please don't hesitate. I'd consider it a great honour.' Deftly, he placed the card on a nest of mahogany tables near the door. 'I'll see myself out – good day to you both.'

Mags stood rigid till the front door banged shut. Then she came lurching forward, grabbing the backs of armchairs for support.

'Jesus Christ, Billy, you can't grant open house to just anybody in this town. Look – why d'you think we installed this security intercom?'

I might've enquired why this security intercom wasn't pointed out to me before I answered the door, but I let it pass. She pushed by me, turned the key in a heavy duty Yale lock, then slid closed a bolt near the bottom.

'I mean, that could've been . . . I dunno . . .' and she looked away distractedly. Then, 'He was here, Billy. In my home. In my bloody home.'

'In fairness,' I said, 'he didn't sound to me like someone who meant you any harm.'

She ignored this and gave the door handle one last rattle for good measure.

'Anyway, why did you not just tell him that you'd made your decision, and that you're taking his case? Wouldn't that have been easier?'

'What? And have him think this was a good idea? That the way to win me round is to come and harass me in my own sitting room?'

'So . . . are you still going to do it, then?'

'Oh, I'll do it. But he won't know till I'm ready to tell him. I'll make him suffer for this – I'll make him sweat.'

She brushed past me again, back to where Cappocci had left his calling card. She regarded it a moment, then picked it up like it was a severed ear. '"Security services, systems and consulting",' she read in a voice dulled by disbelief. 'Heavenly Father! Give me a match, will you?'

I was fumbling through my pockets when something struck me. 'If you don't want that, d'you mind if I have it?'

'What – this? Why?'

I shrugged. 'Ah . . . y'know.'

She shook her head. 'You want to show it off to the lads back home, right? You want to impress some of the hard nuts around Lisdrolin.'

Though I smiled and feigned embarrassment, this was not my intention. However, I did have in mind one former resident of the little village on whom I hoped Mr Cappocci might leave something of an impression.

CHAPTER ELEVEN

Next day, I was first in the household to wake. I peeped into my sister's bedroom just long enough to lie that I had some old college friends to look up and would not be back until the late afternoon. This was greeted by some grumbling and pulling of covers over heads, so I let myself out.

Twice in the public kiosk by the seafront I lifted the receiver, began dialling, then stopped and walked swiftly away. On my third visit, I found the nerve.

The little girl who answered had a Dublin accent so pronounced I felt that she must be putting it on. But she was efficiency itself. After she'd made certain of my message, I could hear her tell grandad that someone called 'Mags' brother' wanted a word. As I heard heavy footsteps approach the other end of the line, my butterflies returned in swarm.

'Hello?' he said, sounding thoroughly intrigued.

'Mr Cappocci?'

'Yes.'

'My name is Billy Walsh. We spoke yesterday at my sister's house.'

'So it is Mags' brother. Little Sara – she doesn't always get these things right. So, Mr Walsh, how may I help you?'

'I was more thinking about how we might help each other. But I'd prefer not to discuss it over the phone.'

'You wish to meet face to face, then?'

'That'd be great. If it's convenient, of course, and doesn't upset any plans you might have had.'

'Plans? My friend, I'm a very old man, with far, far too much time on his hands. A meeting with yourself will be a most welcome diversion. So, what time should I call round?'

'You can't —' I stopped myself short, pretty sure he was unaccustomed to being told what he could or could not do. 'I mean, that's not possible. When I tell you my business, you'll understand why.'

'Fine,' he said, not at all offended. 'Where, then?'

There was precious little of Dublin city that I was familiar with, so I said, 'I went to college in Drumcondra. Apart from there, I'm afraid I'm stumped.'

'Drumcondra's good. D'you know the Capitol?'

I did, rather better than I ought to. The rendezvous was arranged for four thirty that same afternoon.

I arrived early, another echo of my student days. The old place hadn't changed much, still cosily downmarket as these student pubs tend to be. I took a seat in the corner furthest from the bar, and waited. But not for long – I might've set my watch by Cappocci. At precisely half-past four he strode through the main doors, surveyed the entire joint till he spotted where I sat, then made his way towards me. He was dressed as he had been the previous day, though he now wore a pair of dark-tinted spectacles. If the purpose was disguise, he shouldn't have bothered; the glasses only added menace to what was already an intimidating presence.

He took a stool and sat facing the corner, so that his back was to those others present. When a lounge girl flitted by, Cappocci declined my offer of a drink, saying he didn't intend stopping. However, when pressed, he relented to a still water.

'Nice of you to meet me like this,' I said. But he acted as if he'd not heard me – indeed, as if he'd not seen me – not until the girl had brought the drinks, collected the money and left again.

'Now, Mr Walsh,' he said in a low grumble. 'You say we can do business?'

This was nerve-jangling enough without any excess formality, so I told him, 'Please – the name's Billy.'

'Billy, then,' he repeated impassively. I sat straight, then leaned forward with purpose.

'I'll begin with what I've got on offer. Mags Walsh is my only sister. Our parents are both dead, so there's just the two of us. As you might expect, we're very close. She listens to me, as I do to her.'

'Go on.'

'I believe I can persuade her to work for you.' He nodded slowly, his interest obvious. 'I know she's not keen right now, but I'm confident I could swing it. In fact, I'd go so far as to give you a guarantee.'

'That would mean a great, great deal to me.'

'I thought that.'

'Did you have in mind some specific way I might show my appreciation?'

This was the point of no return; abandon it here, or be prepared to see it through to the end. I hesitated, weighing things one last time. Then, 'Yes, I do. I just don't quite know how to put it.'

He sat there unspeaking, unblinking, unnerving. He'd not come halfways across Dublin to coax talk from me.

'The thing is, I'm in a spot of bother with a guy back home. In Waterford, that is.' I expected this might begin some discourse between us but no, nothing from the other side of the table.

'He's been putting the squeeze on me for money. For quite a lot of money. It started out in a small way, but it's gone to a point where he's bleeding me dry.'

Still not a flicker – it was clear he wanted the whole story. But that opened at my father's haybarn one August night a long time before, and there was no way I was starting there.

'Mr Cappocci, I'm not getting into the gory details. But trust me, I'm in trouble, and I can't go to the police.'

'Obviously not. If you could, you'd hardly be trying to enlist an old hoodlum like myself now, would you?' he smiled. And raised his glass to me. I reddened and returned the toast. He allowed the smile to die on his lips – back directly to business.

'So,' he said. 'It's blackmail.'

'Yes, it's blackmail.'

'What's he got on you?'

'I'm not saying.'

'In general terms, is it something embarrassing, or is it criminal?'

'It's criminal.'

'How criminal?'

'About as criminal as it gets.'

He lifted the spectacles slightly from the bridge of his nose, scratched the inside of his eye, examined under his nail to see what he might've extracted, and then said, 'A-ha.' Reaching into an inside pocket, he produced a box of King Edward cigars. Very deliberately he drew one out and began to unwrap it: equally deliberately, he failed to offer me any. He lit up, inhaled deeply and when he spoke again each word came through a small cloudlet.

'So, who's this friend of yours?'

'You want his name?'

'I want every single detail you can give me. Starting with his name.'

'Rodger Doran. He's late thirties, and he lives in Waterford city.'

It was much to my embarrassment that I could add very little to this. Little of relevance, at any rate. Cappocci sat there nodding, indicating that I should – that I'd *better* – elaborate. I dared not disappoint him.

'He's about my height, he's got red hair, he's separated from his wife, he has – he had – one child.'

There. Done. And to signal the end of the briefing, I emptied my pint to the froth and put down the glass with a flourish. Through the fog of cigar smoke, Cappocci regarded me with curiosity.

'Is that it?'

'Well, it's as much as I can think of . . . at the moment.'

'Let me be clear on this. The only significant details you can give me are his name and the city he lives in. Are you sure you actually know this guy? He's not, maybe, someone you saw on a bus and didn't like the look of?'

'I gave you more than that. I . . . I mentioned his red hair, didn't I?'

'Yes. And I can just imagine how, in Ireland, that must make him stand out. Mr Walsh, I don't think you're entirely serious —'

'Look – I'm deadly bloody serious. And it's in your interest to take me seriously.'

'Then for God's sake give me more.'

'What else would you like to know?'

'His address wouldn't go amiss.'

'I don't have an address for him – I'm not even sure if he's got a fixed abode.'

'The best you can do is Waterford city?'

'Yes, I'm afraid so.'

'That's a shame,' he said, thinking aloud. 'I've done some good business in that part of the world. In fact I'm still owed a favour down the sunny south-east. But without a home address . . . This Doran – what does he work at?'

'Nothing. He's a petty criminal.'

At this, the old man made a series of sucking noises between his two front teeth. 'Is he a user?'

'Yeah.'

'What?'

'Heroin.'

'Hmmmm. Now you're talking. So, think hard – I need an address.'

I shook my head. No amount of thinking would wring out what wasn't there.

'OK, then,' he said. 'Just tell me where and when we're likely to run into this person around town.'

He was bending over backwards, willing to go on scraps. But I didn't even have those.

'I'm . . . not certain. But, like, the place isn't all that big.'

Pointing out that Waterford city is relatively small was never going to be enough. Cappocci smiled sympathetically.

'Go back to Waterford, Mr Walsh, and do your homework. We'll meet here again, same time, one week from today. Do not attempt to contact me in the meantime.'

And he stood. I got to my feet to stall him, to try salvage the sinking ship. One week on, my sister would've accepted the case, which or whether, obviously with no representation from me. My only bargaining chip would be worthless.

'You'll definitely find him, if you ask around a bit. He's a well-known blackguard. I mean, I'm sure that one of your ... of your business associates would have heard ... *Hang on!*' I almost screamed. 'I've got it!'

Giddy, I rifled through my wallet till I came upon a strip of torn Polaroid. The same piece that had been given to me only the day before by Doran's estranged wife. One side listed the good lady's telephone number; the other, crucially, bore a likeness of the man himself.

'There!' I crowed. 'That's him. And you'll find him any night of the week in a pub called ... called ...' I put an index finger to each temple – 'in a pub called the Wild Boar, near the Applemarket!'

Cappocci took the picture from me, studied the subject a while, then produced a silver pen and clicked the cap. Seeing a number already written on the back of the photograph, he tilted it towards me and asked, 'Whose?'

'Nobody. Nobody important. You can cross it out.'

He ignored me and began to talk to himself as he wrote. 'Doran. D-O-R-A-N. Rodger, was that what you said?'

'Yes. Rodger Doran.'

'R-O-D-G-E-R. And that pub again?'

'The Wild Boar. Near the Applemarket.'

When he'd done, he returned both pen and picture to his coat. 'You're one hundred per cent certain of this information?'

I wasn't, not by any means. But at that moment, I was afraid to be anything less. 'Yes. Absolutely.'

'And about the drugs habit?'

'That too.'

'How can you be so sure?'

'Cos I've got a friend . . .' And here I paused as I remembered that Mr Cappocci was of a different persuasion to Conor Furlong. 'I mean, I used to know a guy who was a guard in Waterford.'

'So the police are aware that this Doran is an addict?'

'They are. Is that important?'

'Oh yes, very. If it's a crackhead whose brains are on the pavement, the cops tend not to give a fuck.'

This pronouncement jarred like a prod in the eye. But I stayed resolute as he went on, 'Junkies are at it all the time. One guy stiffs another on a deal, or he puts too much rat poison in the mix, next thing you know there's a war on.'

And it was now that my nerve deserted me. With a cough and a squirm and a stammer, I began, 'I'm not sure, y'know, if you need to go quite that far. I know this bloke, and a good fright would probably be enough to see him off.'

He sighed condescendingly. 'Son, take it from one who does know. You can warn an addict, you can frighten him, you can rough him up all you like. But when you're done, he's still an addict, and he's still got a habit to support. Which means he's just as likely as ever to cheat you, rip you off, thieve from you, or in your case, to blackmail you. So if you do have to deal with these people, you do it once, and you do it for keeps. Get that sister of yours on board, and that's precisely how it'll be done. At no cost to you, I need hardly add. This'll be my treat.'

He got to his feet and left by the door he'd entered. I sat there alone, dimly aware that I'd just embarked on the second most ill-judged course of action of my entire life. But I had realistic hopes that, maybe this once, those two wrongs might make everything right.

Towards the end of that week, the small notice appeared in the national press. A date had been set for the murder trial of

Benito Cappocci Jnr. He would be represented by Margaret
Walsh McGee, SC.

In hindsight, my naivety was almost endearing. I genuinely
expected the deed to be done on the very next working day,
and all that Monday I spent on tenterhooks. Tuesday, I
couldn't even eat for tension. By bedtime Wednesday I was
beginning to wonder if it would happen at all. Lights out on
Thursday and I decided that it wouldn't, that Cappocci had
welched on his end of the bargain now he'd got what he
wanted; it did not sound at all beneath him. On Friday,
cursing myself for having dared to hope, I went to the
Heather Blazing a full two hours before either Dasher or
Leaky and got remarkably drunk. When I woke on Saturday,
it was to the distant rumble of heavy machinery at work. In
the two fields by the road that once were mine, the builders
had arrived.

Morbid curiosity drew me to watch in the midafternoon.
It was a desecration, the way the giant claws ripped into the
gentle even sod as the foundations were scooped out, the way
the entire green pasture quickly turned to quagmire under
the wheels of the dumpers, mixers and mucktrucks. The
noise, the fumes, the whole sorry scene piled insult upon
injury. I didn't stay long.

Back in the house, however, my mood was lightened greatly
by a phone call from my sister. Sounding a different woman
entirely this weekend, and with every good reason. First
impressions of the Cappocci brief suggested it was as lost a
cause as she'd predicted. But far from professional damage or
qualms of conscience, all she'd had was some sympathy and
much good-natured ribbing from her colleagues in the Law
Library. More than any of this, though, it gave her great
pleasure to report an awful misunderstanding, a serious

overreaction. That jacket wherein she'd come upon the condoms turned out, on closer inspection, to belong to some complete stranger. Dermot had taken it home from the pub in error. So there she'd been, suspecting him of picking up some young floozie, when all the while he couldn't even pick up the right coat at closing time.

I was regaling Dasher with the saga in the Heather the following Wednesday night when who should ramble in but Furlong. Accompanied by the man who would take his place at the local station house. It was the first time any of us had set eyes on Garda Barron, as the old stager showed the new boy around the turf. However, they very pointedly came nowhere near where Dasher and I were seated. And not wishing to make the situation any more awkward than was necessary, we drank up and moved on to Ned Law's. Dasher then spent the night fretting over whether or not Furlong would tell the new guy all about us. And if he did, what he might be likely to say. I was unable to set my friend's mind at rest on either score.

A full three weeks passed. Everywhere, winter had bitten deep. This night was pelting frost, but I'd earlier built a great fire and since nightfall had been tucked up close by. It was well gone midnight, and that fire was down to the dying embers, but still I was loath to vacate the hearth, even in favour of the bed. Then the phone rang. I thought nothing – nothing at all – and answered the call with a bright, 'Hello.' The voice on the other end was strange and indistinct. Either the line was woefully bad, or the speaker was covering the mouthpiece with maybe a handkerchief.

'Walsh?'

'Speaking.'

'We got him.'

Still nothing registered. 'Sorry?'

'You heard – we got him good.'

Another second of thick black bewilderment, and then the penny dropped sharply. 'Got him good' – inside my head, the words clanged and jangled like the tongue in a bell, while all around me the room – the whole world – swam.

'Hello – you there?'

'Yeah,' I mumbled.

'It went down like a charm – your information was spot on . . . Are you still there, for fuck's sake?'

'Erm . . . yeah.'

'Good. So what about this money?'

'Money?'

'Don't fuck with me, Walsh. I get paid for this, or my next job will be for nothing. If you know what I mean.'

I was not so addled that I didn't now get the strong whiff of a set-up. Either somebody, somewhere, had got his wires crossed, or else I was being walked into a trap.

'Listen, mate,' I said reasonably, 'you've got the wrong Walsh. I haven't an idea what you're talking about, but I know for a fact that I owe no money to you or to anybody else.'

'Oh, I've got the right man,' came the husky reply. 'And Billy boy, I intend collecting what's due to me.'

'Fair enough. How much d'you reckon is due to you?'

'Huh?' And there it was, that instant of fatal, give-away hesitation.

'C'mon – how much?'

'Em . . . fi – three grand.'

'Three grand!' I whooped. 'Good Jesus. What is it you're supposed to have done for that kind of money?'

More hesitation.

'Well – aren't you going to tell me what you want paying for?'

Now it was from the other end of the line that all the confused silence was blaring.

'Look,' I said firmly. 'It's late. Why don't you try that number again, after I hang up.'

'Don't you dare hang up on me, you bastard!' he cried, and as he did, the muffler slipped from the mouthpiece.

'Doran?'

'Walsh, I know fucking well that you had —'

'Doran! In God's name, what d'you want at this hour of the night?'

He hummed and hawed a moment, deciding how he should proceed. Eventually, 'I was attacked tonight.'

'So? Hardly the first time, I dare say.'

'First time there was a gun involved.'

'A gun? You must be moving up in the world!'

'If I was there, Walsh, you wouldn't be half as smart!'

But he wasn't, so I went on boldly, 'Is there some point to this conversation?'

'Well, there may just be. Y'see, I've got to thinking about who would want to see me dead. And for some reason, I keep coming up with your name.'

'No offence, but I'd be amazed if I was the only one.'

'Yeah. That's hilarious. The thing is, when I put it to you just now, you took your time about denying it.'

'How could I deny it, for Christ's sake, I didn't even understand it.'

'I'm not sure I believe you.'

'I'm not sure I care.'

'Oh, you should, Billy. You should care. Cos this close

shave made me realize just how convenient it'd be for you if I was to end up on a slab in Ardkeen. So just before I made this call, I rang my solicitor. He wasn't in the office, naturally, but he did have his answering machine switched on. And, oh boy, what a message he's got waiting for him in the morning. Although strictly speaking it's not for his ears at all. I made it quite clear that it's only to be heard by the police in the event of my passing away in . . . let's say *dubious* circumstances . . . You've gone all quiet, Bill. Not so funny any more, is it?'

He took a short time out to bask, I imagine, and to gloat. And to allow me to appreciate how I'd been outflanked.

'Don't you even want to know what the message says? Now, stop me if you've heard it before, but it's a story about a runaway who didn't get very . . .'

'God damn you, Doran!' I seethed. 'What d'you hope to gain by this?'

'Me? Nothing. I'll be dead, remember.'

'So why, then? As God is my judge, I had nothing to do with what happened tonight. You've got to believe that.'

'But that's the problem, y'see. I don't.'

'Well, what would convince you? There must be something I can do.'

He thought a while. 'You could pray.'

'Pray?'

'For my continued good health. As long as I stay fit and well, you've nothing to worry about. On the other hand . . .'

'Listen, you bastard. I've done nothing to harm you. And I've done nothing to deserve this.'

'So?'

'So it's . . . it's not fair.'

There was a splutter of laughter into the other end. 'Fair? Of course it's not fair. Life isn't meant to be. Billy, Billy, Billy, you must be thirty-five years old. Don't tell me you're only figuring that one out now!'

The line went dead. And I all but followed suit. I fumbled the receiver back on to its cradle, then slumped to the floor like a wet overcoat. For a time – a long time – I was too numb, too shell-shocked to feel even the cold of the tiles beneath me. But as, by degrees, I came round, I knew there was a call that I myself must make. The hour was late, but it wouldn't wait till morning.

'Jesus Christ, what time is it?' came the voice made hoarse by sleep.

'Mr Cappocci, I'm sorry to disturb you, but it's important.'

'It goddam well better be.'

'This is Billy . . .' I hesitated to identify myself fully. 'We spoke in the Capitol a couple of weeks back.'

'Oh? . . . Oh. Yes. Yes indeed. I'm afraid things didn't go well tonight.'

'I know. And that's why —'

'It might've helped,' he interrupted testily, 'if we'd been told that the pub was underneath a pool hall. When our man's machine failed to function, he was faced by some angry people, all of them with cues at the ready. He ended up getting out with his life, but only just.'

'I'm very sorry. But whatever about that . . .'

'Your friend got lucky tonight. But there'll be other nights.'

'That's why I'm calling. I want you to forget all about this. Please . . . please just let it be. Call . . . I don't know who they are, but call them off.'

'You sure? I can guarantee no slip-ups next time.'

'Oh God, I'm sure. The situation's changed all of a sudden.'

'You and what's-his-name have patched things up?'

'No,' I sighed. 'Far from it.'

'He's still . . .?'

'Yeah, he's still doing it.'

'In that case, you'd better be warned. Our man was forced to abandon that job in a bit of a hurry, and he . . . let's just say he left his tools behind him.'

'He left what? What d'you mean? You're not saying that Doran's now got his hand on the gu —'

'It's like I said: be warned.'

Doran's urge to prayer was surely not seriously meant. If only he'd known. Each day after Morning Offering, fifth and sixth classes would join me in reciting a Hail Mary for a privately nominated special intention. That intention now became the long life of a man I hoped would one day die slowly and in great pain. What strange times those were.

Needless to say, Doran's belief that I'd tried to have him shot didn't make him any more frugal as he set about squandering the rest of my money. On the next Visa bill, the bottom line had me scrambling for my calculator to check if the decimal point was in the wrong place. It wasn't – the total was for real. My bank account, even recently bolstered, ran to nothing like such a sum. I had no choice, then, but to realize some assets. Or, as I quickly concluded, all assets. It made no sense to dispose of my land piecemeal, a parcel now and a parcel again. Each notice of mine that appeared in the newspaper involved fresh commission, fresh advertising charges, and fresh tongues a-wagging. Better by far to sell the lot as one lot and have done with it.

A new and amended cover story was now called for. I began studying the property and planning disputes from the local civil court as reported in the regionals. Borrowing a by-law from this case, an objection from that and some boundary judgements from another, I quickly concocted something crude and basic. It still required a bit of work, this new yarn. But I was prepared to gamble that even the first draft would be good enough to hoodwink Martin Houlihan. It was crucial that I get Martin to go quietly. The land was never going to make a fortune, but with a sitting tenant it'd not be worth tuppence. Anyway, running it first by a holy innocent like Martin would be a useful dress rehearsal for higher hurdles to come.

At about five o'clock each evening, he returned to the old van for a sandwich and a thermos of tea. This day, I was lying in wait.

'Going for the break, Martin?'

'Aye – I likes th'oul' cuppa about now.'

'Why don't you come in – I've a pot just made.'

'Oh God no, not at all. I'm grand.'

'Ah, come in outa that. Bring the flask with you, if you don't trust my brew.'

He removed his cap and scratched his head like Stan Laurel used to. 'Are you sure 'tisn't too much trouble?'

'Too much trouble? Will you stop! C'mon.'

He almost wiped the soles off his wellingtons on the grating outside the door, then followed me inside cautiously.

'Sit down anywhere at all,' I said.

He fixed upon a suitable parking spot, but before sitting he brushed as if trying to remove the back pockets from his old blue jeans. When well dusted, he checked the state of his hands. It only added to his already great unease to say, 'Billy, I'm afraid th' oul' paws aren't the cleanest.'

'There's a sink through there,' I said, pointing out the bathroom. Seeing him stooped over the basin, so carefully lathering, so fearful of leaving a splash on the floor or the mirror, I felt nauseated at what I was about to do. Martin was the very last man in the world I would've wished to put to the wall. But my wishes counted for nothing.

'You have the place looking smashing, fair play to you,' he remarked as he now sat himself at table.

I poured the tea and said, 'No better than it should be.' I shoved the milk, sugar and biscuits his way as we both made stabs at conversation.

'How's the missus keeping?' was my opener.

'Ah, sure she's elegant.'

'And all the care.'

'Oh, getting big and brazen.'

'What about the eldest girl?'

'Marie?'

'She's still in Trinity?'

'No – UCD, I think.'

'UCD, of course. What was she doing again?'

'I'm not rightly sure – something to do with science, as far as I know. Her mother would be better able to fill you in about that. The only time she ever talks to me is when she's looking for money.'

And we both got on with sipping our tea as the dustcover of silence fell over us again.

Again, I scrabbled for common ground.

'Will Wexford do the business in Leinster this year?' I ventured, not at all hopefully.

'How d'you mean?'

'I mean, will they be good enough to beat Kilkenny in the championship?'

'I couldn't tell you – don't follow it much.'

'D'you never go to the games, no?'

'An odd one.'

Enough, I decided. It was time. 'Martin, there's something I need to talk to you about.'

'Sure, no problem. But can I say one thing first, before it goes clean out of my head?'

'Eh? What?'

'Well, 'tis the wife's idea, really.'

'What is?'

'Now, I know you've a sister married in Dublin, so I won't be at all offended if you say no. But, you're a single fellow, and Christmas is coming, and I don't know if you've any plans made. If you haven't, we'd be delighted if you'd come and spend it with us.'

I blanked. Talk about having your guns spiked.

'Y'know – in Boolavogue. You could come down the night before, we'd slip out for a few oul' pints, and then you could have the grub the next day. The wife isn't a bad cook at all, when she puts her mind to it.'

If he noticed the horrified look on my face, it didn't halt his spiel. 'Anyway, I'll leave it with you. If you want to come join us, you're more than welcome.'

'I . . . am . . . I don't think so, Martin.'

'Ah, sure why not?'

'You've enough mouths to feed without the likes of me at your table.'

'Will you give over! Sure isn't the more the merrier. As well as that, I'd like to have one other man at the dinner who could eat a blast. Last year, I was getting turkey leftover till damn near Easter.'

'Thanks all the same, but I kinda promised Mags I'd go to Clontarf.'

'Well, I understand that completely. Mind you, the wife'll

be right disappointed. She was looking forward to meeting you, after hearing so much about you. The eldest girl too; she's above there in college, and sure you're not too long out of college yourself. You'd have a lot more to talk about with her than either myself or Eileen. The bit of education is a great thing all the same. To tell the truth, I was kinda looking forward to it myself. I don't know how much Furlong ever told you, but I haven't very many friends around Boolavogue. So . . .' He shaped to go, taking his cap from his knee and fixing it on his head. 'Anyway, I'll say no more. Have a think about it, won't you?'

'Martin.'

'Yeah?'

'Martin, I'm selling the farm.'

At first, he looked at me enquiringly, as if I'd spoken in a foreign language or in a code he couldn't decipher.

He stammered, 'Th – this farm?'

'Yes.'

'You mean another piece of it?'

'I mean all of it. The works.'

'Jesus. When?'

'As soon as I can. Right away, in fact.'

'Fuck me!' He looked away, looked back and 'Fuck me! I know it's none of my business, but . . . why?'

'Martin, I'm so sorry about this. The decision's got nothing to do with you, I've always been happy to have you here – you know that. But it's a long story.'

He sat, unmoved, his expression set. Not exactly challenging me to elaborate, but not prepared to be fobbed off so lightly or with such condescension. So I began, 'This Galway deal. The hotel is coming along nicely. It's a smallish place, so it's been easy keeping inside the budget. Now, at the back of the building there's this old warehouse, completely disused and dilapidated, and we never paid it any mind. Until lately, when we got tipped off that a German was trying to buy it, and turn it into a meat plant. Now, you can imagine what having a slaughterhouse at your back door would do to a hotel's trade? The long and the short of it is, we've had to outbid him and buy it ourselves. And we've decided to go the whole hog and convert it into a proper function hall. It's meant, of course, that the costs have gone flying off the clock. And none of us is pleased about it but – what could we do?'

'What can I do?' he quivered. 'That's a better question. No bank will touch me, and where am I going to lease land without money upfront? This little farm was my life's blood.' The colour drained from his face and he sounded dazed as he continued, 'I've got a family to feed. I've got a daughter to keep in University . . .'

'I know, and I'm gutted about all this. But, Martin, we had to move like we did, or our business just wasn't going to survive.'

'So 'twas either it or me,' he said bitterly. Now he did stand, looked a long while to the ground and then said, 'I'm sorry, I didn't mean that to sound . . . I'm very grateful to you for these past few years, you're a decent man and I know that if there was any way out of this, you'd do right by me.'

How easy it is to go on lying once you've started. How natural, almost, to make cruel and empty promises, to plant seeds of hope in the certain knowledge that none will ever flower.

'Listen, Martin, I wasn't going to tell you this, because I couldn't make it a binding condition of sale. But I asked my solicitor to put a recommendation in the contract that the

276

new owner allow you to hold on to your lease.'

'You did? God, Billy, you didn't have to do that. I mean, you've enough on your plate at the present time without trying to look out for me as well.'

'It was no trouble. I just wanted it noted that you'd been a good tenant, and that in my opinion you should be allowed to continue as before.'

'Well, nobody could say fairer than that. When he told me about this farm first day, Conor Furlong said I'd be dealing with a gentleman. And he was not wrong.'

'Now, Martin, I can't guarantee anything'll come of it.'

'If it doesn't, then it won't be your fault. And we'll not fall out over it.' He extended me his hand, big, broad and calloused.

'That invitation still stands, by the way. Call down to us at Christmas. In fact, any time you're passing through Boolavogue, there'll be a cup of tea for you in the pot.'

Even before he'd closed the door behind him, I could feel the gorge rise in my throat. Seconds later I was kneeling over the toilet, hacking and lurching, but managing only a dry retch. A false alarm.

CHAPTER TWELVE

As arranged the fresh 'For Sale' signs went up soon after. To any locals who asked, I was vague, saying only that complications had arisen in the western deal. This usually discouraged further enquiry. It was with great trepidation that I rang my sister, to inform her that the place where she'd been born and brought up was about to pass from the family. But to my astonishment she took it on board, whole and entire, and with barely a murmur. In no time at all, the subject was closed and we were reminiscing about my recent trip to the capital. Again, she apologized for her foul humour, for the drinking that had helped fuel it, and for the civil war she'd walked me into. Again, I insisted that no apology was necessary, that I'd enjoyed myself thoroughly and would be back early in the new year, if she'd no objections. I asked how she was faring, making ready a defence for Benny Cappocci. As good as could be expected, she told me. Which was to say, a thorough waste of time. The guy hadn't an earthly. And it was on that note I was forced to cut short the call as I heard a vehicle coming cruising into my yard.

I hung up and came to the door. A white car was describing a very brisk, businesslike three-point turn, so brisk that I couldn't tell the occupants till it came to a halt. Then out leapt Conor Furlong. He thundered the door closed behind him, as from the passenger side there emerged a middle-aged woman not known to me. With a couple of strides, Furlong was in my face.

'You are one gutless bastard, Walsh!'

Everything in his demeanour had given warning of just such a broadside. I was ready. 'I see your promotion hasn't improved your manners much.'

'Same as ever – too goddam smart. But you've got nobody fooled this time. So c'mon, out with it, tell us what's going on?'

'Eh? You come tearing like a madman on to private property, you set upon me at my own doorstep – and you're asking *me* what's going on?'

At that, the car's back door opened and as the last passenger joined the fray, a familiar voice called, 'This is none of my doing, Billy.'

Furlong turned fiercely towards Martin Houlihan. 'Stay out of this, I warned you!'

'Leave it so, Martin. Say nothing. Say nothing at all.' The woman was speaking for the first time. Then to me, 'I'm Eileen Houlihan, Martin's wife. Pleased to meet you, Mr Walsh.'

She was low-sized, broad and weatherbeaten, a woman who looked no stranger to hard work or to hard times.

'How d'you do, Mrs Houlihan?' And I held out my hand saying, 'I'm only sorry we had to meet under —'

Furlong stepped forward and slapped sharply down on my forearm. 'Sorry? Are you fuck sorry! If you gave a damn about anyone or anything except yourself, none of this would be happening.'

Without even a hint of a reaction, I went on, 'Mrs Houlihan, it's a pity you decided to bring this let-out with you. I'd like to have the chance to explain . . .'

'Explain? You mean lie, lie and then lie again, you cowardly bag of shit!'

Eileen Houlihan came between the pair of us and said, 'All right, Conor, I'll . . . Mr Walsh, Sergeant Furlong is here as a friend of my family, and he's only trying to do his best for us. I'm sorry if you're . . . upset.'

'Upset? I'm not upset. I'm not even listening. If he was making any sense, it'd be different, but this is easy enough to ignore. No, Mrs Houlihan, as I was saying, I'd like for us all to sit down in a civilized fashion,' and here I shot Furlong a sidelong glance, 'not like escaped lunatics, but like normal human beings. Then I know I could make you see why I had to do what I've done.'

'Martin's already given me a pretty good account of it. You bought into some property, and now you need hard cash or you might lose the lot.'

'That's about the size of it,' I said resignedly.

'Well, we're here today to tell you that if it's a question of money, we can pay more. Double the rent, if we have to – this land is terrible important to us, Mr Walsh. So we're prepared to go up to . . . why don't you say a price and we'll see what we can do?'

She looked at me, imploring and heartbreaking, but with her great simple dignity unscathed.

For one moment, I could feel my resolve show signs of buckling. But how could I about-face now, and in this company?'

'It's not that straightforward, Mrs Houlihan. You don't understand.'

'Not meaning to be pushy or anything, Mr Walsh, but can you try make me understand? You said your problem is money – we're offering you money.'

280

'I know you are, but I need to get my hands on a lump sum immediately.'

'So tell us how much . . . please, Mr Walsh.'

I could bear this no longer. Changing my tone from the conciliatory to the purely informative, I said, 'I need at least thirty grand, up front by the end of the month.'

She paled. 'Th – thirty grand?' she whispered. 'Jay, I didn't realise it was . . .' She shook and shook her head. 'Like, Martin never said . . . Thirty? God, that's a lot of money – a lot more than we could ever afford. Still, I suppose if you have to have it, you have to have it, and there's nothing more to be said.'

'Except maybe this,' Furlong steamed in. 'That there is no money needed to rescue a property development out west. Because there is no property development out west. Well, none that you've any interest in – is there, Mr Walsh?'

I smiled, cold and amused.

'But he does need the money, that part's true. For what? That's a different story.'

'And a good one, I'm sure,' I mocked. 'But right now, I don't have the time.'

'Maybe not right now, but before long you'll have plenty of time, mate. You'll have all the time the judge gives you.'

I forced myself into a long, loud guffaw, and, 'I must say, I'm tempted – it all sounds absolutely fascinating. But if you'll excuse me . . .'

'Oh, consider yourself excused. After all, you know this tale inside out. But these two poor people have never heard it. It all begins way back in 1982. Billy was only a youngster then, and I suppose one day he'll plead that he didn't know any better.'

Mr and Mrs Houlihan were now regarding me with some curiosity.

'This is bullshit . . .'

'Nah, Bill, it's the old hotel that's bullshit. The truth is that, way back then, in '82, there was a colleen named Suzy Deane who lived not far from here. Until one night, when she just vanished off the face of the earth. She was killed, obviously, and her body was very cleverly hidden. Billy was involved. So was his friend. Y'know Dasher Morrissey, he lives near the railway gates? – him. There may have been others, I only know for sure about those two. Unfortunately for the lads, I'm not the only one who knows. There's a drug addict in Waterford city; Doran is his name. He's got the full low-down. And he's been blackmailing the boys ever since. He's given up on Dasher – with all those kids, that man has scarcely enough to eat. But good old Billy here has been a real cash cow for him. Although not for much longer, eh, Bill? I mean, once the last of the land is gone, there's not a lot of blood left for him to suck, is there? And what'll happen then, I wonder. Don't tell me it hasn't crossed your mind too.'

How my expression must've changed with each of Furlong's direct hits I'm not sure, but I fancy that my cool amusement was well wiped. Still, I was not about to be bested, not here, not now, and not in front of witnesses. So I affected a look of concern, of sympathy. Like it saddened me how this delirium had taken hold.

'Conor, we were friends once. And it's in the spirit of . . . well, friendship, I guess, that I'm saying this to you now. You've been on this hobby-horse as long as I've known you. Can't you see that in all that time it's got you nowhere? It's got no legs, Conor. It won't run, it won't walk, it won't even fucking crawl.'

'Well, let me say this back to you – *friend*. You will crawl. To me, before this whole business is over.'

'The day I have to crawl to the likes of you, Conor, will be one bad day for me.'

'Expect more than one, Billy. There's several in store for you, I promise. In fact, I give you my word of honour. D'you remember honour, yeah?'

And so the 'For Sale' stayed in place. Though not for long. The land may have been poor, craggy and remote, but land is land and there's only so much of it to go round. The asking price was being met within days, whereupon the bidding started among the interested parties. In the end, it went for thirty-three and a half thousand. I would've liked to keep this information to myself, but the buyer was a local man, Milo Irish. Milo was known to be a bit of a card, which is the polite way of saying that he turned into the most insufferable loudmouth when he had drink taken. Soon, everyone in South Kilkenny knew to the last penny what had been paid for Murt Walsh's old place. Everyone in South Kilkenny, and one or two beyond.

Christmas came. I spent it alone. It was pretty joyless, though I don't imagine the dinner I'd passed up in Boolavogue was any more festive. But worse than being on my own was the cloud that now filled the sky above my head, the one Furlong had so gleefully pointed out with his final taunt; namely, what was to happen when the well ran dry this time. In terms of the bank account Doran and I effectively shared, this was the last lap. Once this haul was spent, I'd nothing left to flog. And my salary would never support two adults and a lively heroin habit. For better or worse, the end of the road was not far off. What lay there, I honestly could not say. Nor could I take too much time agonizing over it, as I had other, more pressing matters to attend to. Like how to explain to my nearest and dearest that I'd managed to dispose of almost fifty thousand pounds, with absolutely nothing to show for it.

As if to forebode great trouble on the near horizon, that dream returned again. Even in the deepest sleep, there was a judder of unease as I found myself again outside my front gate, waiting among friends I didn't know for the arrival of my grandmother. From that point, it was raw, mounting panic till I eventually removed *Calculus* from the library shelf, only to expose Suzy's mutilated head. I never did get to learn what happened next, as it was now I roared myself awake and bolt upright. With the lather of my sweat already turning cold, with every shadow in the room twitching, with the clock glowing red at three fourteen. And with sleep a distant stranger for the rest of that night.

The new year ticked by, work progressed agreeably enough, my money continued its haemorrhage, and as it did, the day of reckoning edged closer. I'd long given up on all notions of rescuing myself; I merely prayed in a vague sort of way. For what, I don't know. I didn't even know back then. Remembering the booby trap Doran had set in the event of his death, I could see that it'd take a miraculous amount of God's grace to turn this around. However, the power of prayer should never be underestimated. Out of nowhere, a small slice of luck came my way.

I was sat in Ned Law's one afternoon. All alone, with just the newspaper and the occasional company of Ned himself. There'd been an important race meeting on the same day and, returning from Gowran Park track, the Bolands came barreling in. They were rednecks-made-good from over Knockowen way, and it was clear they'd enjoyed a profitable day against the bookies. The tallest of them called loudly and roughly for drinks all round. And then added, 'Sure, give a pint to Basil Fawlty while you're at it.'

I looked up.

'You'll have a pint with us. From what I hear, you need all the charity you can get.'

This type of boorishness was perfectly typical of him and all belonging to him, so I took no offence. I did ask, 'Why? What did you you hear?'

'Ah,' he leered, 'people are saying that your hotel deal is dead.'

'Are they really. And what are they saying killed it?'

'Now,' and he smiled round on each of his brothers, 'I'm only telling you what the dogs in the street are barking. That your accountant split and took all your money with him.'

I reeled on my stool. This was more preposterous even than the yarn I'd been peddling.

'Yeah,' chimed in another, this one short and jowly. 'I believe he took off with a twenty-year-old blonde. And she wasn't the only one to get a good screwing.'

At this, the walls of the little alehouse rang with laughter. I was about to laugh with them when some instinct made me hold off. And realize that an open goal had been handed to me, ribbon-tied.

'So anyway,' crackled the tall one again, 'is it true or what?'

Setting my face like thunder, I snatched up my newspaper and stormed towards the door, pushing through the assembled Bolands as I went.

'You know what you can do with your pint,' I spat as I passed.

All round me there were intakes of breath, winks, nudges, and one audible, 'I told you, didn't I?'

And so it was sorted. I could confidently predict that I'd

never again need to account publicly for those missing thousands. Not in Lisdrolin, at any rate.

In jigtime, this nonsense was all over town. Where it originated, I don't suppose I'll ever discover. But it wouldn't have been the first time that, in the absence of any genuine information, somebody improvised. Nor the first time that people chose to believe – and to pass on – what was juicy in preference to what was likely. But wherever it sprang from, it was soon common currency. And cast-iron confirmed by my failure to deny it when given the chance. Not that anybody ever again mentioned it to me; quite the opposite, in fact. Where once it was chucked into the most casual conversation, it was now skirted in detours that were often gauche and embarrassing. Even those close to me, like Dasher and Leaky, said nothing, not wanting to touch what they thought must be a very raw nerve. All things considered, the rumour mill proved mightily effective, creating so much smoke no one could see that there never was any fire.

But it was a meagre respite. Fundamentally, nothing at all had changed. My small fortune was rapidly coming down to size, as each week that passed saw the cupboard that much barer. Spring turned to early summer with the balance dipping into just four figures. June beamed in, the month of the sports day, the school tour, the long, long holidays, and the bank statement advising me that my financial reserves now amounted to three hundred and thirty-three pounds and change. The game was just about up. And I figured I may as well call time today as the next day. With immediate effect, I cancelled the credit card.

If the effect was immediate, then it was a safe bet that the response too would be prompt. Somehow, despite all he'd said, I didn't believe he'd run to the law. At least not right away. It was not in Rodger Duran's nature to look for a policeman as a first resort. If he did, he'd need to do better than just drop hints like before; he'd need to name a name. And if he did that, of course, the golden goose was dead meat. That would be in nobody's interest, least of all his. So I readied myself for early contact. Early and direct.

If I had gauged things correctly, then for once both the timing and the location were in my favour. The school was closed, and would remain so for two whole months. Unless he was prepared to wait this length, he'd be forced to come and confront me where I lived. Home advantage at last.

So when he did make his appearance, it was almost a relief. Though on that midsummer's evening, I wasn't granted much time to be relieved. No sooner had the rust-red top gone flitting past my window than the front door began rattling as if in the teeth of a gale. Seconds out.

'There's no use trying to hide, you bastard,' came the cry from the yard. Followed by a thud as he went charging against the door. With the door coming off a clear winner.

'Open the fucking thing or I'll kick it down!' he roared. But I saw little danger of that; he was making plenty of noise, but no real impression. So only when I was satisfied that my old hurley stick was out of sight but within easy reach did I put a hand near the latch.

'I fucking know you're in there, cunt!' He sounded winded, dispirited, and the accompanying assault was feeble. I breathed deeply and opened up.

'Yeah, I'm here. What d'you want?'

Doran looked shocking. He'd lost, I'd say, one-third of his body weight, so that his grimy, rumpled clothing flapped and billowed in the easy breeze. His hair was wild and tangled, like a burst mattress, while the devilish eyes of old were bloodshot and unfocused. His skin was grey, blotched here by a carbuncle, there by a running sore. The lips, too, were cracked, and rimmed by old, dried blood. What teeth he retained were rotted to black flattened stumps; his breath reeked like carrion.

'I spent all day yesterday, Walsh, trying to decide whether to turn you in, or just break your fucking neck and have done with it. So, pal, you've got about thirty seconds to explain to me what's gone wrong. And thirty seconds more to put it right again.'

'Sorry, Rodger. No can do.'

'What?' He almost laughed.

'It's over. Finished. The money's gone, and this time there's no more where that came from.'

He gave me a sympathetic little smile. 'Billy, Billy, Billy poor man. What do you mean?'

'I mean, Rodger, that you're not getting another cent off me, cos I don't have another cent to give.'

'Walsh, you're talking now as if I don't fucking exist. As if, all of a sudden, you're running this show.'

'Show's over, Rodger. The land is sold, the money's gone, there's nothing else. You've left me with barely a roof over my head.'

He swayed a little, looked blearily round and mumbled, 'The roof over your head.' Then, having scanned and surveyed it thoroughly, he announced, 'It's too big.'

'What? What is?'

'The roof. The house. Too big for one person. You've gotta sell it.'

'And live where?'

'I dunno. A flat in town, maybe. It's good enough for me, so I'm fucked if it isn't good enough for you.'

It was the arrogance, the casual contempt that did it. That, after all this time on the brink, finally pushed his luck too far. It had been so long since I'd lost my temper that I had no idea what blind rage might provoke in me. And with Doran so close, so weakened and so asking for it, I feared for the consequences. Through gritted teeth I growled, 'Get off my property and don't come back.'

He raised an eyebrow, as if watching a mouse attempting to bark. Then, 'Billy I don't think you understand what you're saying!'

Away went the last restraint. I lunged for him, took him by the throat, whirled him round and slammed him against the doorpost.

'Get out of my yard before I boot you from here to the fucking village!'

The look of agony drooped, he went perfectly limp in my hands and for a moment, I did think I'd killed him. But the prospect mellowed me not a whit. My hands were still tight around his windpipe when the rancid breath again issued and some small semblance of life returned.

'OK, OK,' he urged. 'Let go, for fuck's sake.'

I pushed him from me and towards the front gate. He shrugged, straightened his collar and took another step away.

'Oh, you'll pay for that,' he drawled. 'Christ, Walsh, will you ever! You can act as big as you like. And you can kid yourself that you've put me in my place. But I'd advise you to think hard about your situation.'

'I've thought about it all I'm going to. And it's like I said – not another red cent.'

'One week, Billy,' he announced. 'Just one week. Then I go to the police.'

I turned back into the hallway and from the low table

picked up the phone set. The cable just stretched to allow me to thrust the thing into his midriff. 'Go ahead,' I said. 'Do it now.'

'W – what?'

'Do it. Why wait a week. Call them now.'

He squirmed and jiggled some, then puffed his chest and, 'You think I won't? I'll fucking show you!'

'Yeah – you show me. Nine nine nine should do it, but I've got the number of the local barracks written down somewhere inside. That might be quicker.'

He was breathing hard. And looking more disorientated as the encounter went on. Placing this call made no sense, but if his mental state was anything like his physical, then nothing did. Slowly, clumsily, he lifted the receiver and with the index finger of the same hand, found nine on the keypad.

'Bluffing, am I? You just watch this!'

In a twinkling, he'd pressed the nine key three times and put the phone to his ear. 'Now who's fucking bluffing, eh?'

It was like he'd doused me in petrol and had just struck a match, as a tiny voice crackled in his earpiece, demanding which service he required. He bared his mouthful of teeth, broken and discoloured, and wheezed, 'C'mon, Billy boy. Talk to me. But make it quick.'

'Your call, Rodger. I've told you where I stand.'

He shaped to speak. The operator grew more insistent. Doran began, 'I'd like . . .' but pulled up short. Slowly, drowsily, he lowered the receiver till it rested against his chest. His eyes slitted in one last attempt to refocus, to think straight, and he took another broad look all about him. Then, with a sway and slight swagger, he handed me the phone – both parts separate – and said, 'OK.'

'OK?' I cried. 'OK, what?'

'OK. OK. If you say there's nothing left, then maybe there isn't.'

'So . . . so . . .' I could barely compose the question. 'Does this mean we're finished, you and me?'

He considered a while before, very matter of factly, saying, 'I guess. Though you never know. This world's a funny place.'

And with that, he turned his back on me and began to walk away. I stood like someone who'd narrowly avoided being hit by a train, and watched him go shambling out the gate and along the boreen that lead to the public road. But as gradually my stupor receded, it occurred to me that there was something unresolved. I took off at a gallop and caught him before the end of the lane.

'One more thing. What about the tape?'

'The tape?'

'The one you made for the solicitor.'

His expression was blank and seemingly genuine.

'You made a tape for your solicitor to be handed to the cops if ever anything —'

'Ah, get real,' he said contemptuously. 'Do I look like someone who's got a solicitor, for fuck's sake? Jesus, Walsh, what a bozo you are. What a sad fucking sap. Where will I find as soft a touch again! Here's a good one – someone once tried to have me shot, and I actually thought it was you.'

'Here's a better one, Rodger. It actually was.'

I left him to ponder this, to believe it or not, and I returned home well satisfied with my afternoon's work.

In my little corner of the world, the sun rose again. Everything around me suddenly looked different, more vivid, more immediate, more reassuring. Of course it would've been nice if I actually owned any of what was all around me. But mourning past glories would get me nowhere. I had a life to get on with.

Before the month was out, that life took a sizeable turn for the better. It came on the back of another man's misfortune, and not at all how I would've wished it, but them's the breaks. Ciaran Croker, the school principal, my old mentor of many year's standing, suffered a massive heart attack. He'd survived, but only just. And the duties, cares and stresses that went with his old position were not deemed conducive to good cardiac health. For that reason, he'd been forced into retirement. I was his vice-principal. The school board had its reservations, but the top job was mine if I felt up to it. I did not need asking a second time.

Principal elect of Lisdrolin BNS. And even before I could convey my good tidings to Dublin, there came better news in the opposite direction. Dermot McGee called to say that his wife, my sister, was with child, due some time around the turn of the year. I extended my warmest congratulations and we exchanged some general observations on the nature of parenthood. However, he hung up without inviting me to stand for the child as godfather. He had no family that I knew of, Mags had only myself, so it was clearly an oversight. But a damn inconvenient one, as it meant that I couldn't contact my sister without appearing to be touting for the gig.

While I waited for that call to come, there were some odds and ends to hand that needed attention. The front door, for one, was due – overdue – a lick of paint. It still bore scars from Doran's assault, and now that I knew I'd be keeping hold of the old place, it was OK to be houseproud again. I put Mags' glaring omission down to the fact that the Cappocci case had just come to court. For weeks the country looked on as he was tried, found guilty and given a

mandatory – and deserved – life sentence. Leave to appeal
was denied, the brouhaha gradually subsided and my sister
returned to a life away from the front pages. And still I'd not
heard from Dublin. The rest of the summer idled by.
September came, and down in the Boys' National School I
eased myself into the boss's chair. My first decision of any
note was to close the school for a Monday of public rejoicing;
Lisdrolin had beaten Goresbridge to claim the county junior
title for the first time in our history. Leaky and I followed the
cup as it did circuits of the pubs in the weeks that followed –
many's the sore head was incurred on its account. And still
there was no communication with my sister.

The more late summer turned to early winter, the more
the situation galled. They surely intended having the child
christened; for that, a godfather was traditional. So why had
I not been asked? Come to that, why had I not been told the
news by Mags herself? I had to hear it from Dermot, a man
I barely knew and liked even less. As the long evenings drew
in, allowing me more and more spare hours in which to sulk
and brook, the resentment festered. This was no accident or
oversight, this was a very deliberate snub. Trouble was, I had
no idea what I'd done to earn so cold a shoulder. But I meant
to find out. So with my pride deep in my pocket, I made the
first move. I rang her.

'Oh. Howya?' she said flatly, as if she could take this or just
as easily leave it.

'Fine,' I replied. 'You?'

'OK.' I waited for some elaboration; none was
forthcoming.

'Well, I just said I'd check in with you. And congratulate
you, of course. It's great news.'

'Yeah.'

'I . . . em . . . thought you might have called me when you found out.'

'I did.'

'Your husband did.'

'We had so many people to tell that we divided up the phone list.'

This was bullshit. No matter how such a list was divided, my name simply *had* to be on her roster. But I let it pass.

'So when're you due?'

'Not for a while.'

'R – right. And you're keeping well?'

'I just said that. Now, I've got things to do here. So, was there something else?'

'No . . . no. Just to say again, well done, and I'll be seeing you sometime between now and the big day. If not, I'll definitely go to Dublin when the baby arrives, please God.'

'If you like.'

'And sure it won't be long till you're taking junior with you down here to Lisdrolin.'

'And why would I do that?'

'I beg your pardon?'

'Why in God's name would I ever again want to go anywhere near that place? What would the point be, exactly?'

'The point?' I said tentatively. 'I dunno . . . maybe someday your child might like to see where you grew up. Where you played when you were just a little girl yourself.'

'Except I can't do that, can I? Not without traipsing and trespassing all over some stranger's land.'

Suddenly, everything was clear. The crime she held me guilty of. The poison in her tone. And the reason she'd shunned me all these months. She went on, 'Y'know, maybe

I should take a spin home. And sometime soon, what's more. I'd like a last look at the house I was reared in – before you cash that in too.'

'I won't be selling this house, Mags. And that's a promise.'

'Wow! So what d'you want – applause?'

I wasn't going to fall out with her. But I wasn't going to keep on turning the other cheek either. If this line of dialogue continued much longer, things would be said on both sides that we'd live to regret. So I bit my lip.

'I can see I've called at a bad time. You're obviously not yourself.'

'Not myself?' she shrieked. 'How dare you! How dare you condescend to me like that. Not myself! And what d'you suppose is the matter? Some . . . woman's thing? Morning sickness, perhaps? Let me tell you, the only thing turning my stomach right now is this conversation.'

'Now you just hold on one minute . . .'

'Oh go to hell!'

She didn't just replace the receiver, she clattered it back down on to its cradle with what force she had. My handset now buzzed like the flatline of a life-support machine. I waited till the proper tone was restored, then I stabbed at the redial button. Like it or not, she'd hear me out.

'Hello?' It was Dermot.

'Put her on.'

'D'you mind if I say —'

'Just put her the fuck on!'

On she came. Before she could draw breath, I was off. 'You think I wanted to sell the farm, do you? You reckon it was something I enjoyed doing?'

Typically, all her guns were still blazing. 'Don't tell me, let me guess; it hurt you more than it did anyone else? Well, if it's sympathy you're after, you've dialled the wrong number.'

'Oh, I wasn't expecting sympathy. To sympathize, you'd first have to understand. Fat chance of that where you're concerned.'

'Really? And why would I not understand?'

''Cos you've been gone too long – too many years since you washed your hands of myself and riffraff like me. You're gentry now, the regular lady of the manor, behind your security gates and CCTV, with more fucking money than God.'

'Woah! So it's my fault now, is it? You sold off the family farm as soon as you got your greedy hands on it, you trousered the money, and all because I've done pretty well for myself?'

'That's not what I'm saying.'

'Well, what the hell are you saying?'

'I'm saying that with your pampered, privileged existence, you've forgotten how the other half lives. You earn more dosh in one afternoon than Joe Soap can expect in six months, and more power to you. I know of very few people who have it as good. But I know thousands who'd kill for what you've got.'

'And?'

'And with the likes of myself, hard work alone was never going to get me there. So when the chance came my way, I confess – I took a gamble. Oh, I knew the score. If all went well, I'd be laughing. If not, it'd cost me my shirt.'

'Wait,' she demanded, her dander rising. 'Wait one minute. Where's this leading? Not to the hotel in Galway, surely? You're not still banging that old drum?'

'Y'see,' I said, resignedly, 'you say you want to understand, but when I try to explain, you just . . .'

'Billy – enough! I've given up the booze, I'm almost off the fags, I try to eat healthy and I'm cutting back on the workload. This little life inside me is very fragile. So I'm damned if I'll risk having it contaminated by you and these lies of yours that are as pathetic as they are despicable.'

She spoke with iron certainty. She *knew*.

'What's wrong, Bill? Got nothing to say for yourself?'

'N – no,' I muttered after considerable effort. 'I'm . . . confused.'

'Ha! Well, I'm afraid your confusion goes back longer than you think. Did you not realize that a property deal like the one you fabricated would involve not one but several solicitors? I work hand in glove with solicitors all the time. If that transaction was taking place, I'd know. If it was taking place and involved a brother of mine, I'd know before he did.'

I was rumbled. And speechless.

'I've been on to you from day one, almost. I wanted to look out for you, to make sure that this investment was sound and that you weren't being sold a pup. So, on the quiet, I spoke to a few people out west. And discovered that you weren't actually being sold anything at all. That there wasn't a single grain of truth in your entire story. It came as a bit of a shocker, let me tell you.'

'Why did you never challenge me about it?'

'I dunno. I was curious, I admit. I wondered what the truth might be. And why you were so anxious to keep it hidden. But in the end I decided that if you didn't want to tell, that was your business. We're all entitled to our dark side.'

Tension crackled and swelled in the silence that followed. It was she who blinked first.

'So where did all the money go?'

'It's like you just said – I am anxious to keep that to myself.'

'Ah c'mon, will ya!' she chided. 'Lighten up, eh? Everything is gone, for Christ's sake. What've you got to lose?'

'That's another thing I'll be keeping to myself, if you don't mind.'

It was as if she'd not heard me.

'Let's see, then. Fifty grand. Back to zero. Nothing left. And nothing to show for it. Well, you're not into the horses. You don't do drugs. George Best couldn't have drunk that much and survived. And if you'd blown it on the kind of prostitutes they've got around Waterford . . .'

'Listen, I've already told you; you're wasting your time. I'm saying nothing.'

'Yeah, yeah, yeah. But I'm a pregnant woman, OK? A wee bit deranged, not at all my logical self. So humour me while I think out loud for a bit. Right, then – could you be paying child support? Possibly – but you'd never be paying that much. However, there may be a woman involved. Is there, Billy? A new girlfriend with very expensive tastes? . . . Nah, I didn't think so – you'd have mentioned her. Which leaves us with . . . nothing much. Nothing, except . . . except what? Except what?'

'Mags, didn't I hear you say earlier that you had things to do? May I suggest that you go do them, and stop playing . . .'

'Except blackmail.'

My heart stopped. For a long, long moment it stopped, before restarting with a heavy thud that she couldn't *not* hear.

'Blackmail? Good God, that's it, isn't it? Now, no more fibs, Billy. Tell me the truth or tell me nothing at all.'

I sat there, paralyzed, telling her nothing at all. 'Oh stop it, will you!' she exploded. 'The time for this fuckacting is well past. You need to put your cards on the table, and quickly.

Cos if you don't, I guarantee that one day you'll be hiring me or someone like me. Someone who'll have a job keeping you out of prison.'

In as much as I could see straight, I could see she was right. And I began to consider how best to word a clean breast of things. But while I did, I could not get over how inspired her final shot in the dark had been. She'd run right out of options; then this incredibly lucky guess. Unless luck had nothing at all to do with it.

'Have you been speaking with Conor Furlong?'

'Who?'

'Conor Furlong. Have you spoken to him?'

'And who might Conor Furlong be?'

'He's a policeman.'

'I may well have. I speak to cops all the time.'

'He was stationed here for years.'

'In Lisdrolin? Garda Furlong? No, doesn't sound familiar.'

'But did you speak to him?'

The phoneline was good. I could hear her stall, then struggle for breath just a little.

'Same rules for you, Mags. No fibs.'

'He . . . am . . . called a few months back, yeah.'

'Bastard! Fucking sneaky bastard. He wasn't able for me, face to face, so he went snivelling behind my back.'

'Billy, he's only trying —'

'He's only trying to further his own career, that's all. He's slithering up the greasy pole. If you can help, he'll crawl into bed with you, if not he'll put the knife between your ribs, no better man. I'll give him this, though; he knew just where to turn to find a like mind.'

'And what's that supposed to mean?'

'It means that when he ran yelping to you with his . . . lies and delusions, you took his word for it without question. You didn't even have the courtesy to hear my side; you just broke off all contact, there and then.'

'Excuse me – delusions? Lies? So far, everything he's told me has proved right on the mark.'

''Yeah? Well, for your information, I didn't kill Suzy. It wasn't me.'

After a delay there came a second crack of cannonfire along the line. But now the receiver had not been thrust down. It had been dropped.

'Mags?'

'Suzy Deane . . . was *killed?*'

'Did Furlong not . . .?'

'No. He said you'd been up to something shady and . . . Billy, you were involved, somehow, in the murder?'

'Involved in trying to prevent it, that's all. I swear, I didn't kill her.'

'But you know who did?'

'Yeah, I know who did.'

'So why did you not go to the cops?'

'It wasn't that simple.'

'Not that simple? For God's sake, what could be more simple than putting the person who murdered our neighbour's child behind bars?'

'I was . . . protecting someone.'

'You were protecting yourself!'

'Typical you! Take anybody's side except mine. You know nothing about this, and already your mind's made up that I'm in the wrong.'

'So convince me that you're in the right. Tell me who you're supposed to have protected?'

'I can't give up that name.'

300

'Of course you can't, because there's no name to give up. I remember you and Suzy – you'd have turned in your own mother sooner than see a hair on that girl's head harmed. There was not a person in this world . . . unless Dasher Morrissey. Dasher Morrissey?'

'Dasher didn't kill her.'

'I know he didn't. Because you did.'

'No.'

'You're a liar, Billy. It must've been you, or you'd not have kept quiet all these years. You'd have told what you know, you'd have allowed Suzy a decent Christian burial, you'd have let Joe and Rita mourn . . .'

'Just a minute there, Miss High and Mighty. Now *you* know that I was there, that I was involved – I've just confessed to you. Will you be going to the police to pass this information on?'

'Don't you tempt me.'

'You won't open your mouth, Mags. Because for all your sanctimonious, craw-thumping shit, you're no different than I am.'

'Don't tempt me, I'm warning you. And don't ring here any more. I'm having this number changed, just in case you try.'

'Let me save you a job. Hold on to your precious number. I won't be using it again. You have my word on that.'

CHAPTER THIRTEEN

I had long been dreaming of a life free of complication and intrigue. I certainly had that now. No longer bedevilled by any property to speak of, my days as a landlord were done. Doran had quit the scene, gone, it seemed, without a trace. While my sister, the last person alive I could call family, was a stranger, and very likely to remain one. Now that the storm had passed and the dust settled, I was left with next to no one and next to nothing. Every day it pained, some worse than others. I still had my work, of course, my new and exalted position to grow into. But even that transition came a little too easy, with no awful grinding of gears or upheaval. There was the odd parent who came looking for a fight, the odd inspector to be appeased, and the small band of young blackguards who regularly needed their knuckles rapped. Otherwise, it was all pretty grey. Funding was the great preoccupation; by and large, I saw to it that we stayed comfortably in the black. In fact, it provoked comment locally, that I could be so astute with school finances when I'd made such a terrible hash of my own.

On the social side, things were equally stagnant. There was no woman in my life, I could scarcely remember the last time there had been. Even my merry men of old were a spent and depleted lot nowadays. Seamus Gunning's marriage still held firm, and he'd not been seen on a lads' night out in years.

Kevin Wrafter hadn't ventured home from England in even longer. Furlong was a memory, and not an especially pleasant one either. Leaky was Leaky, still the loudest, the most boisterous of the bunch. Still the first to try his luck whenever fresh talent rambled into town, though in this last endeavour he was hampered by a bald patch that was spreading like ringworm. But whatever his hairline might've suggested, he was no closer to maturity now than the day when first he'd shaved himself. To be honest, I'd well outgrown him, and common interest was becoming harder and harder to find. He saw nothing at all wrong, or pathetic, about chasing girls not much older than the shirt he was wearing. And when I failed to join in the pursuit, he'd chide me for being 'as dry as shite', or having 'no craic at all in me.' We still drank the occasional pint together, but mainly for old times' sake.

Which, of the old brigade, just left Dasher. Dasher by that time had about the saddest, sorriest excuse for a life that I knew of. He morphed into, not so much the typical Irish father, as the typical Irish mother. He didn't socialize. He didn't visit me, nor I him. I dreaded even running into him in the street, as his world had shrivelled to exclude all bar his wife and kids. So every time he loomed into view, my heart sank, while I readied myself for another long and thorough grilling. There'd be queries on reading schemes, standardized testing, social development, staysafe programmes and other aspects of school life that I was unfamiliar with as yet. Invariably, I'd walk away after the encounter with my head spinning but my soul thanking the Lord that it was Dasher and not me. After all, there was a time when we were not that dissimilar.

And so I'd reached my mid-thirties in a curiously ironic fix; my locally high profile put me on nodding terms with everybody, but I scarcely had a friend to my name. Then shortly before that Easter, I put a toe back in the water when I began seeing a girl named Colleen Leigh. She was a set designer with the Red Kettle, a highly regarded theatre company based in Waterford city, and she'd visited the school to plug their children's production of *The Salmon of Knowledge.* I can still see her sitting cross-legged on the table, with the loose gypsy dress, the pretty smile framed in corn-coloured wringlets, and the earrings as big as CDs that swayed as she fielded the questions that came her way. I do remember idly wondering what she must be like in the scratcher, but never expecting to get beyond the wondering stage. After she'd delivered her spiel, we got to talking, and she asked if I'd be taking my own kids to see the show. This was unlikely, I told her, as I'd stayed single. When she replied, 'Good God – how have *you* managed that?' the impact sent the bolt rocketing along the beam to loudly ring the bell up top. I asked her out. It just went from there.

There was no breathless, dizzy romance; it was never like that. But we were comfortable together, at perfect ease in each other's company, and a well-made match all told. We were also of a similar age, give or take, and both seemed happy to settle for what we'd got. Before too long we were a couple, established and accepted. She spent more time in Lisdrolin than she did in her Waterford bedsit, and was soon putting her artistic bent to good use, refurbishing a couple of my bedrooms that were long in need of a makeover. Once a week, we'd call on her clan – a mother and two brothers – at their home in Poleberry. Occasionally, she'd broach my own family, and ask why she'd not yet met my 'famous sister.' Or been to see her new baby (like the rest of the country, I had to learn from the newspaper how I'd become an uncle to a little boy, Garvin). Every time, I'd explain that it was no big thing, that my sister and I had simply grown apart, nothing more dramatic. That this was how life worked out sometimes.

We were together for, I think eight months. Rarely did my life go by on such an even keel, rarely did I feel so rooted, so stable. But ever since one August night of my eighteenth year, these periods of stability were mere hiccups, brief interludes to the mayhem. My dalliance with Miss Leigh was fated no better.

It was Friday 14 May. Leo McCabe, a recent addition to the staff, had been in town that morning keeping a dental appointment. It was something routine so I expected him back around midday, in time for the afternoon session. Twelve o'clock break duly arrived, but not McCabe. When the bell rang thirty minutes later to call the children back to classes, there was still no sign. From my own window I had a good view of the main road outside, and it was there I kept half an eye for most of that afternoon. But as the minutes ticked past one thirty, nearing two, I gave up on him. We finished at three, so an appearance at this hour was scarcely worth his while. With the result that, when his car did swing through the front gate, it was the children who saw it first.

We watched as he leapt from the driver's door, then sprinted to the building and through to my room. Before I could even ask what had delayed him, he'd grabbed the radio-cassette player – the school's one and only – and was already fiddling with the dial.

'It's gone berserk in there,' he wheezed. 'Like something from *Bonnie and Clyde*. WLR . . . WLR . . . WLR, where are you?'

WLR – Waterford Local Radio – was generally a fairly harmless mix of news and chart music. So when McCabe settled the tuning needle and stood back, I first assumed that he'd mistakenly stumbled upon the frequency at which the police communicate. Nothing but sirens, static, blind panic and a man's voice cautioning those present to, 'Keep back, keep back.' I looked to McCabe and said, 'What the . . .', but he shushed me with an open palm.

'So, as the ambulance moves away, bound for Ardkeen hospital,' came the radio commentator, 'the latest we have on the attempted raid at the Ulster Bank is as follows. One of the two raiders shot and wounded, possibly critically. The second arrested at the scene and in police custody. One handgun recovered. Initial reports suggest that a member of the Gardaí sustained gunshot wounds, though that injury is not thought to be life-threatening.' And with that, he handed back in the ongoing chaos. I switched off the radio.

'You weren't caught up in it, were you?'

'No. I was getting the car from beside the cathedral when it all started.'

'And what was the first thing you heard?'

'A voice through a loudhailer. I thought it was some bloke canvassing for votes, so I paid it no heed. But then the shots started.'

'What did they sound like, sir?' asked one lad.

'Pretty tame, actually. Like a capgun being fired.'

'Were there many shots, sir?' asked another.

'A good few, but it all seemed to happen fairly quickly. By the time I got there, one robber was down, the cop was struck, and the second bad guy had given himself up.'

I said, 'And that guy who was hit – what kind of shape is he in?'

'Not good. I didn't see, but people who did said that he was shot in the head, and that there was blood everywhere.'

My crew that year were far from squeamish. But this, the image of a hoodlum dying on the pavement not four miles from where they sat, had a very sobering effect. Leo, noting the lull in questions and sensing his chance, got to his feet.

'Well, that's enough excitement for one day, I guess. Time I went and did some work.'

'You've really livened up a dull Friday,' I said aloud. 'We must send you into town more often.'

The children laughed nervously, still not quite on terms with it all. When McCabe had left the room, we had a long discussion about robberies, and the safeguards banks were employing nowadays in their fight against crime. I then distributed sheets of A4 paper and had them design the front page of the *Munster Express* and imagine how it might report the day's events, complete with banner headline and appropriate photographs. They took to the task with a will – for once, the final bell seemed to come too early.

But come it did. The building was cleared of pupils and staff, I'd locked up for the weekend and was almost homebound when, from inside, I heard the faint ringing of the phone. I was tempted to let it ring. But after quietly cursing the inconvenience, I opened up again, took the receiver and identified myself.

The caller needed no identification. And though a long stand-off and good deal of ill will stood between us, he came straight to the point.

'You're aware of what's just gone on in Waterford?'

'The bank robbery?'

'Attempted robbery. Have you heard the latest?'

'Yer man's dead, yeah?'

'He was killed outright. But he isn't the one you should be concerned with.'

'No?'

'His accomplice – the guy who was arrested – it was Doran.'

If Conor Furlong had somehow managed to get his fist down the phoneline and club me between the eyes, the impact could not have been greater. Still, I had to try and sound unflustered, I had to have myself heard above the hammering of the blood in my ears. I took a steadying breath, then calmly remarked, 'Wow. So the bold Rodger's really gone and done it this time.'

'He's done it all right. But now he's making a damn brave bid to undo it.'

'How?'

'I've just come from the interview room. There's Doran, there's his solicitor, there's Detective Forbes – my superior – and there's horsetrading going on like you wouldn't believe.'

'But . . . wasn't he caught in the act? So what's he got to tra —' And everything went deadly quiet. First, a great shiver passed the length of my body. Once it had gone, I instantly felt feverish, as if burning under several layers of clothes too many. After that, nothing; a numbness, a detachment, like I was watching the whole episode through the glass wall of an aquarium. The office window looked right across the valley to Tory Hill. It had never been so clear, in such sharp focus – I could almost read the number plate on the tractor that was winding its way along the track three-quarter way to the summit.

I slumped back into the swivel chair by the desk. The jolt returned me to my senses in time to hear Furlong go on, 'Doran's got his hands on a map of Boher townsland. He's indicated the spot on what was once Morrissey's – some kind of disused sand quarry. He says that's where the body is buried.' He paused briefly, then: 'As well as that, he claims that we'll find a plastic bag containing the bloodied clothes that you and Dasher Morrissey wore when you murdered her. Billy – will we?'

Through half a lifetime of lying, denying and prevaricating, I'd stayed one jump ahead of this man. But I'd run out of things to hide behind. The game was up.

'Yes,' I said quietly. 'You will.'

'Hmmm.' Then a deep sigh. 'I was afraid we might.'

'But you've got to listen, Conor. I swear —' He halted me with a rueful laugh. 'I don't expect you to believe me, I've no right to. But if you'll let me now, I'll tell you exactly what happened.'

'What happened isn't important any more. It's what can be proved. And according to Doran, every shred of hard, physical evidence is going to point directly to you.'

'That's just how he rigged it the night he killed her. D'you believe that?'

'Whether I do or not is beside the point.'

'But do you? Believe it was him?'

'I know it was him. I've always known it.'

'Well why in the hell then did you spend the past seventeen years trying to nail the wrong man?'

'Who – you? I wasn't trying to nail you, for Christ's sake. I only wanted you to come clean before the others did. There were three of you involved – that's two too many for a secret to hold indefinitely. And the one who got his version in first was the one most likely to be believed. As you'll find out to your cost when you make the acquaintance of my guv'nor.'

'Who is he?'

'He's Detective Sergeant Ray Forbes. He'll be running the show. And Billy, be warned: he's a devious and unprincipled glory-hunter. He'll chase straws, smoke, shadows – anything – to the ends of the earth if he thinks there's a headline in it for him. The man has wet dreams about cases like this one.'

'Wh – why this one?'

'Because he's got his dead body. He's got his star witness singing like a canary. He's got plenty of forensics to back everything up. But it's the target that'll excite him most. Not some drugged-up lowlife – those are ten a penny, so there's fuck-all publicity. No, now he'll be hunting somebody who's somebody. A primary school principal, Billy. Whose sister just happens to be a leading senior counsel. Think about the press coverage when you go in his trophy cabinet.'

Thinking – just plain thinking – was difficult enough at that moment.

'How soon can I expect to hear from this guy?'

'As soon as he gets what he needs from the old sandpit. Which won't take very long.'

'And what then?'

'He'll snap arrest both you and Dasher. Separately and simultaneously. Element of surprise, you know – gives you no time to compare notes. Then interrogate you individually. Get you contradicting each other. Maybe even blaming each other, if he's lucky.'

'You said surprise? You shouldn't be making this call, then.'

'Strictly speaking, no.'

'So whose side are you on?'

'His, of course. I'm a high-ranking police officer now, don't forget.'

'But if anyone finds out you tipped me off like this . . . you're putting your job on the line here.'

'That's a possibility, yeah.'

'Conor, why? No offence, but after all that's happened between us, why would you want to do that?'

'I don't know if I told you this when we were still on speaking terms, but my dad was a cop too. And he always said, "Do your job second. Do the right thing first." And this is the right thing. Billy, when I came to that village not knowing a sinner, you looked out for me. When my neighbour needed a few acres and the second chance that no one else would give him, you looked out for me there, too. All I ever wanted was to do the same for you in return. And Christ above, I did try. But you knew better. You wouldn't let me.'

And for the first time since, I think, the death of my father, I cried. Quietly, to myself, and grateful that the conversation was being conducted over the phone. After a moment, I cleared my throat and part of the quiver from my voice.

'I'm sorry,' I said. 'For being so fucking stupid. For not trusting you. For lying to you, deceiving you . . .'

'Woah! Don't flatter yourself, eh? You may have lied to me, but I wasn't fooled for long. Anyway, this'll hold. Pull yourself together and go round to Dasher's, pronto. Get those stories straight.'

'Fair enough. I'll call him . . .'

'I've done it. He's expecting you.'

I could've, and should've got there quicker. But typically, my first instinct was a selfish one – I tried to contact Mags. I could think of no one better to have in my corner. And if now wasn't the time for old rifts to be forgotten, then we were surely fated to die at loggerheads.

The phone was engaged. I waited a while, tried again and got only her answering machine. Frustrated, I hung up without leaving a message. All in all, a good ten minutes had elapsed since Conor Furlong told me to make tracks.

Mary it was who answered the door. Half-joking, whole in earnest, she pretended not to recognize me; it had been some time since I'd last called, but not all *that* long. I was scarcely in the mood, but I played along. And when I'd established who I was, she said, 'Come on in. I'll get my husband and the two of you can be reintroduced.'

'Actually, he's the man I've come to see,' I said very pointedly.

'He's on the phone,' she told me. 'The one in the bedroom.' She went to the bottom of the stairs and hollered, 'Dash? It's Billy.' I could hear nothing in reply, but Mary sat herself opposite me and said, 'He'll be down in a minute.'

The smile I'd fixed was becoming painful to hold, but I could think of absolutely nothing to say to the woman. She, however, was her usual, convivial self, gushing on about the good weather, enquiring after the children's academic progress, teasing me about the state of my love life. After a series of replies that were short and very distracted, I craned my neck to see up the stairway and said, 'Taking his time, isn't he?'

'I don't know what could be keeping him. I don't even know who he's talking to. It was a man's voice that I didn't recognize. Dash?'

Just then Niall, their youngest, came through the door pushing ahead of him a sturdy tip-up truck.

'Niall,' she said, 'run upstairs and tell your daddy that we've got company.'

'Daddy's in the garden.'

Mary stood, peered through the window and said, 'No, he isn't.'

'He is. I saw him go out, and he didn't come back.'

She took another look and decided, 'Oh, he must be in the shed. Go out, like a good lad, and tell him Billy is here.' Niall disappeared. 'What was it you wanted to see him about – or is it any of my business?'

'It's . . . to do with this bloke we both were in school with. He was caught today taking part in an armed robbery at the Ulster Bank on the quay. He was lucky – his accomplice was shot dead.'

'Eh? Slow down a sec! What armed robbery?'

She'd heard nothing of the earlier commotion in town. I'd now have to tell her the whole story, wasting time I could not afford.

'Switch on the radio,' I said. 'You can hear it as it's happening on WLR.'

There was a hi-fi on the floor beside the chair where she sat. She pressed something, turned something else, then young Niall stuck his head into the room and announced, 'I can't get in – the shed door is locked.'

Mary thought this over for a moment, then said, 'Niall, there's no lock on the shed door.'

'Well, then it must be bolted on the inside.'

'There isn't any bolt on the inside, silly! Did you push as hard as you could?'

'Yeah. But it was still stuck.'

'Did you ask your dad to open it?'

'Uh-huh.'

'And did you tell him Billy was here?'

'I did, but he didn't answer.'

'What – nothing?'

Her brow furrowed, part in puzzlement, part in concern. 'I'd better go check this out,' she said.

Without asking or being asked, I followed. The door was indeed stuck fast. Mary rattled the handle and began calling her husband's name. But she fared no better than had her son. There was no visual access to the shed's interior – not a window, not even a keyhole. When she'd done rattling and calling, she turned to me and spoke with a shortening breath.

'Maybe he's not in there at all.'

We both knew this to be impossible; the door, the only point of exit, was still secured from the inside.

'I'll break it down,' I said, a decision, not a suggestion. She clasped a hand to her mouth and stood aside. Just then, Niall set foot in the garden and called, 'Well, did ye find Daddy?'

'Get back in the house!' she yelled.

'But did ye . . .'

'Get back in the goddam house when you're told!'

We waited till he had, then she nodded grimly in my direction. I took a step or two away, charged, and struck the door just above the handle with my shoulder. It gave maybe half a foot, then rebounded me on to my back some five or six yards away. Well shaken, I got to my feet and tried again. This time, the give was more pronounced – a foot, possibly eighteen inches. On the third charge, the old broom that had been jammed under the door handle gave way. I went careering through, failed to hurdle the small tricycle in my path, and crashed head first into the shed wall opposite. But I was instantly returned to my senses by the bloodcurdling shriek from the doorway behind me. Turning where I lay, I found myself looking directly at a worn old pair of deck shoes dangling just above the ground. It had been simplicity itself. After buying himself time with the broom wedged in the door, he'd climbed on the saddle of the tricycle. He'd tied one end of his belt to the middle crossbeam, the other around his neck and then eased the tricycle to one side.

Mary took him round the midriff, attempting to lift him and so slacken the noose, all the while screeching at me to for Christ's sake hurry and get him down, that he was still alive. He was still warm, but nothing more. So precise, so deliberate and so coldly calculated, this was no spur of the moment act; this was, I believe, something he'd been planning almost all his adult life. If and when the day of reckoning came, and with it his world came crashing, this was to be his cyanide capsule, his emergency exit.

It was I who called the ambulance, while Jamie, the eldest child, was dispatched across the fields to fetch the parish priest. The ambulance arrived first on the scene, but Mary became hysterical when it was proposed that the body be moved without being seen by Fr Hughes. Her husband was entitled to have his last rites given in his own home by a friend of long years' standing, not by some duty chaplain in a grey hospital morgue. Nobody dared argue.

In any case, there wasn't long to wait till the old priest was on hand. Puffing, sweating and panting, he came through the summer heat, still wearing the same old brown workboots in which he'd just been tending the garden. He hadn't brought a missal, but he didn't need one – he knew by heart what was required.

Kneeling over the body, he made the sign of the cross, bowed his head and began to speak in a low, earnest whisper. When he'd done, he rose, crossed himself again, and then indicated to the attendants that it was time for Dasher to begin his last ever journey to Waterford City Infirmary.

Once the ambulance had gone, the priest reassumed

charge. After a word of condolence with each of the family in their turn, he blessed the little wooden shed, and bade us kneel with him on the concrete floor to recite one decade of the rosary. When the Hail, Holy Queen was said, he asked if he might share with us one or two of his thoughts. We stayed on our knees and listened.

Death, he told us, is always tragic, but the death of a young person is particularly so. He himself was never meant to bury anyone he'd baptized, yet he distinctly remembered welcoming Michael, as a tiny infant, into the Catholic faith. And it didn't seem like too very long ago either. Yet here he was today, administering to Michael his last rites before God. And why? What was it all about? What purpose of the Lord's was served by calling home this young man, a good husband, a good father, and a good friend to many. It seemed so pointless, so totally incomprehensible. However, in the fullness of time, we would know that it was neither. That like every person upon the earth, the date of Michael's death was ordained by God at the very moment of his conception. If we didn't understand this right now, it was because we weren't meant to.

To finish, he asked that the same God grant to Michael a just and merciful judgement, mindful of the Christian way he'd lived his life rather than the manner in which he'd departed it.

At this point, voices were heard at the front gate, then the chime of the doorbell. Alerted by the sight of the ambulance, the trickle of neighbours had started. For an instant, none of us spoke, none of us even moved. We understood that once the door was opened to the sympathizers, everything changed. It would no longer be a matter of private grief: it would be public property, to be discussed and mulled over by firesides and on barstools the length and breadth of South Kilkenny.

Mary looked up from the ground. The tears, the hysteria, were gone; either she was incredibly composed or else stuck senseless. Heaving a sigh, she said, 'Good God, what am I to tell these people?'

Fr Hughes got to his feet, helped her to hers and said, 'You needn't tell them anything. Go upstairs and have a lie down. We'll take care of things.'

The doorbell rang again.

'Go on,' the priest urged. 'Don't worry about the kids, don't worry about anything. Get your head down for an hour, then come face the neighbours.'

'I don't think I'd get very much sleep right now, Father, to be honest.'

'You've been through a lot Mary – give yourself a rest. You're going to need all your strength for your family in the coming days.'

The doorbell rang again, more sustained this time. She thought it over a moment longer, then said, 'Jamie, go answer that. Thanks all the same, Father, but . . . there isn't very much more I'll ever be able to do for Dasher; at least I can do this. Anyway, he never let me down in life – I won't have anyone thinking he's shamed me in death.'

'Are you sure?'

'I'm sure. You can go on, Father. And you too, Billy. You've been real friends in need. But I would've expected no less from you.'

'Why don't we just stay with you until —'

'Please. This is something I've got to do alone. Thanks again. I'll never forget you for this.'

Fr Hughes and I slipped quietly through the early-comers.

Once outside, I offered him a lift back to the presbytery. He declined, saying he needed a walk to clear his head and to try gather his wits about him. Not another word passed between us as he shambled away, cocooned in his thoughts. Then suddenly, there came the snarl as three squad cars went hammering by in convoy. Two were regular, the middle one unmarked, all roaring up the Boher Road like they were responding to a nuclear meltdown. It would not be long now.

So much that I should've done. Or that I should've done differently. I should've got there quicker before the fact. When it was over, I should've gone straight to Pat and Bridget Morrissey, his elderly parents, to give them the news before the whole world learnt it. But I didn't. I raced up the hill in the wake of the police cars, got inside the house and then locked the door behind me. There I slumped to the tiled floor and sat a long while in a strange kind of calm. Not mourning my friend, not dreading the inevitable next step, but carefully and dispassionately considering one question: did Dasher have the right idea? Arrest, charge, trial, prison, disgrace – all loomed large on my horizon, while at a stroke he'd side-stepped the lot. Wherever he was now, could it possibly be so much worse than this? The phone rang to disperse such thoughts.

'I can't really talk,' Conor muttered, 'I'm on the mobile, and I mustn't be seen making this call. But we've just found the body.'

'Dasher is dead.'

'What?'

'Dead. He hanged himself right after he'd done talking to you.'

'Oh, Jesus. Oh, my Jesus Christ.'

'I've just come from the house. The ambulance —'

'Hey! Save it, OK? I don't want to sound callous, but d'you realize where this leaves you? Dasher was your big hope – the one person who could back your story. Now, you're right up against it.'

Not till that moment had this occurred to me.

'If you stay where you are, you'll be arrested within the hour. So get yourself to Waterford, to the copshop in Ballybricken. Go voluntarily.'

'And do what?'

'Walk in there, say you've got information about a crime and want to give a statement. And just tell the truth. Y'know – better late than never. Oh, and get yourself a solicitor. A good one.'

As advised, I left the house at once. Waterford city was big and impersonal, I looked well dressed and unremarkable. So I could avoid arrest for however long it took and face the music only when I was good and ready.

I needed a solicitor. Liam Prentice had twice acted for me regarding the sale of land, but this always struck me as being the limit of his ability. I had to find a criminal specialist, and I had to find one who'd drop everything and come running. It was a tall order. I knew of only one place to begin looking.

As I entered the payphone, my silent prayer was as fervent as any of my entire life. On the third ring, it picked up.

'Mags Walsh speaking?'

'Mags, it's Billy.'

Silence. Then a cold, formal, 'Yes?'

'Mags, it's happened. The cops have found Suzy's body.'

No response.

'Dasher's dead. He committed suicide a couple of hours ago. I'm here, on my way to Ballybricken station . . .'

'You've been arrested?'

'No. Well, not yet. I've come of my own free will.'

'A very good move. Hardly your own *idea*, I dare say.'

'Mags, I need help. I need a good solicitor. Can you recommend one who'll get here, now?'

'Sit in your car across the road from the station, and leave it with me. Billy – don't open your mouth till he gets to you. Not to anyone, understood?'

'Understood.'

'Good man. There's nothing I can do for you tonight, but I'll be there early in the morning.'

'You're . . . you're coming down?'

'Of course – unless you don't want me to.'

'I do. Thanks.'

'That's OK. Now remember; not a word to anyone.'

But I couldn't even do that much right. I drove to the station, I sat across the road and waited. Ten minutes passed, maybe more. A skinhead went in carrying his driver's licence – for presentation, I'd guess, because he re-emerged almost immediately. Again the street fell silent. Then, faint and distant, I heard a voice. Voices. I looked up and, as I did, Conor Furlong, in full regalia, came striding round the building's corner. By instinct, I pushed open the car door, climbed on to the road and called his name. He jerked his head to the sound, but when he saw who'd hailed him, his features contorted like it was the Antichrist he'd seen. Taking his prompt, I jumped back into the car and out of sight. But too late; others had followed round the corner in his train, some uniformed and some plainclothes, all now glaring in my direction. One stepped right off the pavement for a better look. He was in civvies, not as tall as Furlong but broader in the shoulders and possibly fifteen years older. Not much of his blond hair survived, and the bushy eyebrows thatching the pinched features made him look quite villainous. He studied the car, noting the make and registration number, then turned to Furlong, who'd come to his side, and grabbed him roughly by the lapel. Words were exchanged, after which both men began across the street towards me. At once, I stepped from the car. Furlong got to me first.

'This is Billy Walsh,' he announced. 'Billy, this is my boss, Detective Forbes.'

'Billy Walsh,' he beamed, but falsely.

'Detective.'

'*The* Billy Walsh. Well, how about that. We've just been to your house, looking for you, and you were here all the time. Coincidence or what?'

I didn't answer.

'So, Billy. Or Mr Walsh, B.Ed., to give you your full and proper title. What brings a busy, professional man like yourself to our humble station?'

'I've got information about a crime. And I'd like to make a statement.'

'Now, isn't that very civic-minded of you,' he said, that nauseating grin widening. 'Something recent, yeah?'

'No. It's something that happened a good many years ago.'

'Don't tell me! You've got something on the disappearance of Suzy Deane. How did I know that, eh? Isn't it uncanny!'

'Isn't what uncanny?' came a low, fruity voice from behind my back. I'd not heard the speaker approach, nor had I laid eyes on him before. But Forbes blanched slightly and gulped, 'Mr Oglaza.' I myself stood suitably in awe, for there could only be the one. Nicholas Oglaza. From the countless times I'd seen his name in print, I'd envisaged someone bigger. But he was less than imposing in stature, standing only about five feet tall and with a physique that was frail and fragile. His grey hair was tufted around three sides of a pink, shiny dome, and on his rather large nose he wore black-rimmed bifocals. And yet, in his presence, those policemen round about came to attention like privates on parade. Oglaza was the best in the business, a scourge of unwary prosecutors and slipshod Gardaí for nigh on half a century. Mags had truly delivered.

'Do tell, Detective Forbes. What's uncanny?'

Forbes wasn't to be easily cowed, and quickly rediscovered his brass. 'I was only remarking to Mr Walsh here . . .'

'Mr Walsh? My Billy Walsh? Pleased to meet you. Nicholas Oglaza – I'll be representing you, if that's acceptable.' We shook hands. 'Please continue, Detective. You were remarking to my client . . .?'

'Just what a day of coincidence it's been. We've gone to his home, and all the time he's here at our place. And why's he here? Because he wants to tell us what he knows about a missing girl. This young lady's been missing for seventeen years now, but only today does he finally decide to get it all off his chest. And – can you credit it – today just happens to be the day we find the girl's body. On his neighbour's land, what's more!'

'We can well do without the sarcasm, Detective,' Oglaza smiled. 'As you rightly point out, my client has come here of his own volition, and so is free to leave at any time.'

'Not any more, he isn't.' Then, to me, 'Billy Walsh, I'm arresting you in connection with the death of Suzy Deane . . .' And he proceeded to read me my rights, to the great and public amusement of my solicitor.

'Yes, yes, Detective Forbes. Very dramatic. And very impressive. I'm at a loss to tell who you're trying to impress, but knowing you, there'll be someone.'

'Oh, I assure you, Mr Oglaza, this is all strictly in the line of duty. I've got my job to do.'

'As I have mine. So perhaps I might be allowed to consult with my client. Alone, and in private, preferably.'

'We've got a holding cell that ought to prove ideal. And I'll be seeing you both in interview presently. Sergeant Furlong, I'll be seeing you in my office. Now.'

The cell was small, the bunk was hard, and that's about all I remember from there. I had little chance to note the decor; Oglaza was all business, all about the matter in hand and demanding of my full and undivided attention. He began by warning me to tread carefully around Detective Forbes, describing him as a man of little integrity but high intelligence and considerable cunning. He went on to say how pleased he was to oblige my sister in this way, as in their dealings he'd found her honest, forthright and trustworthy. This, however, was no attempt at sweet-talk or flattery, but a setting out of the standards he now expected from me. Once satisfied that we understood each other, he bade me begin. The whole story, with nothing fudged, fabricated or omitted.

I started with the night of 19 August 1982. And, stopping to clarify only occasionally, took him right up to the point at which he himself had entered the story. I was as truthful and as thorough as I felt necessary. Which is to say, I told him everything, short of my engaging a contract killer to shoot Rodger Doran; I was gambling that this could never be proved. So when I'd finished, and Oglaza asked me to consider well, to think if there was anything further I'd like to add, I looked him in the eye and said no. Whereupon he summoned the desk sergeant to advise him that we were ready.

'Mr Walsh, I'd like to take you back to 19 August 1982.'

The interview room was carpet-tiled, its bare block walls

painted white. The only furniture was a medium-sized wood and chrome table, with some chairs of a similar style. On Forbes's side there sat two other Gardaí. Both were introduced at the top of proceedings, though I recall neither name. One had pencil and A4 pad, and would occasionally take a note. The other did nothing much. On that same side, a fourth chair stood empty. Furlong's breach of discipline had cost him his place.

'Granted, it's a long time ago. But I understand that for a number of reasons it may still be fresh in your mind. So take your time and tell us everything you remember.'

'It was on 19 August that the calls to third level were out. It also happened to be the day that Michael Morrissey, a friend of mine, turned eighteen. Both he and I had had letters from the Uni. that day, telling us we'd secured the places we were after.'

'Those being?'

'National teaching in my case. Engineering in his.'

'Hmmm. Impressive. It called for a celebration, I dare say.'

'Nothing major. We rang around a few mates and arranged to meet in a bar called the Heather Blazing.'

'Was Suzy Deane one of those you rang?'

'No. We just happened to bump into her there.'

'How exactly?'

'She'd heard our good news, and she came over to say well done. She couldn't really talk, because she was in company, but she suggested that all three of us meet up again after pub closing time.'

'Did she say where?'

'Yes. By my father's hayshed.'

'And did she say why?'

'Not that I recall.'

'Were you surprised by this?'

'Very.'

'Why?'

'Because I'd known her all my life, and she'd never before suggested anything of the sort.'

'Really? So what was your initial reaction? What did you read into it?'

'That . . . possibly she had more in mind than just some cosy conversation.'

'How much more, did you reckon?'

'I reckoned it was likely that there might be some sexual activity involved.'

'Some sexual activity – how very delicate. Just what did you think was on the cards that night, Mr Walsh? In layman's terms.'

'That she was up for having sex with one of us. Maybe even both of us.'

'That was quite an assumption to make, wasn't it? After all, she was just fifteen years old.'

'That never bothered her.'

'What d'you mean?'

'If you'd seen her in action, you'd know exactly what I mean.'

'You'd seen her in action, then?'

'More than once.'

'And did you yourself ever get in on a piece of this action?'

'I'm afraid I was never fortunate enough.'

'You wouldn't have said no, then, if the opportunity arose?'

'I don't know of any bloke in my situation who would've.'

'Why so?'

'Because Suzy Deane was the best-looking girl there's been

in this part of the country. She's nearly twenty years gone, Detective, and in all that time I've never met anyone who could hold a match to her.'

He smiled, an oily grin. 'Nearly twenty years, as you correctly point out. And still you sound a little bit lovestruck.'

'Do I?'

'You do. I can only imagine how intense your feelings for her must've been back then. And how you must've envied – even loathed – Rodger Doran.'

'Loathed, yeah. Envied? Well, I wouldn't have swapped lives with him.'

'You do acknowledge, then, that Doran and she were an item?'

'She kept a few other irons in the fire. But yeah, Doran was as close as she came to a steady. Mind you, that was over too.'

'What?'

'She'd finished with him. She said that she was fed up with Doran and the way he treated her, that she could see he'd never be anything other than a gouger, and that they had no future together.'

'When?' Forbes shook his head. 'When was this parting of the ways alleged to have taken place?'

'Nothing alleged about it; they were through, just like she told us. I even heard her tell him as much.'

'Yes, but when?'

'That very night.'

'And since, by morning, Suzy was dead, this can never be verified. Or contradicted. How convenient for you.' He took a long breath and went on, 'I should tell you, Mr Walsh, that I'm treating this with the utmost scepticism. It does not tally with my information. However, let's carry on. The rendezvous is arranged – what happens now?'

'Dasher – that's Michael Morrissey – and I got there first. We lit a couple of cigarettes and waited. After a while, Suzy appeared.'

'Was she on foot?'

'Naturally – she'd come across the fields.'

'Why had she not taken the road?'

'The other way was shorter.'

'And she'd come alone?'

'She had.'

'When you'd spoken to her earlier, was she drunk at all?'

'No, she wasn't.'

'You're sure?'

'Because of her age, some pubs wouldn't serve her alcohol.'

'She was stone-cold sober, then. Whereas yourself and your buddies were pretty well cut, yeah?'

'We were in good form, it's true.'

'How many of you were there?'

'Seven, eight, I can't be certain.'

'I read a survey somewhere recently. Some women were asked what it was they feared most. Drunken men came top of the list.'

'Is that right?'

'But you claim Suzy just waltzed in among almost eight of you and handed out this saucy invitation anyway?'

'The invitation was only for two.'

'But boys will be boys, Mr Walsh. And a tryst with Suzy Deane was a mightily attractive proposition. So what was to stop the other six tagging along for a peek? Or maybe something more?'

'Nothing, I guess.'

'And Suzy would've known that risk, of course. By your own

327

account, there wasn't a lot she didn't know in matters like these.'

My solicitor harrumphed loudly and said, 'Detective Forbes, I'm afraid I find this line of questioning slightly mystifying.'

'If you're mystified, Mr Oglaza, then you aren't the only one. Personally, I can't understand your client; he's a learned man, he's had most of his life to think about it, and this is the best he can come up with? A fifteen-year-old girl, perfectly sober and with all her wits about her, comes across ditches, hedgerows and fields in the very dead of night and without a living soul for company. To a place where she knows that a mob of slavering drunks may well be lying in wait for her. None of whom, I understand, she's ever previously shown any interest in, drunk or sober. Mr Oglaza, if I may say, you're a veteran of our court system and legal process. You must know that no judge, jury or sane person in this entire land would for one moment believe anything so plainly ludicrous.'

'Do you dispute, then, Detective, that Ms Deane was actually there that night?'

'On the contrary, Mr Oglaza, I know she was. I know, also, that she died there.'

'So how do you propose that she got there, if not as my client has described?'

'I've heard a version that's rather different, and rather more plausible, than that which your client has described. But more of that later. For now, Mr Walsh, the floor is yours. So Suzy shows up. What next?'

I hesitated; he'd got me rattled. It wasn't so much that he was pulling my evidence apart like candyfloss. What unnerved me was this plausible alternative. What could Doran have concocted that sat so much more easily than the truth?

'In your own time, Mr Walsh,' he smarmed. 'Don't you hurry yourself on our account.'

'OK,' I mumbled, distractedly. What was Doran claiming? Was he implicating anyone else? Maybe putting himself at the scene from the start. Or maybe not at all.

'Mr Walsh!'

'Yeah, right. Let's see. After that . . . where was I again?'

'Look,' he snapped. 'I appreciate how dull you must find this, how difficult to give it your full attention. But if you could just stay tuned a while longer . . .'

'I'm sorry,' I said. 'I didn't mean to . . . I'll go on.'

'Thank you. Suzy Deane appears at the place appointed . . .?'

'That's right. First thing she did was to ask for a cigarette. So I lit a Major – my last one – and gave it to her. When I did, we all sat down and just began chatting.'

'How would you describe her mood?'

'Pissed off. Really down in the mouth. Saying how she wished she was a few years older, and had just got the breaks we'd got. Then she'd have a legitimate way out of Lisdrolin, and into the wide world beyond. As things stood, she was reduced to making a run for it every so often.'

'Of course, in the immediate aftermath when tracks needed covering, it was staged to look as if she'd made a run for it that very night. A most convincing illusion, Mr Walsh – it kept the police well off your scent. I mention it purely in passing. Do continue.'

'The conversation then came round to the fact that it happened to be Dasher's birthday. Suzy said she was sorry, that she'd not got him a present, so a kiss would have to do. It was dark, so I'm not entirely certain what happened then, but the next thing I knew she'd straddled him and the two began to

329

kiss in earnest. I saw her whisper something, they both stood up and she began leading him up the ladder to the haybench.'

'Right. And how did this make you feel?'

'Jealous. Very jealous. And a bit angry too.'

'Angry? What was it got you angry?'

'That would have to be when Dasher arrived back down the ladder to ask me for a condom.'

'Oh! I see. You provided the condoms.'

'I provided one. I'd found it – taken it – from a flat in Dublin some months earlier.'

'Did you have any sexual experience to that point, Mr Walsh?'

'Not . . . the real thing.'

'So this might've been your first time, all going well?'

'Please, Detective Forbes!' Oglaza objected. 'I really must ask how my client's previous romantic forays, or lack of them, have any significance in this case.'

'I'm just having some further difficulty with this evidence, Mr Oglaza. I cannot for the life of me believe that any normal, red-blooded teenage virgin would happily hand over his one solitary condom – and with it his one glorious chance – to a friend . . . to *any* friend.'

'I never said I handed it over.'

'Oh? So what did happen?'

'Well, Detective, like any normal, red-blooded teenage virgin, I refused, and we began to argue. But Suzy stopped us, saying she didn't want to use one. That it'd only get in the way and spoil the fun.'

Forbes leaned forward, rested his elbow on the table and his chin on his palm. 'Now I'm afraid I'm rightly confused.' Nobody enquired why, so he went on, 'At her age, and at that time, there's no way she could've been on the pill. So she was about to risk pregnancy, single motherhood, venereal disease – any one of which would have fairly put a stop to her gallop. Might even have ruined her entire life. Yet, when given the option of a condom – of safe, protected sex – she'd have none of it. Now, how would you account for that?'

'I . . . I can't.'

'You can't? You haven't thought this bit through very well either, have you?'

'I was there, Detective. I saw what happened. I've never needed to think anything through.'

'Well, maybe you ought to consider it now, then,' he smirked. 'Because frankly, Mr Walsh, your evidence is like a madman's crap – it's all over the place. D'you want us to break for an hour while you get it straight?'

To my dismay, Oglaza turned towards me, his expression urging acceptance. I clenched my teeth in indignation and growled, 'No, I do not.'

'My client declines this offer out of hand,' Oglaza stated as he adjusted the spectacles on his nose. 'Furthermore, he greatly resents the implication carried therein.'

'Very well. You know best. But you must understand if I chalk it down to another gaping hole in your client's story. Anyhow, you were saying, Mr Walsh. Your friends are about their business. You're alone, left as the third wheel. A position you'd become well acquainted with in the years to follow.'

I'd been warned not to rise to it, but this was beginning to grate just a bit. Only after a nod and a wink from my counsel did I say, 'It was then that Rodger Doran came on the scene.'

'What was he doing there?'

'He'd come to steal some of my father's hay. He dealt in scrap metal, using a horse and cart. So he'd rob a few bales

331

every once in a while to fodder the animal over the winter.'

'He must've been surprised to find someone on the premises at such an hour. And he must've been curious as to what you were up to.'

'He was. I told him it was none of his business, and to get off our property.'

'How did he react?'

'He became jumpy and apologetic. And very ingratiating – trying to butter me up, giving me cigarettes, that sort of thing. He was afraid I'd go and get my father.'

'Why did you not go and get your father?'

'For one thing, it would've left me with a bit of explaining to do. For another, I didn't want to walk away and leave Dasher at that guy's mercy.'

'At his mercy, Mr Walsh?'

'I knew that if Doran were to chance upon the shenanigans just above his head, that there'd be hell to pay.'

'But why should Rodger Doran be enraged? Hadn't you been assured that Suzy and he were yesterday's news?'

'Yes, I had. But I knew enough to know that these things are rarely so straightforward. Just because one party calls time, it doesn't always follow that the other accepts this.'

'Oh, my! What a mature understanding you had of inter-personal relationships.'

'Thank you.'

'I didn't actually mean that as a compliment.'

'That's OK – I didn't actually mean to sound grateful.'

'Touché,' he said breezily. 'And on that last point, incidentally, we're in agreement. Had Rodger Doran sussed the carry-on in the haybench, then there would certainly have been hell to pay. Because he was still going out with Suzy Deane, and well you knew it.'

I shook my head, slowly and emphatically.

'Did any of your friends from the pub hear her say that she'd ditched him?'

'No.'

'Did any of them hear her arrange this famous late-night engagement with yourself and Mr Morrissey?'

'I don't believe so.'

'Very unfortunate, wouldn't you say, that nothing or nobody can corroborate a single word of your story so far. But carry on – it's fascinating.'

'I'm glad you like it.'

'I do – a remarkable feat of imagination. So, you and Doran are sitting there in the dark, just mulling over the ways of the world. As you do. And then?'

'Doran heard the commotion overhead. He immediately put two and two together, he knew what Dasher was doing – what we were both doing . . .'

'And who he was doing it with?'

'No. I said it was some woman we'd picked up at a disco in town.'

'Did he buy this story?'

'He seemed to. In fact, he insisted he be allowed to join the queue.'

Forbes spluttered a loud guffaw. 'Oh, I'm sorry. I beg your pardon. Please, don't stop. Not now.'

Oglaza put a hand across me, signalling his intention to speak.

'It's rather discouraging, Detective, to find such crass ignorance at so high a level of our nation's police force.'

'Oh, I assure you, Mr Oglaza, that my other attributes have always tended to more than compensate for my lack of social graces. In any case, I do believe I've apologized to your client.'

Oglaza scowled contemptuously, then nodded in my direction.

I went on, 'About then, Dasher appeared down the ladder, straightening his clothes and tucking his shirt in. As he did, Suzy put her head over the edge of the bench. Doran saw her and . . . that was the start of it.'

'Of what?'

'He ran at Dasher, hit him full on the jaw, absolutely poleaxed him.'

'And to Suzy?'

'Nothing, right away. He was still spitting fire, but she just reminded him that there was nothing between them, that he had no claims on her any more. They shouted a bit, swapped a few insults – I thought it might just peter out into a slagging match. Until Suzy passed some remark about Doran's people being travellers. Then he completely lost it.'

'Go on.'

'He stormed up the ladder and smashed his fist into the side of her face. She toppled off balance, collided with the eave of the barn roof and fell headlong on to the concrete that supports the main girder. I went to her, got to my knees and tried to . . . tried to do anything I could, tried to lift her away from where she'd fallen. But when I put my hand behind her head, I felt the skull bone. It was completely crushed, completely driven in, and I knew . . .'

'You knew she was dead?'

'It was hard to think straight just then, but yeah, I had a pretty good idea.'

'You seem to have remained reasonably calm.'

'Calm? Jesus, no! I was bloody petrified.'

'So why did you not scream the place down? Someone would've heard, wouldn't they? Someone would've come.'

'Before I could do anything, the two lads were standing beside me. I told them right away I could see no sign of life, and that we'd better go and wake my parents.'

Forbes said nothing but leaned further forward, his two elbows now resting on the table.

'The next thing I remember, Doran had caught Michael Morrissey by the hair, held a penknife to his throat and warned me that if I didn't do what he wanted he'd, y'know, cut him open.'

Forbes' features tightened. He looked to each of his subordinates, and then back to me.

'This is nonsense, Billy. Absolute nonsense, and an insult to my intelligence. Even if it were tru —'

'It is.'

'Even if it were, you can't expect me to believe that this – *this* – forced you into covering up a murder?'

'I don't see that I had any choice.'

'No? Well, let me put one. You could've jumped him. Two fit, able young men, against one bloke armed with little more than a hatpin. I'd take those odds.'

'He would've had Dasher slashed from ear to ear before I'd even got to my feet. And I was in no doubt about it – he'd have done me next.'

'Did he say as much?'

'No, but . . .'

'But it was still enough to scare you into submission. Billy, I've a maiden aunt who wouldn't have been intimidated by that. Mind you, I shouldn't be surprised that you were. I've seen you play hurling.'

'Is that so?'

'I was a young guard in Higginstown, and I was training our minors when we played against you lot that summer. You were wing forward, right? I remember you had a great turn of pace; as fast as a hare, you were. Unfortunately, you were about as brave as one too. Even your own people knew you had no chance of making it, because you were yellow to the core. "The Jap?" Isn't that what they used to shout at you from the sidelines?'

Oglaza very deliberately caught my eye, reminding me – imploring me – to keep a lid on things.

'No, no, no, Detective,' I said with a broad, easy smile. 'Not me – you've got the wrong player. About the turn of pace, though, you're spot on. I don't mean to boast or anything, but I was pretty quick in those days.'

'Quick enough, I suggest, to have dropped the body and made it to your own front door before Doran could get anywhere near you. You could've woken your dad – he was a licensed shotgun holder. Now, a good old-fashioned double-barrel would've settled all arguments, would it not?'

'I did think about making a bolt for it. But it was Dasher – he was crying and gibbering, begging me to do as Doran said, pleading for his very life, the poor bastard. What was I to do?'

'Did you honestly believe that Rodger Doran was going to kill him?'

'You're bloody right I did. I'd already seen him kill one person that night.'

Forbes opened his mouth but could not find a riposte. I'd won the point. 'Carry on,' he said sulkily. 'She's dead, you're going to bury her. How?'

'I got a slurry shovel —'

'A what?'

'A slurry shovel. It was big and flat and used for moving cowdung. I took it from my dad's dairy, which adjoined the barn.'

336

'And with the body?'

'There were fertilizer sacks – plastic – still lying around since earlier in the year. I put the body into one.'

'All by yourself?'

'Yeah. She was small, it wasn't difficult.'

'And once you'd got it in the bag?'

'I lifted it into the boot of Doran's car. Dasher was forced in alongside it, with instructions to keep the mouth raised so no blood would spill.'

'The area where Suzy landed after falling – was that not bloodstained?'

'I'm sorry – I've skipped something. I gathered up all the loose hay from the bottom of the girder, and stuck it into the bag too.'

'Did you take much time, much care over this?'

'Not especially. I just raked up armfuls of it and rammed it in.'

'And yet you managed to leave not a single trace behind you? People passed that way next day, but nobody saw even a speck. And you accomplished this in a hurry, in the dark, and completely on your own. Is that possible?'

'It must be, cos that's what happened.'

'But is it possible in any form of reality that the rest of us might be familiar with?'

I shrugged.

'You *helped* dispose of the body and clear the scene of evidence. You didn't act alone, because you couldn't have. Which means your friend was assisting you. Which, in turn, means that there was no knife to his jugular, no threat to his well-being. In short, no duress from a third party. Sounds a bit more believable, wouldn't you say?'

I shrugged again.

'Billy, I'm no expert at this. Compared to the man you've got sat next to you, I'm a rank amateur. And yet at every crucial point of your evidence, I'm finding gaps that the train could run through. Can you imagine what a good barrister will do to you when he gets you into the dock?'

'I thank you for your generous compliment, Detective,' Oglaza said with a slight wheeze. 'But in building me up, you mustn't put yourself down so. You've done well here – you've certainly managed to split some hairs in my client's recounting of seventeen-year-old events. Oh, nothing damning, nothing incriminating, just a few points of evidence that are, at worst, unlikely. No barrister could do any better, not with the kind of straws you've been clutching at. Detective, you're trying to build a case out of smoke.'

'I can assure you, Mr Oglaza, what I've got is a good deal more substantial than smoke.'

'Well, tell us what you've got, then. That way we'll know how best we can assist you.'

Forbes' smile never quite reached his eyes.

'I've got just about everything I could want. A dead body, a crime, a witness, a suspect, an accomplice who committed suicide rather than face justice – and I can buttress it all with pretty good forensics. We've found articles of clothing, obviously not belonging to the victim, but in a remarkable state of preservation. The shirts are on their way to the lab as I speak; it won't take long to determine who owned them. And who owned the blood. And whose pocket we found the condom in. Though I don't imagine the findings will come as any great surprise to your client.'

'Beyond reasonable doubt, Detective – that's the standard of proof you'll require. You know you're still some way short of that.'

'And you know, Mr Oglaza, how these things work. The crime's been uncovered, the suspects are blaming each other. It now comes down to whose story rings truer, and best fits the facts that are known. I've said my piece about your client's effort, I think it's time you were made aware how the other side tells it.'

Then, after a pause for dramatic effect, he lowered his voice to a murmur and began.

'Rodger Doran's version also starts in the Heather Blazing. He remembers noticing you both there that night. It would've been hard not to; after your academic achievements became known, you were the toast of the town. And making the most of the sudden celebrity – you were drunk, you were loud, and you were chatting up everything in sight. It would've nicely crowned your finest hour if you'd ended up behind the ball alley with some accommodating bit of skirt – one of you certainly came equipped for the possibility. But your luck just wasn't in. Or at least it hadn't come in by the time Rodger Doran left the pub. He thinks it was gone one o'clock; being the night that was in it, the party was in full swing, the bar still serving. He drove his girlfriend up the Boher Road to her home. Outside the house, the pair sat in the car saying a long goodnight. When at last Suzy opened the door to go, a voice from someway down the road caused her to look round. After peering into the darkness, she muttered something like, "Oh, Christ, not those two. And they've seen me. I'd better wait and say hello." At this point, Doran left her and drove off about his business.'

'Business?' Oglaza claimed. 'And what manner of business pursuit could he possibly have been engaged in at such an hour?'

'He was stealing hay,' Forbes replied, unblinking. 'But like

Messrs Walsh and Morrissey, he too struck out. The prevalence of silage-making meant that old, traditional meadows were few. And of those that remained, many were already cleared, it being late August. He'd have to raid a barn, but that was risky. When he tried one up near Tullogher, a barking dog woke the household and he had to flee empty-handed. So he turned for home, down to his last resort; Walsh's hayshed. He'd spotted it while visiting Suzy. It was off the beaten path, just about visible from the road and too close to the dwelling for comfort. But all else had failed – tonight he'd give it a go. On his way back, he turned left into the laneway. To avoid alerting anyone, he disengaged the engine, put his shoulder to the front column and pushed the old Avenger along the track and through the gateway, nearer and nearer to the shed. But to his dismay, he heard a voice. Then a second, this one he recognized as belonging to Billy, son of the house. Now he was in real trouble, Doran felt sure. With the old car in tow, a quick and stealthy getaway was out of the question. His only chance was to sit tight, keep still and hope that the others moved off.

'But they didn't. And in a while, Doran forgot his own predicament and let his curiosity get the better of him. Peeking round the corner, he saw Billy Walsh, as he'd identified, and Dasher Morrissey, as he might have guessed. Both crouched to the ground, bent over what seemed at first glance to be a stricken animal. Till Doran had a better look . . .'

Here Forbes took a break from the narrative. 'Billy, compare the two versions – yours and mine – to this point. You admit that it was extremely unlikely Suzy would've come alone at that hour to so desolate a place. I say she didn't. She was taken there; maybe coaxed, maybe lured, maybe even

340

forced. As you've acknowledged, she was no heavyweight – a little coercion would've gone a long way. Similarly, you can't explain why she declined the offer of a condom. I contend that she was never given a choice in this either.'

Oglaza scratched the dome of his crown, his expression incredulous. 'You're saying . . . attempted rape?'

'I'm saying *rape*. So is Rodger Doran. So is every shred of evidence and stem of common sense. As to what happened afterwards, we can only speculate. It could've been accidental; she fell to her death while trying to get away. Or it could be that she was pushed, to prevent her from ever talking. Either way . . .'

The words stung like needles about the temple. So this was what Doran had been keeping so long at the ready, his fall-back for when the shit hit the fan. Of the three protagonists, it appeared I was the only one who hadn't made a contingency plan for this day.

'No flaws so far, Mr Oglaza,' Forbes preened. 'If there were, I'm sure you would've said.'

'Perhaps not, Detective. Though I can hardly wait for the next twist. Man finds girlfriend murdered, and promptly throws his lot in with the killers!'

'In that same man's own words, his "head was done in" by what lay before him. Once he'd ascertained that the girl was Suzy, and that she was dead, he could do no better than meekly ask what had happened. He was told that wasn't important; the only thing that mattered was to cover it up as quickly as possible. Disorientated though he may have been, Doran wanted no part in a cover-up, but it was now that the other two proved too slick for him, too persuasive. Taking full advantage of his confusion, his lack of education and his well-known dislike for the law, they managed to talk him round. Better to keep the cops out of it, they convinced him. They'd only make a bad job even worse. Call them in, and three families are destroyed; keep them away and there needn't be any. Then came the dangling carrot – both Walsh and Morrissey had just secured places in university, the first step on the road to prestige jobs and fat salaries. If Rodger would just help them out of this jam, he'd not regret it in the years to follow.'

Again, Forbes stopped for a breather. And, I think, to give our side a chance to refute. But Oglaza could find no fault, any more than I could. Whoever cobbled this together had done a tidy job.

'You know the rest. Doran complied. But only in as much as to drive the car. A discussion ensued over where best the body might be buried – six weeks of complete drought had left the countryside as hard as iron. Then Morrissey remembered the old overgrown sandpit. Problem solved. Rodger Doran had never in his life been in that part of the parish, and could not possibly have known of the existence of such a place. So to suggest that he was directing operations at this point is absolutely laughable. Instead, he merely watched as the other two did a thorough sweep of the area where Ms Deane had fallen. They then loaded up their cargo, and guided the driver to the spot selected. There they disposed of everything, including the bloodstained clothes they'd been wearing.

'As they go, this plot succeeded better than most. Suzy was famous for her itchy feet – one more disappearance hardly raised an eyebrow. For the killers, life continued onwards and upwards. For Doran, the hush money arrived as promised. Morrissey funded for him a brand-new beginning in Australia, then on his return Mr Walsh was equally generous. But your finances couldn't hold out forever, could they Billy. And neither could your luck. Which is why we're all gathered here today.' His case was stated, his last card laid on the table. Now he sat back, saying nothing more. It was our move.

With growing impatience, he waited.

Finally, in mock astonishment, he said, 'What, Mr Oglaza – nothing? No objections at all?'

'Just the one, Detective. Namely, that you appear to be pinning everything on the word of a convicted and dangerous criminal, who also happens to be a drug addict.'

'I grant you, he's no saint. But then again, unlike some, he's never claimed to be. Hypocrisy tends to go down badly with a jury.'

'Oh, come on, Detective Forbes. Rodger Doran could be facing charges of armed robbery and the attempted murder of a policeman. Obviously, he'll say anything. So what's his testimony going to be worth?'

'On its own, very little. But supported as it is by all the forensics, and a good deal of the circumstantial, it takes on quite a solid look. And when it's held up to the light beside the hogwash your side is offering, I think it's got a chance, don't you?' Without losing a beat, he turned intently to me and said, 'Well, don't you, Billy? Reckon it's got a chance?' I flustered, looked to my counsel for guidance, but the detective powered on, 'It's something you ought to have a serious think about. Because your own chances don't look at all healthy right now. However, there may be one – just one – left for you.'

Still, there came not a flicker from the old man by my side.

'Y'see, Bill, you claim you never touched, harmed or interfered with Suzy Deane. But Doran isn't saying you did.

343

My point is that the two versions may not be totally incompatible. If you could only see your way to remembering things a little differently. Morrissey was older than you, so naturally he'd have been the leader, the dominant one. Bringing Suzy to the haybarn would've been his idea. It was with him she was struggling when she took the fall – you never even climbed the ladder, right? And Doran is swearing that it was Morrissey who directed the cover-up and chose the burial site. Billy, it's past time to start looking out for yourself in all this. You can corroborate Doran's account and still come out looking like one of the good guys. You were seventeen when it happened – since then, your record is exemplary. If you hold your hands up here and now to one or two lesser charges that I'll suggest to you, then I guarantee you'll never see the inside of a prison cell. But if you insist on forcing this into court, putting that girl's elderly father through a long and harrowing trial, and then you're found guilty – which I'm pretty certain you will be – well . . .'

And why not, I thought. Where would the harm be? What need did Dasher have of his good name any more? And why should I be concerned with him or his reputation, considering the lurch he'd left me in? When all was said and done, Forbes' proposition was at least worth a hearing.

I looked to Oglaza and nodded, 'Sounds fair enough?'

'What sounds fair enough?' he glowered. 'Were you straight with me when we spoke earlier?'

'Yeah, of course, but . . .'

'But d'you have any idea what these lesser charges will amount to? They may include procurement. False imprisonment. Assault. Attempted rape. Accessory after the fact. You want to cop for these, despite being innocent? Assuming, of course, that you are innocent.'

'I am. I swear it.'

He studied me a while, his eyes narrow, his lips pursed. 'No, sir,' he whispered. 'Not while you're a client of mine. Detective!' he then announced. 'This interview is over, as far as Mr Walsh and I are concerned. There is no earthly purpose to be served by prolonging the dialogue – your mind is obviously closed, and you seem intent on nothing other than worming yourself a false confession.'

Above Forbes' left eyebrow, a tic began to pulse. He tried to force a smile, but the frustration, falling so close to the finish line, wouldn't permit one. 'What about the statement, then,' he snarled.

'Statement?'

'The goddam statement he came here to make.'

'No, he won't be making a statement. He's already said plenty. So, Detective, your call. Charge him – if you think you've got enough.'

'Oh, I'm pretty sure I do. But I'll need it confirmed by a higher authority. Have no fear, Mr Oglaza, the t's will be crossed and the i's dotted. You won't turn me over on a technicality. In the meantime we'll be holding Mr Walsh, while we decide upon these charges.'

Seeing the puzzled look on my face, he now managed a smile, this one genuine enough.

'We've got twelve hours, Billy. Which means you've got a night in the cells coming. But don't worry, before long this won't seem like too much of a novelty.'

Oglaza put a comforting hand across my arm, but I was in no great need of comforting; the prospect didn't bother me unduly. So I muttered something, to make light of it all, and we shaped to stand.

'Just one other thing,' Forbes remembered. We settled back

down to hear. 'Rodger Doran was the intended victim of a contract hit two years ago now.'

Oglaza's eyebrows arched comically. 'Someone wanted that man dead? Detective, words fail me!'

'They didn't always fail your client, y'know. He had lots to say on the matter – when he was boasting that the contract was his.'

'I'm sorry – I beg your pardon?'

'Your client has been heard to brag that he took a contract out on the life of Rodger Doran.'

Mouth agape, the old man turned towards me. At once, I struck an expression as close as I could to his.

'Really, Detective. Heard by whom?'

'By Mr Doran himself.'

'Oh, for God's sake, you're not intending pursuing another of these drug-addled ramblings.'

'Again, Mr Oglaza, we'll follow and see where it leads. We're off to a flying start with this one though – we've got the gun.'

'How . . .?'

'When the attempted hit went wrong, Doran seized the weapon and kept it as a kind of memento. Kept it until this afternoon, when we relieved him of it outside the Ulster Bank. It's going to Dublin in the morning, to see if we can establish a ballistic match.'

'A match with what, pray?'

'Well, you'll be aware that your client has a sister who's among the leading barristers in the land. Glamorous though the work may be, it occasionally involves rubbing shoulders with some pretty unsavoury people. Doran's gun was a Browning 9mm semi-automatic. It's quite a common weapon of choice among Dublin's criminal fraternity. Now, if the lab was to find that this same piece had been used previously in some gangland operation, and it just so happened that the gang in question had at some time or other retained Margaret Walsh, SC, to represent them on their day in court – I think you see where I'm going with this. If we can establish a definite link . . .'

'Millions and millions and millions to one, Detective. But follow it by all means. It's as good as anything else you've got.'

The day had started unremarkably. It had remained so till the midpoint of the afternoon. But in those hours since three o'clock, there had been more incident than in the previous ten years of my life. And there was yet more to come as they led me away to spend my first night in police custody.

CHAPTER FOURTEEN

That first hour deprived of my liberty ought to have been my darkest. With nothing else to do, I should've been thinking hard on my plight. Contemplating how the world had gone through the looking glass, how everything was twisted and subverted, how even the gun intended for Doran now looked likely to nail me instead. Wondering how many nights I'd spend watching the moon through a barred window, or how I'd preserve my sanity when all around me had so clearly gone mad.

However, it's possible that I myself was beginning to lose the plot a wee bit already. Because, truth to tell, I found that first night inside made quite a diverting change of scene. The room itself was sparse but functional. And no sooner had I been shown to my quarters than I was fed; rashers, grilled tomato and brown bread, as I recall, and at least as palatable as anything I myself could've rustled up at that hour. I was a bit wary of the tea, remembering from the book *Error of Judgement* how one of the Birmingham Six had his cuppa urinated in while detained. But when eventually I braved it, I found it an excellent brew – a little on the strong side, but that's how I like it.

After I'd eaten, a doctor arrived to take samples of my blood, saliva and body hair. And when he was gone, Conor Furlong – no doubt in further defiance of his superiors –

stuck his head round the door. It was a flying visit, to tell me how we'd made RTÉ's main evening news. A foiled bank heist, the shooting dead of a would-be robber, the suicide (though they didn't actually call it suicide) of a middle-aged father of four. And the finding of a body, believed to be that of a young girl some seventeen years on the missing list, in a remote boghole. 'Gardaí are refusing to say if these incidents are in any way linked,' the broadcast had proclaimed, thereby inviting the entire nation to get busy joining the dots.

The bed was hard and it smelled a bit. The station house boomed, clanked and echoed throughout the entire night. But none of this mattered a whole pile; sleep never even ventured near. Not because I wasn't tired – on the contrary, I was absolutely jaded. But though the body was ready to shut down, the brain still had miles to go. Relief, I think; that was it, mainly. This was hanging over me all my adult life. Today, the sword had fallen. Tonight, there were no swords left to fall. And 'tis indeed an ill wind that blows; this day had finally reconciled me with Conor Furlong and with Mags, my sister – two people who'd meant a great deal to me in times gone by. Reconciled only after a fashion, of course. We could hardly be called intimate yet, and it was far from inevitable that we ever again would be. But this was a start.

Strangely, I'd not yet managed to begin grieving for Dasher. We hadn't been close recently, in fact we'd grown quite a distance apart. But when a guy's been your best friend for thirty years, the notion that you'll never see him again takes time to harden. Perspective, too, takes time. At that moment, all I felt towards the man was anger. For turning tail at the first inkling of trouble. For not toughing it out and lending his voice to mine. I'd not yet spared even a thought for his aged parents. Or for the wife and young family he'd

left behind. The memory of it shames me even now. Doran
was not the only villain of this piece. But by God, he was a
villain, rotten to the core and bad to the bitter end. Grudging
it may have been, but Dasher and I had provided for him
pretty handsomely over the years. Yet the instant his sky fell
in, it was on us that he turned his guns. And for what? The
deal he'd struck, the concessions he'd hoped to gain by it, I
could only guess at. But it was unlikely that he'd walk from all
this a free man. Any more, it seemed than I would.

Outside my window, the weary city slowly wound down.
Then first light broke shortly before five. I lit another
cigarette. I didn't smoke very many back them, but since
they'd bolted the door behind me, I'd lost count. The sun
rose, peeping above the skyline, and the world again began to
stir. At around seven there came the sound of fresh activity,
of animated conversation from somewhere within the
building. Then the approach of footsteps, loud and urgent
along the corridor, the jangle of a key in the lock, and
Detective Forbes was back. He couldn't have slept very much
more than I had, but he looked none the worse for that, fired
as he was with adrenaline and with purpose. After a curt
exchange of greetings, he requested that I arise and
accompany him to the front desk. There he lengthened his
face suitably and told me that after consultation with the
DPP, it was decided to charge me. With manslaughter, with
conspiring to pervert the course of justice, with other charges
pending. A special sitting of the District Court, he said, had
been convened for eleven that morning. If I needed to
apprise my solicitor of these developments, there'd be a
telephone put at my disposal.

Not knowing how Oglaza might be contacted, I rang my
sister instead. I caught her as she was readying the little fellow

prior to dropping him to the babysitter's; in the background I could hear him chirp away contentedly, the first time I'd ever heard his voice. Briefly, I explained to Mags what had transpired. There was no reaction, not as much as a expletive. She merely said she'd have Oglaza meet me outside the courthouse at eleven and that, all going well, she'd be there too. She then asked if I had my passport with me, as there was the likelihood I'd be called to surrender it. I didn't, but I described to her the drawer in my bedside locker where she'd find it as she made her way south. Conveniently, she'd retained a key to the old homeplace through all the years and despite everything.

When I'd done, I chanced one quick call to Colleen Leigh, the woman I'd been seeing. But I got just her answering machine. This was odd, I thought; the only reason she'd ever be incommunicado at that hour of the morning was if she'd spent the previous night with me in Lisdrolin. And I knew with some certainty that *that* had not happened. Only as I hung up did I remember that this was how she screened her calls when the occasion demanded. Several times over the next few days I would try that number, each with the same result. After that, I stopped. I can take a hint as well as the next man.

The lack of sleep, coupled with the sour nicotine aftertaste, left me with no semblance of an appetite. So when breakfast was offered I declined all bar the tea. The desk sergeant let me have his copy of that morning's *Star*. I read it from cover to cover, which didn't take long. We got no mention; it appeared the news we'd made came too late for publication. There followed more cigarettes, more hours of waiting and contemplating as the clock ground towards midmorning. Finally, it was time.

351

I took my place in the back of the squad car flanked by two young policemen, the same two who'd sat silent through my interview of the previous evening. Neither had found his tongue overnight, and even Forbes in the front passenger seat had little to say for himself. Nor was the driver offering much in the way of conversation, so barely a word was exchanged for the duration of the journey. But that journey was mercifully brief, the District Court being just a stone's throw away in Catherine Street.

Our featuring on the national news brought out the crowds. Or if not the crowds, exactly, then a good assortment of gawkers to the front steps of the courthouse. They were largely subdued, however, gathered more in curiosity than in outrage, and only a low murmur passed among them as I stepped from the car. The media too were there; manslaughter was not that uncommon, but this was no common manslaughter. Not likely, when the accused was a university graduate, a pillar of the community – a primary school principal teacher, no less. And as of today, of course, no more. Nothing like a juicy bit of scandal to lay low those plaster saints, to cut them down to size. Suddenly the realization hit home, and hit hard, that no matter how things might eventually pan out, my life as I'd known it had ended. I was ruined.

Inside the building my sister was waiting, Nicholas Oglaza by her side. Other than that, I remember little. I did confirm my name and address, then listened as the charges against me were read. As other charges were pending, I was remanded to appear again one month on. Bail was unopposed, though conditional. There'd be a ten-thousand-pound bond, a similar amount in independent surety, an undertaking to sign on at a Garda station every day till my next appearance, and the surrender of my passport. In all, it took just minutes. Backstage immediately afterwards the passport was duly handed over while my sister, with her famously deep pockets, saw to the financial impositions. Nothing remained, then, but for the police to drop me back to Ballybricken station to retrieve the car I'd left there the day, the lifetime before.

Mags was back at the house ahead of me. The obligatory cup of tea was not a comfortable affair. We hadn't spoken in almost a year, and the single topic now ripe for discussion was one that neither of us was keen to broach. So the talk was kept very small and very mannered. She enquired how I was coping with the demands of my new job. I enquired if her's was treating her as well as ever. She asked after some neighbours she remembered. I asked after her recently extended family. This reminded her that she needed to go make a quick call to the babysitter, a routine check. She returned saying all was well, and we drained our teacups in suffocating awkwardness.

Once she'd finished, she announced that she was going for a stroll over the old farmstead. No question as to my plans for the afternoon, and certainly no invitation to accompany her, she just upped and left. In a matter of minutes, she was back. She'd forgotten, she said. The farm wasn't ours any longer. Was the new owner agreeable to having ramblers on his land? Shamefacedly, I assured her that it wouldn't be a problem. She left again, and this time stayed gone.

From an upstairs window I could see directly into Morrissey's yard. There were six cars there, more abandoned than parked. Two I knew: the white Peugeot belonged to Pat, Dasher's father, the red Corsa to Mary, the dead man's wife. The other four I didn't recognize, but I assumed belonged to relatives who'd dropped by to help get the house ready. The remains were being brought to the church that evening, and a certain amount of the mourners would be invited back to Boher after the service.

At some stage, I knew, I would have to stand among his people, offer my sympathies, and take whatever was coming to me. In fact, I considered going down there now, before the crowd descended, before the evening went into a complete spin. But I thought better of it. Or, truth to tell, I shirked it. I'd wait, I decided, till Mags was with me. It'd be easier that way. And in any case, she would want to pay her respects too. We could make arrangements when she returned from her trek.

Hours passed, and I'd just begun to worry slightly where she might be. Then, she rang. A little out of breath, and more than a little tipsy by the sound of things. Apparently, on her travels she'd run into someone she knew – an old friend from her secondary school days who now lived in one of those new houses further along the Ross Road. Mags was taken back there and then to meet the husband and children, the talk of times past inevitably began, a bottle of wine was uncorked, and an invitation to stay for dinner gratefully accepted. The two women intended to round things off with a few drinks in the Heather Blazing later in the evening. I could meet them there, if I had a mind. Around nine. But what about the funeral, I asked. Would I not see her there beforehand? No, she told me, she was giving it a miss. The burial was taking place next morning. She'd show her face there. That'd do.

From back in the upstairs bedroom, I watched the cars, one by one, leave Morrissey's yard. It was time then; time for the removal from Waterford city morgue. Time to escort the hearse to the little village cemetery, to Dasher's final place of

354

rest. They'd left early – the cortege was not due in Lisdrolin till seven thirty, still about two hours away.

So, I'd be going it alone after all. There'd be no support, no one to take my side when I'd come face to face with Mr and Mrs Morrissey. With Mary and the children. With the general congregation, a public in which I'd been masquerading as a beacon of propriety for so many years now. What possible excuse could I offer to those parents who'd left children in my care, who'd entrusted me with their moral development . . . and then, oh Jesus, then it occurred to me. Joe Deane would be there. About the only thing capable of prising him from his sheltered accommodation these days was a funeral. Here was the death of a neighbour's son, not unconnected with a certain loss of his own; if the old man had a pulse this night, he'd be there. And, doubtless, he'd be wanting a word with me. In God's name, what was I to say to him?

Six thirty. Just one hour to go. I needed a shower. I needed to shave. I needed to change out of the clothes I'd spent the night in. And with the clock ticking down, I needed to get up and get a move on.

Unless.

Unless I was badly misreading the situation and about to make a great mistake. Because maybe, just maybe, it was too soon for those confrontations. Maybe wiser to postpone them a while. Not for my own sake, of course, but for the sake of the old folk. Only the day before did the Morrisseys suffer their bereavement; only then, too did Joe Deane learn of his. Was it right or Christian to have me, the sole survivor, paraded before them at this time? Surely not. Surely such an act would be insensitive. Provocative, even. And of benefit to absolute no one. My appearance in public would only

355

provide a field day for the gossips and rubbernecks, not to mention the huge distraction it would bring to a solemn religious ceremony. For a last hurrah, Dasher deserved better.

And so in next to no time I'd justified it, convinced myself that the decent thing to do was to lie low for a spell. Though not for too long a spell; I didn't intend becoming some kind of recluse, I couldn't keep my head down for ever, and the longer I did, the more difficult a return to the fold would be. After some further consideration, I decided to take up my sister's invitation to join her in the Heather later that evening. I'd be among friends, I could keep it brief, and without risking too much, I could gauge the mood of the people, and see how the wind was blowing.

I left it late, very late, almost to the call of last orders. Even as I approached, I could tell that the place was quite full. The music that was customary on Saturday nights had been cancelled, but the chatter was audible from the street. I eased open one of the swing doors and stepped inside. Those seated adjacent fell quiet an instant, but no great hush descended on the entire gathering, nothing so theatrical. I ordered a drink. As I did I caught sight of a knot of twenty-somethings up the bar with whom I had nodding acquaintance. I duly nodded in their direction, they replied in kind and returned to their own company. Once my pint arrived, I began to scan the crowd for Mags and her old pal, or indeed anybody I might park up beside. Then through the throng I spied Leaky Roche at a table near the big open fireplace. He'd been to the church, I could tell by the Sunday suit he wore. And he was deep in conversation with some people who weren't known to me. Still, it was a mighty relief to see a face so familiar. Without a second thought, I made for the corner where he sat.

I'd just taken a step or two when I stopped short by a rough heavy hand on my upper arm. I turned around, not expecting anyone in particular, but never, ever expecting Pat Morrissey. He wasn't a pub-goer of any great renown – in fact, up till that moment, I wasn't sure if he even took a drink. But he'd taken one or two tonight. Clasping both hands on my shoulders, he swayed a little, wheezed neat whisky into my face, then tightened his grip till he held just fistfuls of my clothing. And now the crowd around did fall silent.

'Is it true, Billy? Is it?'

'Is what?'

'What everyone in the bloody parish is whispering behind my back.'

'What are they whispering, Pat?'

'That 'twas yourself and my young lad killed Joe Deane's daughter.'

'No, that's not true.'

'No?'

'No.'

The look became more crazed, more intense, the trembling more marked.

'So what did ye do, then?'

'Nothing. We were there, that's all. Neither one of us harmed a hair on her head.'

Slowly, he let go one shoulder, then the second and took a steady, almost sober step away.

'Will you swear to me that that's the God's honest truth?'

'As God is my judge, I swear it's true.'

His hand went first to his mouth, then to his eyes and with a thumb and forefinger, he wiped them clear.

'I knew it,' he said, first to the ground, then to the onlookers round about. 'I knew that wouldn't be in Mick's nature. He wouldn't be capable; there wasn't a bad bone in the lad's body. I knew it, I knew it all along.' But then, turning back to me he said, 'And you knew it too, Billy. You've known it for the past seventeen years. So why, for the love of Christ, did you not say something? If nothing else, the Deanes were entitled to give their little girl a decent burial. In seventeen years, why did you not once open your mouth?'

From every direction, the eyes now bore down on me.

'Jesus, boy, d'you realize the trouble, the grief you've caused? Poor oul' Mick was too soft entirely – he'd never have had the gumption to come forward off his own bat. But he looked up to you like no one else. All you had to do at any stage was give the word and he'd have been with you every step of the way. But you didn't. You carried on all this time like you'd nothing to tell or nothing to hide. And look what it's led to. Tonight, instead of one family wearing black, there's two.'

'Yeah!' came the shout. 'And the fucking pity of it is, there's not three!'

Pat and I both looked, aghast, to where the voice had come from. As we did, the crowd parted to allow this latest entry to the fray. I'd not seen him before, I'm fairly sure I'd have remembered. He was young, low-sized, barrel-chested, without any neck visible, and slavering for fight. The naked aggression sobered Pat up even further. Warily, he studied this brute, shaking his head and asking, 'Who . . .'

'Who am I? Kavanagh is my name. Ned Kavanagh from Carrigeen. Does that ring a bell?'

He took a step closer, his arms hanging by his sides like a gunslinger ready to draw.

'Well? D'you know who I am?'

Neither of us answered.

'My mother's maiden name was Faye – she was a sister of Joe Deane's wife, Lord have mercy on the pair of them. Suzy was my first cousin. But I never got to meet her; she was murdered while I was still very young.'

Under the weather he may have been, but Pat Morrissey still knew trouble when he looked into the whites of its eyes. He took a few small steps backwards and stammered, 'You have my sympathy.'

'You can stick your sympathy up your arse. I don't care how sorry you are, I hope that son of yours burns in Hell. Hanging was too good for the bastard, and I hope he's suffering, wherever he is. Still, I suppose when the time came, he had the decency to do the right thing. Not like some.' Slowly he shifted his gaze. 'What's the story, Walsh? Could you not find a rope strong enough to do the job? Mind you, I'm not surprised. You must have a neck like fucking brass to ever show your face in this village again.'

I had this bad feeling that if I as much as opened my mouth, I'd have every last one of my teeth rammed in. Still, I couldn't let him go unanswered. 'You should wait to hear the facts before you go making these accusations,' I said evenly. But as I spoke, I must've raised my index finger to him because, quick as a snakestrike, he'd seized my wrist and pinned it like a vice to the counter.

'Who the fuck d'you think you're lifting a hand to – huh? You're not dealing with some little girl now.' He snorted once or twice through gritted teeth and flared nostrils, then closed the other fist, cocking it by its shoulder.

'Jesus, mate, I'd love to! You wouldn't believe the pleasure, the fucking hard-on it'd give me to smash that smug face of yours.'

Chris Scanlon, the middle-aged publican, could see that

he'd not be round the bar in time to prevent trouble. So he stretched across the counter, trying to get between us as best he could.

'That's enough!' he shouted. 'Give it up now. Do what ye like outside the door, but in here I'm having none of it.'

Kavanagh let go resentfully. 'I'd do time in jail for you, you murdering bastard. I'd do it willingly.'

'I said leave it at that, Ned,' the barman warned.

Before he could retort, a small familiar voice interjected, 'That's pretty good advice. I should take it, if I were you.'

Mags was on the scene, with quite a sup taken, and consequently more belligerent than usual. To the great curiosity of the audience, she stood herself up to her full, intimidating four-foot-eleven and went on, 'This man' – she pointed to me – 'has been convicted of no crime, and is perfectly innocent before the law. That same law, Mr Kavanagh from Carrigeen, is very clear on matters like slander and threatening behaviour. So keep a rein on that tongue of yours, or you may find yourself doing time in prison, willingly or otherwise.'

Kavanagh furrowed his brow and looked at her like she was something that had just fallen down the chimney.

'I know you,' he said, surprised at the breadth of his own knowledge. 'You're that lawyer – that dirty slag who works for the gangsters. I've seen you on the news. What's the matter? Are child killers and rapists gone so scarce in Dublin that you've got to come all the way here looking for business? By the way,' and he winked archly, 'that guy, Cappocci – he was giving you one, wasn't he? Up the arse, I'd say. Up the bum, no harm done, eh?'

If he was trying to scandalize with his choice of language, he'd picked on the wrong woman.

'Mr Kavanagh.' She smiled, her diction suddenly crystal. 'Let me put this in terms that even you may understand. Shut up and shove off, or I'll call the police and have you arrested, clear?'

'Ah suck my dick, you stuck-up cunt!' and he put his palm on her face and pushed her away easily as if he was shifting a gearstick. Immediately I lunged at him and in the brief melee that followed I like to think I landed one solid right somewhere in the region of his jawbone. But it was all over in seconds. By then, Chris Scanlon had come outside the counter and, with the help of one or two able bystanders, restored order.

'Right,' he said once he'd got his breath back, 'that's that. Ye're barred, the whole fucking lot of ye. Drink up and get out.'

Mags, still wound up and raring to go, began, 'Excuse me, but —'

'I'm not fucking listening!' Scanlon shouted. 'I'm barring you, you and you. That's all about it.' He stopped, calmed himself somewhat and said, 'So finish them drinks and leave. You're not being served here any more.'

I didn't deserve this, I knew, but the barman's dander was up, and there was no reasoning with him. However, just then I saw Leaky Roche approach, looking like a man about to do some interceding.

'Hang on a sec, Chris. Don't be too hasty here.'

Scanlon didn't speak, but he did seem to be listening.

'Ned only said what everyone in this pub is thinking. If you put him out, then you might as well clear the whole place.'

I looked at Roche, words failing me utterly. He boldly returned my gaze.

'Yeah, you sneaky bastard. Everything he told you goes for

361

me too. Goes for all of us. Why don't you just fuck off and find some other community to tear the heart out of. Because you'll never again be wanted in this one.'

A low grumble of assent seemed to come from every corner, and rose at my back as I left without even bothering to finish up that drink.

Upon rising next day, my first chore was to call the police in Waterford and notify them of the change of my plans. I'd not now be signing on daily in Lisdrolin station after all; it'd be at Clontarf. Once this new arrangement was acknowledged and approved, I asked that it might be conveyed to Sergeant Conor Furlong. He'd know from this that I must've gone to stay with my sister. He'd probably manage a fair guess as to why. And he could contact me there if the need arose; he did have the number.

This done, I began to pack a few things. I worked as noiselessly as I could, careful not to disturb my sister as she attempted to sleep things off. Presently she surfaced, plenty the worse for wear, but anxious to make tracks with as little delay as possible. I'd already brewed up a pot of tea, and poured her a cup for the road – she slurped it down impatiently, without speaking, without even sitting. And then she was gone.

Before following her, I took a minute to look the premises over one last time. To see that the windows were bolted, upstairs and down. That taps were off, plugs out and appliances disengaged. I then ran an eye around the outhouse doors and recalled how, as a little boy in the long long ago, this had been my area of responsibility. To check of an evening that the hens were in, the dog now chained up and fed, and that the young calves in the corner byre had water. All dilapidated now, stone crumbling, wood rotting and silent as the grave – what had become of the farmyard that once ran with noise, with colour, with life. And what, indeed, of the dutiful little boy. As I locked the front door behind me, I remember wondering if I'd ever spend another night under this roof. Wondering if, after God knows how many generations, the house had been occupied by a Walsh for the last time. Then, driving away, I caught sight of the place in the rear-view mirror and could only think how small it looked, how old, how familiar and reassuring. And yet, it was already taking on the appearance of a house deserted. Smaller and smaller it grew in the distance, till at last the tiny speck vanished altogether. Eyes front, then for Dublin.

The days that followed were boring beyond belief. I was grateful to my sister for providing me with sanctuary, but she might've done a little more to make me feel at home. She might even have trusted young Garvin to me for an hour here and there – from the little I saw of him, he seemed a most agreeable wee fellow. But no. She left the house each day with the baby in tow, never returning till the late evening, by which time she herself would've dined out, and the child was ready for nothing but bed. And once she'd tucked him away, she rarely did more than pop her head around the living-room door before retiring to her study with armfuls of files. I suppose she'd not reached the top of her profession without hard work. And she could hardly expect to stay there without more of the same.

But hard work was something that never frightened her, which was more than could be said for her other half. He would rise any time from about midday onwards, generally speaking. He would then take up station before the TV, chain-smoking cigarettes, drinking cans of Heineken, starting the occasional crossword, and subsisting solely on what he could microwave or what he could have delivered. Thus it would go till the very small hours each morning. Every once in a while, he'd claim to have had an offer of work; never anything too specific, but he'd be gone for the entire afternoon while he followed it up. Invariably, he'd return footless drunk, potless broke, and just as unemployed as when he'd left. Just as unemployed as me, come to that.

Those few hours between my sister leaving for work and her husband vacating the bed were all I truly had to myself. I'd make a little breakfast, then catch up with the news and sport, watch some of the truly desperate midmorning TV, and generally act like I was back again in a house I could call my own.

Dermot's rising was my cue to make myself scarce. That meant a good deal of killing time, but I could've been in worse places with time to kill. Many an hour slipped easily by as I strolled the well-tended greens of the promenade, or followed the causeway and the small wooden bridge that led to the great white flats of Dollymount Strand. Then, as the evening drew in, I'd buy the daily paper and repair to the Sheds or the Yacht for a few pints of stout and, even if nobody spoke my name, for a little cheer. Indeed, I was often sorely tempted to make a night of it by the alehouse fire, to stay on the stool till the shutters came across. But I made a point of resisting. That would've been an easy road to go down. And, from what I know, an extremely difficult one to climb back up.

It was the morning of my ninth day in Dublin. I was alone in the kitchen when the phone rang. This wasn't unusual – in the forenoon I doubled as a glorified answering machine, logging my sister's calls. But this one was for me.

'Billy? Conor here,' it said. 'How's the craic?'

'Not bad. You?'

'Ah, fair enough. Dublin treating you all right, then?'

'I'm bored. I'm very bored. Still, better fed up than strung up, eh?'

'I did hear that the natives got a bit restless. And that you had something of a contretemps in the Heather the other night.'

'What did you hear, exactly?'

'That the Bull Kavanagh and yourself exchanged some pleasantries.'

'The Bull? You know of him, then?'

'Know of him? You could set your watch by him being hauled in here on a Saturday night. He's seen *Match of the Day* more often in this nick than he has in his own living room.'

'Well, give him my regards when you see him this coming weekend.'

'Will do. Anyway, enough about that. I've got some news for you.'

'Yeah?'

'Yeah. They haven't managed to make a match on the gun. Ballistics couldn't come up with anything.'

'That's interesting. But no real concern of mine.'

'Really?' he prodded.

'No!'

'OK, well try this, then. It seems your girl, Suzy, was pregnant. About three months gone.'

'Christ – pregnant? It wasn't mine, I hope you know.'

'I do. Wasn't Dasher's either. In fact, it wasn't even Doran's.'

'So whose was it?'

'We've no idea.'

'Are you going to try find out?'

'And what good would that do? In any case, I'm not sure how we'd go about it, short of taking samples from every middle-aged man in the south of Ireland. And even that . . .'

'OK. Well, thanks for keeping me posted. But none of this is terribly relevant, is it?'

'I wouldn't say that. It may not turn the case on its head, but it does prove one thing.'

'Oh – what?'

'That you were telling the truth when you said she wasn't keen to use a contraceptive. We know now that there wouldn't have been much point. But I understand that in your interview Forbes made great capital out of this. He reckoned it just wasn't possible that a good-time girl like Suzy would ever risk an unwanted pregnancy if she was offered the chance to avoid it. It was one of the reasons he was so sure you were lying.'

'And this is going to convince him that I wasn't?'

'Oh, Christ no, not him. But it's got one or two of the rest of us have a rethink.'

'"Us"? What's this "us" about? You're not telling me that you ever had your doubts?'

'Let's just say I kept an open mind. You've not always been straight with me, Billy, remember? Even now, you're not telling the whole story.'

In the silence that now roared between us, I desperately tried to calculate. He had something. But what could he possibly have?

'The bag,' he answered, unasked.

'The bag?'

'The bag. Suzy's. That great big red herring that prevented this bloody case being properly investigated in nearly twenty years.'

'Oh, that bag. What about it?'

'It'd be nice if you told us where it is.'

'I don't know where it is.'

'OK, then, what did you do with it?'

'Do with it? Conor, I never even saw it.'

'Bollox. She had it with her that night.'

'Not when she came to the haybarn, she didn't.'

'Billy – please! We know for a fact that she took it from her house that night.'

'And I'm telling you for a fact that I never laid eyes on the goddam thing. It wasn't there, I swear it . . . I swear to God, that's the truth.'

He paused an age, deciding how he should treat this. Then, to himself almost, 'So what the hell became of it? Could it have been in Doran's car?'

'Maybe . . . or – no, it couldn't. I saw all around the interior, and Dasher had a really good look inside the boot. Nothing.'

'R . . . right. Well, c'mon, help me out here. You must have some theory about what happened to it – I mean, you've had half a lifetime to mull it over.'

'And I spent half that lifetime dreading the day it'd turn up – then everyone would know that Suzy never got away that night. The truth is, Conor, I don't have a clue. What about yourself?'

'OK. Off the top of my head; she hid the bag in a bush or a ditch nearby. Some stranger stumbled upon it and took a liking to what he found.'

'Well, whoever he was, he must've been quick off the

blocks. Because the very next day, myself and Dasher searched the place high up and low down.'

'Hmm. It could always have been lifted that night.'

'Funny you should say that.'

'Why?'

'In the middle of all the pandemonium, when Doran had the knife to Dasher's throat, we thought we heard something move in the rath behind the haybarn.'

'Jesus! Why did you not say this till now?'

'Cos we looked there and then, but could see nothing.'

'Well, what did you expect – it was fucking dark!'

I didn't answer.

'That's got to be it, doesn't it? Someone on his way home from the pub gets taken short, stops in to Deane's rath to drop a load, finds this smashing kitbag full of gear, puts it on his shoulder and walks away.'

'But that person must've seen and heard everything. He'd have witnessed a killing. D'you honestly think he'd have stolen crucial evidence from the scene – and maybe landed himself in nearly as much trouble as we were? Conor, if someone had been there, he'd have been standing in a copshop telling his story before daybreak, not running off with the victim's property.'

'Not necessarily true. Like, he might've, I dunno . . . Ah, shit! Yeah, you're right, of course you are.' He laughed a little. 'I'm glad you pointed that out, actually, because it could've misled a stupid person.' Now we both laughed. 'I'll let you go, Bill. But before I do, can I put one other thing to you?'

'Sure.'

'Why did you not just ask her?'

'Ask her what?'

'Ask her where her bloody rucksack was.'

'And why would I do that?'

'She tells you she's running away from home and . . .'

'Woah! She never said that.'

'Billy, it's in your evidence.'

'Nah, nah, nah. She only spoke in general terms. That she intended running away. That she wished she was eighteen like Dasher, so that nobody could force her to come back when she did.'

'Hang on! If you didn't think she was about to do a runner that very night, why did you spend all the next day looking for her travelbag? What made you think she'd even packed one in the first place?'

'Her father told me.'

'What?'

'Joe told me. The next day I was working with my dad, God rest him, when Joe came into the field and said that Suzy was gone, and she'd taken her stuff with her.'

'So . . . if that's the case . . . it must've been Joe who passed on that information to the police as well.'

'Had to be. He was the only one who knew. Apart from his missus, obviously.'

'Now there's another strange thing. I'd safely say I read that file fifty times. There isn't as much as a single, solitary word of a statement there from Mrs Deane. She refused to have any dealings with the law whatsoever.'

'There's nothing strange about that, Conor – she just let her husband do the talking for both of them. That's how things worked in their time.'

'D'you remember a lotta years ago, young Willie O'Connor, I think it was, claimed to have seen Suzy travelling by Inter-rail through Greece? And when I told this to Joe, he was like a child with a birthday. But his wife was having none of it. Kept saying, "You can't fool me." Absolutely adamant she was, remember?'

'Yeah, but . . . so what?'

'If it was like you say – he called the tune and she just sang along – how could they be this much at odds?'

'What're you driving at, Conor?'

'I dunno . . . maybe nothing. I've got to go – I'll be in touch.'

Some hours later, on the afternoon of that ninth day, a further call was to come for me. I wasn't there, as I'd gone to sign on at the police station, so Dermot took the message. The caller, who – it was emphasized – spoke with a broad rural accent, preferred to remain anonymous. But he did say that he knew who I was, where I was and what I'd done. And added that he'd be round one night, late, to burn me in my bed. Dermot was well spooked – understandably, given that only a light interior wall separated his bed from mine, and that he did spend the greater part of his life there. But Mags was unfazed. She heard it all before; in her line of work, this kind of thing came with the territory. It's just that, till now, it hadn't come to her own home, as she was ex-directory. But not to worry, she said. If it happened again, she'd simply get the number changed.

However, Dermot remained far from reassured. And compounding his unease was the fact that the threat had been made in an accent not local to Dublin city. As he was unable to tell one regional brogue from another, we all sounded much the same to him, much like certain IRA men he'd occasionally heard on the TV. That entire night, he harped back to the call, becoming more fretful

370

as he did. Next morning, he was up before I was with all the appearance of a man who'd not got a great deal of sleep. And the instant I returned from signing on that evening, he was near hysterics as he confronted me on the doorstep.

'All right,' he panted. 'Enough is enough. This has to stop.'

'What has to, Dermot?'

'This. You staying here.'

'Huh? You want me to leave?'

'I'm sorry, yeah, but . . . yeah. You'll have to go.'

'I see. When d'you want me out?'

'As soon as you can. Tonight – tomorrow at the latest. It's nothing personal, but my mind's made up.'

'Fair enough – it's your house,' I said without irony. 'But what's happened?'

'I'll give you one guess,' he told me, no less agitated. 'He was here, that's what.'

'Who was?'

'Pah! Jesus Christ, like he was going to leave his name and address!'

'Well, what did he want, then?'

'He wanted you.'

'Why?'

'Why d'you think, for fuck's sake. It was the same guy who made that phone call yesterday.'

'Are you sure?'

'Course I'm sure. I'd recognize that thick fucking culchie accent . . . Oh, hello there!' he called weakly over my shoulder. 'This is the gentleman . . .'

I turned around to see Furlong, for once out of uniform, advance up the darkened path and into the light from the porch.

371

'Billy!' he said.

'Hiya. I believe you met my brother-in-law, Dermot.' They shook hands, Dermot nodding and smiling like a simpleton. 'This is Sergeant Conor Furlong.'

'Sergeant? Y'mean, like . . . a cop?'

'A cop is right,' I said sternly. Then, to Furlong, 'Shame on you, ringing up Dermot like that, telling him you're going to set fire to the place!'

'What?'

'Oh, nothing.'

He shook his head as he saw that I was the only one appreciating the joke. Then, 'C'mon, I'm parked across the road. I've got something to tell you. And someone for you to meet.' And he strode towards the car without even bothering to check if I was following. There'd been a breakthrough, something significant; I could tell by that strut in his step.

'So where are we going?' I asked as he turned the ignition key. He didn't answer, but headed straight to the seafront, there taking a right for the city centre. Staring straight ahead, as if his passenger seat were empty, he proceeded no more than half a mile before swinging into the grounds of the Clontarf Castle Hotel. Once there, he disengaged the engine and killed the lights.

'The news is good; your story checks out.'

'Checks out? Conor, checks out against what?'

He smiled. 'Let's go. We've got an appointment to keep.'

He stepped from the car and began across the gravel. When he heard me disembark, he activated the central locking and continued towards the hotel entrance, with me snapping away at his heels.

372

'C'mon, for Christ's sake. You said "checks out". What does that mean?'

He stopped. 'What d'you think it means? It means that we've come into possession of a statement that corroborates yours almost verbatim.' And he set off again.

'What?' I shouted. 'Like, who? Did Doran change his story?'

'Did he hell. But now he's going to have to.' With one hand on the hotel's big front door, again he halted. 'Billy, I found your Peeping Tom.'

Time stood still, the frame frozen. But could I possibly have misheard?

'Y . . . you've found him?'

He grinned, he nodded, the clouds parted, the world lifted from my shoulders. Small wonder I began to feel light-headed and dizzy. For support, I put my hand on the pillar that flanked the main entrance. Furlong's words came to my ears as if from the bottom of a deep pool.

'Yes, sir, I managed to track him down. And you were spot on; he did see and hear it all. Well, all of it that matters.'

Now things were in focus. Now I wanted to raise my arms aloft and run roaring the length of the seafront. And then find a convenient rooftop from which to holler.

'Don't you want to know who he is?' Furlong smiled.

'Yeah, but first things first. You're certain that he's prepared to stand up and say what he saw?'

'He's done it already. Billy, the charges – well, the main ones – are dropped. Gone. You're off the hook. Now, if you'll follow me, there's someone in here who's anxious to talk to you. This case may be closed, finally, but the air still needs clearing, don't you think?'

To the right of the foyer was the public lounge. Furlong led the way. Though roomy and plush, it was sectioned along the side wall by partitions of oak and stained glass, making a series of small, intimate alcoves. Walking some yards in advance of me, he stopped when he reached the fourth of these stalls and spoke to the person secluded there.

'Joe, d'you know this guy?'

I almost ran the last few steps, and craned my neck round the screen. God, Joe Deane looked feeble. The little that remained of his hair had turned a kind of shop-dummy yellow, while about his face the skin hung loosely, all blotches, liver spots and the general wear and tear of eighty years' living. I would've told him not to bother getting up, but he was already labouring to his feet.

'Billy, is it?' he asked, and he extended a hand that looked like a talon in a latex glove.

'Yeah, Joe, it's me. Can you not recognize me?'

'I can't really see you, boy. The oul' lamps aren't what they used to be.'

As we shook hands, I struggled frantically for something to say. Even if I was about to be exonerated, I owed the old man an explanation.

'I'm sorry, Joe.'

He looked into my face with those vague, sightless eyes and nodded.

'I should've done something that night, and Christ knows, I should've done something in the meantime. But I was afraid, I suppose. Afraid that the story wouldn't come out right. And afraid of what might happen to me even if it did. But I swear to you, Joe, neither myself nor poor old Dasher . . . look, I'll say no more. I'll wait and let you hear it from

Conor's man.' To Furlong, 'I take it you told Joe you've got someone who can verify this?'

At that instant, a lounge girl arrived at the table. Conor ordered teas and gestured for me to take a seat. We sat, the three of us, in silence a while, with the old man staring blankly into the middle distance. The more I watched him, the more he looked distinctly unwell, or at the very least, uneasy. The tremble in his hands became increasingly pronounced, and his eyes began to brim till great tears ran in crevices down his cheeks. I went to attend to him, but Furlong shook his head crossly, a signal that I should stay out of it. When at last he spoke, the voice came out like a death rattle.

'I heard her come in that night. Herself and Doran were fighting, and all the screeching and the slamming doors woke me. She wasn't inside five minutes when I could hear her sneaking down the stairs again and opening the front door as quiet as she could. So I got up and looked out the window. And there she was, crossing the road and getting over the ditch into the rath field. I thought I'd better go after her, in case she was running away again. She'd tried it twice before, y'know, and she caused so much bloody commotion, the whole place was up in a heap. So I wanted to grab hold of her and bring her home, by the ear if I had to. But by the time I was dressed, she was gone – I couldn't see her anywhere. I didn't want to start shouting for her, and go waking the neighbours at that hour of the morning. So I set off across the field, and as I did I heard these voices in the distance. I followed the sound, and when I got as far as the rath, I saw . . . Well, you know what I saw.' And he lifted his eyes to meet mine.

'What!' I gasped. 'It was you?'

I looked to Furlong, for some indication that the old man might be raving. When I could not see a flicker of doubt or scepticism, I went on, 'But why, for God's sake?'

'I told you why.'

'No, I mean why didn't you step in and do something.'

'I was like you, I suppose – afraid. Doran was a rough, tough, hardy gorsoon. He was after killing one person that night, so he had nothing to lose. I was no young man at that stage, remember. He'd have knifed me there and then, and it wouldn't have cost him a thought!'

'That's fair enough, Joe, but once he'd left, you could've raised the alarm. You could've gone to the police the next day. Or the day after. Why didn't you?'

'And what good would that have done? Suzy was dead, and nothing I could do or say was going to bring her back. One young life was destroyed – what was the point in destroying three more. Especially when 'twas yourself and Mick Morrissey. Ye were just starting out with great things in store. You were going for your teaching, and Mick, I believe, was off to be some class of an engineer. Well, if this business had to get out, ye could kiss goodbye to all that. Not to say what 'twould do to the mothers and fathers that reared ye. Now, I wouldn't have done the same for everyone, but Jesus Christ, ye were neighbour's children. I knew ye from the day ye were born, and I knew ye weren't bad lads. Even young Doran – he might've been a bit wild, but he came from decent people. I know it was wrong, but I thought that, at yer age, ye were entitled to a second chance. So I went home and slept on it, and this is what I decided. If either of ye went to the police, I'd be straight down there after ye and back up yer story. If ye didn't I'd keep yer secret, and let ye get on and make something of yourselves. And God forgive me, didn't I get the notion that nothing would ever come to light if only I could make it look like she was after running off again. So I took some things from her room, and this oul' travelbag she had, and I burned the whole lot in the half tarbarrel out the backyard. When I went to the guards, I told them she was missing, that some of her stuff was missing as well, and I let them work it out from there.

'And, y'know, for nearly twenty years, no one could say I did wrong. You went off to Dublin, you came back an educated man and a credit to this parish. Mick Morrissey, God be good to him, reared four of the nicest children you'd meet in a long day's walk. And poor oul' Doran – I know he wound up going a bit astray, but I don't think that was all his fault either.'

What? I thought. Had he just said these words? Had senility ravaged him to a point where he could even think them? I leaned forward, the better to study him. But he continued to stare at the same spot on the table, as he'd done throughout the monologue.

'Would I be right in thinking,' Furlong began, 'that you never even let your wife in on any of this?' The old man shook his head. And after he'd flashed me a that-explains-that glance, the policeman did the same.

'Misguided loyalty,' he sighed. 'That's what the judge is most likely to put it down to.'

'Judge?' I asked. 'Will Joe have to appear in court?' All of a sudden, the prospect didn't fill me with optimism.

'Mainly to tie up a few loose ends. You'll be making an appearance too, by the way. But nothing you need lose any sleep over.'

Just then, the waitress returned with the tea for three. I

took the pot in hand and began to pour. When I did, Furlong got to his feet.

'None for me, thanks. I've got some things to do. I'll leave you guys to it – I'm sure you've got plenty to catch up on. I should be back in about an hour, OK?'

Once he'd gone, I passed Joe the milk jug and pushed the biscuits towards him. He thanked me and took from each as required, then sat himself more comfortably, his composure by now well regained. His eyesight, too seemed to have improved somewhat, as he located the sugar unaided and applied the little sachets without a bother. Back to his old self, then. As if he'd ever been away.

'That fellah, Furlong,' he cackled. 'He's a shrewd one, I'll tell you. No flies on him.'

'He's gone now, Joe,' I said quietly. 'There's just me and you.' His eyes gave a nervous dart around the room as I went on, 'So there's no need to pretend any more. You can cut out the bullshit and tell me what really happened.'

His hand on the table began twitching again.

'That's what happened, Billy. I *was* there.'

'Oh, you were there, I've no doubts about that. But being there – that's the only bit of your story with even a grain of truth in it.'

'Are you calling me a liar?'

I had to consider my answer. But not for very long.

'Yeah, I am. For starters, like my own father and every other farmer around, you never went anywhere without a penknife that was nearly the size of the butcher's cleaver. That little toy that Doran was waving about would not have scared you. Anyway, even if you'd only your bare hands, you'd have been more than a match for him. You know me since I was born? Well, I know you almost as long, remember? And you'd have wiped the floor with that guy, armed or not.'

'Ah now, that's easy for you to say . . .'

'Leave it out, eh? You told Conor that you kept quiet because you didn't want to ruin our prospects. But that night, you had no idea what our prospects might be. It wasn't till next day, when you came into the mountain field where myself and my dad were loading hay, that we told you. So you couldn't have been acting to protect our university places – you didn't know we had any.'

That shake of his was worsening.

'And what's this about Doran coming from decent people? The Dorans were the greatest crowd of thieves and villains ever seen in the south of Ireland. And it was on the way to a match in Mullinavat, when I was a very small boy, that I remember you saying as much. In fact, you were the first person whoever gave me the low-down about that family; maybe that's why it's stuck in my mind all these years. So c'mon, Joe. What's the story? Why did you not step in that night?'

He looked me boldly in the face, his eyes narrow and his jaw in a very determined set. 'I've said all I'm going to say. You're in the clear, aren't you? So what more d'you want to hear?'

'I want to hear why you let Dasher die. You could've saved him if you'd only had the courage to speak up.'

'Oh, Jesus, and aren't you a fine one to be talking! You didn't only give up your best friend, you let go a whole farm of land sooner than tell the truth. Anyway, why didn't Morrissey say something himself? Hadn't he a tongue in his head too? If that young man is not alive today, it's no fault of mine.' The exertion, the aggression, left him wheezing slightly.

'So,' I said. 'This is how it's to end, is it? The whole truth about Suzy's death will never be told. Joe, don't you think you owe her that much? Don't you think she's entitled to rest in peace?'

'Fuck her!'

'What? What did you just say?'

'I said fuck her. Why should she know peace? D'you reckon she gave myself or my wife even five minutes' peace, with her drinking and her whoring and her gallivanting? We took her in when her own family wouldn't have her, and what did we get for our trouble? Fifteen years of purgatory! D'you really want to know why I kept my mouth shut? Because I was fucking delighted! There's no one who ever deserved to come to a bad end more than that sly, conniving little bitch. I'm telling you now, 'twas the hand of God that shoved her off that haybench!'

And across twenty years, my foolish blood began to rise.

'Joe, that's another dirty lie. Suzy was nothing like that. She was . . .' I hesitated as I saw him smirk. 'Well, whatever she was, she's dead, and she deserves better.'

'Better than what?'

'Better than to have her memory blackened by some malicious old fool who ought to have a little respect.'

'Oh, my! I must've struck a nerve, Billy. Was there a bit of an oul' shine there all those years ago?'

'I liked Suzy, yeah.'

'Liked? Only just liked? Oh, come on now – she's dead, she deserves better?'

'OK, then, God damn you, I loved her. Happy?'

He must've been, because he immediately began to quake with breathless, tubercular laughter.

'What's so bloody funny?'

'You loved her, did you? And I suppose she loved you back. And she loved young Morrissey as well. And that's why she came to meet you that night. Oh, my poor man, may God give you sense!' And he laughed some more.

At that moment, I wanted nothing so much as to catch him by the scrawny neck and squeeze the last puffs of life out of him.

'What d'you know about it, eh?' I trembled.

'More than you think, oul' son. A lot more than you think. I crouched there in the rath that night, watching the whole carry-on, thinking to myself, "Good girl – now you're fishing in the right stretch of the river!" Sweet little Suzy, y'see, was pregnant. And she hadn't all that much time. In a few months, she'd need to have found a stooge, a father for the child. So she was on the hunt. Before morning, she'd have had her hooks in one of the college boys. Oh, you're dead right, Billy. I didn't know that night that you'd been called to university. But I'll bet, she did. You told her, didn't you?'

'I . . . mentioned something.'

'Mentioned something? Billy! My own eyes are damn near useless, but you're as blind as the back end of a horse. Christ, boy, for fifteen years she wouldn't piss against you for shelter. But suddenly she was all about you. And she wouldn't have you use . . . one of those things.'

'A condom?'

'The very fellah. And of course, you know why – cos she had to make it look convincing. Oh, you can take it from me, I knew her as well as any man, and I knew there was nothing that girl wouldn't stoop to. It was like she was giving trials to yourself and Morrissey, and whichever one of you she settled on, well . . . God help him. She'd have

381

been back to you a couple of weeks later with her story, and there'd be no way out for you – you'd wind up marrying that deceitful little trollop, and rearing another man's child. Billy, I know you had it rough, with that tinker taking your money and your father's land off you. But believe me, you got off light. If Suzy had to live that night, things mightn't have turned out a whole lot better.'

What remained in his teacup must by now have been stone cold but he emptied it anyway, as if to signify that proceedings were at an end, that he really had said his piece. Placing his hands on the table, he began the preliminaries to the pretty arduous task of getting to his feet.

'And now, I'm afraid, you'll have to excuse me. I'm not used to being up so late – I'd sleep on a clothesline this minute.'

I should've gone to help him up, but I didn't. Something was still not right, something he'd still not told me.

'Your friend,' he volunteered, 'was good enough to book me a fancy room here. Sure, I'm very glad of the break from th'oul nursing home.'

His face reddened as he forced himself towards a standing position. It looked to me like he was in a most unseemly rush to make his exit. And just as determined to keep up the small talk till he could manage it.

'I suppose 'tis devil the luxury hotel I'll ever again see at my age. Still, 'tis nice . . .'

I reached across the table, placed one hand on his shoulder and eased him back into his seat.

'One last thing, Joe. You just said you knew she was pregnant before she died. How could you know – did she tell you?'

He stalled, then stammered, 'I can't remember rightly.'

'You can't remember?'

'Well, I suppose she must have. Yeah, now that I think of it, she did. On the quiet, like.'

'It *must've* been on the quiet, because nobody else had any idea. Your wife told my mother everything, but she never told her that. Because she didn't know, did she?'

'I . . . don't think so.'

'So – Suzy confided in you, but not in Rita. I didn't realize you and Suzy were so close.'

His face froze like a condemned man awaiting the fall of the axe. Instantly, I could tell I'd nailed him. Almost as soon, I knew how.

'Was the baby yours, Joe?'

The expression didn't change.

'Oh my Jesus, she was carrying your child!'

He gasped frantically for breath.

'It's not what you think – not as bad. Like, she was never my flesh and blood. And Lord knows, she didn't take very much persuading.'

'But she was only fifteen, Joe. You were old enough to be . . . You *were* her father, for fuck's sake. And how long . . . I mean, how often?'

'A couple of times – three at the most.'

'Three times in fifteen years? Get out of it!'

'Upon my life. The first was only that summer, I think maybe in May. It hadn't rained in weeks, and there was a fox doing the rounds. The hunting must've been bad in the wilds, because he was coming down into the farmers' yards. He killed some hens on your mother, and two ducks that my missus was only after buying. So this night I put a cartridge in the gun and waited up for him. At about four o'clock in the morning, Suzy came downstairs in her

nightshirt. Said she couldn't sleep . . . A couple of times –
three at the most,' he repeated.

'But even that, Joe,' I said. 'How could you?'

'How could I? he spluttered. 'Christ, boy, that's rich!
Weren't you trying to do exactly the same thing?'

'Not the same thing, Joe. Not the same thing at all! I was
young and I was single. Your wife, the woman you were
married to for twenty-five fucking years, was asleep in the
bed upstairs!'

He shrank back into the seat and, before my eyes began
drifting away, tuning to a more agreeable wavelength. The
prerogative of old age. Push any harder and I'd lose him. If
I'd not done so already.

'I'm sorry,' I said contritely. 'You're right – I'm no one to
judge. Go on with the story.'

Slowly, disdainfully, his eyes returned to mine.

'Please,' I urged. 'I need to know. After . . . after a while,
she came back to you and told you – what?'

He hacked loudly, considered a while, then, 'That she was
expecting, and the baby was mine. Simple as that.'

'It couldn't have been just as simple as that. You knew – you
must've known – that there were other men in the picture.'

'I did. But she said it was my doing. And her saying it –
that'd be enough to damn me.'

'So what arrangement did you come to?'

' 'Tis she drew up all arrangements. I'd have to let her go
where she wanted, do what she wanted, see who she wanted
to see, and give her money any time she asked. In return
she'd say nothing to Rita, and she'd do her best to find a man
who'd be a father to the child. If she did, no one need ever
know the truth.'

'And if she didn't?'

'I suppose I'd just have to support her baby, as well as her high living – she had no intention of giving up either one. I was rightly over a barrel, she knew it, and she was going to play it for all she was worth.'

'So when you saw what happened that night, you really weren't too sorry.'

'Sorry? I thought all my Christmases had come together. There was only one thing worrying me; that they'd find the body. Cos if they did, they'd find the baby. And, like, I knew they could do this test – this paternity test – so I was afraid of my life —'

'Of course you know now that you'd nothing to be afraid of,' I said, interrupting.

He stopped short, tightened his features and asked, 'What? What're you saying?'

'All they had in those days was a blood test, and that'd only show conclusively if you *weren't* the father. The technology wasn't there yet to prove if you were.'

Slowly, very slowly, the truth seeped through and understanding began to dawn; I could tell by the way the face fell, and the crushed, broken look that came about him. Everything: his grand deception, his years of unshakeable silence – his entire past life, even – had been for naught. It was a long time before he spoke again. When he did, it was in a voice bereft of all consolation.

'How was I to know that, Billy? I was a poor man's son, who left school at eleven to try scratch a living from a few stony acres. How was I to know what the world of science could or could not do? As far as I was concerned, that body had to be buried, and had to stay buried. 'Twas just lucky for me, I thought, that ye hit upon that very plan too. So I did what I could to help ye – unbeknownst, of course.'

Now it was my turn to see the dawn of a little understanding. 'So you tampered with the scene when we were gone, didn't you? I could never work out how there wasn't a single trace lying around next morning.'

'I waited till there was some daylight, till I could see what I was doing. Then I washed down every surface where there was even a speck to be seen. After that, I got another of your father's old fertilizer sacks, stuffed in every rib of hay that was bloodstained, and took it away with me. When I got home, I shoved it into this tarbarrel where I used to burn rubbish. I was about to set light to it when – I dunno, 'twas as if God, or someone like Him, whispered in my ear: "Take some of her things and burn them too. Then everyone will say that she ran away again. And they'll never think to look for her around here."'

He stopped, slumped back into the upholstery and breathed deeply a while. His story truly had been told, his piece said at last.

'So there you have it, young fellah. You know how 'twas done, and now you know why. Your friend seems to think 'twas misguided loyalty – let him keep on thinking that, eh?'

'Oh, don't you worry. He won't be any the wiser on my account.'

I summoned the waitress and called a round of brandies, large ones. When they arrived, I raised mine, said, 'Cheers,' or the like and took a sip. Joe lifted his glass to within inches of his mouth, then stopped and held it there, before slowly returning it to the table. I had no idea what, but something more was on his mind.

'She never spoke to me again, y'know.'

'Who didn't?'

'Rita. Never again. Not after that night.'

'Why . . . why not?'

'Because she was watching from the bedroom, and saw what I was up to out the backyard.'

'You mean when you burned all the stuff?'

'That's right. Oh, I never noticed her at the window. But when I came indoors, she was waiting for me. Me, with blood all over my hands.'

'So, she probably thought . . .'

'That 'twas myself that killed Suzy, and did away with the body? Well, what was she supposed to think?'

'But did she not ask you?'

'Ask me?'

'Confront you, then. Demand to know what had happened.'

'Jesus, boy, there were times over the years when I'd have given the world just for that. Just to have her say something – anything – even if it was only to accuse me of killing her child. But no; not another word passed between us from that good day till the day she died. She moved into Suzy's old room, 'twas there she spent most of her days, and all of her nights. Oh, breakfast, dinner and tea would be there waiting for me at the usual times – but not her. She wouldn't lower herself to eat off the same table.'

'Because she mistakenly thought . . .'

'Mistaken, yeah. But I suppose she knows the whole story now, wherever she is. And the day won't be long coming when I'll be there with her, please God. Maybe then we'll be able to patch things up again, and be like we were once. She didn't always hate me, y'know.'

'I'm sure that'll happen,' I said. 'God is good.'

And we sat silent for a while, both – I imagine – wondering when He might think about demonstrating this to either one of us.

387

At the far end of the lounge, the doors swung open and Furlong came bustling through. He undid his jacket as he approached, then threw it into the windowsill behind Joe's head and sat amongst us once more.

'That's my business taken care of – how about you two?'

'Yeah,' I said. 'I think we're just about done here.'

'Very good. Joe – bedtime?'

Furlong and I got to our feet and gingerly eased the old man to his. When he was standing independently, I extended an open hand across the table.

'Thanks, Joe,' I said. 'I'm . . . very grateful.'

He quivered violently as he clasped his hands around mine in a determined but frail grip. On each line of his face, I could see his search for something to say, for the words on which to end this whole sorry affair. But the words wouldn't come, and with his distress growing increasingly obvious, Furlong stepped in.

'Right, c'mon you. If the nurses back in Thomastown find out that you were in a pub till this hour, it's the last gate pass you'll ever get.' And he linked the old man towards the foyer and the elevators.

I was left alone. At first, I remember thinking only how different this place looked now from the place I'd entered a couple of hours earlier. How much easier the atmosphere, personable the staff and clientele, softer the streetlight I could see through the frosted-glass window. It was as if, for the first time in a long time, the world had lowered its guard and loosened its collar. I snuggled a little deeper into the leatherette and called for beer. The pint arrived with Furlong not far behind it.

'Pick it up,' he told me. 'We'll adjourn to the residents' bar.'

'Can we? I mean, are you staying here too?'

'Course I am. What did you expect?'

'I just wasn't sure if the station's expenses budget would run to a second suite in this kind of opulence.'

'What station's expenses? I paid for this.'

'You did? Out of your own pocket?'

'Well, it is the only pocket I'm allowed access to.'

'Conor, this is very good of you.'

'You'll think of some way to make it up to me,' he smiled. He reached on to the windowsill, retrieved his coat where earlier he'd tossed it, and was just a little irked to see a second one under his.

'Forget his head, he would, the dozy old twat. Will I take it up to him now in the room?' he wondered aloud. 'No, I'll hold on to it till morning.' And so doing we made our way to the nearby residents' bar. Furlong slapped his room key, his accreditation, up on the counter. I took two twenties from my wallet and placed them alongside.

'Tonight's on me,' I said. 'I insist.'

'Oh, I'm not going to argue with that. In fact, I think you should go on jollying me for the rest of your life,' he answered, but in jest. Then, suddenly serious, 'I found him, y'know. He didn't come to me.'

'What cracked it for you – was it the bag?'

'Course it was. When I thought about it, it was obvious that it never existed. So the bould Joe must've invented it. From there, it was only a matter of collaring him to ask why.'

'Jesus, mate, you're a lifesaver. That was brilliant police work.'

He mumbled something, blushed a little and took a long draught from his pint. 'I wonder what the real reason was, though,' he said then.

I gulped hard and went, 'Huh?'

'I mean, why did he do what he did?' and he looked me squarely in the eye.

Despite myself, I gulped again. He let me stew in it for maybe half a minute.

'Obviously, you aren't as grateful as you let on.'

I did my best to look mystified.

'C'mon, Bill. It wouldn't kill you to tell me that it was his baby Suzy was carrying. Or, at least, that he thought it was.'

Here was something I'd just sworn never to divulge. But it mattered little; my silence was eloquent enough.

'It's the only way any of this makes sense,' he went on. 'Loyalty will only drive a man so far.'

'Can you find out for sure if the kid was his?'

'I could. But I don't know why I'd want to.'

'You won't be taking this to your top brass, then?'

'No way. To hell with them. I worked it out for myself, they ought to be able to do the same.'

And just then, I wondered how on earth it could be that he was still a uniformed officer. Did the detective corps of the Irish police force already have such an embarrassment of talent that they could afford to disregard the likes of him? Somehow, I thought not.

'You've gone very quiet,' he said suddenly. 'Something on your mind – something else you're keeping from me?'

'Not really – I think you've more or less got it all. Part of the reason he sang dumb was because he wasn't too unhappy to see Suzy get her comeuppance. She hadn't been black-mailing him, exactly, but she'd threatened to tell his wife the whole story unless he kept her sweet . . . which I suppose is kinda the same thing.'

'If you say so, Billy – I understand you're a bit of an

authority on the subject!' And with a broad smile, he raised his glass to me. It was something of a gloat, but I didn't begrudge him his moment.

'Yes, very droll. By the way, there is one other thing, but I'm sure you've got it figured as well.'

'What's that?'

'It seems there's a possibility that Suzy may not have found me totally irresistible after all.'

'That's preposterous!'

'She'd cut a deal with Joe, y'see. In return for his generous and continued indulgence, she'd try to con some poor sucker into thinking that the sprog was his. With a view to lasting friendship, marriage, and a life of absolute misery, I'd imagine. That's where myself and Dasher came into the picture.'

Furlong shook his head in mock astonishment and was about to speak – something sarcastic, I dare say – when his eyes narrowed as if a bulb had just gone on behind.

'Joe was fully aware of this, yeah?'

'Obviously. It was all part of the bargain he'd made with her.'

'And did he have some preference as to Suzy's prospective husband?'

'Are you joking? He didn't care if she took up with the wild man of Borneo, so long as it got her out of *his* hair. Come to think of it, I well remember him saying to my dad, round about that time, that he'd even stopped objecting to Rodger Doran. Now that makes sense too.'

'So why did he follow her that night, then?'

'Sorry?'

'He knew where she was going, right? Or at least, he knew why she was going. He must've known he wouldn't enjoy what he was about to witness. And he'd have to come up with a bloody good excuse if his missus woke before he got back. So – he leaves his bed, dresses himself, and then goes creeping around the undergrowth in the small hours of the morning, just to see who's having it off with his girl, when, at the back of it all, he doesn't really give a damn? Billy, something doesn't add up here.'

Put like that, even I could see the faultline.

'He isn't some kind of pervert, is he?' Furlong asked. 'Y'know, a voyeur?'

I could dismiss the suggestion, but not the stone under the door. Something did not, indeed, add up. And it rankled.

'Jesus Christ, Conor, I had him here two minutes ago, wiping the slate clean. He'd have told me. If only I could've thought to ask.'

'Ah, you did well to get from him all you got. He'll never again open up like he did tonight. Not to you or anybody else. Forget it – the chance is lost.'

I sighed. 'You're right, I guess. That book is closed, and it's not . . .' I stopped. Something – maybe something I'd said – had set Furlong's inner alarm ringing a second time.

'That book,' he muttered, 'that book,' as he reached round and took Joe's overcoat from the back of the stool where he'd draped it.

He then looked guiltily about the room. 'This is highly unethical,' he whispered, inviting me to object. Once I'd signalled that, whatever it was, was OK by me, he began to run his hands through the pockets. It did feel a bit despicable, but I was too curious to cry halt. And more than a little disappointed when Furlong emerged from his rummage holding nothing more sensational than an old, old missal, without a cover to be seen or binding worth speaking of.

'Conor, it's a prayerbook.'

392

'That's right. A prayerbook. This morning, after I'd collected Joe from the nursing home, we'd driven past Paulstown – about twenty miles – when he realized he'd forgotten this wee book.' Here, Furlong waved it at me like a referee administering a caution. 'And – get this – he made me turn the car about and go back to Thomastown for it. I thought he had to be kidding and drove on. But he got all stroppy – took a right hissy fit – and said that if I wasn't prepared to take him back, then to let him out of the car and he'd make his own way there. I couldn't believe it.'

'What's so unbelievable? He's religious. Most of his generation were.'

'Billy, he's almost blind, and look at the size of this print. It's like the bottom of a dodgy insurance policy – in this light, even I can't make it out. And you reckon he's religious? Now, think about the man we're dealing with here. And some of the things he's done in his life. He's hardly going to be a shoo-in for canonization when the time comes, is he?'

Carefully, almost surgically, he began to leaf through the loose and mildewed pages. Every once in a while – maybe six times in all – he stopped to scrutinize an entry all the more closely. Not once throughout the trawl did his expression change, not till he reached a point close to the end. Here there came a lengthy delay, a slow nodding of the head and a look as if he'd just been reacquainted with a very old friend.

'Well?' I urged. 'What's it say?'

'It's not what it says – it's what he's got between the leaves.'

I raised myself on the stool to get a better look. 'Memory cards?'

'That's right,' and he began to draw them out and lay them on the counter. 'Here's your father. And your mother. This one's Rita, his wife . . .'

393

Rifling through the old man's intimate possessions was bad enough, but at this I drew the line. 'Of course he keeps them in his prayerbook – now put them back there, will ya!'

'Just bear with me a while longer. He's got four or five others in here; neighbours of yours, I'd guess. Nothing strange about that. But then, just inside the back page, there's this.'

The Polaroid that Furlong now brandished was in such poor condition that I had to peer to discover the subject. But when I did, there was no doubt. It was her – as maddeningly, mischievously, heartbreakingly beautiful as I remembered from that summer so long, long ago. And just for an instant, I was once again that naive, lovelorn gawk who worshipped the ground she walked on. And who never stood even a ghost of a chance. However, I snapped myself out of it when I noticed Furlong taking some mean pleasure in my reaction.

'So, what d'you want me to say?'

'Don't you see? Among all the pious, sombre remembrances, he's got this. A photograph. A holiday snapshot. Does that tell you anything?'

'Yes, as it happens. It tells me that since Suzy's been confirmed dead only in the last couple of weeks, there probably hasn't been time to get her card printed.'

'Oh, very good, Walsh. Very sharp. You may well have a future in this game. Now, take another look at the photograph.'

This I did. And continued to do. 'What am I supposed to be looking for?'

'Whatever. Any general observations.'

'Apart from the fact that it's in absolute rag order . . .'

'Exactly. Whereas all the other bookmarks – see – are pristine. Mint condition, like the day he put them in there. But this,' he went on, 'this is dirty, it's dog-eared, it's worn almost to the point of being transparent. And he's pawed it and mauled it so often that the image is hardly recognizable. Another thing – have you noticed these lines? – it's been folded over more than once. Like, maybe, from being kept in a pocket of his working coat, in those days when he used to work. D'you want to know what my guess is?'

'Go on?'

'For the past seventeen years, the man carried this face with him wherever he's been. It's the first thing he looks at each morning, the last thing each night, and the only thing that's kept him going through many a lonely day. I reckon he was obsessed with the girl – stone crazy about her. And that's why he was following her that night.'

'In that case, he's a helluvan actor, old Joe. Cos ten minutes ago, when he said he hated the living sight of her, he certainly had me convinced.'

'Oh, I'm sure he did hate her, in his way. But does one thing necessarily rule out the other?'

'Nah, you've got it wrong, Conor. If he was so very besotted, would he really go spying on her when he knew he'd have to watch some other bloke on the job? And anyway, back then Joe was desperately trying to cover up his involvement with Suzy. Not draw attention to it by prowling around in the bushes like a jealous boyfriend when she was getting down to it with someone else.'

'I do believe he wanted nothing more to do with her. I just don't believe he could help himself.'

'You're way off beam, y'know. There are a thousand reasons why that photograph is in the condition it is. Joe swore that what happened between himself and Suzy was a brief and terrible mistake; that's good enough for me. Because I can tell you for a fact that, up to the night Suzy died, Joe was as happily married as any man in the land.'

'I don't doubt that either. But I do remember his missus, and I can tell *you* for a fact that she looked nothing like this babe.'

Again, he waved the photograph in my face. 'You've got a great old saying down Lisdrolin way, Bill. "A taste of fresh grass makes a rogue of the beast". When Joe had a slice or two of this, he discovered a liking for . . .'

'THAT'S MINE!!!'

We looked round to find him almost upon us. In the halflight, we'd not seen him coming, but to judge by the murderous look on his face, he'd seen plenty – failing eyesight or not.

'Mine! What right have you got?!' he spluttered, all pain and anger and delirium, like he'd been knifed in the stomach and was breathing his last. 'Tell me, you sleveen! Who gave you the authority?'

'No one did, Joe.'

'Then get your dirty hands off it!'

He lurched between us, swiping the photograph from Furlong's hold, pressed it to his chest and retreated a step. His breath was still dangerously shallow, but he was making no effort to rein himself in. Not while his honour remained unsatisfied, is fury unrequited.

'You've disgraced your uniform this night, Sergeant. In my time, the police were men. You're not a man, and you never will be.'

By now, almost all those present were craning to take a look, with much of the attention drawn to the old fellow's attire. He'd hastily pulled on his slacks and cardigan, but the pyjamas underneath were still visible, while inside open-laced shoes his feet were bare.

'And you,' he seethed, 'I expected nothing better from that two-faced cur. But from a neighbour, I expected more.'

'Sorry, Joe,' I said weakly. 'We didn't mean anything by it. It's just . . . it fell out of your pocket.'

'Young man,' he announced, his voice heavy with disappointment, 'you do no credit to your parents' memory. They were honest people.' Another short pause, then, 'So, lads, are ye finished going through my things?'

We both mumbled something in the affirmative.

'You're sure now?' he spat. 'Have another snoop, why don't ye, in case there's anything you've missed.'

Around the room low whispers passed behind hands and knowing glances were exchanged. The weight of embarrassment and humiliation caused Furlong to fumble once or twice as he began gathering Joe's other accoutrements from the bar where he'd spread them. But the old man wasn't interested, wasn't even waiting he'd got what he'd come for. With Suzy safely in his grasp and with one last withering glance, he turned away and rattled towards the exit. Every eye in the room followed the progress of the stooped figure inching across the floor, clutching whatever it was he'd left his bed to rescue.

Tramore beach, 1982. High summer. The young girl by the water's edge is laughing, tossing her tousled black mane, maybe posing, maybe not. She wears a loose white T-shirt, and her jeans are pulled up past her knees. Not yet a woman, but long past being a child, she is very, very beautiful. No amount of folds, blemishes or cracks on the faded snapshot can obscure that. Not ever.

*

We could guess, we could speculate, we could conclude what we pleased. But we could never be sure. Joe knew. He alone had the story, whole and entire. He was surrendering nothing more. It would go with him to the grave.

EPILOGUE

Winter here in Toronto took me unawares with its sheer brutality. I thought I'd seen cold weather in my time but – Christ Almighty! Many's the night I lay shivering, chattering, swearing that come first light I'd be on my way out of this godforsaken tundra. To anywhere – anywhere, so long as it was a little more southerly, a little more habitable. Which covered damn near everywhere. But I stayed, consoling myself all through with thoughts of how beautiful summer in this city must be. Today, June's dawned. It was worth the wait.

That said, even winter could've been worse. Practically all my work was indoors as I tended to a plumber, a Tipperary man named Lonergan. He hired me on spec, cash in hand, following a conversation in a bar one night, and he proved himself a decent fellow, a reasonable taskmaster, and an excellent man to pay. I had little cause for complaint; unlike the previous winter, my first under the new identity I'd assumed. Though strictly speaking, I did nothing so shady as to adopt an alias – I simply elected to go under the Gaelic version of my name, which is the right of any Irish citizen. Billy Walsh translates as Liam Breathnach; the two names look nothing alike, so I was off to a good start. This I bolstered by growing a beard, wearing a crew-cut, and getting myself the pair of weak prescription glasses that I'd been resisting for some years. So when, in due course my passport was reissued in its Gaelic form I thought the transformation complete. I left Ireland, and with it, I hoped, the sins of my past life.

I first fetched up in Luton, half an hour's train-ride from central London. And what a mistake that turned out to be. A vibrant Irish stronghold it may have been, but its emigrants all seemed to come either from Kilkenny or Donegal. I was unmasked almost immediately. The Kilkenny folk wanted to interrogate me relentlessly, the Donegal mob wanted nothing much to do with me, but when drunk both factions wanted to beat the shit out of me. So I soon packed my things and headed for Glasgow, where I spent Christmas and saw in the new year on a wretched landfill not far from Govan.

But these casual labourers tend to get around. It was the fall of that year, I was beginning to consider myself settled, and had even been to Parkhead once or twice as the new football season kicked off, when who should arrive on site one day but a gang of my old tormentors up from the south of England. Time, I knew, for me to move along. It was then that my landlady alerted me to Canada and its possibilities. No entry visa was required, the standard of living was excellent, and there was plenty of work for the willing. Not alone that, but her son lived in Toronto, and she arranged to have him meet me off the plane and give me a bed and board till I found my feet. I was on the next flight out of Glasgow.

Even after events in the Clontarf Castle Hotel, there was still some distance to go, some charges to be answered. In my case, those amounted to attempting to pervert the course of justice, and accessory after the fact. In return for my guilty plea, and in respect of the evidence newly come to light, the Probation Act was applied and I walked free. In passing sentence on Joe, the judge dubbed him a naive and unsophisticated man, bewildered by what he'd witnessed and blinded by deep-seated tribal loyalty. He ruled that nothing was to be gained by imprisoning a man so old, and so otherwise exemplary of conduct. Joe, too, was free to go. Once the judgements had been handed down, I tried to make my peace with him. But he rebuffed me, just as he'd rebuffed every conciliatory effort by Conor Furlong on their return trip from Clontarf to Thomastown. At the time of writing, he was confined to a Kilkenny city hospice, now totally blind, totally bedridden, still not talking.

When eventually Doran came to trial I was in Glasgow, but could follow proceedings in the Irish newspapers widely available throughout the city. The charges against him ranged through blackmail, manslaughter, and attempted armed robbery to the attempted murder of a policeman, with several drugs offences tacked on almost as an afterthought. Wisely, I think, he chose not to contest things. Twelve years was the court's sentence, of which he can reasonably expect to serve about eight. I intend using that time to put unbridgeable distance between myself and Ginger Rodger Doran.

I offered what remained of the old homestead to my sister, thinking she might want it kept in the family. But she wasn't keen. If anything, she was even more anxious than I was to be rid of it. When it did come under the hammer, it sold quickly but cheaply; the package no longer included my land while the buildings were, at best, in need of refurbishment, but more likely fit for nothing other than demolition.

My days in exile pass tolerably enough. The nights, in the main, tend to find me in one pub or another; I am, after all, an Irish navvy, so it's no more than the done thing. It doesn't worry me unduly – my drinking would probably be classed as heavy rather than problem. The problem only arises when I stop, go home and take to my bed. Because since the day I left Ireland, the dream's been coming again, with awful regularity and real vengeance. It starts just like before; a great crowd has gathered together on the tarmac outside my old front gate. The atmosphere is carnival. I'm with friends; nobody I can identify, just a feeling that the spirits are kindred. The mood heightens with the appearance of my grandmother, the old woman who'd so doted on me in her lifetime. She's carrying with her a medal of honour, ready to be presented, and as she draws near to me, everybody smiles in expectation. However, indignantly and with her nose in the air, she carries on striding right by, to pin the medal on another. I don't see who the recipient is, but the low grumbling of the mob tells me that it's time I got myself out of there. So I try to slink away unnoticed. After a few paces, my attempt at escape is twigged, the low grumbling becomes a great cry for blood and I begin to run, ducking into the first door I see. I now find myself in the library of St Pat's College, and with the roars of the rabble filling my ears, I dodge desperately between bookshelves. Turning left into one aisle, I'm confronted by an angry wall of humanity; I try to double back, but my exit too has been cut off. Now I begin to plead. I've done nothing, I tell them. They've got the wrong man. And to prove my innocence, I reach to an upper shelf, to a maths book with its broad spine facing outwards.

And there behind Spivak's *Calculus* sits the gruesome evidence of my guilt – a rotting, worm-eaten, severed human head.

Except these nights, the head is no longer that of Suzy Deane.

It's mine.